THE FIEND IN
HUMAN

JOHN MACLACHLAN GRAY

ST. MARTIN'S GRIFFIN 🕮 NEW YORK

www.minotaurbooks.com

Library of Congress Cataloging-in-Publication Data

Gray, John, 1946–
    The fiend in human / John MacLachlan Gray.
        p. cm.
    ISBN 0-312-28284-2 (hc)
    ISBN 0-312-33526-1 (pbk)
    EAN 978-0312-33526-7
    1. Prostitutes—Crimes against—Fiction. 2. London (England)—Fiction.
3. Journalists—Fiction. I. Title.

PR9199.3.G753F54 2003
813'.54—dc21   2003046833

First published in the United Kingdom by Century
The Random House Group Limited

First St. Martin's Griffin Edition: September 2004

10 9 8 7 6 5 4 3 2 1

Contents

"You can't expect fellows like them murderers to have any regard for
the interest of art and literature. Then there's so long to wait
between the murder and the trial, that unless the fiend in human form
keeps writing beautiful love-letters, the excitement can't be kept up. *We* can
write love-letters for the fiend in human? That's quite true and we
once had great pull in that way over the newspapers. But Lord love
you, there's plenty of 'em gets more and more into our line. They
treads in our footsteps, Sir. They follows our bright example."

– A Running Patterer

From *London Labour and the London Poor*, by Henry Mayhew.

Acknowledgements

My heartfelt gratitude to my editors from three countries: Anne Collins (Canada), Hope Dellon (USA) and Oliver Johnson (UK), and my agent Helen Heller, for their insight, support and friendly advice. Couldn't have done it without them.

Nor could this book have been written without the collaboration of Henry Mayhew (1812-1887) who wrote *London Labour and the London Poor*.

And I wish to acknowledge my wife, Beverlee, who puts up with a lot.

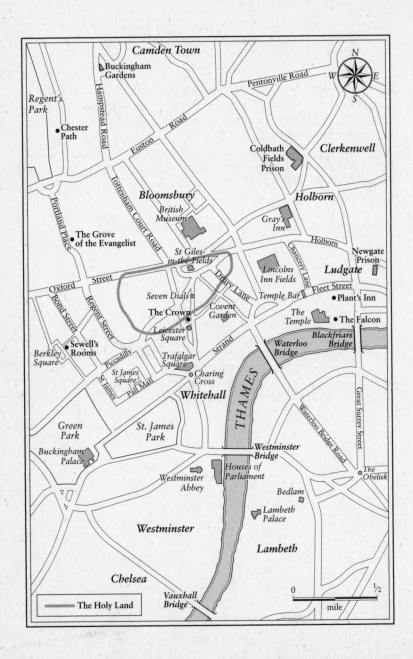

N
W E
S

Camden Town

Buckingham
Gardens

Regent's
Park

Pentonville Road

Chester
Path

Hampstead Road

Euston
Road

Coldbath
Fields
Prison

Clerkenwell

Portland Place

Bloomsbury

Tottenham Court Road

British
Museum

Holborn

Gray's
Inn

Holborn

The Grove
of the Evangelist

St Giles-
in-the-Fields

Lincolns
Inn Fields

Chancery Lane

Newgate
Prison

Ludgate

Oxford   Street

Regent Street

Bond Street

Seven Dials

Drury Lane

Temple Bar

Fleet Street

Plant's Inn

The Crown

Covent
Garden

The
Temple

The Falcon

Leicester
Square

Strand

Blackfriars
Bridge

Berkley
Square

Sewell's
Rooms

Waterloo
Bridge

Piccadilly

Trafalgar
Square

St James
Square

Pall Mall

St James

Charing
Cross

Whitehall

THAMES

Great Surrey Street

Green
Park

St. James
Park

Waterloo Bridge Road

Buckingham
Palace

Westminster
Bridge

The
Obelisk

Westminster
Abbey

Houses of
Parliament

Bedlam

Lambeth
Palace

Westminster

Lambeth

Chelsea

Vauxhall
Bridge

The Holy Land

0   ½

mile

A HANGING AT NEWGATE
Notes While On The Town

by

Edmund Whitty, Correspondent
The Falcon

LONDON, 11 May 1852

For the better part of Monday 10 May the vicinity of Newgate Prison took on the aspect of a seasonal fair. Beginning at nine the previous evening, pilgrims crowded onto the square, past the abattoirs of Snow Hill and the approaches from Newgate Market, while surrounding streets echoed with the heavy boots of the great unwashed. Some came by rail, some by cart, still more on foot, from Hackney, Newham, Greenwich and Hammersmith, as well as the extremities of Greater London (Stinking Lane, Pie Corner), where the potteries, ironworks and slop shops, as though commanded by the chimes of St Sepulchre, disgorged their working poor for an unscheduled treat.

After all, what could provide a better tonic for the oppressed human spirit, than to witness the fate of one more wretched than oneself?

> *Cold fowl and cigars, pickled onions in jars*
> *Welsh rabbit and kidneys – rare work for the jaws*
> *And very large lobsters with very large claws*
> *And there is McFuze and Lieutenant Tregooze*
> *And there is Sir Carnaby Jenks of the Blues,*
> *All come to see a man die in his shoes!*

Few retired to rest that night and all were too excited to sleep, passing the hours over draughts and cards, rattling the dice box while indulging in insulating potations, those who drank deepest jarring the night air with chorus after chorus of that depressing anthem for a hanging: 'O My! O My! Think I've Got to Die!' Among them wandered enterprising businessmen, renting out the last of the better positions: *Beautiful prospect! Excellent situation! Favoured view!*

As a professional your correspondent was permitted to observe the proceedings from a privileged position opposite and above the gallows, from which viewpoint the quality gather to take in the spectacle at £10 per seat. Indeed, the two young gentlemen beside us, Oxford men with an eye for the ladies and a patrician taste in cigars and brandy, seemed to regard the spectacle as existing purely for their own edification and amusement.

Below, more frugal enthusiasts paid in discomfort what their pocket-books could not afford; as early as two in the morning they took up their posts, stubbornly withstanding the pelting rain through six weary hours. Haggard and pinched they appeared by morning, especially the wretches accustomed to the airless factories and unwholesome abattoirs, with starved cheeks, toothless jaws and a moist milkiness of the eye. Not that the fellmongers, the glue-renderers, the carpenters and shoemakers appeared any more hardy or vigorous.

None the less, never did a more willing audience assemble to witness the most extreme penalty England has to offer the public other than a drawing and quartering – and the latter, while still a sentencing option, has not been performed in fifty years.

To the chagrin of my two lusty companions, few females honoured the company with their presence, only a few gaudily dressed kept women with skin like peeled fruit, their more foresighted escorts having procured their company as an enjoyable prelude and epilogue to the coming event.

As a trickle of pale sunlight appeared between the clouds and over the slate of the eastward rooftops, an impatient throng could be discerned monotonously tracing the outline of a circle six persons deep, as though working a treadwheel, backed by the shadow of Newgate, their faces self-consciously gloomy in keeping with the enjoyment of sorrow. Within this moving wall of woe, children disported in the first rays of the sun, like drab butterflies, mistaking the aroma of gin for flowers.

No matter their physical occupation, every mind in the square turned in the same direction: to imagining the event to come, to savouring the knowledge that such horror was about to be inflicted upon somebody else.

In a few moments the clock of St Sepulchre will chime, and he will ascend the scaffold steps to the drop, a temporary machine connected to the wall of the prison by means of iron hooks; where a rope will be drawn through a chain and around his neck; and when the Chaplain pronounces the dreadful words, *In the midst of life we are in death*, Executioner Calcraft, as dusty and as dependable as death itself, will draw the pump-like handle, release the bolt, and a carcass will be all that remains of a man named Christopher Walden. Thereafter, the body will be cut down, to be interred an hour later within the walls of Newgate, dignified by neither coffin nor shroud, covered with lime and water, then buried and the ground smoothed so that, within the shortest time possible, the Fiend in Human Form – this week's edition at any rate – will have been erased from the face of the earth, like a mistake in spelling.

And yet as a regular spectator of such public offerings at Newgate of a Monday morning, your correspondent cannot but wonder whether a second Fiend is brought to life by the elimination of the first – a Fiend unconfined to the material remains of Christopher Walden, free to spread and drift like the black smoke from surrounding chimneys, to be inhaled by the population as a whole.

Not that the earth will be any the poorer for Walden's absence.

Swell, fraud, corrupter of any misfortunate with whom he came into discourse, our man stands condemned for a brutal murder, under circumstances which your correspondent must refrain from repeating, by order of the Chief Magistrate of London. Let it suffice to note that Walden's hanging is an eventuality akin to a long-standing infection laying claim to a voluptuary.

Yet again one wonders where the malignancy stops. In what society does such a Christopher Walden encounter a person of the rank of Arlington Fogg, an in such circumstances? What explanation exists that might entirely remove this blot to the legacy of Arlington Fogg? Like blood on bed-sheets, the stain will remain. A *frisson* of scandal to heighten the coming drama and to entertain the throng, while business is transacted for profit.

First come the refreshment peddlers, with food and drink made from putrid ingredients or adulterated with toxic substances. Next come the flying patterers and balladeers, to market their similarly unwholesome chronicles at five pence a page. In decades previous, when a man was condemned on Friday and summarily hanged on Monday, there was no time to prepare and print a 'Last Confession'; now the condemned man is given at least a week's grace and sometimes two – and a commercial opportunity is born.

Prominent among these merchants of false news stands an author promoting a work entitled *The Sorrowful Lamentation of William Ryan, Otherwise Known as Chokee Bill*, an account distinguished by its utter disregard for the fundamental requisites of journalistic veracity, a work of fiction in all but name, whose unabashed purpose is to exploit the macabre achievement of its principal (in comparison to which Christopher Walden is a Piccadilly pickpocket), and the public dread it inspired, to lucrative effect.

As the clock at St Sepulchre tolls in measured monotony, somewhere within those walls the door of a death cell is flung open and the condemned prisoner, freshly shaved, wearing the suit of a bridegroom and a pair of white Berlin gloves, sets upon his bleak promenade down the dimly lit passage to an elaborate iron staircase leading to the basement, down which he trips with exaggerated vigour, like a schoolboy at playtime.

But now he stops and the false bravado disappears, as a door opens and reality greets him with the watery light of morning.

From the open door to the machine is not greater than a hundred and fifty feet, which distance he covers as though in a trance, stiffly, arms strapped to his sides by means of leather belts. At each corner of the scaffold stands an official dressed in black, bearing a long wand in one hand, like an inquisitor in some medieval exorcism. Upon seeing the prisoner, the crowd lets out a low moan, punctuated with cries of *Down in front!*

The Chaplain reads aloud the solemn service for the Burial of the Dead. As the procession reaches the ladder, the voice falters and quavers appropriately.

The prisoner climbs the ladder, to be met at the summit by Mr Calcraft – who, before acquiring his current post, flogged boys for a living. Above his dusty beard, the executioner's facial pores appear to have been pricked repeatedly with pointed sticks.

Now the cries of the multitude shrink as though for want of air, to the dreamy murmur of a sea-shell; now one's ears throb with the unnatural silence, broken by the drone of the Chaplain who prays for the departing sinner, and by the incongruously amorous patter of pigeons, fluttering across the pavement and nestling on surrounding eaves.

Now the Chaplain pauses in his reading, as though advancing a final plea for mercy from the Almighty. Now he whispers an inaudible question to the condemned man, to which the latter replies aloud, with a measure of impatience: 'I have nothing to say to you, Reverend. Thank you for your interest.'

Now Christopher Walden, of his own accord, steps into the centre of the trap, under the beam. He pauses, blinking rapidly as though in unaccustomed light, his face shining as pale as a candle. A smile appears at the corners of the lips, together with a slight shrug of the shoulders, as if in dismissal of some blunder, as though to say, *Not to worry. It doesn't matter now.*

Now his face grows puzzled, perhaps uncertain whether what is happening around him is genuine or imagined. The bell tolls inexorably. The people bend forward with tightened stomachs and straining eyes. Now the hangman grasps the rope – Walden bends his head to assist him. Now the noose is slipped over, and the head returns to its former upright position; the prisoner moves his neck about like a man with a tight collar. Now the hangman hurries to the ladder – but then remembers something he has forgotten. He returns to the drop and places the cap, which resembles a too-large night-cap, upon the patient's head.

'God bless you. Goodbye,' says the patient in a husky voice, extending one pinioned, fin-like, white-gloved hand. In response, the hangman takes the hand and shakes it as though it were the normal way. Now the white cap is pulled over Walden's face; the pointed edge moves with his rapid breathing.

The executioner descends the ladder to take position beneath the drop.

Now the bolt is drawn with a metallic click. Down falls the drop with a dull crash, and a man falls through the opening, elbows thrown out, fists clenched. Now the body spins below, where the hangman seizes the legs and pulls. One knee bends spasmodically upward, as though attempting to hop over a wall.

The chest heaves convulsively. The close-fitting white linen cap takes on a momentary, peculiar strain, as if a bag of blackberries has been bruised, which quickly sags into its normal contour and its natural hue.

After a moment the hangman looses his hold so that the body spins more slowly, until it comes to rest, a shapeless, dead thing, lit by the morning sun.

From the seats of the quality, applause.

Notes in Passing: Your correspondent salutes the bracing egalitarian spirit which has overcome some of the most fashionable households in London following published concern at the availability of over-the-counter poisons – especially arsenic and strychnine – in the light of the Redding case. About the estate of Lord Throttle, for example, Her Ladyship having previously made such a scene at Bishop's over the pudding, it is now the custom that servants be served before, and not after, their betters, and from the same cooking-pot as well.

Lord Throttle's servants have never eaten better.

Soho

A pity the discovery was made so soon after breakfast, thinks Mr Macklin while holding the long coat-tails of the younger policeman away from the mess, holding them out to either side as if carrying the bridal train in church.

'Gone queasy, have we, Mr Dick? Nasty, was it?'

'Oh dear Jesus,' moans the younger man while wiping his mouth with his handkerchief. 'Hideous, it was. She were like a . . . a piece of . . .' Whereupon the mental picture returns, producing a renewed heaving, as more of Mr Dick's breakfast splashes upon the cobbles.

'If you sees a little brown ring pop out,' says Mr Macklin, 'that is your arsehole.'

'Very good, Sir. Very nice indeed.' Having cleaned his face, Mr Dick fumbles for the top hat he cast aside in the emergency, Mr Macklin releases the coat-tails, and the two policemen contemplate the narrow strip of pre-dawn Prussian blue in between the surrounding rooftops, considering what is to be done.

'Just a bit of humour, Mr Dick, no offence meant. I had not realized this were your first. Be assured, you'll get quite used to it.'

In this dirty and disreputable part of the city, at this silent hour when even the horses are asleep, this is the time and the place for it, thinks

Mr Macklin, this is when you find them. And yet it always comes as a surprise, always they catch a man off guard, as though, like their assailants, they have been waiting for the right moment.

'She were . . . sliced, is all I can say. Carved, like your Christmas goose.'

'An unseemly comparison, Sir. No need to bring Christmas into it.'

'Look at her for yourself then.'

'Only if necessary, Mr Dick. Tell me one thing: were there a scarf?'

'A scarf, Sir?'

'Were she choked with a scarf?'

'There were no neck to choke, Sir. There were no place to put a scarf, if you get my meaning.' Pissing against the wall, at first he had thought it was a pile of bloody rags beside him, so far had it strayed from the appearance of a human being. By the time he bent down close enough with the torch to see what it was, he could smell cheap lavender, and then he knew.

'I do not think strangulation had anything to do with it, Sir. He would not have gone to the effort if she were already dead.'

'Very good, then, let us be back to the shop before first light, and I shall send out Mr O'Malley with the cart, to remove it. Or dump it in the Thames, if the morgue is full.'

'Sir, the woman has been murdered. She did not do this to herself.'

'I'm aware of that, Mr Dick.'

'We must make a full report. The murderer must be apprehended.'

'Oh, is that so? And where do you propose we begin? Shall we ferret out the twenty or so gentlemen our judy there may have serviced this once around the clock – the nameless clerks, sailors, drapers, not to mention your fellow Peelers getting a bit for free? On the night after a hanging, business is brisk. Or perhaps we should begin with her toff, whoever he may be, who may have become tired of her, for that is all it takes with that sort. Or her whoremaster, with rent owing and the need to set an example for others. Or her fancy man, alive with drink and jealousy. Or a rival judy over the Devil knows what. And while we comb the district from Haymarket to Soho, and Soho to Leicester Square, let us send a team of inspectors to her home village, wherever that may be, to interrogate the families she has disgraced by her own ruin.

'Shall we mobilize the entire force over the slashing of a whore? You decide, Mr Dick, and be quick about it – for you'll see another just like that one within a fortnight, and another after that. With this class of woman, it isn't whether, but when.'

The younger policeman turns toward the darkness of the alley in which he found her, splayed out on the cobbles like a doll. He can still see her in his mind's eye, as if she is calling to him. 'Do you suggest, Sir, that we leave it at that? We simply walk away from a murder?'

'Mr. Dick, if I were to show you a deep hole you might fall into, and were you to do so, who do you suggest is at fault for the mishap?'

'I should certainly blame myself for failing to listen.'

'Precisely. Such women murder themselves, is my way of looking at it.'

'And yet it is a very high price to pay for not listening.'

'May I remind you, Mr Dick: had you not taken it upon yourself to have a piss on a public thoroughfare, you would never have seen it and we would not be having this discussion.'

'True for you, Sir, you're right there. But what was it about the scarf?'

'Which scarf, Mr Dick?'

'I mean, seeing as Chokee Bill is in Coldbath Fields, awaiting execution, what were the meaning in your question about a scarf?'

'Force of habit, is the answer. The newspapers, Mr Dick. These journalists have power, they hook the mind while rubbing one's face in excrement. It is not easy to turn the page.'

'And yet, turn the page we must, is your meaning.'

'Well said, lad. You have a future with the Metropolitan Police.'

I

Camden Town

There is something unspeakable in Whitty's mouth. Is it a dead animal?

No, it is his tongue.

The correspondent opens his mouth – carefully, for the lips adhere to one another and the skin in one corner has cracked. He refrains from opening his eyes, for the lids have been secured by two sharp objects.

He slides gently over the edge of the bed, flops to the floor with a wet thud, and gropes blindly for the commode. He relieves his swollen bladder while remaining on all fours, for balance. He rolls onto his side, arms and legs splayed in front, heaving in short grunts.

He has transformed into a dog. That would explain the terrible taste. A dog will put any deuced thing in its mouth. He remains still, eyes closed, thinking things through ... Sometimes of a morning he imagines himself having fallen prey to some malevolent night sprite, a temperance fiend perhaps, which sneaks into his bedroom carrying a disgusting substance, maybe faeces, with which to punish people who sleep with their mouths open, having imbibed deeply.

On the other hand, maybe he has become a dog.

He burrows his head under the rug for warmth. He sneezes on a ball of dust and experiences the sharp sensation of a wire tightening around his skull. Placing one paw on his head, he presses his temple with his thumb. . .

A thumb. He has a thumb. He is not a dog.

For a moment, he thought he was a dog.

Whitty reawakens with a ball of dust in his mouth – the result of lying beneath a carpet which has not been beaten in years. Why, he asks himself, would he be lying under a carpet? Is something biblical happening? It was Jael who concealed the Canaanite general under a carpet, then drove a tent peg through his head. Was the Canaanite choking on a dust ball at the time?

Why is he thinking these thoughts of choking and death?

Choking. Death. The public hanging. Newgate. One by one, like candles at a festival of Druids, the events of yesterday illuminate the inner passage of his mind. A steady diet of weekly hangings, while necessary to sustain life in a slow news period, is like oil of vitriol to the human spirit. Unlike other sensational events, one does not become inured to a hanging – rather, it is quite the opposite, as though a layer of skin is removed with each repetition of the spectacle.

Naturally, following yesterday's proceedings, restorative cordials were taken earlier than usual, in the company of two companions whose names escape him for the moment. In addition, unless he dreamt it, certain other tonics were taken, which indulgence disturbed the natural rhythm of his body, the equilibrium of stimulants, depressants and opiates which sees him through the day. Consequently, other than the hanging itself, yesterday is a blank wall . . .

Oh, the dread. Where did he go? What did he do? Whom did he do it with, or to, or over? More urgently, at some point in the day did he turn in his copy? On time? *Did he?* Apprehension grows like a boil: does he still have a profession? If not, what will he do with what remains of his time on earth? Where will he go? What will he drink? With no purpose in life other than one's occupation, one is no better than an animal.

A thread of drool moistens the worn stubble of the rug beneath Whitty's chin, where he lies dormant, seeking scraps of remembered events, like a jilted lover reassembling a letter torn apart in a jealous rage.

Plant's comes to mind. The rear snug at Plant's. Words exchanged in anger – with whom? He must speak to Mrs Plant, who keeps an inventory of his excesses and transgressions, for future reference.

A misgiving: something about Mrs Plant.

Following the most recent misfortune, his latest monumental blunder, it has been Whitty's practice to let no one know precisely where he lives. Instead, he frequents regular haunts at which, at times of his choosing, he may be found. Plant's Inn, situated just off Whitefriars near the offices of *The Falcon*, is his preferred address – an open-pit mine in which journalists root for nuggets as part of their professional day.

He spent the evening at Plant's. Therefore he must have visited the office earlier in the day, for that is the way of it, a gin or two as a nominal reward for some trifling achievement – such as a completed and submitted report on a hanging; which visit can extend into the evening, spending the fruits of one story in hopes of another, sniffing the brains of his colleagues for truffles of information, and being snouted in return.

So there it is. He was at Plant's, therefore he turned in his copy. Therefore he still has a profession. Despite whatever indiscretion or excess, life may continue, such as it is.

His relief liberates other memories rendered blurry by an evening of gin and medicinal snuff – which activity ended with a few drops of laudanum, whose purported blessing, a sound sleep, is undercut by the most terrible dreams. . .

. . . as a regular spectator of such public offerings at Newgate of a Monday morning, your correspondent cannot but wonder whether a second Fiend is brought to life by the elimination of the first – a Fiend unconfined to the material remains of Christopher Walden, free to spread and drift like the black smoke from surrounding chimneys, to be inhaled by the population as a whole . . .

Whitty awakens with a start. What was that? Who wrote it ? Did he write it?

. . . an account distinguished by its utter disregard for the fundamental requisites of journalistic veracity, a work of fiction in all but name, whose unabashed purpose is to exploit the macabre achievement of its principal (in comparison to which Christopher Walden is a Piccadilly pickpocket), and the public dread it inspired, to lucrative effect.

Trenchant stuff: what on earth was it about? Something on poisoning?

His body and mind throbbing like an inflamed nerve, Whitty crawls on all fours to the grate in the opposite wall, gathers the last few lumps of coal from the tin scuttle, sets them alight, and curls up before the fire in such a way that his entire body may occupy a pool of uncertain warmth.

Once he was a dog, now he is a cat. As his mind clears with its recollections of the previous night, he suspects that he may have been, at some point, an ape.

Mr Darwin, if rumours of his current premise serve, is only half-correct when he postulates the necessary evolution of the species. It is possible to devolve as well as to evolve. Depending upon your poison.

Whitty is now upright, though uncertain how the feat was accomplished. Temporarily, his intestines have found equilibrium. And he has had a wash. *Capital.* Nothing to tone the system like a hot bath, a cup of strong tea, a restorative dose of medicated snuff – and a teaspoon of

Acker's Chlorodine, a useful mixture of opium, marijuana and cocaine in alcohol.

Feeling human now (whatever that means), the correspondent brushes his side-whiskers to their requisite sleekness and shaves the edges, resisting the perverse impulse which he imagines every London clubman to experience while shaving of a difficult morning – to turn the razor sideways, slit the throat and be done.

For the second time since awakening he reflects upon the bleak insufficiency of his one-dimensional existence. A clock with one hand loses perspective; a man with one leg topples over – but what to do? Should he marry? Take a commission in the Dragoons? Re-commit to the Church of England? Ha!

Hallo. A slight swelling on the right cheekbone, as though from a blow of some kind. From someone left-handed, presumably. Not a good sign.

He dresses carefully: fresh shirt and collar, silk cravat, the customary salt-and-pepper trousers; putrefaction within, perfection without – the secret to worldly success . . .

Hallo. What is this? A stain on the left buttock, indicating possible contact with the floor. And a ripped seam as well.

He finds spare trousers and a fresh waistcoat. He retrieves his coat and hat, noting that the coat is clean, the top hat uncrushed. Whatever happened, it happened indoors.

Courage.

Streaks of watery sunlight trickle over the surrounding roofs and tree-tops of Camden Town, illuminating the stucco horror that is Whitty's current lodging, with its front entrance (dual ringers for Guests and Trade), its patch of withered vegetation surrounding the backyard privy, its second staircase for Mrs Quigley's sole, emaciated servant.

Widowed and with a modest endowment, Mrs Harlan Quigley maintains a close watch over all that rests within her province, in the way that a spider keeps in touch with its web, sensing each tremor as an extension of her own plangent body, whether it is the sound of a hoop removed from a pail in the back kitchen, or a rumoured change in the financial position of one of her guests.

'Good afternoon, Mr Whitty. Two gentlemen, *sniff*, to see you last evening.'

Owing to a set of wooden teeth which might fly from her mouth in an unguarded moment, the widow habitually pushes her vowels through pursed lips as though through a tube; no doubt in compensating for this necessary constriction, her nostrils are given to punctuating her speech in short, meaningful sniffs.

'Two gentlemen do you say, Mrs Quigley?' Whitty's heart sinks. He does not need this.

'Two large gentlemen, who voiced concern about a confidential matter. Something about, I regret to say, rats.'

Blast. Can they have tracked him down already? 'Rats, do you say, Madam? Some mistake, surely.'

'Would that it were so, Mr Whitty. Buckingham Gardens does not permit an association with gentlemen who wager, nor with gentlemen who concern themselves with rats.'

'I beg, Madam, that we may discuss this at some later date, for I am unwell, and have urgent business in the city.'

Mrs Quigley blocks his passage, a formidable woman in pagoda sleeves, a crinoline, multiple petticoats and a skirt like a black umbrella. Like any man brought up by a governess, Whitty represses the instinctive urge to flinch in anticipation of a blow from the flat of her hand.

'*Sniff*. A word if you please, Mr Whitty.' The proprietress inserts herself between the correspondent and the front door with the surprising speed of a rhinoceros. 'I shall speak plainly, Sir. Having noted, and not for the first time, certain disturbances, certain improprieties on your part, having taken complaints from Mr Stedman and other guests, furthermore having noted the balance outstanding in your account . . .'

Whitty's crushing headache has returned along with the residual anxiety, the impending sensation that he is about to tumble into a chasm. 'Forgive me, Mrs Quigley. Something disagreed with me. The mutton at dinner . . .'

Wedged between Mrs Quigley and the entry wall, Whitty recoils from the pressure of her body, redolent with stale lavender – which he finds, in his present condition, insupportable. Distorted visually by the throbbing in his forehead, she towers above him, backed by multiple shelves of hideous porcelain miniatures, like a Chinese dragon in some pagan version of Hell.

A waking nightmare and so early in the day.

'Madam, I take your complaint with all seriousness, yet I beg you, important business calls . . .' Thinks the correspondent: such as the need to heave.

'Mr Whitty. This establishment caters to temperate, respectable, working gentlemen, for whom a restful night's sleep is of the utmost importance. Hence, I am afraid, Buckingham Gardens requires you to seek other arrangements, immediately.'

'Madam, you push me too far. This is not a convenient time.'

'You are not welcome here, Sir. Is that plain enough for you? If I have to summon a constable, I intend to see you vacate the premises with dispatch.' Mrs Quigley folds her substantial arms beneath her bosom, flushed with the assurance of power over her domain in Camden Town.

Whitty takes a deep breath. It has come to this. And so early in the day.

'I thank you, Madam, for you have done me a service. Namely, you have set me free to speak my mind and to write frankly. As it happens, I was about to undertake an exposure of the degraded state of suburban lodging. Naturally out of loyalty to Buckingham Gardens, I intended to spare our readers a full account of the conditions here. A moral compromise that weighed upon my mind; but now, thanks to you, I am at liberty to tell the truth, and damn the consequences.'

Mrs Quigley's wattles tremble over her starched collar. 'Sir, I will have you understand that Buckingham Gardens offers accommodations of the first rank.'

'So you may have deceived yourself, Madam, the wretches in your care being for the most part clerks, necks like bent umbrellas from a lifetime of subservience. However, upon this occasion you have drawn to your bosom a member of the Fourth Estate. You have taken a step up and I congratulate you. See that you do nothing further to jeopardize your position.'

Whitty traverses the walkway to Ampthill Street, swinging his walking-stick with feigned nonchalance, as the door to Buckingham Gardens slams behind him with impressive force. He turns down Ampthill Street, bending against a chilly wind, feeling vaguely corrupt.

After London became uninhabitable for the leisure classes, who now venture into the city only in season, white-collar workers likewise began to desert the city for suburbs such as Camden Town, a community of middle-class strivers whose motives for immigration are a mix of pastoral Utopianism, everyday pretension, and a desire to impose upon the rural landscape their vision of gentility.

It was a mistake to flee to Camden Town. It is neither natural nor healthful that a London clubman should dwell outside the West End. He could have stayed ahead of the chase by moving from one shabby nethersken to the next, or talked his way into a club under an assumed name: anything would have been preferable to this flight to the edge of the earth.

He trudges past hastily erected, identical buildings of yellow brick, with titles such as Kent Corner and the ubiquitous Shady Nook, with dates below the eaves, like headstones. As is usual with denuded landscapes, the wind lifts the dust, which swirls about him as an abrasive counterpart to the London fog. Whitty feels the dust insinuate itself into his clothes, there to itch him for the day. He reminds himself that, for the talented correspondent, every experience, however unpleasant, is crisp copy. He tells himself to view Camden Town not as a curse but as a social experiment; material, perhaps, for an exposé on the sterility of the suburbs such as the one he just described to Mrs Quigley – a narrative with greater potential than most, of late.

In his mind, Whitty composes a tentative paragraph:

> *In accommodating the catastrophic tide of immigration from the country-side that occurred over the past decade, as well as the exponential growth in the power and wealth of business, whole new areas have grown, seemingly overnight, out of rubble and open space. Greater London grows ever greater in sprawling suburbs of semi-detached dwellings and rental accommodation, all with the same look of mass-produced gentility, defined by the one aspiration cherished by Britons of all classes – the desire for private, secure space, uncontaminated by the next class down. . .*

A decent opening. Trenchant stuff. Crisp copy. Pip, pip.

A cab is nearly as scarce as a pub in Camden Town. Drivers find little custom among the ink-stained wretches who commute on foot the three miles to the city each morning, unable to afford a lowly omnibus, much less the new double-decker buses, with decency boards to prevent pedestrians from looking up the skirts of the ladies. Hence, the grinder he manages to flag as it emerges from Mornington Crescent is a most dissipated vehicle, whose cabman, in cracked riding boots, a horse-blanket for a mantle and a whip, peers down at Whitty like Shakespeare in livery. 'Where's it to then, Guv?'

'Fleet Street, my good man, if you please.'

'Yor be the press if I'm not mistaken.'

'Indeed, you're correct.'

The cabman produces a greasy copy of *Dodd's*. 'I likes to keep up with the news. Shockin' business on the hangman what starved his mother. Well done, Guv. Right fly.'

'Thank you very much.' He accepts the compliment, although the piece was written by Fraser, a rival he holds in contempt. He recalls that the hangman was in fact a bootseller whose mother died of worms, that Fraser's account contained more fiction than fact by a generous measure; yet such was the response, *Dodd's* was required to print extra editions. He wonders, not for the first time, if there is any point in reporting actual events at all.

The grinder's spindle-legged, moth-eaten horse, hairs on end like porcupine quills, whisks its tail into his face as Whitty mounts the runner; the cabman flicks his whip with a practised movement of the wrist so that the abrupt forward motion flings the passenger rudely into his seat, even while closing the door. Bracing himself for the bone-rattling trip down Hampstead Road to shabby Tottenham Court Road to precious Oxford Street, the correspondent settles into a deepening apprehension and gloom.

Clearly the cab has been out all night. One of its silk window-curtains has been torn from its fastenings and flutters in irregular festoons on the inward wall. The velvet cushions, worn shiny by a thousand trousers and the pomaded hair of a thousand heads, are powdered with cigar-ashes. He notes a theatrical pass-check under his feet, and the dirty fingers of a white kid glove stuffed down the back of the seat.

He leans back, closes his eyes and falls into a half-sleep, in defiance of the vehicle's unpredictable lurching. In his half-dream he is speaking, or rather orating, to a restless throng at some sort of political rally. The phrases issuing from his mouth are in a foreign language and he is unable to discern his own text. Now it comes to him that he is standing not on a platform but on a gallows, in the courtyard of Newgate Prison. The air is swirling with pigeons. One of the birds flies straight at him from the slate roof opposite, striking him hard on the cheek . . .

A particularly deep pot-hole jars the vehicle so that Whitty is nearly thrown from his seat, and now the sounds of wheels surround him like waves of the sea: the clatter of hansom wheels, the rattle of the brougham, the groan of broad cartwheels, the latter leaving behind the fragrance of green peas and country earth. He hears a babble of voices, excited, angry, pleading, a not-quite musical roar like the sound of a large marriage party, or a political gathering, or a livestock auction.

He rubs his eyes and peers through the window as the grinder makes a right turn onto Regent Street and south to the city. Beyond the rattling omnibuses, saddle horses and drays are fine ladies in flounced skirts, sleek gentlemen in twice-about neck-cloths and black top hats, gliding up and down the walkway like moving columns, pausing at the superior shops and furniture galleries whose square-paned windows glint like spectacles in the morning sun.

A mustard-coloured chariot with a trail of liveried servants stops in front of a chemist's. The delighted shopkeeper dashes across the pavement to open the door with the sweaty enthusiasm of a man who has recently stepped back from the brink of financial ruin, his fall checked by the arrest of William Ryan, otherwise known as Chokee Bill, the Fiend in Human Form.

It is impossible to overestimate how truly unbalanced London became during the Chokee Bill panic. Yet the cognizance that a murderer walked the streets, and the lurid nature of the murders themselves, would never have produced such an extremity were it not for their artful treatment in the sensational press, notably by Edmund Whitty of *The Falcon* – who, through a vivid, not to say lurid, reconstruction of the murders, the murdered and the murderer, stirred the London reader's torpid imagination into imagining the violent death of a fallen woman as something notable, or even abnormal.

In fact it was not until three women had been murdered while plying the trade, murdered with the same scarf and the same mutilations, that the *Telegraph* stooped even to a mention that the murders had anything in common. (And there have been two in as many months since: God only knows how many anonymous wretches died previously by those same hands.)

Even at that, with the wilful myopia only editors achieve, only two of the four commonalities were deemed relevant: the fact that all three were women, and the fact that all three were whores. Hence, the *Telegraph* chose to present the murders, not as the work of a single fiend, but as though violent death and mutilation were a fate of all who choose that style of life, and that these three women together sound a dreadful message to women who would follow the path to ruin. As far as the *Telegraph* was concerned (as well as the Metropolitan Police), the identity of the murderer, whether one or several, was largely irrelevant.

It became clear to the correspondent that, if these wretched women were to cause any notice whatsoever through the fog of reflex moralism, it would be necessary to shift public attention from the victim to the murderer. Further, until such time as the identity of the Fiend in Human Form was known, it would be necessary to invent one.

Thus it came to pass.

Lying in his bed with a serious case of morning sickness, and with a deadline looming over him like some dreadful bat, Whitty partook a medicament from his chemist, fell into a slumber . . . and through the opium haze, before his mind's eye, slouched the inspiration, the man of the hour, the figure who would lift the murder of whores into the realm of the newsworthy: Chokee Bill, the Fiend in Human Form.

In supplying a name for the murderer, Whitty had no sure estimation of the potential of a symbolic character to rivet the public imagination and focus it on a narrative; none the less, this soon became apparent. Within a matter of days, so entrenched and so vivid had the Fiend become in the public mind that, had any man claimed to have created Chokee Bill, he would have been made a laughing-stock.

It was as though a resounding chord had been struck by the sound of the name itself, which Whitty borrowed from a half-remembered childhood rhyme:

> Up the river, over the hill
> Into the village is Chokee Bill
> With (something, something) and graves to fill. . .

Perhaps the name served to reawaken some ancient, common memory, some long-forgotten, Gothic bogeyman. In any case, Chokee Bill permeated the city like a miasma, causing business to contract as though the plague were upon London.

For the economic slump to follow, Whitty feels not a shred of remorse and more than a little of its opposite. The wave of public alarm – and the attention of the constabulary – would not have required the name Chokee Bill to effect, had the victims been shopkeepers, and not whores . . .

Whitty peers through the curtains at the passing parade of expensive fabric, the magenta satins, the bottle-green velvets. By unfocusing somewhat and thereby altering his field of vision, he can discern the thin shapes of sneak thieves, beggars and sweepers, darting out of the crannies between buildings, scuttling sideways like crabs then retreating into the shadows.

He observes a girl no older than six, in rags, crying in distress over what appears to have been a beating, a performance which she enacts on a daily basis. As always, he marks with heartfelt admiration her portrayal of hopeless despair, the theatrical sweep with which she gesticulates, clasping her little hands together and pressing them to her breast.

A magenta dress with its side-whiskered escort swishes by the child without pause. Lacking the Fiend in Human Form to disconcert them, they have no reason to notice.

2

Fleet Street, west of Ludgate

The cabman tosses Whitty's coin into the air and catches it with an impudent wink, then, sensing the possibility of a fare in the middle distance, whips his foaming wreck of a horse and tools off, leaving the correspondent warily scanning the streetscape off Chancery Lane for suspicious parties, while identifying the beggars and performers who occupy customary tracts under the arches and porticoes, as though by inheritance.

A solemn, sharp-featured young prostitute watches traffic from a second-floor window while tearing a newspaper into strips for curling-papers; behind her a young man yawns and buttons his shirt. On the walkway beneath her a Hindoo, in a voluminous turban, orange caftan, worsted stockings and hobnailed boots, sings a foreign ditty while beating a tom-tom with stoic monotony.

At the corner beside the tobacconist's, an Italian organ-grinder, hirsute and sunburnt, churns out airs from *I masnadieri*, 'The Old Hundredth' and 'Postman's Knock', cycled throughout the day like the chimes of a clock. Nearby, a coarse-featured woman, in a Scotch cap adorned by a thatch of rusty black feathers, dances the highland fling, while her partner, a shabby operator with one eye, produces a shrill howl from a set of etiolated bagpipes.

Each of these parties is familiar to the correspondent, having from time to time served as paid eyes and ears supplying fragments of information, to be connected like scattered dots into a coherent picture, from hearsay to rumour to fact.

Other spaces and terraces along Fleet Street are occupied, as always, by costermongers.

The Irish fruit-seller with his cart, for which the loan (at two hundred per cent interest) has been nearly paid. On the street, such a thing approaches the acquisition of a building. Next to him the clothes-man, tall and skeletal beside racks of men's and ladies' apparel, freshly stolen from the clothes-lines of the better districts.

In less-favoured locations stand less-favoured retailers, all wearing the same quiet expression of melancholy struggle – slowly starving to death, keeping out of the workhouse one more week in the last gasp of their independence. Their cries, none the less, are a confederacy of hearty optimism.

Paaaaper! Any of the morning paaaapers!

Strange news from Sussex!

Fine pictures, show stunning!

Will you buy!

What d'you lack?

The choice is yours!

As though to provide a visual counterpart to the vocal din, the walls around these melodious hawkers are themselves a clutter of messages:

Malt whisky from John Howse!

Can you help me out?

Rose Swingle is a drunken cunt!

Suspended above the heads of the prospective buyers and sellers rushing in all directions are the signs of shops, scarcely nine feet above the ground, large enough to nearly touch one another in the middle of the street, each sign proclaiming a rare and precious commodity or service. Beneath one's feet even the drain covers carry a message of some kind.

Whitty confines his attention to the specific object he seeks, or dreads: specifically, any person who might conceivably deal in rats, or associate with people who deal in rats, or search for clubmen who have failed spectacularly in their efforts to profit in rats.

Thus far, the coast is clear – thanks, perhaps, to the frock-coated Peeler standing patiently at the opposite corner. (Whitty reminds himself to write in favour of an increased police presence at the earliest opportunity.)

Hallo. The correspondent's survey pauses at the patch of street formerly occupied by Stump Conners, the armless musician and informant, able to play the violincello with his feet. In his stead (dead probably, Stumpy has not been looking well) now stands a man Whitty has never seen before: robust yet melancholy, fresh-coloured yet weary, with full whiskers and a broad sandy brow, wearing shiny corduroy trousers, a jacket whose seams have been strengthened with brass studs, a pair of stout hobnailed boots, and what was at one time a fine stovepipe hat but is now the colour and consistency of soot, careening at an odd angle to the left as though having suffered a chimney fire. In the hatband are inserted several sheets of paper; other papers fill the crook of his arm. Around his neck is the red handkerchief typically worn by costermongers.

A standing patterer by trade, announced by the sandwich-board he carries (divided into compartments illustrating the merchandise on offer), and by the roar emanating from his mouth (among standing patterers it is a rule that the greater the bellow the better the chance of a sale). Not that it is possible to ascertain what the man is announcing, it being the way that only isolated words (*Barbarous, Wicious* and *Full Particulars*) can be discerned.

A typical specimen, excepting that this particular individual appears to be directing his attentions solely in Whitty's direction. As the correspondent steps off the kerb (slipping a ha'penny to the Indian crossing-sweeper to preserve his boots), even with his back turned he can sense those watery blue eyes watching him, while a stentorian voice breaks off from its barrage of syllables to recite, with perfect diction, an excerpt from a ballad:

> *Hark! the solemn bell does summons*
> *The wretched murderer to his fate,*
> *Let us hope he does repent,*
> *His sins, before it is too late.*
> *See the hangman is approaching,*
> *No one present can him save,*
> *While his victims are in Heaven,*
> *Whitty fills a murderer's grave.*

Hallo. The correspondent pauses; no doubt his mind is in a dreamlike state, as frequently happens when suffering from morning sickness; yet he thought he descried a familiar name.

He shakes off this mild hallucination as he turns up the narrow court to Ingester Square, a nondescript patch of grass containing a forlorn plane tree, with a decrepit bench beneath for minimal shelter from the weather.

Below the square, the byways wind down the embankment to a series of steps containing a warning – 'Clothing Must Remain Decent' – and thence to a number of open sewage drains, where boy mudlarks forage for objects to sell; where, to the left, through a mist like hothouse steam, one can see the half-destroyed hulk of Blackfriars Bridge, once the route for children on their way to visit their parents in Marshalsea, the debtors' prison.

His father's investments did not lead him quite so far down as that institution – or perhaps one should say that they took him far beyond it. A solicitor by profession, Richard Whitty had attained a measure of craft sufficient to entangle his holdings in a devaluation dispute at the

Chancery, a web of such intricacy that the matter is unlikely to be sorted out this century; which stratagem afforded ample time for a relocation in the New World – where, Whitty has no doubt, a substantial nest-egg awaited. When last Whitty heard from Mother (Father having ceased communication over another matter), they had settled in California, having joined a railroad syndicate. Next came a curt announcement from Father that his mother had died 'of natural causes'.

And, as mad Hamlet put it so well, the rest is silence.

At the far side of Ingester Square sits a queer, dumpy, blank old building, like a warehouse that has been sat upon; which inconspicuousness confers an immense advantage, for the challenge of finding it allows irate readers plenty of time to cool down. *The Falcon*'s headquarters is further diminuated by the two churches adjacent, as well as by the proclaimed headquarters of two fine-sounding companies which have never been heard of except by their directors.

He stops at a nondescript door in the corner of the squat building, marked with a single word: FALCON. Before entering he turns once more to scan the square, for he has an uneasy impression of being watched.

In the churchyard, the man in the crooked hat deftly slips out of sight behind a monument, and remains motionless until Whitty has disappeared inside the building.

3
Sewell's rooms, off Bruton Street

Nestled in a suite of mahogany-panelled, second-floor rooms opposite Berkeley Square, following an English breakfast of kipper, kidney, toast and jam (it is well past noon), two young gentlemen settle into their coffee, cigarets and a bit of a read.

Reginald Harewood, in ill humour, groans at something in the latest *Dodd's*: 'Oh dear. There's another fellow gone.'

Immersed in a volume of Browning, Walter Sewell absently stirs an unwholesome amount of sugar into his cup.

Harewood lowers his newspaper with an expression of reproach. 'You might at least muster sufficient interest to ask the poor chap's name.'

'Sorry. Who was it?'

'It was Swan-Thackeray.'

'Charlie? Oh dear. How did he die?'

'Not dead, married.'

'Married? Oh.' Sewell shrugs. 'Well, as St Paul put it, *Better married than burn.*'

'No scripture, please, old boy. As I have said on numerous occasions, we received a lifetime's worth at Chapel.'

'Quite.'

The two young men – one handsome, one not, one tall, one not, one whiskered, one not – have taken their meal courtesy of the less attractive but better financed of the two, born Walter Sewell, patronized by fellow Oxonians as 'Roo'.

Reginald Harewood – 'Reggie', as he is known by friends, teammates, competitors and a succession of willing young women – spoons a dollop of gooseberry jam onto an end of buttered toast. 'Deuce of a thing, marriage. Don't disagree with it in a general way, of course . . .'

'Such arrangements seem to be the rule,' comments Sewell, who decides to risk another biblical reference. 'Adam's rib and all that. Even Noah's animals went two by two.'

'Poor examples. You're leaving out of account the thrill of the chase. What would become of fox-hunting if it were always the same fox?'

Sewell puts one hand to his cheek, where there should be whiskers were he able to grow them. 'I'm afraid I don't get you.'

'The pursuit of the opposite gender. The unmentionable act. The fur of the fox. I say, old trout, how many euphemisms do you require?'

'Oh. That. Oh, I see.'

'Love is a drab business once it has lost its mystique.'

'True.' Sewell turns his teacup pensively in its saucer, as though the saucer is the dial of a clock and time is running out.

Harewood lights a fresh cigaret and smiles at his unlovely, inexperienced friend: 'There, there, my good fellow. We'll make a clubman of you yet.'

'Do you really think so?'

'No doubt about it. I vote we begin with a spot of brandy – though it's rather early, I admit.'

'A restorative, you mean. To steady the system.'

'Exactly.'

'An excellent suggestion. Woke up rather liverish myself.'

In fact, the previous evening was a disaster. Having come up empty-handed at the hanging, lacking a suitable assignation, they took too much claret at Plant's, where some unpleasantness with the correspondent for *The Falcon* marred what might have turned into a jolly evening.

'Bother that fellow Whitty,' says Harewood. 'A melancholy, misanthropic, moralistic, rum sort of fellow. Never liked him at all. Stretches the old school tie a bit thin if you ask me.'

'Surprising success, though, all things considered.'

'Not a gentlemanly sort of success.'

'Of course not. Still, I shouldn't get on the wrong side of him. Pen and the sword and all that.'

'Sound advice, Roo. Remind me next time.'

'I shall do so.' Sewell knows only too well his friend's ability to arouse the jealousy of lesser men; thus does fascination become both a blessing and a curse, depending upon one's audience.

The two young men discovered one another as boys while freshmen at Eton, after witnessing a fellow New Boy undergo Ordeal By Birch for one of the many offences collectively known as 'shirking'. (*Hallo! There's going to be a swishing!*) This, at the capable hands of tiny Dr. Keate – who, famously, would dress up for the occasion, sometimes in the manner of Napoleon, sometimes in the manner of a widowed woman; at such a moment an Eton freshman discovers exactly just how alone it is possible to be, how alien the world can seem.

Not long after, in their dormitory following Evensong, Harewood rose to the unathletic orphan's defence by disrupting a form of arbitrary victimization known as 'blackballing' – a self-explanatory practice incorporating shoe polish. Together they fought off four assailants, during which encounter both boys had the skin taken off their noses with the rough end of a bolster.

Sewell, the less advantaged physically, had acquired a protector; Harewood, neither aristocrat nor scholar, nor provided with a gentleman's income (despite the Governor having grudgingly paid the double fees of a 'gentleman commoner'), had acquired a benefactor. Thus do even the most devoted male friendships rest on a foundation of self-interest:

> Thou preparest a table before me
> In the presence of mine enemies:
> Thou anointest my head with oil;
> My cup runneth over.

Harewood drains his glass, which his friend refills without prompting. 'Speaking of the female gender, there is a favour I wish to ask, old fellow.'

Sewell affects the expression of a man of the world. 'Certainly. Ask and it shall be given.'

'It concerns my cousin Clara.'

'Clara. Of course.'

'We're two men of the world, Roo. Never forget that.'

'Quite.' How he wishes it were true.

'And I count on your discretion.'

'Goes without saying.'

Harewood leans forward and lowers his voice, while searching for le mot juste. 'There have taken place, upon occasion, between myself and my cousin Clara, certain conversations of an intimate nature . . .'

'Oh. She's not in the . . . in the family way, I hope?'

Harewood lights a fresh cigaret off the preceding and drains his second glass: 'Sprained her ankle? Good heavens no! As I've told you many times, only a cad goes out without a skin in his purse.'

'Quite.'

'The devil of it is this: the Governor has found out, and has come down rather hard.'

'Of course, you're first cousins. Although that has never been a problem with the Royals.'

'It is worse than that. Upon my soul, I'm blessed if he don't want me to marry the girl!'

'Oh, I say!'

'It's no bloody joke, I tell you. The Governor holds the purse-strings – insufficient as they are – and I'm damned if he'll give me a penny until I'm in chains.'

'The impudence of it!'

'The Governor has never been what you'd call the horn of plenty, but a trickle has become positively arid.'

'What can he be thinking of?'

'It's the old man's fancy, in his dotage, to bring the Greenwells back into the fold at my expense. Harbouring one's poor relations is one thing – but marry her? Marriage ain't a game of cards, old chap. When a man plays and loses he can deal another hand and perhaps win; but when a man gets a wife without money, he's knackered for life.'

'Mind, you stand to inherit a substantial estate . . .'

'But if I were to marry Clara, I should be submitting to blackmail. A fellow must have principles, Roo. Without principles we're nothing.'

'So I take it you feel on the horns, as it were.'

'Rather, I should say.'

'And what does your pretty cousin think of this?'

'Oh, Clara's all right. Marvellous girl, with no capacity to understand such matters.'

'Reggie, you're a cad – even with a skin in your purse.'

'No worse than other men, I don't think.'

'I meant it as a compliment.'

'Ah. Well, yes, I do seem to have a way with the ladies. Dashed if I know what it is.'

'You haven't given her a promise of any sort, I hope? In return for her . . . favours?'

'Blessed if I have. None beyond the usual "love you madly" sort of thing. Still, with matters about to come to a crisis, no telling what ideas will creep into that pretty little head. To give you some sense of the spot I'm in, listen to this.' So saying, he produces a piece of embossed stationery and reads aloud, while doing a superb imitation of his unlettered *paterfamilias*:

> *You may be well aware that you have disgracefully disappointed me in every plan that I have formed with regard to you. Of your career since Oxford, suffice it that your shameful reputation has eclipsed my honourable one, though the latter was achieved by far greater effort . . .*

'Oh dear. I see what you mean.'

'The old fellow goes on to suggest that I shall marry Clara or die "penniless in a brothel, of some loathsome disease".'

'That is very hard, but rather droll as well.'

'Droll it may seem to you, but not to me.'

'Anything I can do? Ask and ye shall receive.'

'I'll be frank. Being temporarily short of funds (damn the Governor), I've had to take a bunk at the club. Insufferable bother, but there it is. So I'm strapped for a rendezvous, and I'm blessed if I shall take the girl to some flea-pit on Leicester Square. Not the thing for a lady, don't you see.' So saying, Harewood admires the room, especially the wainscoting, which has been waxed to a shine a fellow could shave in.

'That would be unthinkable. Of course you can make use of my rooms.'

'It would be a few hours a week, nothing more.'

'I shall have a duplicate key made. You can come and go as you please with absolute confidence.'

'Capital thought. Provide some breathing-room. A chance to think things through.'

'Quite.'

'Good old Roo! Who can a fellow rely upon, if not his best damned friend in the world?'

4

The Falcon

In the narrow, dark hall (tunnel, really) to the inner office, the correspondent sidles gingerly past the previous visitor, a uniformed electric telegraph messenger whose perfunctory nod suggests an unbecoming smugness in such a young man. Pausing to mould his features into an expression of confidence, Whitty pushes open the green baize-covered door and steps into a large, cheerless, heavy room, redolent of cigar smoke and ink, with a pattern of circular smudges in the ceiling thanks to a century of evil-smelling tallow candles jammed in tin sconces, which the Editor prefers to the disconcerting brightness of gas.

Removing his gloves while waiting to be acknowledged, he surveys the aged Turkey carpet, splashed with dried ink and littered with piles of newspapers both home and country, crumpled by fists and eviscerated by scissors. It occurs to him that a visitor is but a momentary variable in a room as unchanging as the cemetery next-door – excepting that in this case the bone-yard is one of ideas, perished in their infancy.

Three creaking bookshelves crammed with tattered brown volumes of reference fill one wall, with the flaming cover of the Post-Office Directory like a star in a patch of mud; the wall opposite is papered with area maps, shiny with finger-grease; on the third wall an old clock hammers away, above the begrimed plaster bust of a previous eminence, hair powdered with dust, glaring with chilly disapprobation straight into Whitty's wasted life.

In the geographic centre of the Turkey carpet squats a battered desk covered with letters (open and unopened), publishers' copies of books (to be demolished by reviewers), and several baskets containing cards of invitation for a wide variety of desperately important events. To the right of the desk is a leaden inkstand like a bird bath and a sheaf of pens; to the left, a huge waste-paper basket, filled to overflowing with envelopes. The entire room vibrates from the machinery below – like a distant earthquake, punctuated by that awful clock.

Whitty massages a tightening knot of pain in his temple with finger and thumb.

The Editor's capacious and well-tailored girth (though precisely

Whitty's age, the former is more prosperously built) occupies a cane-bottomed armchair surrounded by his good men and true, in the form of a sub-editor and a series of sub-sub-editors, all of whom hunch over smaller desks on either side, faces hidden by the pages of competing newspapers. From behind the sheets, disembodied voices exchange commentary as though calling from separate rooms.

Having arrived in the midst of a discussion, Whitty gathers that the electric telegraph messenger brought in a report of the wreck of a steamer with all hands lost, off the north-east coast of Ireland; which urgent and dramatic narrative must compete for pride of place with an ugly knife murder in Haverfordwest, a salacious foreign rumour, an unpleasant coroner's inquest following a fatal accident, the worrying (rising or falling) price of railway or mining shares, and the growing of the largest turnip in the history of Scotland.

Algernon Sala and Edmund Whitty go back a good distance, having suffered through Rugby together and having rowed in the same eight at Oxford. Though separated by subsequent events, the two friends opted for parallel paths, with the result that both men, each in his own way, are established figures on Fleet Street, albeit occupying vastly dissimilar positions in the institutional hierarchy.

At this moment, as Whitty finds himself wading through another trough in his career (despite flashes of renown, the correspondent is never overmuch in demand), the Editor, as his dearest and oldest friend, represents his best chance of a receptive ear.

'Edmund. Come and take a seat.' Sala does not look up, his mind not having disengaged from the previous topic. His voice, while by no means shrill, is of a higher pitch than one might expect from a man of his size. 'Sorry, old boy, but the fecking electric telegraph takes precedence over everything these days.'

'Certainly your messenger seems to think so.'

'I've ordered a vacuum tube installed at ruinous expense, solely so that I shall not have to look at the little shite.'

Sala adjusts his monocle while presenting the correspondent with a brooding, hirsute face full of black whiskers, and a brow so low it is as if his eyebrows have been grown long, then combed straight back. Beneath the hairline, contradicting its simian aspect, gleam a pair of small, intelligent grey eyes, the left eye magnified by a monocle designed for distance vision. Taken altogether, the effect is of a child within a bush, peering through a telescope at objects of interest.

'That young rascal is our messenger of death, Edmund. Mark my bloody words, Sir. When there is an electric telegraph situated in every home receiving instant news by the hour, I ask you – who will need newspapers then?'

'As usual, you paint a gloomy picture, old chap.' Indeed, thinks Whitty, our man takes a perverse, childlike delight in the prospect of utter ruin. As far as Sala is concerned, if it was chilly this morning and warm by noon, London will be in flames by midnight.

'Think of it, Edmund: since the beginning of history, the maximum distance any object or idea could travel was that which could be covered by a man on horseback. Now it is instant. *Instant!*' (For Sala, the word itself is enough to produce a *frisson*.) 'The electric telegraph will demolish geography. It is the end of the world as we know it.'

'A grotesque exaggeration, but well put.'

'Thank you. Part of a speech I am giving to the Royal Society. They want a prediction or two.'

'Never had a gift for prognostication myself. Always seem to be wrong.'

'Frankly, old chap, it requires no gift to prognosticate your own future, should you continue on your present course. For God's sake sit down, you're the walking dead.'

Whitty clears the high scrivener's stool, only to find the rung broken and one leg about to collapse. Rather than fall to the floor with his legs flying in the air, he braces himself awkwardly against Sala's desk with one hand. His temple is pounding on the side facing the clock; he would not be surprised if it were swollen.

A sudden grunt of approval from beneath the beard: 'Speaking of the dead, tremendous crack on the hanging piece, old boy, trenchant and vivid. Plays to the morally superior, while fulfilling the demands of sadistic voyeurs who missed the show. Delights and instructs and all that. Condemns a thing while marketing it at the same time. Should be taught in school as a model of journalistic balance.'

Whitty comprehends the Editor's ironic subtext, yet Sala has the advantage of him, given that the author of the piece is able to recall it only in fragments. Notwithstanding, he must make an effort to grasp each scrap of praise, carry it to the bank and convert it to a sum of money.

'Decent of you to notice, old chap. Took a fair amount of time with it – more, certainly, than my modest stipend would justify.'

Sala's eyebrows curl like twin caterpillars. 'Of course, it goes without saying that the hanging of a common murderer is hardly another Fiend.

30

No Chokee Bill on the loose, no buxom body bathed in blood, the thing has no legs on it at all.'

Isn't it lovely, thinks Whitty, how one's accomplishments become mallets with which to pound one's future prospects to pulp.

'You make an appalling sight, Edmund. Consumptive and syphilitic at the same time.'

'In actual fact I have been contemplating the water cure – nothing like it to tone the system.'

'Water would be a novelty in your system, I should think.'

'London water is notorious. Gives you typhus.'

'You'll use any excuse to deteriorate.'

'Deterioration is relative. We all deteriorate.'

'Not with your enthusiasm. *The Falcon* is concerned about you, Edmund. You possess – though I may be the only remaining editor in London with this opinion – the sharpest pen in the city, and you seem to be undertaking a tedious form of suicide.'

'Nonsense. The effects of overwork and underpayment are well known.'

'*The Falcon* pays a market wage, Edmund. Supply and demand, say the little shites above.'

'Exactly. Which is why, given your gratifying enthusiasm for the hanging piece, *The Falcon* might see it as being to its advantage to venture an advance.'

'Paid in full, Mr Whitty. Every penny.' Dinsmore, the sub-editor, rubs his thumb and fingers together as though signing for the deaf.

'No balance outstanding.' So echoes Mr Cream, thereby executing his prime function in life, to further his own prospects by seconding any motion put forward by a superior.

Sala shrugs his thick shoulders, as though the matter has been taken out of his hands by some implacable god. 'There you have it, old chap.'

'Quite.'

'Even so, Edmund, *The Falcon* might be able to manage some sort of advance on a future piece. Got anything for us?'

Of the many indignities commonly suffered by a freelance correspondent Whitty finds this one hardest to bear. He will now be required to present ideas, to toss them into the editorial pit one after the other like scraps of meat, to be sniffed at, nibbled, then spat on the floor, having contravened somebody's pet theory as to what cut of meat the public currently craves.

The devil of it is that forming the presentation entails most of the work of writing the deuced thing. Yet this is how things are done, and there is not a correspondent on Fleet Street with the prestige to escape it.

'Shocking bit of business on Halliwell Street, Algernon. A reliable source has it that just around the corner from Exeter Hall, London's evangelical Mecca, operates a bookseller who specializes in volumes from a section of Paris known as the Clitoris of Europe. In the space of a five-minute stroll, one can acquire both a sermon on temperance and a volume of De Sade bound in human skin.'

Comes the sub-editorial chorus, crowlike, from behind their newspapers:

'Naw.'

'Heard it before.'

Dinsmore snorts from behind newspaper: 'You read that in *Dodd's*, old chap. Fraser investigated the human skin angle. Turned out to be the skin of a goat.'

'Fraser is a Scotch buffoon, Sir, who would not know human skin from crocodile.'

Sala lights a long black cigar, leans back in his creaking swivel chair and puts up his feet, thereby signalling that he is looking forward to more entertainment. Nothing to lift an editor's spirits like the song and dance of a desperate correspondent.

'Not bad, on the whole, I like the human skin angle. Clitoris of Europe is charming, but obviously it will never pass.'

'Impossible,' adds Mr Dinsmore, unnecessarily.

'And frankly, Edmund, our readers have seen one too many holiness-decadence cheek-by-jowl exposés in recent months. The line is starting to pall. Anything else, old chap?'

'There's a rumour going around the Mayfair clubs having to do with a lost twin of Her Majesty . . .'

'Oh come, come on, Edmund, not the lost twin wheeze again!'

'This one is rather fresh. It seems the woman worked as a Haymarket prostitute until she learned of her origins from a solicitor who happened to be a client. Through this solicitor, a meeting was arranged at Blenheim Palace, at which Her Majesty is said to have swooned. The twin later committed suicide by charcoaling herself to death.'

'Dear Heaven, that bloody well has my fecking attention! What do you think, gentlemen?'

Dinsmore lowers his newspaper, revealing a narrow face with plump, raw wattles swinging from side to side and a pair of plump, wrinkled hands: 'Royal blood in the veins of a Haymarket prostitute? That will never pass. Not without a palace indiscretion to support it.'

'Indiscretion? Scandal would be more like it,' offers Mr Cream beneath his stovepipe hat. 'Royal bastard might do the trick.'

'Royal bastard from Her Majesty?' Sala smiles wistfully. 'I wouldn't set my hopes up on that one. Rather occupied with the German at the moment, I should say.'

Whitty makes a joke in his turn, although he would like to throttle the two of them with his bare hands. 'Given the German disposition, she might require a servant to clear the cobwebs.'

'Or the manure.'

'One boff per pregnancy is my estimation.'

'Haw!'

'That's quite enough levity, don't you think, gentlemen?' cautions Dinsmore, who plans to relate this tasteless incident to the proprietor, presented as a humorous utterance by *The Falcon*'s rascal of an editor. 'Of course, the decision is yours, Mr Sala. I have every faith in your judgement.'

Upon Dinsmore's expression of approval Sala becomes less enthusiastic about the proposal, suspecting a trap. The little shite is encouraging him to give Whitty too much of a free hand and thereby exhibit a lack of command. The Editor tosses a furtive glance at the sub-editor; there is intrigue afoot, he can sense it.

'I say, Edmund, to be candid, it is a somewhat shop-worn bit of goods. Yet there is no bloody limit to the public appetite for royal skeletons. Put a watch on it. Anything else?'

Thinks Whitty: When the racy ones come a cropper, what hope remains for the high-minded stuff? Oh, what he would give for another Chokee Bill! Oh what he would give for a drink!

'On the legal front we have recent parliamentary concern over the availability of over-the-counter poisons, especially arsenic and strychnine, in the light of the Nottingham case. There exists a suspicion that people may be knocking one another off courtesy of the local chemist.'

'You've already written on that.'

The deuce. 'So I have. But there is more to it.'

'So I should hope. Any facts to offer, an indication of the severity of the problem?'

'No way to tell, given that arsenic and strychnine produce the symptoms of typhus and apoplexy.'

'Bloody Hell, Edmund, are you suggesting that we treat everyone who keels over as a suspicious death?'

'Don't be absurd, Algy. Still, the notion would mesh well with the Inquiry into the State of Girls' Fashionable Schools.' Herewith the correspondent draws his last, least promising card, a small item he obtained from Walter Bigney downstairs for the price of a pint of brandy. At this point Whitty would accept a pint of brandy for the entire work.

Sala scowls, relighting his cigar – a sign of interest. 'Elaborate that last thought, would you, old chap?'

'Thackeray calls them stables for training in fine-ladyism, breeding cows for auction in the marriage market. The report reads as though it were the most dangerous development since the Roundheads. It envisages an entire generation of deceptive Jezebels and string-pulling hags.'

'I see you've been doing your research, Edmund. Are you suggesting that graduates of these schools go on to feed rat poison to their lords and masters?'

'Worth a few afternoons, I should say. Check the attrition rate, look for an increase in instances of hubby keeling over into his soup.'

'I bloody well like that one. What do you gentlemen think?'

'Worth a small advance,' admits Dinsmore. 'Two pounds.'

'Actually, I was hoping for something more like ten. Unexpected expenses have accrued.'

'Haw!' Cruel laughter erupts from behind several newspapers.

'That's a funny comment, Whitty.'

'Very droll indeed.'

Capital, thinks Whitty. Was that not an excellent joke? What could possibly be more risible to a manager than to watch a correspondent on the brink of disaster, dancing a jig?

5

Deverley Lane, off Floral Street

On a narrow street near Covent Garden stands, or rather, leans upon its neighbours, the former town-house belonging to Viscount Deverley, a prodigious spendthrift and a connoisseur of many things French, who squandered his inheritance to the last sovereign before departing this world in the French manner, in the company of a palm pistol. For the next decade Deverley Manor emulated the career of its owner in an extended period of decay, after which the building stood to be demolished by a syndicate in favour of a commercial property. The necessary investment in this project having failed to accrue, and following a scandal as to where, precisely, earlier investments had disappeared (as though the Viscount's ghost were presiding), Deverley Manor thereafter lay in proprietary limbo, a fallow field producing only cud to be chewed by barristers.

Then, like a weed which grows without encouragement, from the baroque rubble of the Viscount's wasted life sprouted an unusually specialized pub known as the Clarabel: whose beverage on offer tends to gin and not ale, whose snug comfort maintains a tattered approximation, not of a gentleman's trophy-room, but a parlour of the upper middle class, complete with swagged curtains, table-covers, an array of china displayed upon the carved mahogany wainscoting, and an oval portrait of Her Majesty above the cracked marble fireplace.

In this haven congregate the judies who work the surrounding neighbourhoods, down to and including the Haymarket. Here they find respite from their labours, or consolation for their lack of the same, there being no male permitted to enter the establishment: neither the punters seeking to badger down the price of service, nor the fancy men who attach themselves to these women like ticks, nor the crushers waiting to take their pleasure as the price of avoiding arrest, nor the 'cash-carriers' – who, often as not, disappear with the cash – nor the gangs of degenerating touts with hardened knuckles who prowl the streets for a lone whore to surround, beat, rape and rob.

Here working women come to chat, in confidence and safety, about men and millinery, decorating schemes, professional adventures, troubles with colleagues and landlords, legends and rumours circulating the district, the latest outrage or perfidy perpetrated by the constabulary – and, of course, to exchange professional advice.

'I've become partial to a half-pound of raw liver,' offers Mrs Miller, a dark-complected woman sometimes known as the Rose of Abyssinia, to the company in general. 'It works something wonderful. You warm it on the grate while he is pissing, keep the lights dim, and Bob's your uncle.'

'Oh, Flo!' whispers Etta to the more experienced friend seated next to her. 'Is she talking about you-know-what?'

'I'm afraid so, my dear. Listen well, for you too will need to settle on a means of having him off but not in.'

'Lor'!'

Within the walls of the Clarabel the women gather as equals, no matter to what degree their circumstances may vary: whether they be children imitating adults, or adults imitating children, or bogus virgins, or gamines who arouse interest by means of a sharp wit and incongruously lewd remarks, or 'country girls' from the rookery, conditioned by overcrowding to indiscriminate sexual acts before they ever thought of hawking themselves on the streets. (Of course the establishment abounds with the daughters of clergymen.)

Whatever one's age and circumstance, whether one plies the trade in a bedroom of one's own, in a room above a divan, in a bawdy-house or standing up against an alley wall, it is substantially the same job.

'I advise against venturing into the Temple, and and especially to avoid the Inns of Court. Not without a cash-carrier, for the place is swarming with rampsmen.'

This from Saint Marie, born Sophie Barker, a canny fourteen-year-old equipped with a rubbery, athletic body and an aspect of heart-breaking innocence. Beside her sits Jolly Pam, a passive mound of flesh whose appeal, such as it is, runs to sailors, for whom amiability and tolerance remind them of their mothers. The affinity between these two women would be a mystery anywhere but the Clarabel, where it is understood that, for all the dangers and drawbacks of the street, unlike the kidnapped girl in borrowed clothes who works the closed brothels in St John's Wood, unlike the scullery maid whose position depends on co-operation with the master, none of these women is a slave.

At an adjacent table, Jerusha Switt (professional name Soft Emma) issues a useful warning concerning a vicious toff distinguished by hair swept in exaggerated jug loops, who likes to pinch to the extent of producing welts all over. 'And I dare say, given sufficient drink and a pocket knife, he don't stop at pinching.'

'The notice said as we're to report such gentlemen to the constabulary, in light of recent events.'

A pause of general disapproval, then: 'Aye, Miss Steeves, and get nibbed yourself, most likely. I'm surprised at you, an experienced woman of the world.'

Miss Steeves concedes the point: 'True for you, Mrs Ogylvie, you are right. If you want to know the time, ask a policeman.'

This draws a laugh which Etta does not understand: 'What does she mean, Flo?'

'It is a joke about the quality of a crusher's watch, my dear. Remarkable it is, how many lushingtons wake up in gaol absent their gold watch.'

The younger woman nods, securing this information in her mind for later use, ever so grateful to her teacher and protector with the new bonnet and the lustrous chestnut hair – and her own hair so dirty brown, and a mole above the lip into the bargain!

Such exchanges between women alone justify the position of the Clarabel in the society for which it is intended, along with its proprietor.

Mrs Ogylvie smokes a cigaret behind the mahogany counter previously removed from the billiards room, a woman of almost reptilian thinness who, through persistence and parsimony, has taken her investment beyond the confines of her once voluptuous body to the outer world of investment and enterprise. Having (like a remarkable number of former whores) emerged uninfected from her myriad and arbitrary commercial encounters (owing, perhaps, to advice from such as the Rose of Abyssinia); having subsequently declared herself immune to men for life: Mrs Ogylvie dedicated her remaining years here on earth to erecting, maintaining and improving the Clarabel. Curiously, from the moment the establishment began to flourish, its proprietor began to grow spare, to dry like a piece of candied fruit, which does not rot but hardens. Crouched before an array of inexpensive alcoholic beverages – displayed in what was once a bookshelf in the Viscount's upstairs library – the emancipated Mrs Ogylvie grows ever more desiccated, having already achieved at the age of thirty the sinewy toughness of an indestructible old woman.

Flo is well known to Mrs Ogylvie and a regular of long standing at the Clarabel; not so the girl beside her, a poky field-mouse who would prefer to turn liquid and trickle down a crack in the floor; yet she too will come to frequent this place regularly, to find dignity in the china, solace in the company, and hope in the triumphant compression of Mrs Ogylvie.

While not possessing resources of the first rank, by no means is Flo among the least-favoured. She does not form associations with sailors, soldiers or people with peculiar tastes, her custom being for the most part shop people, commercial travellers and the better sort of clerk – clean, respectable married men, albeit with a distaste for marriage. (Once she spent the week with a stray clergyman from Exeter Hall, who was most generous.)

Flo has only once given herself for free, and not for drink nor supper, either. She will never be a dollymop, she will die first. Nor is she susceptible to the illusion of romance.

That was her error. Bored footless by the drudgery of her father's shop, she encouraged a young gentleman of property in the neighbourhood and yielded to his desires. Word spread, as word will; a girl has only to make one such mistake.

Naturally, having had his way, he treated her like a dollymop; she expected otherwise. Still, she is wiser for the experience. By the end of their association she was as eager to leave him as he was to get rid of her. The disgrace proved hurtful to her parents, who are stupid people of no interest. She was glad to be rid of them too.

Soon after this episode she made the acquaintance of an introducer, a proprietor of a tobacco shop named Mrs Mansard, who examined her teeth, pronounced her all right, and presented her through the Royal Mail to various contacts as a fresh country virgin, which was nearly true. By this means, and for payment of half of what she earned, she acquired two admirers – a Covent Garden butcher and a shopman from the Strand. They doted on their little country virgin as a pet, paid for her lodging, she even learned to play the piano a little; but this soured eventually. Men are flighty creatures who quickly lose interest in what is readily available.

By then it was time to part ways with Mrs Mansard, for, although undeniably pretty, she no longer appeared quite so fresh as to pass for a country virgin.

Thereafter, she attempted to make her living in a respectable fashion as a seamstress. In a busy period she found she could stitch seven or eight pairs of trousers at eight pence apiece, but once thread and lighting were paid for she barely managed to clear three shillings per week. Thinking her problem to be a matter of money management and not slow starvation, she sought the advice of other seamstresses, only to find that they made ends meet by selling their favours to the lowest sort. Heeding this warning, she returned to her first profession.

She does not regret having worked as a seamstress, if only because it confirmed her original choice as to which occupation, managed skilfully, offers the better prospects for an unmarried woman with no gift for the stage.

She does not associate with pickpockets, nor is she reckless. She puts something by every week. She will one day have an establishment, as does Mrs Ogylvie, a tobacco shop or cigar divan with living quarters above; already she has her eye on one. Unlike Mrs Ogylvie, Flo will not grow dry and hard, for she plans one day to chose a man – a well-bred man of settled character, not a fancy man. She will put up with no opium, nor heavy drinking.

Her father and mother remain unaware of what she does to support herself, though if they had any penetration they would guess. She lets them know she is alive in a language they can understand, by sending money . . .

In the meanwhile, at the Clarabel the general conversation has turned, as it has so often in past months, to a catalogue of the recently absent. This is a mobile profession, often with only rumour to indicate whether someone is missing because she has moved away, or is preggers, or has got herself a toff and is on the randy, or has chosen to make herself scarce for any one of a hundred other reasons.

'Do you know what's become of Lucy, Cora? With the pug nose? She hasn't come in this last fortnight.'

'That's true, Mrs Ogylvie, neither have I seen her. I heard she went away.'

Notes Jolly Pam: 'I seen her brat down Pudding Lane, downy little mutcher he is, can't be more than ten.'

'She can't be gone away, for she wouldn't leave the brat.'

'Heaven only knows, then.'

'True for you there. I shall ask Mrs Sidler to look for her in the cards. Remember when she saw Twin Becky in the hospital and sure, there she was with fever.' This produces a murmur of agreement, for it is a common thing to consult Mrs Sidler.

'I hear we is to report such disappearances to the crushers.' This suggestion meets with silence.

'So I did over Agnes Bottomley's absence, and was three days in the spike for nothing.'

'Any flam to save them the bother.'

'True for you, Mrs Ogylvie, the Peelers is a nest of idle buffoons for sure.'

'Nor was Mona taken notice of, and all her things in her room like she had only just stepped out a moment.'

'And would Fancy Diana leave behind six pairs of shoes?'

There follows a general murmur, for there is not a judy in London without a similar story.

Pipes up Etta, without thinking: 'If you want to know the time, ask a policeman.'

A merry laugh around the room to break the tension. Etta smiles, pleased with herself.

Good, thinks Flo. Already she is beginning to fit in.

Remarks the Rose of Abyssinia while lighting her clay pipe with a lucifer: 'A gentleman of mine 'as seen the ghost of Dark Anza, the black Irish girl – missing, oh, easily a year or more. Took him to a gattering, filled him with whisky, then to an accommodation house. He turned to remove her cloak and she disappeared. Or so the gentleman 'as it – as 'ave others. Well-bred gentlemen, of settled character: they walk in the door, turns, and she is vanished.'

'Aye, I've heard that one. In the version I know, she bleeds first.'

'Bleeds where?'

'Where her throat was cut.'

'So you believe it, then?'

''T'was the hairless man at the jerry-shop told it to me. Said as he heard it from a standing patterer.'

'So many stories as where they go.'

'I heard from Miss Enright who reads the papers that they wants to put up camps for such as us "fallen women" – the "excess female population" they calls it.'

'Do you think that is it? That the crushers take them away?'

'Nonsense, Cora. That's as absurd as the ghost of Dark Anza, home to repeat her last trick.'

'So many stories, Mrs Ogylvie. All with a ring of truth to them. Who's to know?'

'It is your nerves, Cora. It is not an easy thing, to settle in one's mind to that Chokee Bill is nibbed.'

'True for you, Mrs Ogylvie, you're right. Like Dark Anza, he stalks the quarter still.'

6

Plant's Inn

The walnut panels that cover the room from floor to ceiling seem in their advanced age to be fraught with confused memories. In a reverie (such as is commonly evoked by hot spiced gin), in the cold, dusty light from the front window, one can discern the outlines of faces, row after row of them, seemingly etched or branded in the wood grain – ancient correspondents perhaps, long dead of dissipation and worry, their newsworthy exploits long forgotten, their criminals and informants and disgraced aristocrats long consigned to Fleet or Marshalsea or the family churchyard.

Yet despite these spectral reminders of past degeneration, the establishment itself, though scarcely bigger than a hackney coach, draws living journalists to its bosom as eagerly as the sight of their Mum, here to situate themselves near a warm fire, surrounded by plump casks, fragrant nets of lemon and tobacco, jewel-like bottles glowing in the most friendly shades of amber and red and green, courteous beer-pulls nodding agreement with everything they say.

'A healer of hot gin and water if you please, Humphrey, and a large soda-water as well. Quickly, for I'm unwell.'

Glimpsed through a fog of cigar- and pipe-smoke, distorted by what Whitty suspects might be a slight fever, the barkeeper's face frowns over the counter more in sorrow than in anger; a weary man with a lifetime of overheard secrets stored in sacks beneath his eyes, Humphrey has seen and heard too much to be surprised ever again.

Inexplicably, he places before him only soda-water. 'Afraid your money's no good, Mr Whitty, Sir. Mrs Plant has declared you out of order.'

'Out of order in what way, Humphrey?'

'In a serious way, I should think. Madam has a fondness for you, Sir, which is not necessarily an advantage.'

'How so, Sir?'

'She holds you to a higher standard than the regular custom.'

'I see.' Whitty adjusts his whiskers in the mirror, then turns in the direction of the snug by the fire with the small table within – its crisp, white cloth perpetually laid, sheltered from the rough world by a glass partition etched with the outlines of angels, from which position the proprietor and manager customarily exercises control.

Empty, for the moment.

What has he said or done? Nothing unredeemable, hopes the correspondent, for he has begun to experience an unprofessional fondness for the proprietor.

In any case, a customer would have to be utterly maddened with absinthe to initiate a quarrel with Abigail Plant – which she claims as her married name, although her origins (and the identity and fate of Mr Plant – she claims widowhood) are anything but distinct. Rumour has it that she is ruined Irish gentry; something about the clarity of her gaze, her unaffected, direct demeanour, and above all her spirited firmness when angered, inspire men to instinctively uncover their heads, though barely in condition to locate their hats.

Whitty turns back to the bar, massaging his temples, for both sides of his head are pounding now, the effect of this morning's medicament having diminished long before he left the offices of *The Falcon*. He suspects this difficulty with his publican to have something to do with the mysterious injuries to his cheek and trousers. (Blackouts are a damnable business.)

'Refresh my recollection please, Humphrey. What do I have to apologize for?'

'Begging your pardon, Sir, but Madam made it clear that an apology will not suffice in this case.'

'Oh, come now. Surely you will at least give me a hint.'

The barkeeper leans forward after glancing toward the entrance furtively, as though at serious risk simply by continuing.

'Evidently at some point last evening, a suggestion or request was made.'

'What sort of request?'

'Of an objectionable nature, I'm led to understand. One to which Madam took extreme exception if I may say so, Mr Whitty.'

'Whatever the misunderstanding, I'm certain it can be cleared up. Where is the good woman at present?'

'Not on the premises, Sir. I believe she has gone to Confession.'

'I see. Then surely there can be no harm in slipping me a hot gin and water in the meantime.' Whitty is desperate. His vision is beginning to tunnel. 'Surely you cannot be expected to make note of every face in the establishment.'

'I have specific orders not to take your money, Sir. However, I notice Mr Fraser holding forth in the back snug, in the company of some others of your profession. Were it another gentleman's money involved in the transaction, a hot gin and water might be served to whomever.'

'An excellent suggestion, Humphrey. And we will clear up our misunderstanding with Mrs Plant immediately upon her arrival.'

'I doubt it will be as simple as that. As you know, once Madam makes up her mind there is little that will shift it. My employer is a woman of character.'

Past Crocker of the *Spectator* and Stubbs of the *People's Friend*, Whitty passes through a low door into a small room shaped like a three-cornered hat, into which no ray of sun or moon penetrates, a room regarded by journalists as their private sanctuary; here, seated around the deal table at its centre, affairs of state are decided by better minds than presently occupy the House.

Prominent among the company is Alasdair Fraser, columnist for *Dodd's*, whose genial, avuncular exterior and Lowland sociability belie a heart that longs for a return to the Bloody Code – not for the utility of hanging in reducing theft, but for the salutary effect of death as a general social tonic. In Fraser's mind, regular public executions, whatever their pretext, provide an object lesson for the lower classes, whereas a dearth of hanging invites misbehaviour.

Fraser sits rooted at the head of the table, a compact party with tiny, shrewd eyes and no neck to speak of; Banning and Cobb are seated on one side and Hicks on the other; the former operatives contribute criticism to the pages of *The Illustrated London News*, while Hicks writes occasional social accounts for *Lloyd's*. One might wonder how each manages to produce the number of narratives appearing under his name; Banning and Hicks are rarely spotted outside these panelled walls, while it has been several years since Cobb favoured high society in his perpetually drunken state, having offended everyone who matters.

'Ah, Whitty, just the man. Good show.' Fraser makes an attempt at civilized English vowels, yet the savage burr of his heathen ancestors slips through none the less.

'You seem in a boisterous mood, Mr Fraser. Has someone been killed?'

'Good cut! Humphrey, fetch a hot gin for the gentleman, he looks like he could use it.'

'Certainly, Sir. A hot gin for one of the gentlemen present.'

'Whitty, sit down and give us the benefit of your thoughts on the Stork proposal.'

Whitty sighs inwardly, knowing that any discussion with Fraser is a contribution to Fraser's column. It is a high price to pay for a drink.

In a widely circulated pamphlet entitled *A Proposal for Disbursement of the Surplus Female Population*, Sir Henry Stork argues for the establishment of camp facilities for single, unmarriageable women, wherein Britain's unplucked flowers might exercise their maternal instincts on foundlings and orphans. Sir Henry proposes thereby to kill two birds with one stone, providing aid to the impoverished while circumventing the unfulfilled woman's natural tendency to duplicity and malice. Predictably, the scheme has considerable support among back-benchers in the Conservative rump, for whom Overpopulation has become code for the swelling ranks of the destitute.

Whitty considers the matter over his gin. 'It seems as if we already possess a number of the matronly establishments suggested by Sir Henry. If I am not mistaken, they are called brothels.'

Banning, Cobb and Hicks chuckle into their cigars and look to Fraser for a reply, notebooks and pencils poised beneath the table.

'Surely you don't suggest that all unmarried women are potential prostitutes, Sir. That would be a Calvinist position indeed – hardly the Whiggish way.'

Another chuckle from Banning and Cobb, who repeat the words 'Whiggish way' as though this mundane alliteration were a rhetorical gem. Whitty drains his gin and holds the glass up for another as the price of a response. Fraser, with characteristic thrift, signals the barkeeper to charge it to Marshal, who is too groggy to notice.

'Give it time, Alasdair,' continues Whitty. 'Even Stork will be hard pressed to keep up with the growth in the supply and demand for matronly services. It doesn't require genius to see a profitable connection between the surplus female population, the bastard population, and the moneyed population. I believe it is called poverty and license, the fastest growing industries in London.'

The pencils of Banning, Cobb and Hicks scratch away, all having heard the rumour that Fraser has illegitimate offspring in Aberdeen, for which he pays a small pension to the former governess of a niece.

'Poverty is intrinsic to the human condition, Edmund. It is the cane of discipline in the school of life. About this, the demented Mr Darwin is correct. Natural selection is the key to progress, and we inhabit an age of unprecedented progress. The poor are its necessary by-products.

The dilemma Stork is attempting to address, which seems to have eluded you, if I may say so, Edmund, is nothing other than the spread of disease – of infection both moral and physical, to which women are self-evidently prone when wandering about the streets on their own. In their insatiable time of the month they are capable of infecting men in frightening numbers.'

'I bow to your superior expertise, Sir. Now let us examine Mr Stork's plan – another gin if you don't mind, Hicks – and savour its beauty. Envisage the encampments of fallen women, these municipal wet-nurses, infected or not as the case may be. What sort of structure does Stork plan to erect? A prison? An army barracks? A devil's island, or perhaps a ship – like the reeking prison hulks at anchor within sight of Waterloo Bridge? Is that where we would raise these fortunate innocents, the future guardians of England? And what should we do with them upon graduation? Send them all to Cambridge?'

'The problem with you, Whitty, is that you lose yourself in detail and cancel yourself out. It is the story of your life. You have no principles and no faith.'

'Most of all I lack your vision. I swear, Alasdair, you will not be satisfied until you have every Briton in prison or in transportation – leaving yourself and a few associates to run the realm.'

Pencils on either side of him scratch busily, then pause, in the expectation that Fraser is about to launch another version of the social infection theme which has sustained his column for three years now. It is only a matter of time before he brings up the dowager who died of consumption because the infected slop-worker who made her evening gown slept in it; a complete cock without a doubt, yet the issue of its truth is outweighed by its instructive intent.

Whitty signals for another gin, large this time, sponsored by Cobb. In looking to catch a glimpse of the barkeeper he notices a young woman – or, rather, two young women, one luminously pale and somewhat solemn, the other more developed. Both young women wear long dresses fashioned of pieces from several other dresses; poor as mice surely, yet they appear surprisingly pretty. They have been watching him – assessing him, rather; whatever can it mean?

Prostitutes? Seemingly not, for they return his look with a simultaneous, barely perceptible curtsey, then disappear.

Very strange.

Dorcas and Phoebe emerge from the establishment in a businesslike manner, climb the stone steps to the walkway and squeeze past two young swells climbing into a hansom on their way to an evening at Café Royale. Dorcas, the more extravagantly endowed of the two, stops to flirt with one, while Phoebe slips into her sleeve the silk handkerchief she just nicked from his coat pocket; now she lifts her skirts and darts across the street to the shadow of a doorway, where a man in a crooked hat and corduroy suit leans against a pillar.

'Still accounted for, my girl? Hasn't slipped out the back drum, has he?'

'Still there, Father. Drinking gin and shooting off his mouth with some other gentlemen of the press.'

'And who is buying for him, I wonder? Not himself, that's a certainty. By the way he conducted his affairs today, our man is dreadful short of cash. Counted his shillings like they was his own teeth.'

'At present his credit is stood for by the party from *Dodd's* with conservative views.'

'Well observed, my angel. No doubt his credit will run dry with the discussion. Then he will stagger forth and then we will see.'

Dorcas joins them now, and Phoebe sees the frown pass over her father's brow, a slight wince, like the pain of a bad knee or some other injury as she smiles her sweetest smile.

'When he comes out, Henry, do you wish that I hits him with the cosh? I shall ask him the time o'day, then make a few remarks in the way of a gay proposition, and when he bends over to speak to me I stuns him cold.'

He holds a blunt forefinger before her face for emphasis: 'Never you mind the cosh, Dorcas. Nor do I approve of that kind of smutty talk.'

'It was only in jest, Father,' says Phoebe.

'What is done in jest is done in mind, and what is done in mind is soon or late done in deed.'

'That may be so, Henry, but still he should get a good coshing after what he done to you. Deserves to be served out proper for it, he does.'

'That may be so, child, yet I will not see you stun the man. For in truth it is not so simply done and you could as easily kill him. Besides which, from what I seen of him there will be no need – by the time he finds his way out of his booze-ken, he'll have stunned himself.'

7

The Haymarket

Having dined on beef pie, duck and sherry, Reginald Harewood alights from a coach at the corner at Orange Street and the Haymarket, followed by Walter Sewell, both men in a state of high excitement, albeit for different reasons.

Sewell watches his friend, as he often does, with a kind of wonder: tailored to perfection, fragrant as a lily, inhaling the unwholesome night-time miasma as though it were country air. (For his part, Sewell expects to come down with a fever at any moment.)

Harewood drinks deeply from his silver flask, replaces the stopper, smoothes his impeccable whiskers with the back of a chamois glove and turns to his friend, eyes sparkling with that merry light that draws women like insects.

'*She walks in beauty like the night, Of cloudless climes and starry skies* . . . How's that for a turn of phrase?'

'It was Byron, actually.' Indeed, Sewell can imagine his friend as George Gordon, seducer of Europe, which impression is enhanced by Harewood's slight limp, the consequence of a rugby injury of which he is very proud; excepting that his friend is not a poet so much as he is a man about whom poems are written; to Sewell, it is his friend who walks in beauty like the night.

'Can you feel it, Roo? The *frisson* in the air – a quivering of creatures of the night, begging to be worshipped and ravished?'

'Your *frisson* is misplaced, Reggie. I do not know how you can find such excitement in the prospect of an intimate association with a fallen woman.'

'You do have a rum way of expressing yourself sometimes.'

'They are not the cleanest creatures on earth, nor are they the most discreet. Does that not worry you? I certainly worry on your behalf.'

'The devil take your hygiene, Roo. We'll find some romance in you yet.'

Near Leicester Square is an angular street, unilluminated by gaslight, where whores retreat to relieve their bladders. (Peelers ignore this trifle as long as it is not done in the main thoroughfare.) They retire in twos for this necessary process, so that one woman will act as a screen, standing alongside until her companion is finished, then taking her turn. In this convenient setting the two Oxonians join a queue of merry gentlemen, alone or in pairs, waiting to select their companions of the evening.

'How do you maintain an appetite, Reggie? Imagine if this were a dining-room.'

'Dash it Roo, you're a fountain of unpleasant imagery. Very well, to the square – though the selection there is not half so convenient.'

Crossing Oxendon Street they sidle their way between slowly moving hansoms and grinders, avoiding hooves, wheels, and manure. Regretting the absence of a sweeper, Sewell employs the edge of the opposite kerb to scrape the shite from the sole of his boot, then hurries down a narrow lane after his friend, whose fawn-coloured boots reveal not a speck of muck. Sewell watches his friend's back in its triangular elegance, walking-stick swinging in a brisk arc, the other gloved hand holding a cigar, whistling beneath his whiskers, his slightly uneven gait seemingly in rhythm with the melody. Sewell notes as well the contrasting glances of passers-by, of welcome or envy depending upon the gender, and the moment is sufficient for him, he needs no more, he would happily return to his rooms off Bruton Street and spend the rest of the evening with a book.

Past the Comedy Theatre on Panton Street, the preponderance of female traffic increases, until by Leicester Square they face an ample array of women of every description, examining shop windows with curious intensity, their reflections in the glass exchanging seemingly accidental looks with the men walking by.

'Not to be a prig, Reggie, but what do these ladies possess that your cousin lacks?'

'Upon my word, Roo, a fellow cannot be always asking himself why he does things. Takes the fun out of life.'

As they stroll around Leicester Square, Sewell does his utmost to avoid the implied invitation of an array of physical types:

A brunette with sturdy shoulders and a noticeable moustache simpers coquettishly from within her bonnet, followed by a woman who bears a slight resemblance to a bulldog, with compressed features, little close-set eyes and separated teeth. A prospective paramour with the little nibbling face of a mouse bats her little black eyes at him. Now he hurries past a long, white, slug-like creature with a head like a little ball and a small dark nose like the ace of spades . . .

'I suppose there's no rhyme or reason to it,' says Sewell, 'when one is simply looking for a hole in which to spend.'

'Roo, if you weren't the best friend a man could have, I might give up on you entirely. These women are the poetry of the age: young lovelies, brimming over with desire, unspoilt by education and manners, living for the moment . . .'

Abruptly, Reggie Harewood points with his walking-stick in a way that reminds Sewell of fox-hunting. 'Oh I say, look what we have here.'

'Which one do you mean, Reggie?'

'See the two little creatures reading the Empire playbill? Dark hair on one of them, quite pretty in a prim sort of way? And her friend beside her, blonde, tits nearly falling out of her bodice? I say, Roo, the little dark-haired one might be just your cup of tea. Spirited little piece, be great fun once you get the clothes off her.'

Before Sewell can protest, his friend has already commanded the rapt attention of both young maidens.

'If I may be so bold, Ladies, we are two gentlemen from the country who are rather at a loss this evening.'

Speaks up the blonde girl, conspicuously eager: 'If you're lost, Sir, my friend and I are more than pleased to give you directions.'

Reginald Harewood smiles, eyes sparkling in that way of his. 'How utterly kind of you.' He offers the blonde girl a drink from his flask, which she accepts. 'Please permit me to introduce my friend, Mr Stanley.'

'How do you do, Mr Stanley. Please might I introduce you to my friend, whose name is Phoebe.'

Mr Stanley reddens in reply.

'What an utterly enchanting name,' prompts Harewood, offering the young lady a drink. 'Is Phoebe not an enchanting name, Mr Stanley?'

'Enchanting,' replies his friend.

'Why thank you, kind Sir,' replies the darker, smaller girl, admiring the silver flask and smiling prettily. 'Unfortunately, we both are currently engaged. Instead, why don't you go and pork your little fat friend?'

'Reggie, these people are animals.'

'Indeed, were I not so enchanted by her friend, I should have taught her a good lesson with my walking-stick.'

'In truth, old chap, I am feeling ill, and in the mood to retire.'

'Nonsense. A temporary disappointment is part of the hunt. See?

Look there – already we are in luck.' Harewood grips the arm of his friend, turning as if to glance into a shop window displaying bonnets, situated a short distance from two young women, similarly partnered.

Sewell watches his friend direct a beam of charm straight at the tall one with the rebellious head of chestnut hair, whose lack of a corset and straight, peasant's waist gives her an unaffected, upright air – unaffectedness being Reggie's principal fetish. Sewell would judge the young lady to be something over eighteen. Her companion, whom he fully expects to have foisted upon himself, cannot have attained her fourteenth year. The one shows a pleasing eye and a fair set of lips, whereas the younger girl is the worst kind of Irish drudge, features prematurely set in an expression of resentful disappointment.

While the taller girl exchanges pleasantries with his confident friend, Sewell takes an intense interest in bonnets.

All too soon, Harewood taps him on the shin with his walking-stick: 'I say, damned impolite of us not to introduce ourselves.' With a wink, he turns back to the two young women.

'I am Mr Brighton. And I am pleased to present my cousin from Kent, Mr Stanley.'

Mr Stanley screws his face into a smile.

'Very pleased to meet you, Mr Brighton.' The taller girl offers her gloved hand to the handsome, tipsy young clubman. His teeth are excellent. His whiskers complement a set of features that fall just short of aristocratic. There is something luxuriant in the way that his eyes linger upon her white arm, which she displays in pleasing contrast to the dark velvet of her cape. She squeezes his hand before letting go, for he is a relatively attractive prospect and not unpleasant to service, though he can barely contain himself and will require careful tending for maximum return.

'Confound it, Ladies,' says he, 'I'm utterly charmed by your company, as is my friend – am I not correct, Mr Stanley?'

'Quite,' murmurs Sewell, resigned to the fact that Reggie must have her, and have her tonight.

'I say, this is damned bold of me, but might you trust yourself in a coach with us?'

'I am sorely tempted, Sir, and pleased that you find me engaging, but it is my duty to see to my sister. Etta is a country virgin unused to the city and I am responsible for her honour and safety.'

'Upon my word, we mustn't see your sister unescorted. I assure you that my companion Mr Stanley would be only too delighted to accompany little Etta – protect her, set her on the right path and all the rest. Am I not right, Mr Stanley?'

'Undoubtedly,' mumbles Sewell, leaning into the shadow of the doorway, for his cheeks have turned crimson.

'Capital. Then it is settled.'

The taller girl turns for a private word with the solemn young thing, who stands close by as though hiding behind her skirts.

'What do you think of the pudgy fellow, Etta?'

'I does not think he likes me,' whispers Etta.

'Nonsense. Look at the blush on him. He is a baby, wetting his wick for the first time, he doesn't know what he likes or doesn't like. Straighten up, Etta, it isn't as though I have not told you what to do. Get yourself in order and do as he wishes, but don't be too willing and don't be too quick. I shall meet you later at the usual place.'

'I'll try, Flo. But I has my doubts.'

'Do not worry. Plant him a kiss with the tip of your tongue in it, and you will have your way.'

Carefully closing the curtains of the hansom against prying Peelers, Flo adjusts her bonnet in the way that allows her chestnut hair to fall over her velvet shoulders, and turns to smile at her Mr Brighton. 'Your friend is a bashful gentleman, Sir. I fear I cannot tell what my sister will make of him.'

'Never worry, my dear, the old trout will pay well. Indeed, he pays for nothing as far as I know – though he'd die if anyone found out. Dashed good fellow, Roo, but a mere child in the ways of the world.' Smiling, he offers her his silver flask.

She smiles back and sips the brandy after wiping the flask with her glove. 'But you gave me to understand that his name was Mr Stanley,' she says, for she likes to tease men, and prides herself on her powers of observation.

'You can call him whatever bloody thing you like.' A note of sharpness, then his voice drops to a soft burr. 'Still, I am utterly fascinated by all that you say.' So saying, he places her hand on his thigh; she removes her hand after giving it a squeeze.

'Well, my blossom, what do you say to the Crown for champagne? Damn me, it'll be a pleasure to be seen in the company of such loveliness.'

'To be candid, Sir, I don't drink in the way of business. For that I have haunts of my own, and other sort of men for my pleasure.'

His smile tightens, as does his grip on her thigh. 'I say, getting saucy are we? I don't like impudence in a girl.'

'I am only looking after my own interests, Sir. Surely you would not expect otherwise.'

The hand on her thigh relaxes. 'Quite. Assume the standard arrangements of course. Five shillings – or more, depending.'

'How much more might that be – depending?'

'Oh I should think as much as ten.'

'Unlike your friend, I can see that you are a man of the world.'

A bargain having been struck, they retire to one of the many rooms for rent above the nearby coffee-houses, which no one supposes are meant for a good night's sleep.

Alone with him in the room, she feigns modesty, pushing him away at first, then permitting him to loosen or remove a bit of her clothing here and there. So it proceeds. As the charade becomes more playful she intrudes upon his person as well, with accidental touches and lingering glances, while persistently refusing to submit. Notwithstanding his evident state of readiness, she increases the boldness of her teasing – until, unexpectedly, there occurs an abrupt change in the young man, as he pushes her backward suddenly and roughly onto the bed and clutches her throat in a way that is neither comfortable nor gentlemanly.

'What is it, my blossom? Eh? Do you wish to be forced? Is that the way of it?'

'Why no, Sir.' Despite the shimmer of fear in her bosom she maintains an aspect of calm innocence, for that is the best way with gentlemen who are prone to turn mean. 'It was just a game, Sir, and I thought you were fond of playing it.'

His hand relaxes as he reconsiders. 'A game. Of course. My dear, I am terribly sorry. That was wretched of me. Though you do bring up the beast in a man.'

'That is the entire point, is it not?' She relaxes now that the danger, if any there was, is over.

By the end of it she has earned her shillings painlessly, having satisfied his requirements by means of her hands and thighs, and him sufficiently fevered with randiness and drink not to detect the absence of actual penetration.

While he lies against her, satiated and limp, she thinks about his display of meanness and the way he took his pleasure. Many men, in her experience, love women as much for malice as for lechery. Still, a girl does not have to like it, nor does she have to put up with it.

So she decides she will rob him, not so much for monetary gain as a form of trophy-taking.

However, her young stallion will not co-operate. In a surge of renewed vigour he proposes to rendezvous with his companion, who will provide him with funds for further refreshment and entertainment.

Having hired another hansom and having instructed the driver to return to the Haymarket and Orange Street, she watches her Mr Brighton sink at last into a sodden sleep.

After making certain the curtains are well closed, she goes to work, deftly removing his silk handkerchief, gold ring, pocket-watch – and of course the now-empty silver flask with the coat of arms. She takes care to place each object in its own pocket inside her cloak, so that they will not bump one against the other.

She unlatches the door and prepares to jump – hesitant, reluctant to damage her good shoes on the cobblestones – when Providence comes to her assistance, as the cab abruptly pulls to a halt on a narrow street to permit another coach to pass. While the drivers exchange the time of day, quality of business and hours of work remaining, she climbs softly down onto the cobbles, silently refastens the door, and hurries up the lane in the direction of Leicester Square, smiling to herself . . .

'You there, Miss! Just a word, if you don't mind!'

The unmistakable voice of the Metropolitan Police. The sudden stab of fear causes her to gasp, for here lies a greater danger than anything she experienced with her young man this evening.

'Yes, Sir? What is it you would have of me, Sir?' As usual when there is trouble, she chooses an aspect of innocence and ignorance as her best defence.

'Step under the lamp where I can see you, if you don't mind.'

'Yes, Sir. And what is it you wish? For I am but a poor woman. Please, if you're a thief I have no money to give you.'

'Don't play the idiot. State your business.'

In the light of a nearby lamp, by his height alone she recognizes Mr Salmon, who is well known on the Haymarket and whose presence bodes well or ill, depending. Mr Salmon is not a regular Peeler but another kind of policeman, which means that he will not bring her in capriciously as a prostitute; but should he suspect her of some other crime, he can be bribed neither with money nor with flesh. This too is well known. She is ever so glad to have packed her stolen things in separate pockets where they will not rattle, for they are enough to bring her ten years' transportation.

Standing in his long shadow, she understands why Mr Salmon is called an 'inspector', for she can feel his eyes looking her up and down as though she might be a stray animal or a possibly stolen cart.

'I'm a lacemaker, Sir. On my way home from work. I live in Perkin's Rents.'

'A lacemaker, do you say? Who is your employer?'

'I work for Mrs Blossom of Whitechapel.' Indeed, Flo once worked for Mrs Blossom, who operates one of the better-known slop shops in the city. Lies are always best when they stop just short of the truth.

'And what might a lacemaker be doing, travelling about London by cab? And why should she disembark in such haste?'

He saw. That is why he stopped her. Now she must think quickly, for the rest of her life hangs in the balance of probabilities as he weighs them back and forth.

'It was a young gentleman, Sir. Of the quality. He invited me to take supper at the Crown, and I accepted because I was hungry. But on the way there he made an improper suggestion, and improper advances too, so I left him. That is the honest truth, Sir, I swear.' Indeed it was a young gentleman, and he was heading for the Crown; again, she chooses near-honesty as her best defence.

'A chance meeting, was it? For that is not the dress of a lacemaker.'

To this she has no reply.

'Very well, Miss. I see that we've come to the truth at last. No, I'm not on a quest to rid London of its whores. Carry on, then, do you hear me? Don't just stand there gaping. Go about your business.'

'Thank you, Sir.' She swallows hard to contain the tears of relief rising up in her.

'Only a moment, while I offer you a piece of advice.'

'Yes, Sir?'

'I would not wander about the empty streets alone if I were you. Not after dark.'

'I understand, Sir.'

'No, Miss. I don't think you do.'

8

The Holy Land

The appalling stench burns his nose and lungs alarmingly and penetrates his eyes, though they remain tightly closed. And he is retching. He was retching even while he slept. This symptom has occurred to him before of course, yet he hates it no less for the acquaintance. As he regains consciousness he becomes aware of a hand, a large, callused hand. How strange – the hand is clutching the back of his neck, holding his head steady within a circular opening about the size of a horse's halter. A stable? No, that cannot be right . . .

In truth, these awakenings are becoming insupportable, the blackouts, the nausea, now this.

'Give him air, Father. He is retching.'

'That is to the good, my dear. The natural ammonia is doing its work. Better than smelling salts, ammonia is. Quick now, my angel, define ammonia.'

The young girl with the pale skin, long dark hair and the dress made from many dresses, transforms from angel to pupil. Daughters of all classes assume such roles for Father's benefit, especially when approaching womanhood. When a girl develops in certain places, she cannot be herself any more with the men of her acquaintance. This is not entirely a bad thing. (Secretly, she plans for a career on the stage.)

'Ammonia, Father, is a noxious gas.'

'Wery good, Phoebe. And where is it commonly found?'

'Ammonia is a by-product of the coke ovens, and from certain . . . bodily functions.'

'Speak it right out, my angel, there is no profit for the scientist in squeamishness. Meantime,' Owler adds, turning to Dorcas, 'do you, Miss, have anything to add to the discussion?'

Holding the correspondent's head down the hole with one hand, Owler removes his own crooked hat with the other, revealing a ruddy bald head and a fringe of reddish hair. He passes the hat to Phoebe's friend, who is of the same age and complexion as her contemporary, but with hair the colour of the sun after rain, and with a languorous quality – a family inheritance no doubt, as is her fondness for spiced gin. The latter tendency he cannot control, alas, for Dorcas is not his

THE FIEND IN HUMAN

daughter but his ward, taken as company for his child when Phoebe's mother drank bad water and they expected the worst.

'Aye, Henry? What is it you wish from me?' Dorcas smiles at him experimentally, in a way a young woman ought not to smile at an older man.

Owler sighs wearily. He has spoken to these two about modesty in dress and the folly of a prematurely provocative demeanour. As with the drink, his authority in such matters is diminished with Dorcas; hence, a wariness on his part, an aspect of decorum in the presence of his daughter's blooming young companion, thereby to safeguard the innocence of his daughter, and of himself into the bargain.

It is the environment to blame, thinks Owler, the time and place we live in, when the poor can no longer afford to be respectable. With every imaginable sort of indecency proceeding in plain view, the most intimate acts on display in the gas-lit shadows of a normal evening, what is left to protect? Having cost the young their childhood, who are we adults to begrudge them their sad, partial sophistication?

And yet the streets are more dangerous now, with all manner of beasts lurking about.

Pushing these troubling thoughts to one side, the patterer removes the head of his guest from its pungent container. 'Well now, Mr Whitty, or should I say, Mr Special Correspondent: are we ready to regain our senses?'

Whitty breathes deeply the comparatively fresh air, while gazing about the small, windowless room (morning light filtering through cracks in the walls), striving to assess the situation. He recognizes the standing patterer, even without his crooked hat, as the party who has been following him all day.

Suddenly the correspondent for *The Falcon* becomes sensible of the nature of the hole to his right, which he has occupied for an uncertain amount of time. 'We're in a bog-house, Sir! You have put my head down a privy!'

'It is indeed a privy, sir,' comes a feminine voice to Whitty's left. 'You should consider yourself fortunate that Father did not throw you into the cess-pit below, for it is over a fathom deep and you would have drowned.'

He turns to confront the speaker – unless it is two speakers. Or perhaps he is seeing double, which would not surprise him in the least. 'I beg your pardon, Miss, but I don't believe I have had the honour . . .'

'My name is Phoebe. And this is my companion, Dorcas. And this is my father, whom you may address as Mr Owler, and whom you have sorely ill-used, sir.'

'Grievous bad,' adds Dorcas, with a pretty smile.

So there are two of them. Having established this fact, the correspondent directs his attention to his captor. 'Have I been kidnapped, Sir? Am I under torture?'

The ruddy, whiskered face assumes a pained expression: 'Nothing so barbaric, sir. A medically necessary procedure, is what. You was in a bad way when we brought you here, was my observation. You was into trouble with an unusual wariety of persons – surely you remember the circumstance yourself.'

'A bad way? What sort of a bad way was I in?'

'There was an assault, Sir. A most wicious assault of which you was the recipient. Hardly what one expects from a member of the gentler sex, if I do say so. The lady proposed to wield a coal-shovel to wery bad effect, as she ushered you out of the building. When the lady returned inside, you was then attacked by two other gentlemen who came out of the shadows – like they was standing in a queue, waiting their turn.'

'Such a popular gentleman,' remarks Phoebe to Dorcas.

Blast. The ratters.

'I'm not one to pry into the business of others,' continues Owler, 'yet had we not intervened I am certain you would surely have suffered a serious injury.'

Whitty massages his pounding temples, for it is as though someone has driven a nail straight through one side of his head to the other. 'Would the lady with the coal-shovel by any chance have been speaking in a foreign accent?'

'Irish I believe, Sir. A handsome people, but with a temperamental streak in my observation. You was in a sticky situation. You was lucky to have escaped without broken bones.'

'I am grateful to you, Sir.' Although at a loss as to how a man and two girls might hold back two ratters, Whitty must take the patterer's word for it, for the scene is but a vague memory of unintelligible voices and terrible curses.

Feigning a gentlemanly calm, the correspondent extends his hand. 'Edmund Whitty of *The Falcon*, Sir, at your service.'

Owler does not reciprocate. 'Oh, I knows who you are. You are the newspaperman.' He spits out the word as though it has a vile taste.

While Whitty considers this alarming utterance, Owler turns to the two young women: 'Now I'll thank you young ladies to be on your way, whilst I have a word with the newspaperman.'

'Certainly, Father.' Phoebe nods to her companion, confirming a private set of plans, the particulars of which her father would prefer not to know. Now she turns to the gentleman guest with her most refined smile: 'Good-day to you, Sir.'

'My compliments to you, Miss. Your presence has been the highlight of my day thus far.'

Thinks Phoebe: What must he think of her, having been held prisoner in a privy?

Alone now with his captor, Whitty's mind has recovered sufficiently to gather that this is the same standing patterer upon whom he heaped defamation in the hanging piece – a far more damning shot, now that he recalls it, than he would deign to aim at a fellow correspondent. For the moment he chooses not to refer directly to this connection, but to affect the aspect of a victim of mistaken identity.

'You done me an injury and an injustice, Sir. Yet life goes on.' Owler gestures toward the door like a head butler. 'And now Mr Whitty, you may accompany me to the dining-room.'

'Excellent. Might one have the opportunity to wash?'

Mr Owler finds the question highly amusing.

The instant the two men emerge through the creaking door of the bog-house, it all becomes horribly clear: Whitty will be fortunate to get away with the clothes on his back; indeed, he will be lucky to get away with his back.

They are situated amid a warren of yards and passages crammed with outcast humanity, a dense mass of worm-eaten houses with walls the colour of bleached soot, so old they only seem not to fall, their half-glazed windows patched with lumps of bed ticking.

He is a man lost in a maze, without hope of extrication by calculation or craft: between these houses curve and wind a series of narrow and tortuous lanes; stagnant gutters bisect the lanes, filled with substances Whitty does not wish to think about; above them is a formless architectural mass, interconnected by an elaborate complex of crude runways between roofs, with spikes located beside the upper windows to permit a party literally to climb the walls. Below ground, Whitty has heard, bolt-holes link one building to the next in a maze of escape routes. The cumulative result is that a fugitive can pass over and under a series of houses and emerge undetected in another part of the rookery in a matter of moments. Should the Peelers or some other authority dare to pursue him, their prey will simply have vanished. Should a foolish crusher follow him into the cellar, chances are good that the policeman will drown in a concealed cess-pool like the one of Whitty's recent acquaintance; surviving that, the constable will in all likelihood place his head in a bolt-hole and promptly lose it.

'My God, it's the Holy Land,' Whitty whispers, turning somewhat paler than normal.

Owler smiles: 'Werily, Sir. And welcome.'

Straddling New Oxford Street, extending from Great Russell Street to St Giles High Street and bounded by a series of frightful brothels, is an immense, squalid warren crammed with outcast humanity – in effect, a foreign country, as though in the core of Empire dwells a race of cannibals from the far end of the Nile.

When ancient trades became obsolete and ancient villages became uninhabitable, families whose existence depended upon them migrated into the city, there to form villages in miniature amid the gracious estates behind Regent Street and the Strand, causing their well-born inhabitants to wonder if London was any longer the place for them.

Meantime the pace of progress stepped up, and with each change more hands went out of work. As the income of the working classes descended, more people and lower people – chimney-sweeps, washer-women, tripe-sellers, beggars – poured into London's centre to pack the back streets, courts, squares and mews.

Naturally, the social tone coarsened. Inhabitants of the quality were set upon by ruffians and had their watches stolen, and the presence of the lower orders became simply too oppressive to be endured. So the quality moved away, leaving their fine houses to be subdivided by agents on commission.

As these houses deteriorated, the subdivisions divided again and again. Whole families moved into single rooms in which to do piece-work to pay the rent, pawning the spoons at the end of each week to make up for the shortfall. As these meagre spaces became insupport-able, parts of rooms were sublet, then beds, then parts of beds. In the meanwhile, primitive shanties were constructed in the back-yard, then let, then sub-let, then sub-sub-let.

By this point the area had become known as the Holy Land, after the impoverished Irish Catholics who poured in as though it were Jerusalem.

It is the common wisdom that no person has any business there who is more than one step away from death by starvation, disease or hanging. Despite a variety of pecuniary and social embarrassments, Whitty has never sunk quite this low.

True, one's chance of being murdered for one's money or clothing is greater in the lanes behind the Ratcliffe Highway, and the opportunity to become infected by an appalling disease is more available on the mud-flats where the sewers empty into the Thames; yet the Holy Land is more feared. In scope it has attained a macabre grandeur, like a canto out of Dante, as though majestic Britain, the pinnacle of civilized progress and Christian virtue, has somehow brought about within its own bosom an equal majesty on the other side.

The patterer conducts his guest across Carrier Square – if the term 'square' may usefully be employed to describe an outdoor space bisected by a drain and cluttered with coster carts, upon which lie the bodies of sleeping prostitutes of the lowest sort, skirts every which way, white legs indecently exposed, dangling over the rims like the necks of plucked geese. In the reeking hubbub of Rosemary Lane, festoons of second-hand clothes wave like pennants from tiny cave-like shops; other surrounding streets – alleys really – emanate from the square like arteries from a heart, filled with sick persons and stick-persons, monuments to the act of loitering.

A woman with a bloated face, a short pipe in her mouth, tiny eyes darting incessantly back and forth and with a wolfish dog by her side, tears rags in strips for some commercial purpose. A young man with a consumptive cough, covered only by a blue rug stolen from a livery stable, cries out piteously while banging a tin alms cup. A group of black Irish keep watch for someone who might profitably be waylaid – assuming themselves already lost to the Devil in this heathen Protestant city.

Having no idea where he is other than somewhere south of New Oxford Street and north of Leicester Square, keenly aware of the potentially fatal consequences of every breath taken in this fetid warren, Whitty determines his best course to be one of discretion: retain a cordial accord with his host on all issues moral and political, express deep regret for harm done, and negotiate the best possible terms of release by agreeing to everything. Not the boldest strategy, but Whitty is not in a bold mood.

'May I ask where you are taking me, Mr Owler?'

'Tea-time, Mr Whitty,' replies the patterer. ''Course, if you prefers to be on your own . . .'

'Not at all. Absolutely delighted to join you.'

Through a set of green stable doors they enter what can only be a kitchen, to judge by the pervasive smell of burnt animal fat and fish. Visually, the room is obscured by thick grey smoke (a loathsome miasma carrying every disease in Europe), pierced by a narrow shaft of light from a hole in the roof.

Whitty has found himself in some appalling hovels, but nothing to compare with this.

'Be it ever so 'umble, Sir. Consider yourself my guest.'

'Most grateful, I am sure,' replies the correspondent as though charmed by the quaintness of it, lighting the stub of a cigar he has found in a pocket, the better to breathe without retching.

As they cross the room Whitty's eyes adjust to the gloom so that he can now make out a blackened chimney, which stands out from a brick wall like the flying buttress of some dismal cathedral. Blackened beams hang from the roof and down the walls, supported by a floor of packed dirt. The two men pass beneath an iron gas pipe whose flame provides a feeble illumination; as they reach the opposing side Whitty can see that the entire wall is a long, projecting wooden bench, in front of which stand a series of tables of various heights, sizes and shapes, with each one of them at some stage of collapse.

Across the tables loll the torsos of at least twenty sleeping men, lying back to back for warmth, knees bent like sleeping infants. At the end of the room, a group of men and women huddle about the stove in blankets and coats the colour of soot. A few are toasting herrings, which smell strongly of overripe oil and add to the unwholesome sweetness of sheep fat. To one side of the stove, three men occupy themselves by drying the ends of cigars collected in the street.

Whitty has never seen so ragged and motley an assemblage in his life – hair matted like sheared wool, unshorn beards slick with grease, pallor approaching a luminous green. Two men – either artists or thieves who stole from artists – wear tatty smocks; another sports a rotting plush waistcoat with long sleeves; another an ancient shooting-jacket.

Even in such company, the appearance of the party who rises to greet Mr Owler defies comparison: his cheeks are so sunken that it is impossible that the man can have any teeth; a skeletal frame covered by an ancient coat, stained black and worn shiny; a shirt so brown with wearing that only close inspection can discern the shadow of a chequered pattern. The sight of the man is of such overpowering wretchedness as to be almost comical. Whitty wonders for how much longer the man will be able to stand up at all, especially with the lady's side-buttoned boots he wears on his feet, the toes of which have been cut out so that he can get them on.

The man executes a wobbly bow. 'Good afternoon, Henry. Lovely to see you.' His voice seems to emanate from some distance away.

'Good afternoon, Jeremy. Mr Whitty, allow me to present Mr Hollow, my former associate – former I regret, owing to illness and infirmity. Mr Hollow is a very fine poet.'

Whitty bows; the hand in his feels not unlike a packet of twigs. 'I am extremely pleased to make your acquaintance, Sir.'

'Jeremy, this is a newspaperman, moniker of Whitty.'

Replies Mr Hollow, 'You have heard of *The Husband's Dream* perhaps?'

'Regretfully, I have not had that honour.'

'Henry, we really must revive *The Husband's Dream*.'

'Should have done so already, Jeremy, but for the cost of paper.'

'Very popular in the streets it was, in its day.'

Owler turns to the correspondent. 'And a stunning instructive piece of work it is, Sir. Imaginatively conceived and cunningly wrought. Consider: a drunkard falls asleep in the gutter and is redeemed in a dream. Simple, true, and wery uplifting to the sensibilities of all as read it.'

'I shall certainly read it at the next opportunity.'

'That will be difficult, Sir,' replies Mr Hollow. 'We have no copies for want of capital.'

'And yet,' says the patterer, 'we must never forget as how the writer lives on in the memory of the faithful reader.' As though to prove his point, Owler begins to recite in a purposeful, resonant baritone:

> '*O Dermot you look healthy now,*
> *Your dress is neat and clean;*
> *I never see you drunk about,*
> *Then tell me where you've been . . .*'

'That is the opening, for your information Mr Whitty,' says the poet. 'It sets the scene of a chance encounter.'

Adds Owler: 'In the next stanza, Dermot recounts as how he dreamt of his wife's sudden death.'

'The dream is, or so it seems to me, a most poetic state of mind – do you not agree, Mr Whitty?'

'I do not doubt it, Mr Hollow.'

'Indeed,' says the patterer, 'the misery of his children as they cry over their mother's dead body is wividly described – one can see it before one's eyes as t'would squeeze a tear from a banker. Now, hark to the redemption:

> *'I pressed her to my throbbing heart*
> *Whilst joyous tears did stream;*
> *And ever since I've heaven blest*
> *For sending me that dream . . .'*

At the concluding line, the patterer's substantial baritone tapers to a whisper as though drained; in response, a ripple of applause erupts among the wretches seated about the stove. 'Of course, with no sheets to sell, even a masterpiece is not worth a farthing.'

'May I take it, Gentlemen, that you are business associates?'

'Mr Hollow were my wersifier for many years, until his infirmity.'

'And what, may I ask, is the infirmity?'

'The eyes, sir,' says Mr Hollow. 'I am nearly blind.'

'That is indeed a terrible affliction, and I am sorry to hear it.'

'You are generous, Sir. I can still compose my verses, but they die with me for want of copying.' Mr Hollow turns to Whitty, who can now perceive a milkiness of the eye. 'As a professional man, what might be your honest opinion of my work?'

Honest? Whitty side-steps the subject, having no desire to undermine the *raison d'être* of a blind man. 'Empty praise is cheap, Sir. Allow me to offer you some small sustenance as a gesture.' So saying, he reaches into his pocket, retrieves the few coppers remaining from the unremembered events of last night, and slides them across the table between Mr Hollow and Mr Owler.

Sighs the poet, transfixed by the sound of money: 'A kind gesture, Sir, most kind. Although material reward is a poet's last consideration, I confess that remuneration of late has reached an unusually low ebb. To make ends meet, I have been occupied in collecting dog manure for use by tanners. I go by the smell, you see.'

Whitty didn't know such an occupation existed. 'A lean business, I should imagine.'

'Not nearly so lean as the writing of poetry, sir.'

'I readily admit it, Mr Hollow.'

'Now, Gentlemen,' Owler announces, 'enough banter, for we are here on a wery sober business.'

He leans over the table (its deal surface has developed into a series of rolling hills, with a long, flat indentation in the centre), removes his crooked hat, sets it upside-down, intertwines his fingers sausage-like and assumes the worrisome aspect he displayed earlier in the privy.

'Mr Whitty, I am not one to mince words or to dance around a thing. I likes to call a thing by what it is, and we are here on a serious matter. Jeremy, this here Mr Whitty, a *newspaperman*, has indicated in the public mouth that my "Sorrowful Lamentation" concerning Chokee Bill is, to put it baldly' (the patterer stammers as though he can scarcely produce the word) 'a c-c-cock, Sir. A flam.'

'Oh dear, Henry, that is very bad.' The poet turns to the correspondent with grave aspect: 'I will have you understand, Sir, that in the trade Mr Owler is known as a scholar of murders who has not missed a public execution in a quarter-century. For sheer devotion to the craft he is without peer, having spent more than an hundred hours altogether with criminals in the death cell, conversing with them in great seriousness on the prospect of that eternal world upon whose awful precipice they sit. You may take my word on it, Sir, Mr Owler shines as a beacon of integrity. Mr Owler has been a steadfast friend to me, Sir – indeed, more than a friend . . .'

Aware that he is not out of danger and with no escape in sight, Whitty chooses an aspect of judicious, measured dignity.

'I accept your estimation, Sir, that the issues of which you speak are of unexampled gravity.'

The poet laughs ruefully. 'I fear that the damage to your reputation will put you in the manure business yourself, Henry.'

'If not the workhouse, Jeremy. And what's to become of the young women in my care? As I am known to say, Sir, life goes on – whether we like it or not. You what has noted those wretched female carcasses in the courtyard, I leave you to your conclusions as to my fears.'

Thinks Whitty: Clearly for wretches such as these, the great fear is not death so much as the cruelty of survival, the consequent suffering when 'life goes on'.

Cautions the poet: 'While your agitation is not without reason, Henry, reason also suggests that you give thought to the disposition of your daughter. A girl of exceptional character if I may say so, I who know her as well as if she were my own.'

'That is true, Jeremy. Both Phoebe and Dorcas will endure cold and wet and starvation before applying to the Union and winding up in the workhouse.'

'It is not right, young girls breaking stones and picking oakum like convicts.'

'Not to mention the attentions of the porter. It don't bear thinking, Sir.'

'The workhouse is for girls who have only their virginity to sell.'

'True for you, Jeremy. Do you agree, Mr Whitty?'

The correspondent nods back and forth, wearing an agreeable, serious expression. It is not a pleasant business to encounter someone who faces ruin as a result of a thing one has written, and is now in a position to do the writer harm in return.

'I beg your pardon, Mr Owler, but I hope you will accord me the assumption of honest intent. I had no wish to do you harm.'

'I assume so, Sir, and in that spirit I shall therefore undertake to prove you wrong. Should I be successful, I trust that you will do the honourable thing and return a man's reputation to him. Does that seem the right course, Sir?'

'Indeed, Mr Owler. Wholeheartedly. If I were proven to be in error, professional ethics require a prompt correction.' Not necessarily true, thinks Whitty, but this is no time for hair-splitting.

'May I have your word on that, Sir? As a gentleman?' Owler puts out his hand, which the correspondent grasps as required. The patterer's palm is like wood to the touch.

'Indeed, Sir, you have my word as a gentleman.'

(In actual fact, the correspondent has reason to doubt both his status as a gentleman and the likelihood of persuading *The Falcon* to retract, it being general policy not to do so unless under threat of a lawsuit, a parliamentary hearing or the imminent removal of the correspondent's kneecaps.)

Owler's face reassumes that open aspect which Whitty finds so troublesome, for there is nothing more mortifying than honest gullibility. 'Now that we have resolved the measure to our mutual satisfaction, Mr Whitty, I propose some wictuals. Well, Gentlemen? Some material sustenance to sustain the wital organs?'

'With pleasure, Henry,' replies Mr Hollow, nearly in tears at the prospect.

'Absolutely delighted,' adds the correspondent, relighting his stub of a cigar against the smells to come.

Appropriating three of the correspondent's coppers, the patterer approaches the stove at the far end of the room and places them into the open hand of the keeper of the stove, a sharp-eyed crone in a brown night-gown, who ladles out three bowls of a thick, steaming substance from an enormous iron pot. Now Whitty stares into the battered tin vessel before him, as blackened and grease-encrusted as the stove itself, wherein lies a thick grey liquid, with a curious lump of something like tripe floating upon its surface.

Owler speaks confidentially: 'In this establishment, Mr Whitty, it is the custom for a patron to supply his own utensils. Your bowl is come courtesy of Mr Elkin there.'

Whitty glances in the direction indicated: seated by the stove, the gentleman in the deteriorated shooting-jacket (with what looks like a small goitre on the side of his neck) waves magnanimously. The correspondent waves a queasy thank-you in return.

In the meanwhile, across the table Mr Hollow sips the precious liquid, delicately at first, then with real urgency, now turning his bowl upside-down so that a long greenish tongue can lick the surface dry, followed by a thorough wiping with a forefinger, to be licked dry as well.

The patterer regards the correspondent's untouched meal. 'Were the wictuals amiss, Mr Whitty? Service not as accustomed?'

'Not so, Mr Owler. My stomach is not constant, is all.' Discreetly he pushes his bowl across the table to Mr Hollow, who accepts with relish, repeats the ritual of the first, then places his head against the wall and falls into a swoon, his mouth pursed in a silent, rhapsodic *oh*.

Taking advantage of the ensuing pause to pack and light his pipe, Owler returns to the topic at hand.

'I'll warrant that, thanks be to Jeremy here and to good fortune, I have well and truly interviewed William Ryan and have endeavoured to obtain his various particulars . . .' The pipe gets going, cloaking the table in an acrid haze. 'I am prepared to furnish such evidence as to prove my adherence to – and I quote yourself, Sir – "the most funda-mental principles of journalistic veracity" in my methods and sources.' Owler glares at Whitty, blowing out smoke at such a rate as to appear almost diabolical. 'Will that satisfy you?'

'Indeed, Sir, if you can furnish such evidence, I can scarcely refuse.'

'If in so doing I must reveal certain trade secrets in confidence, might we shake on that as well?'

'You may rely on my discretion, Sir.' Once again Whitty grasps the thick, dry hand of the patterer.

Owler reverts again to a trusting frame of mind, although how such a disposition remains possible in this environment is quite beyond the correspondent.

'As my first item, I offer you my work in progress, what has a seminal bearing on the matters what lay before us. From the warious facts our man has let slip from time to time over the past weeks, I have assembled a narrative which I believe is not far from the truth of the matter, though I would give much to hear it werified by the party in question.' So saying, Owler produces from within his coat a piece of folded foolscap, upon which is written the following document, smudged with ink and tortuously revised:

The Sorrowful Lamentation

of

William Ryan
Known as Chokee Bill, the Fiend in Human Form

by

Henry Owler, Esq.

O you who claim a Christian name,
Now hear my story true;
O do not shun the face of one
More wretched far than you;
Harken to these words of mine,
My dreadful tale to tell;
My life to end, my soul to spend
Eternity in Hell.

O once I knew a love so true,
Our hearts we freely gave;
Though she was of a class above,
My station she forgave;
But family ties will oft belie
The purest of the pure:
I, in her sight, a shining knight,
In father's sight, a boor.

Corrupt and mean, a libertine,
Ancient, bald and stout;
A suitor from a class above –
For him I was cast out;
And in my wrath then from the path
I stumbled and I fell,
While in her pride, my would-be bride
Did sell her soul as well.

By chance I passed a wayward lass,
I cast a wanton eye,
And promised I would pay her well
If she with me would lie;
While in the act I made a pact
With Satan, curse the day,
The evil shade did me persuade
To take her life away.

In front of me on bended knee
She did for mercy cry,
For heaven do not murder me
I am not fit to die;
But I to look no pity took
I choked away her breath,
Till with her eye still asking why
She stared at me in death.

From the first the Devil's curse
Did urge me more to sin,
The gates of Hell did open up,
And I did enter in;
I killed a second woman then,
My cursèd soul to thrill;
As though to soothe my broken heart
I father'd Chokee Bill.

Thus with the gore of three, then four
My hands were deeply dyed,
The Devil had received my vow,
No more my sin to hide;
Then I killed as Chokee Bill
A woman whom I knew;
Though stoutly I did it deny,
Suspicion round me grew.

Though on the murders at the first
The jury did divide,
Then the judge did bade the verdict made,
And all twelve 'Guilty' cried;
With fetters 'round was I then bound,
And shin-boltèd was I,
Now I'm fast in gaol at last,
No more can I deny.

Death to serve I do deserve
My crime it is so base,
I chose to show to women low

No pity and no grace;
And so I win no grace, although
Of one I'm innocent
And so I from this wicked world
Most shamefully am sent.

You disappointed lovers, whom
The stars refuse to bless,
O do not hate, nor curse your fate,
Nor sink to wickedness;
But look to prayer for strength to bear
The heavy hand of fate;
You may rejoice, you have the choice,
For me it is too late.

'That concludes the werses part of my Sorrowful Lamentation, Sir. I beg you take them, I have made a copy. Though the rhymes within has proved too much for me from time to time, I warrant it is up to standard and ready to be followed with the printed text of his Last Confession word for word, when Mr Ryan takes me into his confidence.'

'By which you mean when and if your verses prove to be true.'

'It is my best connection of the available facts, Sir.'

'And a plausible tale to be sure. But as I understand it, the man claims complete innocence.'

'It is not to be thought of. The party has been convicted in an English court of law. There is no question of his guilt. Time is running short for such speculation, Sir. I have wagered my all in stirring anticipation of a Last Confession on the day of the hanging. Werses to whet the appetite is crucial, and I have sold them all over London.

'Now you, a *newspaperman,* has coopered me in advance! What remains, even should the wile murderer unburden his conscience, now that you have informed the public that anything I record is a flam?' The patterer pauses to collect himself. 'Excuse me, I beg you, for I am in a nervous state. I worry, Mr Whitty. I worry all the time.'

'I understand you, Mr Owler,' replies the correspondent, thinking that the narrative recounted in Owler's doggerel bears a strangely familiar scent (albeit, his memory is far from foolproof these days). 'I have nothing but good wishes for the success of your project.'

'Cold comfort, Sir, when you have done more to cooper it than anyone.'

To which Whitty has nothing to say.

9

Near Waterloo Bridge

Having made their exit onto Covent Garden through a lane (a crack between two buildings really) at the southern edge of the Holy Land, Dorcas and Phoebe proceed south past Temple Bar and across the bridge to Waterloo Road, a row of brokers' shops which they have not visited in several weeks and where they have identified a firm prospect.

They slow down to a dignified pace, assuming the demeanour of two proper young women on a shopping excursion, passing an assortment of household items – ornamental cupboards, fire-screens, copper kettles – as well as an array of heavy carpenters' tools on tables, without showing the slightest interest; such large objects are best left to teams of wiry rogues of seven or eight, in ragged trousers held up by one brace, who travel in swarms, thereby to speedily transport objects of astonishing size and heaviness, over the objections of the most well-armed shopman.

'Shall we tarry here and there, Miss Phoebe, or shall we proceed to the objective direct?' Dorcas has adopted the quality accent they assume occasionally, as an ongoing mockery of the upper orders, as a kind of code, and as a rehearsal for what they hope to one day become; for what girl does not like to imagine herself a great lady, swishing across the best carpets in London?

'Let us take our time, Miss Dorcas. It is a long way to travel for a single purpose. Efficiency is the key to progress, my father says.'

'Oh quite, Miss Phoebe, you does put things in perspective as to the way of it.'

One shop presents a most promising picture – a deal table stocked with cheeses of various kinds and eggs on shelves; rashers of bacon of fair quality lie in piles in the sunlit open window, ticketed variously as 'Fine Flavour' and 'Fresh From the Country'. The grocer standing guard thinks much of his own appearance, to judge by the care given to the curl of his side-whiskers. Propitiously, his eye has fixed upon Dorcas.

'Good-day to you, Sir,' says Dorcas to the grocer, producing her most affectionate smile to test the waters.

'And a good-day to you, Miss,' replies the shopkeeper with a wink, grooming one side-whisker with thumb and finger, much distracted by this comely young lady. 'And how may I help you on this fine afternoon?'

Dorcas crinkles her eyes at the shopman, as though thinking about something pleasant yet unmentionable. Her eyes hold his momentarily. Phoebe does not approve of this method of distraction, but cannot fault its efficacy, as she swiftly and neatly scoops six nice rashers into a concealed pocket sewn into the folds of her patchwork skirts.

Moving on to the milliner's shop next door, they pause to admire the crinolines hung on wooden rods and swinging in the wind, not to mention the table stocked with boxes of feathers of every tint, and the bodice-fronts of various styles.

'Doesn't you admire the notions, Miss Phoebe?'

'Indeed I so admire them, Miss Dorcas,' Phoebe replies, scanning the display, and the surrounding area. 'However, methinks we might discover that the pins to the right are sharper than we might prefer.'

Dorcas casts a casual glance in the direction indicated, where a sharp-featured young woman under the awning has stopped her knitting and watches their every move.

'Quite, Miss Phoebe. I agrees entirely.' And they move on to the next shopkeeper. (It is a rule when working the shops that the women are not nearly such fools as the men.)

A greengrocer, by contrast, is good for three fresh apples during an interval when Dorcas stoops low to examine some pears, thereby causing her unbuttoned bodice to open further than usual. As for the idle young shopkeeper presiding over the furnitureware room, with its gilt mirrors and parrot cages, it will be many hours before he notes the absence of the brass door-knocker in the shape of a lion – good for a shilling at least, a high price for a glance at her creamy softness.

'How much did you show him?' demands Phoebe, painfully aware that she could unbutton her own bodice down to the waist without causing a fuss.

'Just enough, my dear. I hears in the most fashionable circles, it is said that the throat extends to the nipple.'

'That was Miss Menkin, who appeared naked on a wild horse. In a public market, the throat stops well short of the nipple I should think.'

'Oh, Miss Phoebe, you're so *stricter avec la bodice*.'

'Oh, Miss Dorcas, you're so *insouciant avec la décolletage*.'

In truth, Phoebe worries that her friend's bosom may prove a fickle ally, the sort of attribute that attracts the wrong sort. Yet she says nothing, for it would spoil the fun.

Continuing in this mock-sophisticated fashion, our two criminals pass by a row of costermongers selling fruit, fish and tin objects, for they don't steal from costermongers. Their keen eyes scan the street for Peelers on their rounds, in tail coats and high hats, as well as the detectives with their quiet, smooth movements and cautious aspect. Such care is necessary in a city where crimes of property are vastly more serious than crimes of violence, where one will spend many more years in transportation for stealing a man's boots than for crippling him with a club.

Next to a Cheap John selling cutlery from Sheffield stands the object of their expedition: a second-hand clothing store fronted by a series of iron rods containing trousers and coats of all patterns and sizes, fluttering in the wind, their empty arms beckoning passers-by to take them home. Past a row of headless dummies with their coats buttoned up, they stop beside a bottle-green corduroy garment with velvet sleeves and brass buttons, in excellent condition. Phoebe examines the coat as though inspecting the integrity of its seams, while Dorcas strolls over to the shopkeeper, smiling in a friendly way, and bends down to inspect a pair of boots. In an instant, Phoebe deftly unbuttons the coat, glances to the left and right, slips it off the dummy's shoulders, picks up her skirts and glides into the general pedestrian traffic.

An hour hence, in a leavings shop off St Giles High Street, Mrs Ealing accepts the corduroy coat, which is exactly the coat requested by her customer, who had seen it the previous day; she cheerfully pays the two girls about a tenth of its value, along with a measure of spiced gin – of which Dorcas, in Phoebe's opinion, is overly fond. Mrs Ealing enquires as to its acquisition, not from moral fastidiousness but because it gives her pleasure to hear of such exploits, for they remind her of her youth. As Dorcas and Phoebe relate the incident, Mrs Ealing laughs with delight, her enormous breasts quivering over their bodice like bowls of blancmange.

The Holy Land

It is mid-afternoon, to judge by the narrow shaft of light from the ceiling, and the communal kitchen has filled considerably. Several of the fallen women glimpsed earlier have come in for tea with gin to assuage their morning sickness; their discomfort is made worse by the attentions of a raucous team of four young thieves with sooty faces and clothing, in high spirits after having stolen a large piece of salt beef and a number of potatoes from some honest vendor. They proceed to cook the meal, divide it, then tear the meat asunder with their fingers. One youth, scrawny as gristle, upon receiving his portion dances around the room, whirling his tin plate on the tip of his thumb. While passing the correspondent, he pauses, dips his nose into the plate and seizes a potato in his jaws, baring his yellow teeth.

Whitty has attended to the patterer's yarn carefully, partly for lack of an escape, partly not to give offence, but increasingly from mounting interest – and the smell of a series.

'I don't mind saying it, Mr Whitty, business could be better. People are more choosy like – they demands more and more of the nasty particulars.'

'I agree with you, Mr Owler. It is getting so that the news is not driven by facts, but by the fickle taste of the reader.'

'Fickle is the word, Sir. Mark you, Hollet was an exemplary fiend, but he wasn't good business because the wictim was a parson – that put people off the enjoyment of it. Surrell was no go either, not salt to a herring. I put much hope on 'The Horrid and Inhuman Murder committed by T. Dory on the body of Jael Denny', a most shocking thing, worked it every which way – but she didn't take. The weather coopered her, nobody was out on the streets as had a penny to keep warm. There went a shilling's worth of half-sheets, straight into the stove. Under such circumstances, I tell you, Mr Whitty, one can lose respect for the truth.'

Furtively, the correspondent opens his chemist's packet, wets his forefinger and collects the last granules of powder, which he rubs into his gums for the taste and the pleasant sensation of numbness. 'Sir, there's not a correspondent in London who hasn't embellished a story for the sake of a commission. I have succumbed myself, I am ashamed to say.'

'You don't say, Sir! I am shocked to hear it!'

How familiar, thinks Whitty, to circulate a cock for the week's rent, then rediscover one's principles the following Monday. Indeed, if he were to close his eyes (and nose), he might imagine himself speaking with a colleague at Plant's.

'Take the Liverpool Tragedy, now – wery attractive. Bless me, it saved me and my girls from shivering on the streets many a long, cold night. Do you recollect the tale?'

'Indeed. A son comes home from the Indies after thirty years, having married a rich plantation owner's daughter. The young man rents a room in the lodge operated by his parents, meaning to surprise them in the morning. Mother finds gold in his trunk and cuts his throat while he sleeps.

> *This young man he was a sailor,*
> *Just returned from sea;*
> *Down to Enfield Chase he went,*
> *His parents for to see;*
> *Little knew that bloody night -*
> *Would seal his destiny.'*

'Well remember'd, Sir! The old woman severs head from body while the old man places a washing-tub under the bed to catch the blood – these details is stunningly wivid: she washed 'er bloody hands, and then, so that the blood might not lead to detection, *drank* it!'

'Then comes the twist. On the morning after the murder they go upstairs . . .'

'And they discover the birthmark. Sometimes it is a tattoo.'

'The telltale mark! Exactly!'

'They have killed their own son! In agony, they put an end to their existence . . .'

'As I heard it, by swallowing lye.'

'Could be, could be – although self-immolation by fire is fly as well. Once I put my pipe in my pocket and burned the papers by mistake. Sold them as fresh from the fire what killed 'em, with nary a soul contradicting me.'

'Fraser of *Dodd's* took the train all the way to Liverpool to verify that one. Scoured the public record, found neither a coroner's report nor record of a double suicide since 1795.'

'Your Fraser is a fool, Sir. The thing is a total cock and everyone in England knows it.'

'He is not *my* Fraser, I assure you.' Indeed, Fraser has outrun him on many a lead; more, seemingly, of late. 'Tell me, Mr Owler, have you done William Weare?' So saying, Whitty quotes another verse from memory, much-loved as a boy:

> *'His throat they cut from ear to ear,*
> *His brains they punch-ed in;*
> *His name was Mr William Weare,*
> *Wot lived in Lyon's Inn.'*

'Indeed, Sir, I can see you have an eye for the best. Still does rattling business, especially in the country places.'

And now, having set the bait, Whitty springs the trap, though somewhat loathe to take advantage of such a simple soul: 'Another stunning cock might be the verses concerning your Chokee Bill,' he says, and watches as the jab finds its mark.

Owler reddens and is momentarily at a loss for words. '*Touché*, Sir. A good cut. But mark me carefully, for there's a crucial difference. Readers don't come from China, Sir, they knows what's what. Take the Liverpool Tragedy, now: ain't a particle of it ever existed; I knows it, you knows it, they knows it.'

'Everyone except Fraser, seemingly.'

'But do you see, Sir? The story sells on its merit purely as a yarn, not from curiosity for the true particulars of something partially known. Whereas with Chokee Bill, there being hard facts in the public record, the author is held to a higher standard: he must offer the excitement of a stunner with the integrity of hard fact. Can you see the distinction, sir, or are you that keen to discredit me?'

'I certainly do. *Touché* yourself, Mr Owler.'

'Christopher Walden came off badly for just that reason. Mr Walden were stingy in the fact department. Mind that there was no sorrowful lamentation nor shocking testimony offered by me – not for want of trying, let me tell you, pursued the thing like a terrier, sunk my capital in the turnkey, arrived with pencil and paper day after day to listen to Walden blubber his excuses, to get the Last Confession down on kite, don't you see? Walden was not forthcoming. Yet even so, I did not resort to a cock. I rooted for facts to the end, stood right under the drop waiting for him to clear his conscience before leaving this here wale of tears – and what was his last words on the brink of eternity? "I have nothing to say to you, Reverend. Thank you for your interest." Horse shite!

'To be sure, other stationers was bellowing his Last Words before the breath was out of his body, but I had none of it. A man deals in truth or fiction, Sir, one does not mix the two.'

'I am not certain many journalists would exhibit your integrity, Mr Owler, were they similarly cornered by circumstance.'

'I admit the integrity was stretched thin. Fortunately, like Providence answering my prayer, Jeremy here produced an acquaintanceship with Chokee Bill, with new particulars. It was the thing we'd prayed for, me and the girls.'

'How did Mr Hollow acquaint himself with such a notorious fellow?'

To Whitty's surprise, the inert gentleman across the table speaks in a distant, weak voice; the open mouth does not perceptibly move.

'It was several years ago. A serendipitous occurrence . . .'

'Good to see you alert, Jeremy.'

'Only resting, Henry, after the unaccustomed repast. Indeed, a cup of tea might revive me further . . .' Obediently, Owler signals the crone at the stove for tea, one for the poet and another for himself, Whitty abstaining.

After a luxurious sip of the steaming, blackish beverage, Mr Hollow continues: 'It happened several years ago, when my "Demon of the Sea" had attracted considerable attention. I had prospects, definite prospects, though even then my income was not what I should have liked – has it ever been? Accordingly, I had taken up residence in a dismal padding-ken frequented by the lowest characters. Unknown to myself, a group of coiners had set up operation in the garret over my head. One of these coiners was William Ryan – the man who would, years after, become known as Chokee Bill.'

Whereupon Whitty's interest takes on a new intensity.

'Mind, I spoke to the man no more than once in my life. Our association was pure chance. Returning from my day's work, near Seven Dials I recognized an inspector and two crushers gathered on a corner with an eye to my lodgings. Ordinarily I should not have interfered, for it was none of my business. But this was in the days when coining was a hanging offence. Rather than see a young man hanged when I could have it otherwise, I climbed to the garret by the outside wall. I warned Mr Ryan of the danger and informed him of a hiding-place nearby, wherein he might place his materials in case he was apprehended in flight; for as you know, sheer possession of coining apparatus was a capital offence then. I had learned of this place from an uncle in the business of small loans.'

Mr Hollow takes a sip of his tea, wincing at its bitterness. '*The Pelican In Her Piety*, gentlemen. Feeding her young with her own blood. Her own blood!'

'I beg your pardon, Sir,' says Whitty, 'but you have lost me there.'

'Nor did I see the meaning of it then. I who pretended to be a poet . . .' The sightless eyes now glisten as though attracted by some faraway object.

To the correspondent it seems that the man is raving: 'Mr Owler, I confess I am at a loss.' In reply, the patterer puts up his hand, calling for patience.

'Mr Ryan and his colleagues made good their escape,' continues Mr Hollow, picking up the thread as if he had not dropped it. 'Through the window and over a roof. I emphasize that the hiding-place was of great value. Indeed it was a holy place, for it brought about Mr Ryan's resurrection.' The poet laughs, making a dry click in the back of his throat.

'Mr Ryan must have been grateful.'

'Never saw the fellow again. Such a man reduces everything to money, that is the essence of a coiner. They are a separate breed from you and I.'

'Coiners are taking over the world,' adds Owler.

'Twenty years later, a chaunt went about the Holy Land that a William Ryan had gone up as Chokee Bill. Thought I: Thus might Mr Ryan repay me, the stranger who gave him an additional twenty years of life. Thus might I, in turn, repay Mr Owler for many kindnesses . . .' The voice recedes down a hallway as Mr Hollow falls back into slumber.

'So you see, Mr Whitty, thanks to Jeremy here I thought I had another Rush on me hands. By means of a turnkey with whom I had an association over the Walden affair, I gains access to Ryan. He remembers Mr Hollow, and pronounces himself willing to repay his debt of honour before leaving this wale of tears.' Here Owler begins to recite from memory:

In vain he repents, with no friend to whom he can communicate private thoughts and in return receive consolation. Hence his nervous system is fast breaking down, every day rendering him less able to endure the excruciating torments he is hourly suffering, haunted by remorse heaped

upon remorse, every fresh victim Chokee Bill were required to strangle
being so much more fuel heaped upon the mental flame what scorches
him . . .

'The man sounds in a bad way.'

'No, he claims innocence, as you know.'

'How inconvenient for everyone concerned.'

'I remain optimistic that remorse will get the better of him as the big day nears.'

'For your sake, I hope so.'

'Werily, and a white-knuckle business it is.'

Whitty's neck prickles, indicating the presence of crisp copy. Skilfully handled, an association with lowlife such as this could be his ticket to solvency – the story being not about Chokee Bill *per se* (who loses all currency on the day William Ryan is hanged), but about the patterer and the wretches with whom he associates, their occupations, habits, loves . . .

Envisage the patterer as a native guide conducting respectable readers through the jungles of Africa. Envisage a series of articles (entitled, perhaps, 'How The Other Half Lives') concerning the savages who infest that dark country within the country, which respectable Englishmen regard with fascination, yet would no more willingly enter than they would visit a nest of crocodiles.

In Whitty's mind, the Holy Land transforms from a jungle into a garden, whose riches yield a book, a tour of public lectures – not to mention the possibility of a debt-free existence – financial and otherwise. Assuming (admittedly a precipitous assumption) that he can interest the Editor and his grim cabal in the narrative he intends to undertake, convince *The Falcon* that his thematic point is sufficiently sharp as to prick the public fancy, he has every chance of a healthy stipend . . .

Owler's fist pounds the table, jolting the correspondent to alertness. 'Werily, Sir, I swear on the memory of me mother that I'm not done with Mr Ryan yet! Is it reasonable that a man should take such pains as to make another man a figure of legend, walk mile upon mile in the rain to do it, and get hardly a ha'penny for his labour? It cannot be thought on! When the wile and inhuman murderer takes his last walk, I shall be paid my just claims!'

'Mr Owler, after hearing your account I think I can be of service to you. More than by a simple retraction.'

'How is that, Sir? Heaven knows I am open to suggestion.'

'You mentioned the fleeting nature of public interest, the unhelpful incursions of professionals such as myself; yet I may be in a position to come to your aid. If you were to take me to meet this party known as Chokee Bill, thereby to witness your interaction with him, I might whet the public interest for you, while attesting to the veracity of your report.'

'Sir, that would be most agreeable to myself.'

So begins an association between two gentlemen of utterly divergent background and taste. Thus do human beings, out of pure self-regard, come to rely on one another. However implausible – nay, inappropriate – the prospect may have once seemed, a connection, indeed a society, is born.

Chester Path

Owing to the genius of the architect Mr Nash, the town-house occupied by the Harewood family faces onto Regent's Park, providing the property with maximum exposure to the Outer Circle and the gardens beyond, while turning its back on the less favourable addresses to the rear: Gustavus and Stanhope Streets, to say nothing of Market Square, with its stench of old fish and rotting vegetables.

Regent's Park expresses in abundance the traditional English love of nature, the requirement of a semblance of the countryside even in the city. Indeed, looking outward from the front entrance of Harewood Manor, one could be situated on a manicured country estate, scrupulously maintained by an army of gardeners. Seen from behind, however, Chester Path is a blank shield of whitewashed masonry. Homeowners on Chester Path are further protected against intrusion from below by a grid of ironwork fences and gates, each with its own key; which effectively prevented lesser citizens from making use of the park unless by trudging all the way down to Euston Street. Thus can a property become a public facility and a private luxury all at once.

At the same time, there exists a connection between the impeccable house on Chester Path and the worst rat-holes off St Giles High Street – a connection between the investor and the source of revenue, the proboscis and the host.

A mile away in the parish of St Giles, eighty per cent of the houses in the Church Lane quarter (near which Whitty, Owler and the poet took their frugal repast) are owned by precisely eight people. All of these, excepting the Duke of Bedford, live in the area of Regent's Park. All are related by blood and marriage, this family of freehold, whose agents rent entire streets to lesser proprietors, who rent to managers, who rent by the room, and on down to parties who rent part of their bed to people with nothing.

Perched near the middle of the pyramid (though nowhere near its pinnacle, the Duke of Bedford being a cousin of the Queen) are the Harewoods, whose holdings in the Holy Land are of such long standing, and whose leases are so secure, as to comprise, in effect, a massive, obscure annuity, the source of which has been long forgotten.

Once reduced to a dividend, all money looks and smells the same. There remains no lingering odour to trouble the investor.

This ethic of insulation from the source of one's existence is expressed in the decoration of the house on Chester Path, its windows draped in successive layers, each providing protection, symbolic and real, from the coarser elements of the city. Seen from the outside, though packed with family and servants, Chester Path appears as bereft as a tomb.

It is behind such successive tiers of protection that the respectable, well-situated family stores its women, so that their sensibilities may be sheltered, their morals untainted by the rotten world.

Clara Greenwell is the daughter of the elder Harewood's sister – who, naturally, did not inherit; nor did she marry well. Thus inadequately provided for, Clara eagerly accepted her Uncle Miles's invitation to enjoy his protection, thereby to capture the affections of her cousin Reginald (or one of his friends), thereby to assume the birthright denied her.

To this end, once a week Clara is at home to visitors; it is a special day for which she makes herself even prettier than usual, to entertain the compliments of any young gentlemen who might bother to call; chaperoned of course.

Which is not to suggest any indecision on her part as to whom she intends to marry. But Reggie has not yet proposed. It is a foolish woman who places all her eggs in one basket.

Walter Sewell alights from the cab on the Outer Circle and crosses to the iron gate, noting the rustle of an upstairs curtain. Clara has been watching for his arrival, in the way that one might anticipate the postman.

There is no question in Sewell's mind that Reggie must marry somebody, and that, all things considered, it will have to be Clara. He accepts this. Aware that Clara and Reggie were meant for one another, Sewell, in his own interest, invested no small effort in persuading Clara that he had fallen a bit in love with her himself, the better to put her at her ease, to satisfy both her vanity and her preference for control.

However, the tactic succeeded somewhat beyond its usefulness. Clara has come to enjoy Sewell's fond attentions, as a way of topping up her required goblet of flattery. For Sewell, this has turned into something of a chore.

He arranges his face into a pleasant expression, smoothes his trousers, his sleeves and gloves. He reaches for the brass knocker, set in the jaws of a lion: hardly has he executed two strikes when the door swings wide open, as though the servant lurked behind it. Liveried in canary-yellow breeches, the footman inspects the visitor with a practised eye, as impersonal as a fence. He does not appear to recognize Sewell, although the latter has visited on a weekly basis for months.

'A very good afternoon to you, Sir, and may I say welcome to Harewood Manor.'

'How do you do, Bryson. I am very pleased to be here. Is Miss Greenwell at home?'

'Please step in, Mr Sewell, and I shall be very glad to determine that for you.'

The footman admits Sewell into the house – or rather, into an ante-room devoid of furniture, a holding chamber in which to isolate the visitor until enquiries can be made.

Waiting in this marble cell, Sewell regards the framed verse on the wall:

> God moves in a mysterious way
> His wonders to perform;
> He plants his footsteps in the sea,
> And rides upon the storm.

Cowper of course. Poet laureate to the Smug.

With a little squeal of pleasure, Clara Greenwell bursts into the reception room, in a froth of crinoline and lace, her golden ringlets brushed to dishevelled perfection by her chaperone, directly behind – tall and thin, dressed as a widow, a tragically plain woman whose heavy eyebrows gather above an aquiline nose. Indeed, the two women before him make a contrast so remarkable as to be almost deliberate – one pinched and worn at twenty-one; the other, five years her junior, a radiance of creamy, smooth, untouched flesh. Such a grim allegory on innocence and experience! Even Sewell is open to the illusion, though he knows well who is the virgin and who is not.

'Dear Roodie, what a splendid surprise!' Clara's little hand slips into his like a warm dumpling, causing Sewell to redden uncomfortably, and to express himself with an awkward sincerity she finds delightful.

'Miss Greenwell, you have the beauty of Bathsheba and the grace of Mary.'

'You are so terribly sweet. Do you remember Miss Brown, my companion and confidential friend?'

Sewell bows, while grasping her companion's chapped fingers. 'A delight to see you, Miss Brown. I trust the afternoon finds you in the best of spirits.'

'I am well within reason. I am obliged to you, Sir.'

Followed by Clara's black-robed protector, in this muffled atmosphere of successive draperies and protective furniture covers, not to mention covers for the protective covers, the two young people enter a sitting-room containing three chairs, set in a broad triangle near the fireplace. Upon the mantel sit busts of the Queen and the Duke of Wellington, with a portrait of the Saviour between, gazing aloft with gentle blue eyes. Above the Saviour hangs an enormous, elaborately framed mirror, which doubles the weak illumination of gas and firelight (daylight having been banished from the premises), to suffuse the room with a rosy glow sufficient to flatter the most sallow complexion. On either side of the fireplace, a pair of ferns spill over their pots next to stands of hyacinths, the latter producing a moist, sweet aroma.

Incongruously, the mantel is supported by a pair of bare-breasted women, like the prows of ships. Their mahogany colour identifying them as Natives, the display of nudity is therefore as acceptable as with wild animals.

In the centre of the room is a square table containing a partially completed jigsaw puzzle depicting the World, with the Empire coloured red, the rest of the globe in green and blue. A second table by the fire is under preparation by the parlourmaid, setting a tea-tray and plates of wafer-thin bread and butter. As is customary in rooms where members of the opposite sex congregate, the legs of both tables have been concealed by embroidered tablecloths, down to the carpeted floor.

'Thank you, Emma, that will be all.' In speaking to the servant, Miss Greenwell employs the high voice recommended for commanding servants, with a rising inflection at the end to indicate that the girl is not to stray very far away.

For her part, Miss Brown takes a bundle of crewel work from her apron and seats herself in the chair closest to the fire so that the young people will be obliged to converse around her person, as though she is a tree.

'And is life still so very jolly up at Oxford?' asks Miss Greenwell, seemingly unaware that both Sewell and Harewood came down months earlier.

'As it happens, at the end of term Reginald and I took a fancy to do London together. For the moment, Reggie has chosen to reside at the

Fidelium, whereas I have taken rooms off Bruton Street at Number 34.'

Having made a mental note of the address, she enquires further: 'Do you find yourself comfortably situated, Sir?'

'Excuse me, Miss Greenwell,' interjects Miss Brown, 'but I hardly think an enlargement on the gentleman's personal quarters to be a suitable direction for the conversation.'

'Quite correct, Miss Brown,' acknowledges Sewell. 'I am obliged to you. May I say that, toward late afternoon, say around four-thirty, the light shows itself to considerable advantage on the east side of Berkeley Square.'

Miss Harewood's violet eyes widen prettily. 'I love the light at Berkeley Square, and agree that it sets off the garden to good advantage – especially under the plane trees. It seems to me that plane trees lend dignity to a garden – would you not agree, Miss Brown?'

'I have heard Mayfair is a costly neighbourhood,' observes Miss Brown, taking her cue, for which she expects to be paid five shillings.

1 2

The Fidelium

Reggie's club is situated among other clubs while remaining somewhat different from its neighbours, being an older institution whose founding members, their dues paid-up in perpetuity upon their seniority and therefore having nothing further to contribute, have had the effrontery to remain alive. As a result, at the Fidelium new members are assiduously courted, the only requirement being that they be male and somebody, and gambling is encouraged.

So irrelevant have the founding members become to the day-to-day running of the Fidelium that, when an elderly gentleman collapsed in the foyer, patrons took bets as to whether he was dead or in a fit. Upon another occasion, it was not discovered that a founding member had passed on until someone took notice of the fact that the *Telegraph* shading his face was the previous day's edition.

In such a club, even while in disgrace, Reginald Harewood is always welcome.

Sewell finds Harewood in the lounge: 'Sorry to have kept you waiting. Am I late?'

'How should I know?' replies Harewood testily. 'I don't have a watch.'

'Of course. Sorry to have brought it up.' Indeed, Sewell is worried about his friend, who has not been quite the same since the robbery. 'Really, you're going to have to put the incident behind you.'

'I cannot. She robbed me. It is like being raped. She took my rugby ring!'

'A devastating loss, to be sure.'

'An irreplaceable memento, that ring. Really, I should have reported her to the police, if it weren't for the particular circumstances.'

'Indeed, you have displayed exemplary restraint.'

Reginald Harewood signals for brandy and cigars. 'What do you say we dine together?'

'Here?' enquires Sewell uneasily, for the Fidelium is not known for its cuisine.

'I suppose we must, because it is so much trouble to go anywhere else. Could do with a few quid. Financial picture damned rum. Bloody

85

impudent Irish fellow followed me back here yesterday, buttonholed me in the foyer wanting to be paid for something – in front of the company, don't you know!'

'What did the fellow want?'

'By his trousers I suspect he wanted something on account for the horses.'

'Blasted cheek! How did it end?'

'He paused in his damned yammering and I gave him a cigar. While he was biting the end of it, I went straight upstairs. Didn't come back down for twelve hours, by which time he'd got tired of waiting, I suppose.'

'If we might go hunting together, I would pay your groom something to keep him happy.'

'I should like nothing better, old chap, but as I told you, I daren't go outside in daylight.'

'What a nuisance. In the meanwhile, any softening of the Governor's position on Clara?'

'Not a bit of it. Blessed if I've seen a shilling in a fortnight.'

'The way the city is populating, the Harewood holdings will double in value. A marriage within the family will keep it in the family, don't you see.'

'You have a point, Roo. Still, one don't give in to pressure. Not the thing at all. Besides, I'm not ready to go into business, signing this, buying that.'

'You'd be the possessor of a great deal of money.'

'I care not a fig for money – as long as it keeps coming in, of course. Which it is not.'

Sewell, who can see that his friend needs cheering up, presses a five-pound note into his hand. 'On the bright side, I've had a word with your comely cousin, as requested.'

'What did she tell you?'

'It is settled. Four-thirty at Berkeley Square. Provided, of course, she can negotiate a price with that glowering hag of a governess.'

'Well done. There's a good chap.' Reginald pockets the money as though it were his handkerchief.

'You could do worse, Reggie. She's terribly taken with you.'

'I say, Roo, you should be one of those fellows in a French comedy, who carry messages, move things along, unite the star-crossed lovers, all that sort of thing.'

'Without being a lover himself?'

'Not everyone's ticket, is it? One might as well try to teach a person how to be tall.'

'I suppose you're right,' replies his shorter, plainer friend.

By half-past four the London afternoon is transformed utterly by fog, an almost daily occurrence, in which a thick, sooty curtain drops between everyone and everything, noon becomes night, and the city assumes the cloistered gravity of a confession-booth; in which nobody sees anyone else but as a shadow in the mist; when the immanent roar of machines and men is silenced, leaving only the muffled clatter of nearby horseshoes on stone, and the occasional disembodied voice, whose speaker remains anonymous and untouchable.

Today the grey fog has taken its turn, the most common version of the London particular, an eerie grey like the ghost of stone or the lingering shadows of departed walls – the perfect medium for an illicit liaison. When it is the yellow fog, people and objects may be discerned and recognized, albeit with difficulty; but once the grey sets in, the city becomes a well-kept secret, even from itself.

Lit by a weak flicker of gaslight, the fog swirls around a maroon phaeton as it clatters onto Berkeley Square. Nestled under a rug, Clara peers into the mist expectantly, smiling to herself. Perfect.

As a dense cloud of fog enveloped her carriage, she felt a slight flush inflame her cheek, knowing that he awaited to envelop her in his arms, ready to devour her. Already she felt his presence . . .

She taps the bottom of the driver's chair with her umbrella, commanding him to stop beneath a plane tree whose branches hold the fog in tufts, like cotton.

'Remain here, Grimes, if you please.'

'As you wish, Miss.'

As you wish indeed, thinks Clara, having purchased the servant's cooperation with five shillings she stole from the housekeeper, and having ensured her chaperone's silence by making her a present of the romance Uncle Miles gave her at Christmas, in return for a kiss on the mouth.

Reggie must have been waiting behind the tree, for suddenly he is beside her, having vaulted into the carriage in the most graceful manner: now she imagines the two of them as runaways, alone despite the wishes of their parents, moved by their mutual passion, the fierceness of their desire.

She emits a little gasp: 'Oh, Reginald, you frightened me.'

'My darling,' he whispers in her ear. 'You've come.'

He steps down onto the cobbles and assists her out of the phaeton: 'Wait here please, Grimes, there's a good fellow. Miss Greenwell and I wish to take a stroll.'

'Very good, Sir,' replies the driver, watching the two lovers disappear into the fog.

Clara affects a little shiver, inspiring him to hold her more tightly in his arms. 'Darling, you're cold,' he murmurs.

'A little,' she replies, gazing into his face. Her violet eyes widen, prettily.

He kisses her on her lips, made swollen by deliberately biting them. His tongue reaches for hers, whereupon she gently pushes his chest with her little hands. 'Oh, Reginald,' she gasps. 'You're too much for me.'

'Please forgive me, Clara. Don't you see? My love for you is uncontrollable – you must know that, surely.'

She glances downward, modestly.

Clara loves Reggie and is determined to have him, having concluded that handsome, practical men make the best husbands. No Heathcliff for Clara, thank you very much. And although she does not know exactly what it is she craves in her heart, certainly it will be more attainable if she is independently wealthy, and can have what she wants, and make people do what she wants. This much seems obvious.

She affects another little shiver and holds her head so he may kiss her on the mouth again. He has scent in his whiskers. She allows his tongue to remain somewhat longer this time.

'Oh darling, you're still cold.'

'I am a bit, my Reggie. I fear I am not as toughened to the elements as you. Oh my dear, won't you please take me somewhere warm?'

'Of course I will, dear Clara, you mustn't get a chill.'

Clara smiles, while submitting her plump little hand to the strong grip of her future husband and protector.

His hands trembling (she is a hot little treasure), Reginald Harewood fumbles with the brass key to Sewell's rooms, there to be alone together, while the compliant Roo consigns himself to an evening spent walking the streets.

In the reception room, she tilts her head so that he will kiss her on the mouth again – which, of course, he does.

Peering over his shoulder while she allows him briefly to slip his hands where he shouldn't, Clara can see through the open door to the bedroom. In her mind she puts aside her fantasy of Miss Brontë and replaces it with something more French – more like the novel she made Uncle Miles obtain for her while in Paris, in return for her continued silence on the subject of certain liberties taken.

He undresses her, layer after layer, then marvels at the white body beneath, from the tiny foot and ankle upward to the mysterious spots and crevices, which he has come to know but still views with childlike fascination. (As a child he was told that a woman went down to the ground in one piece, like the trunk of a tree.)

The door closed automatically behind him. A soft voice said in French: 'Is that you, mon chéri?'

'Yes, it is me, my love.'

She could hear his heart pounding like a steam-hammer as he stood over the bed.

She lay there, her buttons carelessly undone. He bent down and she embraced him passionately, darting her little tongue into his mouth. His manhood responded to her fingers and he lifted up her skirts.

She parted her thighs. Her legs were bare. A delicious perfume emanated from her skin, mingled with the perfume of her odoer di femmina. He gently placed his hand on her cunt.

She murmured: 'Let's fuck. I cannot wait. Naughty man, you have not been to see me in a week.'

Instead of replying, he pulled out his formidable weapon and climbed, thus armed, onto the bed, ready to train his sights and to thrust himself ferociously into the breach, whereupon she gasped in feigned wonder, then began to wriggle her buttocks while crying out: 'Put it all the way in! You are making me come!'

13

Coldbath Fields

Situated atop Mount Pleasant, Coldbath Fields, or 'The Steel', is of a design pioneered in America, consisting of a building with two galleried wings and a common area in the centre; this arrangement has proved especially beneficial in enforcing the now-standard 'separate system'.

Elegantly simple, the separate system requires convicted criminals to sleep, eat and work separate from one another, and to refrain from speaking for all but one hour a day, an arrangement which contributes to the benefit of all. From the standpoint of the prisoner, reform is achieved through Christian penitence, counting the months with only a wounded conscience for company; for the state, there is enhanced efficiency, a few warders being sufficient to monitor a large number of cells; for respectable citizens, there is the solace and reassurance in knowing that the perpetrators will suffer more than their victims ever did.

In keeping with its philosophy of diligence and order, governorship of The Steel has traditionally been conferred upon officers who have served successfully in the army or navy, who have learned to obey and to command with equal assiduity.

In general, inmates at The Steel serve sentences ranging from two hundred days for serious rental arrears, to fourteen years for the theft of a gentleman's greatcoat. None is considered beyond redemption. All receive the benefit of the most modern theories, in which Governor Cornwallis has taken a keen interest.

Of the fifteen hundred inmates of both sexes currently serving in The Steel, only the current occupant of the condemned cell can be said to constitute a danger to the public, and this of an exceptional kind, being of such a freakish disposition as to murder for the sheer pleasure of it.

The new penal philosophy of incarceration is no longer designed for those awaiting punishment (hanging, flogging), but as a punishment and correction in itself. (Americans, who originated the concept, refer to the facility as a 'penitentiary'.) Thanks to the modern approach, English children no longer scurry beneath gibbets by the roadside on their way to school, nor do their parents take weekly pleasure in the public flogging of their neighbours; instead, a scientific programme of silence, solitude, the treadwheel, as well as flogging and blistering where necessary, improves these disfigured souls, out of public sight.

Whitty has written often about the peculiar horror that ensues whenever the scientific mind turns its attention to public morality and the creation of a better world. Stories about the horrors of prison life are always popular, as the imagined spectacle of physical harm done to another inspires in the reader a pleasurable awareness of his own comfortable position.

Given that it is the usual practice to house convicts awaiting execution in the death cell at Newgate (the site of the hanging itself), the placement of William Ryan in Coldbath Fields has occasioned some speculation. Some see it as an attempt to augment the severity of punishment, at a time when the garrotter has replaced the traditional footpad as a civic bogeyman. Others see Ryan as an object lesson to current inmates at The Steel, who might otherwise contemplate graduating to more serious crimes. Others look to the planned procession from The Steel to the square at Newgate as a revival of a tradition – the public exhibition of the criminal throughout the city, that he may be subjected to the indignation of honest citizens.

'Does our man know we're here?' enquires Whitty, jammed in the insufficient shelter of an obscure side doorway (how aptly named, Coldbath Fields!), trying to remain dry against a frigid, angular torrent of rain mixed with sleet (ah, spring!) which abrades his exposed skin like the blades of tiny knives.

'Mr Hook has never been what you call timely,' Owler admits, it being an hour since the agreed-upon time, the metal door having failed to budge from its sealed position. (The rust, the cobwebs, the state of its hardware indicate a discouraging lack of use.) Whitty observes his companion, pipe in mouth, hands in pockets, water pouring off the brim of his crooked hat, skin as thick as buffalo hide, yet with a curiously fragile sensibility.

'Mr Owler, is this necessary to accomplish our purpose?'

'Mr Ryan is in great demand among preachers, women's societies and likewise. Many would gladly take credit for a condemned man meeting his Maker in a reformed state. Without preferred access we should be lucky to meet with the Fiend once a fortnight. Trust me, Sir: best to make use of my channels what have stood the test of time.'

'Out of curiosity, what *are* these channels? Do you forward a request in writing?'

'Surely you jest, Sir. That would put us both on the treadwheel side by side.'

Whitty thinks he is coming down with a fever, a result of the terrible smells ingested of late. He longs to take to his bed, even if it be situated in Camden Town.

'How the devil do you know the message was received at all?'

'Indeed, Sir, I have wondered that about the electric telegraph. How they squeezes the sentences through such a little wire is a great mystery.' Owler strikes a lucifer to his pipe, filling the tiny doorway with a stench somewhat like burning leather.

Whitty removes a length of spider web clinging to his sleeve. 'Why do we not meet your man at the main door, like other prospective visitors?'

'I explained the legalities only moments ago, Sir. Many unforeseen factors could cooper an enterprise such as this.'

At the door Whitty can detect a faint scratching like that of a rodent, then a teeth-grinding protest as the iron bolt is jerked open, followed by the heavy groan of the door itself. Now a crack appears, and, in the crack, a single eye, framed above and below by a thatch of matted hair.

'Mr Owler, might I presume?'

'You are correct, Mr Hook.'

The crack does not widen. 'We made no arrangement about third parties, Squire.'

'Mr Whitty is a factor in our purpose, Mr Hook. He is fly.'

'In these matters I be sensitive on third parties, whether they be fly or not.'

'Mr Whitty is with *The Falcon*. 'T'will expand our potential wonderfully.'

The crack does not open.

'Allow Mr Whitty access, Mr Hook, and you will have a new pair of boots from the profits. I knows a fine pair on the Waterloo Road what has the name Hook right on 'em.'

The eye disappears momentarily and the door grinds its way to an opening sufficient to allow Owler and Whitty to squeeze through, into the main exercise yard of Coldbath Fields House of Correction.

'What is the meaning of the word "fly"?' asks Whitty.

'It is the language we call *cant*, Sir, and it indicates trustworthiness. Mind, I said you was fly to gain entrance, not because I hold this opinion of you myself.'

The turnkey having forced the door shut again, they now occupy a dark alcove leading to a blank wall – the continuous renovation and expansion of the house of correction having created, in what was once a passage between two buildings, a small, three-sided enclosure, from which they overlook a large open space paved with flat stones. On the far side of the yard stands the hulk of the prison itself, whose surface has been decorated with improving texts designed to uplift offender and officer alike.

GO TO THE ANT, THOU SLUGGARD
CONSIDER HER WAYS TO BE WISE.

Around the yard, walls of squared greystone tower to a height of fifty feet. Just below the top of each wall is a *chevaux-de-frise* – a continuous rod of revolving iron spikes, supported by a horizontal bar armed with additional points which has been drilled into the stone. Along the top edge of the wall are embedded a row of long, sharp spikes, their points angled inward to further discourage an impromptu exit.

To Whitty, the paved expanse has the aspect of a grotesque playground, where about a hundred men have gathered in circular groups of ten or twelve in order to participate in what appears to be a child's game. Within each circle of prisoners sits a concentric circle of twenty-four-pound cannon-balls, evenly spaced; at the bellowed command of an officer, each man picks up a cannon-ball, carries it to his right-hand neighbour, sets it down, then returns to his place, where the cannon-ball formerly belonging to his left-hand neighbour lies waiting for him. He picks up the next cannon-ball and repeats the exercise, again and again, as the cannon-balls go around and around for eight hours of a stretch.

To maximize the tedium and isolation, each man not only maintains absolute silence but also wears 'the beak' – a peculiar cloth cap, the peak of which, also of cloth, hangs low enough that it covers the face like a mask, with two small holes for the eyes. Thus, the men are deprived of communication either by voice or through facial expression. Notwithstanding, so persistent is the human urge to communicate, interchange between the prisoners takes place by means of peculiar movements of the thumb and fingers, in a system akin to the deaf-and-dumb alphabet.

Whitty notes the ever-present pigeons fluttering about the prisoners' feet in the yard, visible beneath the beak; the rainbow-like shimmer about their necks must provide a welcome glimpse of colour to an eye accustomed to none.

'Shot drill,' explains the turnkey, removing his cap to scratch his pate, situated above an explosion of whiskers which sprout in tufts, above which sits an eye, like a robin's egg in a nest – the one and only eye, thanks to cataract in the other, a milky chrysalis which, thinks Whitty, awaits the emergence of a butterfly.

Mr Hook's threadbare uniform of shiny blue serge emits an odour of tobacco, sweat, mutton and wet wool; its tarnished brass buttons barely contain the flesh packed within. From his belt hang a number of objects: a chain containing many keys, a humphrey (a small shot-filled cosh), a policeman's night-stick, a whistle, and a canvas bag packed with personal effects – mutton, tobacco, gin, and a potation which, to judge by the smell of his breath, is Mariani wine, a cocaine preparation.

'I was not always as you see me now, Squire,' whispers the turnkey. 'I would have you know that.'

'I beg your pardon, Sir?' A weariness settles upon the correspondent, for he is about to revisit that almost universal tendency among the lower orders – the urge to present oneself as having once occupied a higher state. Every beggar was once a shopkeeper, every thief plied an honest trade, every harlot is a ravished daughter of the gentry.

'An engineer was I until me sight took for the worse. Depth perception, Squire: without the two eyes you're jiggered where machinery is concerned.'

Whitty ventures no reply, distracted by a flutter of pigeons in the yard, where a man has collapsed. Obeying a barked order from the warder, two inmates roughly pick the body off the ground by the wrists and ankles, carry it to the entrance to the building and toss it onto a blanket like a sack of flour, where it joins three of its insensate colleagues, having likewise succumbed to exhaustion, malnutrition or jail fever. On the wall above them is an uplifting message:

LIFE'S RACE WELL RUN
LIFE'S WORK WELL DONE.

In the meanwhile, the remaining men close the circle and, to another bellowed command from the warder, resume their futile enterprise.

'In your experience, Mr Hook, is shot drill an effective tool in the reformation of a criminal?'

'Most efficacious, Squire. Thanks to exercise and diet, our prisoners grow more feeble and present less danger to the public.'

'I had not thought of nutrition as a weapon against crime.'

'A deep thinker, is Governor Cornwallis. If there is a trend, the master has hitched onto it.'

Whitty notes that Owler is already headed across the yard, eager to get to work, anxious over valuable interview time lost, gloomily conscious of the stakes involved for himself and his wards, leery of his reliance on a party so easily distracted from their intended purpose.

Having passed through a huge square room from which extend two wings consisting of tiers of cells, they enter the treadwheel house, a building resembling an enormous, roaring factory and containing a number of peculiar machines, each of which is powered by the feet of a line of prisoners, climbing a set of moving stairs.

Whitty lights a cigaret as a fumigant to ward off the universal prison smell: sweat and raw sewage, combined with the fumes of burning chloride of lime – an unappetizing preparation designed to keep putrid fevers to a minimum.

'I note that the treadwheel has caught your interest, Squire.'

'The famous treadwheel. Much has been written about it.'

Newgate and Fleet being his normal prison beat, this is Whitty's first view of this latest in correctional thinking (colloquially known as the 'cock-chafer') for which The Steel has become justly famous. Before them stands a long series of compartments, designed to accommodate the labours of five hundred at a time, not unlike the rows of stalls at a public urinal, in each of which a masked convict can be seen treading a turning wheel at a single fixed rate. The focus of their combined effort is an enormous, vented water-wheel, spinning against the far wall without evident purpose. Women in canvas skirts and bonnets work the treadwheel as well as men, their modesty ensured by pieces of linen stretched on a frame behind them, shielding their ankles from immodest display. Below each compartment issue three steps, upon which other prisoners await their turn, without enthusiasm.

'The treadwheel be the pride and joy of our establishment. By tradition, every inmate spends its first three months on the machine. Nobody leaves The Steel without the full benefit.'

'Through labour they see the error of their ways.'

'Well put, Mr Whitty, true for you there.'

'And choking on one's own filth – that also will straighten a man out.'

'Might you be referring to the odour hereabouts?'

'I should be insensible not to, Mr Hook. We are in the midst of one gigantic cess-pool.'

'The odours is a professional drawback, to be certain, Squire. It is not uncommon for the warder coming in of a morning to become sick. Many is the time I have hurled me breakfast, bought at me own expense not an hour earlier.'

'And it must surely be a torture for the women,' observes Owler, pained by his habitual worry for the two girls in his care. 'To allow girls into such a place as this is.'

'Not at all, Mr Owler. These is not women as you'd call *women* in polite society, Squire. These women is the toughest nuts and therefore slow to crack. You wouldn't credit the inconceivable wickedness of these girls, the impudence of them. Simply to maintain respect, a girl's head must be shaved and blistered at the slightest sign of rebellion, otherwise you have the very Devil on your hands.'

'Sweet are the uses of adversity, which find sermons in stones and good in everything.'

'That was of a pretty composure, Mr Whitty,' says the turnkey.

'It was Shakespeare, actually. Are you gentlemen acquainted with Shakespeare?'

'I have heard some speeches,' replies Owler.

Adds Mr Hook: 'I've heard of an eye-gouging that is most shocking.'

'That would be *King Lear*. There is also a hot poker up a bugger's arse in *Edward II*.'

Turnkey and patterer wince at the thought.

The prison bell sounds the quarter-hour, on precisely the same note heard in Newgate, Pentonville and Holloway; prison bells are all cast by the same hands, in the same mould, tuned to the same pitch – a harsh, strident voice expressing callousness and hopelessness in one dispiriting note.

Hearing the bell, Owler grows once again anxious. Urged on by the patterer, the three proceed down a set of iron steps, then immediately back up to ground level, to what appears to be a small outbuilding attached to the rear, like a garden shed equipped with a heavy iron door.

'Now that we are outside the condemned cell, might I impart a caution?'

'Mr Owler, I eagerly await your counsel.'

'There must be no mention of a Sorrowful Lamentation until such time as our man actually confesses. 'T'would be a fatal blunder if you get my drift, Sir.'

'I agree. An innocent man might find it unnerving to hear his confession read to him in verse.'

'Nobody said he were innocent. Or might you be apprised beyond the horizon of my knowledge?'

'Nothing of the kind, Mr Owler, I was only theorizing about the case.'

'There is no theory to be had about the case. There is nothing theoretical about it.'

'They always confess,' says Mr Hook, producing a large brass key from the ring attached to his belt. 'Some confess when I'd of sworn they don't remember they done it.'

'In this case,' says Owler gravely, 'the worry is who will hear the confession. Competition is keen.'

The turnkey having opened the heavy iron door, they enter a surprisingly large room with a ceiling at about three times the height of a man. There is one rectangular window just beneath the ceiling, topped with a rounded cornice and covered with a grid of flat iron bars, allowing a chequered view of the sky.

The wall opposite contains a second door which opens onto a tiny, enclosed exercise yard, bounded on three sides by the building itself and two exterior walls. The fourth wall verges on the prison yard and is lower in height, its purpose being not so much to contain the condemned as to protect him from other prisoners, who, having wives and daughters of their own, and tending to a conservative line on crime and punishment, would cheerfully serve out Chokee Bill for the primitive satisfaction of it, thereby saving Mr Calcraft the time and trouble.

The walls are made of square stones, cluttered with the names, dates and last messages of former occupants, etched in its surface with pieces of rock or metal. In the centre is a deal table containing the remainder of a meal consisting of a mutton chop, a fish and what looks to be preserved tongue, as well as a pudding. Remarkably, the table also contains two bouquets of fresh flowers, newly delivered.

'I say, Mr Hook, the accommodations and victuals seem to be of an unusually high order. Wouldn't mind a stay here myself.' (Whitty watches the turnkey sharply.) 'I understand – theoretically speaking of course – that for the payment of a certain sum by an outside party, it is not unknown for a convict to obtain certain supplementaries.'

Hook's eye grows shifty, aware of its delicate situation and the correspondent's ready pencil. 'True for you, Squire, though we would never countenance it here.'

'No doubt, Mr Hook. I appeal purely to your professional

imagination. Were such a thing to occur, how might it be done?'

'I wouldn't hear of such a thing meself, but it would stand to reason that any such gammy transaction would take place outside the premises – let us say, by means of a package left with the barkeeper of a certain pub.'

'Thereby protecting both the enterprising turnkey and the prisoner's anonymous benefactor.'

'Exactly, Squire. Of course, we be talking of a purely theoretical matter.'

Whitty becomes aware of a sound in a far corner of the room, in whose shadow he can make out the back of a man, who is turning a handle, attached to what appears to be a large grinder-organ – without music – to which he is attached by means of chain and ankle-iron. It is as though our man were playing the roles of grinder and monkey, simultaneously.

'Am I finally in the presence of Mr Ryan?'

'You are indeed,' replies the turnkey. 'The condemned man has asked for the benefit of a machine to himself.'

'Most industrious of him.' Now that the correspondent's eyes have adjusted to the perpetual dusk he can make out more clearly the contraption in the corner, as well the muscular form of its operator, working away.

Owler, meanwhile, crosses to the prisoner's bunk, where the floor has been piled high with evangelist tracts, as well as a number of newspapers and sensational weeklies. 'Observe the leavings of our competition,' he whispers to Whitty.

Having crossed the room, Mr Hook proceeds to unlock the prisoner's ankle-iron. None the less, the convict continues to turn the crank in a regular rhythm, still with his back to his visitors as though they did not exist, although he can surely hear their conversation.

'Gentlemen,' announces the turnkey, 'this be the most modern device in The Steel. Like the other cranks you seen, this one makes use of a drum filled with sand, with a cupped spindle running through it, which the convict turns by a crank-handle. A standard device, but with a modern innovation: the revolutions is counted by clockwork. Thus, a calculation of the total is maintained, with no need for supervision whatever.'

'What, if I may ask, is the intended benefit of the crank to a man who stands condemned to death?'

'Like the Governor says, "While there is breath, there is correction."'

'The gentleman appears to be in excellent health. Unlike the villains we observed on the treadwheel. I should have expected his state to be somewhat enfeebled.'

'That would be the nourishment, Squire. Your condemned party is on hospital rations, unlike the forger or burglar.'

As well as certain supplementaries, thinks the correspondent. 'So the crank does him good,' notes the turnkey approvingly. 'There be no benefit in hanging a man what is already half-dead.'

Whitty observes the regular grind of the crank and the patch of sweat on the man's shirt, indicating genuine effort.

'On what basis does our man claim innocence, Mr Owler?'

'Mulishness, Mr Whitty,' snaps the patterer. 'And a surfeit of cheek.'

Upon hearing the word *innocence*, our man ceases to turn the crank, pauses to work a cramp from one heavily muscled shoulder, then straightens to his full height: clearly a performance for our benefit, thinks Whitty.

The turnkey addresses the condemned man: 'Mr Ryan, you have permission to take a rest, on condition that you give these gentlemen your full co-operation. Satisfy them and you will have a tot of rum for your next meal. Less than full co-operation, and the count you achieve will be halved. Is that clear?'

'Lucid as always, Mr Hook.' The calm, amused voice of the convict indicates a remarkable degree of self-control – perhaps the assumption of an ability to control others as well.

The turnkey turns to the visitors. 'Gentlemen, feel free.'

As Whitty approaches the machine, its operator turns dramatically into the chequered light, providing the correspondent with a first glimpse of his Fiend in Human Form: tall and lean, with a straight nose and intelligent forehead, distinctly unfiendish in aspect (hence, the gift of flowers from appreciative ladies). Whitty notes an overhang to Ryan's brow near the locality of Eventuality – a feature indicating, to the skilled eye of a phrenologist, a trove of hidden animal appetites awaiting satisfaction. As well, he recognizes from experience the habitually composed expression common to men who are prone to watchfulness, for whom potential danger is a given.

'Mr Ryan, may I presume?'

'Presume away, Sir. For that is the name by which I prefer to be called.'

In contrast to his show of good breeding, Whitty adjudges his complexion to be that of a man with hot blood in his veins – a passionate, unbridled, un-British character. Drawing closer, he notes the mane of dark hair as well as the man's level of physical fitness – especially of the upper body. No doubt about it, the party has taken to the crank with relish. What could be his purpose in such a regimen? What does he hope to achieve?

'Please forgive the shortage of seating arrangements in my modest establishment. Feel free to make use of the bed as though it were a couch.' So saying, Mr Ryan seats himself on a stool beside the eating table, takes a long inhalation of the flowers and smiles wryly. 'There is nothing more stimulating to a Christian woman than a condemned murderer.'

'I have heard that you claim innocence, Mr Ryan.'

Ryan returns the correspondent's stare, evenly. 'That is because I am innocent. At the same time, one hates to disappoint a lady.'

Again, the prison bell sounds the quarter-hour. Three-quarters of an hour left, thinks Owler to himself; may God grant him a loose tongue.

'Allow me to introduce myself, Sir. Edmund Whitty, correspondent with *The Falcon*, at your service.'

'I've read your work. If I remember correctly, you're the correspondent who first brought forth the name "Chokee Bill". My congratulations to you.'

'Thank you, Sir.' Like any writer, Whitty is childishly pleased by the prospect of being read by a stranger. 'May I hope that you find your situation reasonable?'

'You flatter me with your concern, Sir. I presume that you, like Mr Owler, have come in search of the elusive Last Confession from the man you journalists are pleased to flatter as the Fiend in Human Form. I'm sorry to disappoint you, but the truth is, I am not your man.'

'So I'm given to understand. However, neither judge nor jury agreed with you.'

'The proof of my innocence will become evident soon enough, though I fear that I shall not be present to witness it. Chokee Bill will strike again, of that I am absolutely certain – if he has not done so already. Until then I can only reiterate my story, not because it will profit me, but because it is the simple truth.'

In Whitty's experience, it is unwise to believe any man who uses the word *truth* more than once in a single conversation.

Owler gloomily relights his pipe.

*

The turnkey having left the cell to attend to other business, correspondent, patterer and convict pass through the door to the condemned
man's private exercise yard, if only to escape the oppressive emission of
Owler's pipe.

Owler produces a small, tattered notebook and a grimy stub of a
pencil: 'Mr Ryan, let us set aside for the moment the question of guilt
or otherwise, since you deem me unworthy of that confidence. So as to
provide me with some reason to continue our association, might there
be any feelings of general regret or remorse to be shared with the
reading public, by way of a caution like?'

Reasoning that if a loosened tongue is required then a little
something will do no harm, the correspondent produces a flask of
brandy. 'Some refreshment, Mr Ryan?'

'Your generosity is appreciated, Sir.'

'Would you care for a cigaret?'

'Thank you, yes. Though I regret that I cannot return the hospitality.'

Whitty chooses one of his special cigarets, prepared by his chemist.
Ryan accepts a light from the proffered lucifer, drawing the delicious
smoke deep into his lungs, nodding with appreciation (the nod of a
connoisseur) and smiling to himself in a secret way, as if thinking, *I
know exactly what you are up to, my friend.*

A shrewd customer, thinks the correspondent. An egoist, who cannot
resist the urge to display his superior traits.

'We was speaking of regrets,' prompts the patterer.

'Indeed, Mr Owler, one need not be a murderer to house a generous
supply of regret. Let me count the ways: I regret my wasted life – which,
while stopping well short of murder, did overstep any number of God's
commandments. I regret a certain meanness and ruthlessness in my
approach to life, in which I take no satisfaction, though it were born of
desperate circumstances. I regret my past inability to see beyond the
immediate satisfaction of material desires, having felt the bite of
poverty. I regret my first crime, born of a free-and-easy nature which
would not settle to any youthful business other than the filching of
handkerchiefs. I regret my first success, in which I stole a silk handkerchief from a gentleman's pocket near St Paul's . . .'

Impressive, thinks Whitty, and yet rehearsed, with a symmetry
lacking in real life.

'I regret my first conviction for theft, that I failed to take instruction
from it – that, following my release from the Old Horse, I practised new
criminal trades acquired in prison. I regret the passing of forged Bank

of England notes – that the gallows held so little terror for me, even after Cashman was topped for passing finnies on Snow Hill. I regret every man I propped upon a highway, crimes for which I might have been hanged twenty times.'

Ryan pauses – for effect, observes the correspondent.

'Yet most of all I regret my conviction and sentencing for the one crime I did not commit. Not because my hanging will be any great loss to England, nor because I do not deserve it on other accounts, but because it provides time for another to continue his terrible work. Chokee Bill is still in London, Gentlemen. I know this for a certainty. Put a Bible on the grave of my mother and I shall swear to it . . .'

Thinks Whitty: Men who swear on the graves of their mothers are mostly liars. Yet just because a man is a liar it does not follow that he is not, upon occasion, telling the truth.

Throughout the above declamation, Ryan has been pacing the enclosure in an erratic, angular pattern – no doubt the stimulative effects of Whitty's medicinal cigaret. However, this energy soon dissipates, and now he leans against a corner of the wall, appearing to study its surface, running his fingers tentatively up and down the rough stone as though by habit. Above his head is a cistern, situated on top of the wall, with the *chevaux-de-frise* bolted to either side.

'Well, Mr Owler, have I provided you with enough regrets for the moment?'

'It is adequate,' replies Owler, without enthusiasm.

The bell having sounded once more and the turnkey having returned, the prisoner escorts his guests to the door as though from his Mayfair town-house. 'I regret, Mr Owler, that my statement has not provided the news value of a confession.'

'To be frank, Sir, it's not worth the cost of printing.'

'I find it odd that you have not considered the possibility of my innocence – if only to spread your risk.'

'Give me a reason to think so, Sir.'

'You have but to weigh the evidence fairly. Unlike others.'

The patterer has no reply, having sunk into gloomy thoughts of the workhouse. Whitty, on the other hand, remains alert and curious, having taken a medicinal cigaret himself. (Stimulants by day, depressants at night – rules to live by.)

'Mr Ryan, allow me to ask you the most basic of questions: assuming that you are innocent, why are you here?'

'For the protection of a lady, Sir.'

'And which lady might that be?'

'I am not at liberty to say.'

'Indeed, Mr Ryan, you are not at liberty at all.'

Now ensues a pause in which they test each other's ability to endure silence, like opponents prior to a game of chess.

'I shall be pleased to enlighten you at some later date. However, I must now entertain a person from the Women's Temperance Union who has every hope of a pledge.'

'If I may pose one last question, Sir: If you did not kill those five women, then who did?'

'I shall tell you that when I can hope to be believed.'

14

The Haymarket

And the hoofed heel of a satyr crushes
The chestnut-husk at the chestnut-root.

The tall young woman with long chestnut hair concealed beneath her bonnet and a deep *décolletage* beneath her cloak, and a complexion unmarked by disease or poverty, strolls the walkway around the perimeter of Leicester Square, stopping at each shop whose darkened window contains a display of bonnets. She likes to buy a new bonnet once a week. The bonnet she is wearing this week is black – the same black as her silk cloak. Removing her bonnet will display her chestnut hair, which is her best asset; removal of her cloak will expose her white skin, which they like to stroke. Her cloak has never been pawned, nor has she had to sell her hair for wigs. Nor is she in debt, and therefore a prisoner of the keeper of her lodging on Romilly Street. She can leave London whenever it pleases her. She is an independent operative, which is more than she can say for such as her friend Etta, a slop-worker who must stoop occasionally in order to meet the monthly shortfall.

Someday Etta will learn, as Flo has, that to become a slop-worker is an uglier and less hopeful fate than this one.

Today she awakened at four p.m. in her room, dressed in a leisurely fashion, then made her way to a supper club, where she danced a little and waited for someone to approach. However, none of the gentlemen at the Holborn liked her enough on this particular evening, so she drank a little in order to dull the feeling that wells up in her when she is ignored. She did not drink overmuch, however, as that makes her sad.

Next she proceeded to the Haymarket, where she wandered from one café to the other, from Sally's to the Carleton, to Barns's, on to the Turkish divans and then back again . . .

Hallo. By the feeling at the nape of her neck, she has attracted the attentions of a gentleman. Yes, there he is – at the window two doors down to her right.

When he turns in her direction, she knows him at once and is about to move on quickly – yet he does not seem to place her in return – all to the good. She reminds herself that, in such situations, it is best to affect an aspect of artless innocence.

'I beg your pardon, Miss, but might I ask you for directions to the Haymarket?'

'Why certainly, Sir. It isn't far, and in the direction you're now facing.'

As he draws closer, his face betrays no sign of recognition. Perhaps he never really looked at her face in the first place, for that is often the case.

'This is good luck, for I find myself rather at loose ends. Might I be so bold as to ask if you will accompany me?'

'Since you are a gentleman, Sir, I trust you to behave as such.'

'You may rest assured on that score, Miss. Indeed, am I to understand that you find yourself alone in the city as well?'

'Aye, Sir.'

'From the country, perhaps?'

'A disgraced millinery girl. Anything you wish.'

'I count myself a lucky gentleman to find myself in such attractive and flexible company.'

'You're generous, Sir, but it is a dark night and perhaps that has deceived you.'

'It is not quite so dark as that. Indeed, you are easily the prettiest girl I have seen this evening. I confess to having followed you while I summoned the courage to tell you so.'

'You flatter me overmuch with these attentions. I am quite overwhelmed.'

'No more than you deserve. Indeed, if we were able to share a few moments in seclusion, I should like to favour you with a small present. As a token of my esteem.'

'How thoughtful. And if I might ask, what might be the value of such a token, Sir?'

'That would of course depend on you, Miss. Might I persuade you to step into this doorway so that I might show you my little present? Which, I am certain, an independent assessment would value at no less than a sovereign.'

Eager to earn such a reward, yet unwilling to risk accompanying him to a room, she takes his hand in hers and draws him into the doorway, placing her other hand beneath his coat, near the bottom button of his waistcoat.

'Actually, it is a scarf,' he whispers, removing his white silk gentleman's scarf from inside his coat and wrapping it around her neck.

'A white scarf. So very pretty. Is it a bit too tight, do you say? Does it chafe somewhat? I am sorry, you will have to speak a bit more clearly, for I can hardly understand a word you say. What beautiful eyes you have. How wide they are – not a trace of a squint. And how rosy your cheeks are becoming. Do I make you blush? Was it something I said? Have I embarrassed you? By Jove, I see you are positively faint. Perhaps you should rest a moment, for you seem to have lost your breath . . .'

He pushes her against a display window containing ladies' shawls and bonnets, with sufficient force to crack the glass. Lying on her back in the shadow of the arch now, she can no longer make out his face, but she knows who it is, and knows he is smiling . . .

> *A still, small voice spake unto thee,*
> *Thou art so full of misery,*
> *Were it not better not to be?*

Crooning verses, he pulls the scarf more tightly and her tongue begins to swell. He is indeed smiling. His arms and shoulders are surprisingly strong – a rugby player, perhaps. As a demonstration of his power, he executes a sudden sharp twist, causing her to lurch sideways, puppet-like. Her bonnet falls onto the steps. Her long chestnut hair splashes across the slate floor.

'Oh you are an impudent one with your pretty little tongue sticking out! Making fun of me are you? Oh, I say!'

15

Coldbath Fields

A thoughtful correspondent, a dispirited patterer and a well-lubricated turnkey make their way in the gloom of evening past the oakum-picking shed, from which a line of female prisoners files past in the company of a warder, having completed their shift, to judge by their red and bleeding fingers.

'A most instructive outing,' Whitty observes.

'Indeed, Squire, I hope it will lead to a most salutary article on the modern prison.'

'At the very least, Mr Hook. Not to mention an appreciation of its heroic staff, performing correctional miracles under trying circumstances – with of course a generous reference to the theories of your enlightened Governor Cornwallis.'

'Oh, that is a stunner, Squire. Such a mention would do me no harm, professionally speaking.'

'Consider it done.'

'Laying it down a bit thick, aren't you?' observes Owler under his breath.

'Only as required,' whispers the correspondent, while the turnkey struggles with the rusted metal door.

'What is your judgement of the situation?'

'Our man Ryan spins a clever tale,' observes Whitty. 'Note his long confession of crimes – falling just short of the crime of which he is convicted.'

The turnkey chuckles. 'They all does that, Squire. Very free they is with their past regrets and their sorry upbringing – it adds to the look of sincerity, don't you see.'

'Very full of secrets they is, too,' observes Owler, who has resumed puffing on his dreadful pipe. 'Always some unsavoury truth, kept secret by Certain Parties, concerning a Prominent Person.'

'Still, Mr Ryan tells his story well.'

'Our man was in the crim-con business, Sir. Such was established in the trial itself.'

'So I understand. In partnership with a woman of ruined character.'

'Name of Sally Hunger,' says Owler. 'A woman not unlike Mr Ryan in character.'

'True for you, Squire. Such women make it their business to appeal to the flaws of a propertied man, for whom a charge of criminal conversation would mean ruin. To effect the dodge they require a male accomplice to play the outraged husband, and to provide protection for the female operative,' replies the turnkey. 'The female party lures the victim into a most depraved situation, then, at the moment of greatest possible mortification . . . you may imagine what follows.'

'Quite,' agrees Whitty. 'Am I to assume that Mr Ryan performed the role of the outraged husband?'

'The same. However, according to Mr Ryan, the gentlemen took exception to the dodge and refused to pay. What is more (and this is where credulity splinters, if my opinion has any credit), our man claims that there is another woman, very near and dear to him, whom the would-be mark will surely murder if Mr Ryan tells all. Of course it is all a cock.'

Cock or no, Whitty's mind has assumed a state of heightened interest, having combined the various impressions of this afternoon with his recollection of Ryan's trial; the result is a plethora of intriguing, plausible narratives, each capable of eliciting keen interest in *The Falcon*.

'Mr Owler, if I recall correctly, did not this selfsame Sally Hunger fall as a victim of the Fiend?'

'Precisely, Sir. Your mind is working at high throttle at last. Sally were found in a lane near the Strand, the fifth victim, choked like the rest and mutilated in Chokee Bill fashion. She were Ryan's undoing, of course. By similar fact, the cloud of suspicion spread to the other murders.'

'It does seem rather a blunder – to kill so close to home.'

'Who knows what rage might move the Fiend? All five was women of low character. All five was choked with a scarf. And there was things done to their faces. The murders was in every aspect identical.'

'But Mr Ryan offers another explanation.'

'Wictimization by the failed object of blackmail, yes.'

'Oh, he has a tale for everything, Squire,' says the turnkey. 'That he will hang rather than see harm come to her.'

'An elegant irony – that the blackmailer should die from extortion.'

'Werily, Sir. Too elegant to be true.'

Comes a contemptuous cackle from the turnkey: 'The protection of a lady? It is not elegant, it is the oldest cock in The Steel!'

'I expect that is true,' agrees the correspondent. 'We all strive to place our ugly little tale in a favourable light.'

'All the same, Squire, one expects better from such a clever man. Sworn to a gentleman's silence? Did you ever hear of anything so fishy in your life?'

Having made their way in silence down Mount Pleasant, our partners in journalism now warm themselves with spiced gin at the Hare and Razor, a small, near-empty pub near Guilford Street, frequented by what look to be Coldbath Fields alumni, to judge by the drawn pallor in the faces and the concentration with which they take their liquor.

About Mr Ryan, Whitty is of two minds. On the one hand, here is a man with as wily and ruthless a nature as one will find on the Ratcliffe Highway, a man spiritually capable of treachery even to the point of killing. Yet there exists a discontinuity between the man and the crime. The correspondent judges Ryan to be, above all, a tactician – a man who does nothing unless it be for money (he was a coiner after all), or some other objective in his own interest. This is hardly the sort of man who kills purely for gratification – as, seemingly, did Chokee Bill. Unless, of course, our man represents a new kind of villain, peculiar to the modern era; something as yet unforeseen.

Whitty signals the barkeeper for another tot, as the nutmeg and lemon are in perfect combination. At the same time he reminds himself to be careful with spiced gin, for experts claim it to be more addictive than opium.

'From what I have heard this afternoon, Mr Owler, I think you can rest more easy on the hanging. That a whole new story is about to erupt around our man.'

Owler stares gloomily into his cup. 'What might produce such an optimistic conclusion, Sir?'

'Our man is an athlete in training – that much is clear. I find it unlikely that he is preparing his body for the grave.'

'True, there is a futility to it.'

'Therefore I have no choice but to conclude that our man is preparing his escape.'

A LOOMING CRISIS IN BRITISH PRISONS

by

Edmund Whitty
Correspondent
The Falcon

Much has been written concerning the failure of the British Prison system, notwithstanding the millions of pounds afforded it, to produce any social benefit other than as a tool for moralists, a playground for thugs and a laboratory for sadistic experimentation. However valid, such objections are soon to be eclipsed by a scandal of sheer incompetence, the which is destined to jolt London to its foundations.

For indeed, despite the righteous huffing and puffing in the Fourth Estate over a 'wave of crime' in the city and the need for sterner measures against evildoers, scant attention has been paid to the incompetent enforcement of those laws which already exist. As a consequence, despite the unprecedented construction of new Houses of Correction and the gaoling of seventeen thousand British men, women and children, no discernible decline in the rate of criminal activity has occurred. More ominously, there is reason to suspect that, in the meanwhile, due to rampant negligence and petty corruption from the highest official to the lowest crusher, the public remains at the mercy of the true fiends who stalk the streets.

Information has reached the ears of your correspondent indicating that the comedy of errors of which we speak is shortly to come to an explosive and sensational climax.

16

The Falcon

Having secured payment of a barely acceptable five crowns for the predicted crisis in British prisons (which may or may not come to pass, Whitty could not care less), and the public uproar to follow (or not, as the case may be) when a certain condemned prisoner makes (or does not make) his escape, Whitty collects Sala's stipend from the ancient cashier in spectacles and eye-shade, and upon exiting the building, negotiates the narrow passage to the rear, where the distinctive pong combines the fragrances of cemetery and inkwell. There he opens a small door and passes down a set of cellar steps, where the dank reek of mildew and wet earth contributes to an already rich bouquet. This is the entrance to the printing-office where *The Falcon* is set in type and brought to press; the firm is under separate ownership from the paper itself, having served a number of organs published in offices currently leased by *The Falcon*; the two companies have thus grown together like two adjacent plants in a crowded garden. The printing-house is by far the senior business, having printed for hire since broadcast began, some of whose workers – including the particular gentleman Whitty has come to see – have been employed here since they were children.

Two floors below, having traversed a short hallway and a set of swing doors, a quite different blend of odours presses onto Whitty's face like the palm of a sweaty hand, an industrial confection of oil, glue, treacle, turpentine, stale breath, fresh paint, sodden paper and leaked gas, steamed together into an indivisible reek not dissimilar to over-cooked cabbage. The noise is enough to rattle your sternum: a hiss on the top of the scale which would puncture your skull, accompanied by the low rumble of wheels on the bottom, with the intermittent rattle of straps and metal bands in between, the totality of which induces a peculiar vibration to the entire building from which nobody within may escape, from the Editor-in-Chief down to the lowest messenger, a vibration so constant that after a few months an employee would swear the building to be as still and as silent as a library.

Bent beneath the oppressive din, Whitty climbs a steep iron staircase in order to proceed along a walkway of the same material, set against a brick wall made shiny with the stains of a thousand inky, oily hands.

Intermittently he turns sideways in order to allow copy boys to pass – dirty-faced and hard-eyed, in paper caps and aprons, their shirt-sleeves rolled high above their elbows to reveal arms like black, stiffened hemp. As he passes an opening in the wall, he momentarily stops to gaze with admiration at the mighty steam engine one floor below, driving the ancient Koening & Baur press, its wheels turning so that flatbeds crash back and forth, causing cylinders and inking rollers to spin – a miracle of furious, untiring co-ordination, a brute symphony of cause and effect, and all so that a sheet of white paper at one end can emerge as a printed broadsheet out the other. The correspondent, who descends from a class well above the printing trades, knows as little as possible about the physical process of putting out a newspaper other than to wonder at man's capacity to manipulate physical laws to advantage – imperfectly in this case, both in the varying quality of the product and in the machine's tendency to break down at regular intervals, bringing the entire organ of public speech to a stuttering, ignominious halt.

'Halloo!' Whitty shouts down to a burly pressman lying on his back, wearing a large black apron over a grease-encrusted suit and cravat, working with an enormous wrench, like a veterinarian tinkering with the kidney of a shuddering beast. 'You, my man! Have you encountered Mr Bigney?'

'Wha?'

'Bigney! Is he here, old chap?'

'Whafa nomen?'

'Bigney!'

'Bigney wibtisset horse!'

'Beg your pardon?'

The man points further down the ramp. 'Tissers!'

'Typesetters? Thank you, Sir!'

Whitty hurries up the ramp extending from the cat walk and turns in the direction of the typesetting room, whose double doors he is just about to swing open when out comes a small party whose skin has been inked as permanently black as an African's. A clay pipe is wedged solidly into the gap provided by a missing tooth.

'How do you do, Mr Bigney. Did you receive the material I sent you?'

'Aye, and yor in luck. Yor on the pig's back for sure.'

Mr Walter Bigney, whose official designation is that of engraver, is a bit over thirty and looks twice that, due to a distinctive quality common to long-standing members of the trade, the result of any number of chemicals handled, inhaled, eaten and otherwise ingested in the course of a working day. However, even had he landed in a different occupation, Mr Bigney would still retain that particular stuntedness of stature common to the low-born, together with a set of black teeth, the result of a lifelong diet of ale, gin, tea, and bread dipped in animal fat.

'Excellent, Mr Bigney. I knew I could rely upon you.' Whitty feigns a heartiness he does not feel, for he does not like Mr Bigney and bridles at being called by such familiar names as 'matey' and 'little prince' by someone so distinctly inferior in rank. One does, after all, retain some semblance of personal pride. Or does one? One might think otherwise, to judge by the company one has been keeping.

Still, the engraver remains essential to Whitty's professional well-being, being possessed of that peculiar faculty more of value in this building than in any other – namely, the ability to locate and combine information, at will. This capacity has, in effect, transformed a mediocre engraver into an invaluable library – or at any rate the nearest thing to such a facility in the building. Having taken to heart the sound business principle that supply and demand determine market value, Mr Bigney is able to command an income far in excess of any engraver in the industry, and a degree of deference far in excess of his station.

Whitty experiences uneasiness whenever he does business with Mr Bigney, a suspicion that the latter views him as but a cog in the larger machinery for social upheaval, all of which has the smell of something French.

Speaking of things Gallic, Whitty first made use of Mr Bigney's service during the Courvoisier case over a decade ago – the bewildering and almost motiveless killing of Lord William Russell by his French valet, which investigation became thoroughly corrupted by the £400 reward offered by the family. Thanks to the engraver's connective facility for incidents of the most miscellaneous nature, Whitty assembled an array of circumstances (the placement of stolen property, the recollection by a servant of a somnolence after consuming beer provided by the suspect, the likelihood that evidence of a break-in was concocted from the inside), which, combined with known and accepted facts about the natural tendencies of foreigners (their childlike avarice in believing that Englishmen carry vast sums of gold; their primitive assumption that by murdering the victim they erase all evidence to convict), created a distinct probability that the valet was guilty.

Hardly had the jury exited the courthouse before the correspondent, then a rank junior in the trade, burst into the sub-editor's office (then a

THE FIEND IN HUMAN

vicious ape by the name of Waites), with a set of articles questioning the advisability of hiring foreigners as servants, which engendered a satisfying panic among the Mayfair set. This triumph secured Whitty the post of correspondent on public hangings over his then rival at the paper, Fraser. The latter subsequently went on to secure a position at *Dodd's*, and has been undertaking a war of attrition ever hence.

'So my little prince would be asking after Mrs Marlowe.' This from Bigney, maddeningly cryptic as always.

'Mrs Marlowe? I don't recall having mentioned anyone by that name.'

'That's why yor'll pay yor friend Bigney his price.' Whereupon the engraver reveals his teeth in what Whitty presumes to be meant as a smile.

'I beg your pardon, Bigney, but I cannot hear above the noise well enough for proper discussion. If I may presume that you have something for me, may we step outside a moment?'

'With pleasure.'

'Your pleasure usually comes at my expense.'

'Get out yor pocketbook, matey, and prepare for an improvement of yor professional prospects.'

In the comparative silence of the outdoors, the correspondent's ears ring like an after-tone of the bell in Coldbath Fields as he follows at a servant's pace behind Mr Bigney on a turn around Ingester Square, in a dismal mist, sheltered by the weary-looking plane tree – which, seemingly afflicted by some wasting disease, reaches for the narrow patch of night overhead like a knotty hand from the grave.

The engraver is a proud man, inappropriately proud, with the false superiority of the accidentally talented – a vague, malevolent smugness.

Whitty reflects upon Mr Darwin and Mr Marx, on animal evolution and the eventual arrival of an Industrial Man – the latter consisting of that which remains of a human being after the removal of faculties incompatible with mechanized production. Before him may walk just such a prototype, Mr Bigney having been whittled down to the minimum necessary for the fulfilment of his purpose. The man cannot hear properly, nor can he appear in society without attracting alarmed stares at the condition of his skin (skin being the currency with which one trades first impressions); and yet, within the confines of this printing establishment, Bigney is perfectly suited to his environment, a bespoke creation of memory, malice and craft.

Whitty considers the faculty known as *hyperamnesia* – Bigney's uncanny ability to locate everything he has seen or read. Such prodigies are by no means uncommon in the hallways of journals and newspapers; every paper in London contains at least one unaccountably vast human storehouse of information – of crimes, scandals, plagues, accidents, together with their leading actors and various connectivities . . .

'Pay attention now, I have not all night to be mooning about with the jabbering class.'

'On the contrary, Bigney, I eagerly await your information.'

'Yor asked to pursue a line of enquiry concerning a certain female admirer what is supplying the Fiend in Human with vittles and suchlike.'

'That is indeed the direction I am taking.'

'It led to a diversity of facts. Collecting the evidence required my attention for most of the day.' Bigney leans against the rusty iron fence surrounding the churchyard and lights his pipe.

'Never mind the cost for now. Who is your Mrs Marlowe?'

'By Mrs Marlowe yor would be meaning Mrs Cox.'

'And who is Mrs Cox? I'd be grateful if you'd come to the point.'

'By Mrs Cox, yor would be meaning Miss Hurtle.'

'Damn me, Bigney, I am beginning to become annoyed.'

Bigney places a black forefinger beside his nose, winking conspiratorially. 'There were a certain connectivity in this Sorrowful Lamentation yor gave me, what struck me as familiar.'

'So it seemed to me, though I couldn't place it.'

'Allow me to refresh yor memory.' Whereupon the engraver recites part of the patterer's Sorrowful Lamentation which the correspondent left with him earlier, pointedly by memory, though having glanced at it but once:

> *O once I knew a love so true,*
> *Our hearts we freely gave;*
> *Though she was of a class above,*
> *My station she forgave;*
> *But family ties will oft belie*
> *The purest of the pure:*
> *I, in her sight, a shining knight,*
> *In father's sight, a boor.*
>
> *Corrupt and mean, a libertine,*
> *Ancient, bald and stout;*
> *A suitor from a class above –*

For him I was cast out;
And in my wrath from the path
I stumbled and I fell,
While in her pride, my would-be bride
Did sell her soul as well.

Here Bigney emits a laugh which is, as always, at Whitty's expense. 'Did yor not make the connection? Ought I to say it in Gaelic?'

'Blast! The business in Scotland. Of course.'

'Further discussion will cost yor a half-crown in advance and a half-crown after.'

'That is a grotesque overpayment for a reference which I could have deduced on my own.'

'Try to sell it to Sala without me news clips. Believe me, my prince, yor onto a stunner. Think I'll hike me advance to two crowns.'

'Outrageous!'

'Ah the fury of the jabbering classes, when the laws of provide and require don't play in yor favour.'

'Bigney, I shall pay you a half-crown in advance and one on approval, but only so that I may be free of your impudence.'

'Done.' The engraver bites the coin with his black teeth to test its genuineness, then leans forward and holds Whitty's eye in his. 'Yor recall the Inquiry on the State of Girls' Fashionable Schools?'

'Indeed, I received a small advance on it this week.'

'Well, consider yorself a lucky man, because now yor got two birds to kill with the one stone.'

'In what way?'

'No recollection at all? Yor wrote it yorself at the time.'

'Surely, you don't mean Mrs Gorton's Academy for Young Women.'

'The very one.'

'A cabal of young ladies blackmailed the servants in order to carry on in a most disgraceful manner, and with the most inappropriate customers. A thoroughly indecent business and a national disgrace. The report never appeared in print, of course. The interesting facts would never pass.'

'Who do yor think was a graduate of that very institution?'

'Not this Mrs Cox you mentioned, surely.'

'Not by that name, matey. Yet she's the one, or I'm not a Christian man. Not only is she one and the same, but she were a large part of the interesting yet unprintable bits yor mention.'

'The young lady who had it off with a young rounder – hired on to do repairs and the like, who made a sideline smuggling opium and romances to the girls.'

'So yor got a memory after all.'

'That man was William Ryan, you say?'

'I'll take that remaining crown before I continue if you don't mind, Guv.'

Cursing his failure to summon the details of such a notorious case, Whitty reluctantly parts with a heartbreaking portion of his cash, bitterly aware that it is worth every penny.

'This will require full documentation.'

'Publication or money refunded, as usual. But there will be no call for a refund. Hark to this: upon her graduation, our young lady returns home just like the entire affair never occurred, or so it would seem to those what knew her, and in less than a year our Miss Hurtle is Mrs Cox – wedded to an auld Scot with a fortune, a laird of the manor that one. Excepting, within a month of the wedding, our Mr Cox is dead.'

'I remember it well. The jury simply couldn't believe that a well brought-up young woman would do such a thing. Found her Not Guilty.'

'In actual fact the verdict was Not Proven – the Scottish way of saying we have not a clue. Created a delicious scandal, of course. One poem deserves another – listen to this:

> *'When lovely lady stoops to folly,*
> *And ancient husband in the way;*
> *What charm will soothe her melancholy,*
> *What gentle art will save the day;*
> *What artful means her sin to cover,*
> *And rescue her from prison locks –*
> *To repossess her handsome lover?*
> *Arsenic for Mrs Cox!'*

Whitty thinks back to Ryan's cell – the improved living conditions which could, by the turnkey's admission, only have been purchased from outside the walls of Coldbath Fields. By an unknown purchaser. For the benefit of a man with a way with women. A man who has formed a bond with a woman sufficiently strong that the condemned man will not reveal her name, even to save himself.

Arsenic for Mrs Cox.

'Pay attention, matey, yor drifting off on me again. You people have no urgency, life's all a dream for you, ain't it?'

'I'm not drifting off, Mr Bigney, I am thinking. Please continue.'

'The rest yor can examine for yorself, assuming yor can still read. It will cost two crowns for the whole packet payable on publication. I'll be pleased to know now if yor have the wherewithal to buy, otherwise Mr Fraser of *Dodd's* has expressed enthusiastic interest.'

Fraser – that predatory warthog crouched by the wayside, waiting to cut him off at the knees.

A dose of restorative snuff to buff up the spirit, then: 'Agreed, Mr Bigney. You shall have it.' The two men shake hands – one black hand, one white (the correspondent will later clean his palm with his handkerchief), after which the engraver reaches beneath his apron and produces a greasy envelope.

The transaction done, Whitty takes his leave with all possible dispatch from this unpleasant, hostile, necessary man. A deep fatigue has come over him, calling for rest and renewal, followed by a period of concentrated, uninterrupted thought.

Standing atop the church steps and in the shadow of the arch, two patient men in cloth caps watch and wait. One party has a barrel chest, a broken nose, arms like legs and hands like clubs. The smaller man is missing a left hand.

'When shall I do 'im then, Norman?'

'He'll pass by at any moment. This here square's a cul de sac, Will, meaning that he cannot be leaving other than the one way. We'll wait for the other gentleman to enter the building. There is no need for a witness to our appointed task.'

So mentally preoccupied has Whitty become, so entangled in Mr Bigney's diverse, almost random information, by the time he notices the two men on either side it is too late; neither fight nor flight are open to him, especially since his feet are no longer touching the ground – rather, he is being lifted by both elbows and propelled into the middle of the square to come to a bone-smashing halt against the lone plane tree.

'Have a quiet word, Jimmy?' A rhetorical question, for the correspondent's neck is about to snap.

'Certainly, Gentlemen, and how may I be of service?' the correspondent pleads through one side of his mouth.

'It is about a spot of money what is owed, Jimmy.'

'Whatever money can you mean, Sir?'

The neck hold becomes firmer, the grip on the arm is tightened, joints are in jeopardy.

'The interest on a certain debt of honour.'

'Best not toy with us, Jimmy. Our mutual friend is fussy about regular payments.'

Of course, thinks Whitty, sick at heart. The ratters.

'I take it that my friend the Captain sends his greetings.'

'Greetings yes, and a small caution,' returns the smaller man. 'A reminder that the Captain emphasizes honesty and thrift as core values in his good work.'

'Quite. Please convey my best wishes, together with my assurance . . .'

Whitty is at this moment unable to continue, for he is slowly sinking to his knees, the breath having been knocked clear out of him thanks to a sharp blow to the left kidney.

'Hit him again, Will. Just so the particular is clear.'

To which Will is only too happy to obey with a fist to the solar plexus.

On his hands and knees, vomiting his luncheon on the trunk of this spare, unwholesome tree, Whitty contemplates his options. Brassing it out seems the only alternative.

'Be careful with me, Gentlemen. I have not been well of late, and a dead client is a dead loss.'

'Ease back, Will. Apparently our Jimmy has not been well.'

Will, who stands ready to break the correspondent's left arm using the trunk of the tree as a lever, interrupts his labour with an impatient exhalation of breath: 'Could I break a couple of his fingers then, Norman?'

'Gentlemen, Gentlemen,' rasps the correspondent, through swollen, fluttery lips. 'None of this is the least bit necessary, for I am assured of a handsome advance within the week. Of this I swear you may give the Captain my unequivocal guarantee as a gentleman.'

'Your unequivocal guarantee as a gentleman? Within the week?' The smaller man smoothes a whisker with the stump of his right forearm.

'We can count on that, Jimmy?'

'Will is trying to convey to you that, in the case of default, the Captain's response will be interesting.'

Will smiles. 'Especially interesting for Rodney.'

'Rodney? I regret that I have not had the pleasure of meeting Rodney.' Massaging the numbness from his left arm, Whitty glances from one face to the next: the larger man appears hairless underneath his top hat, the face seemingly composed of scar tissue.

The smaller party smiles more broadly. 'How neglectful of us, Will. Let us introduce Rodney. Mr Whitty really must meet Rodney.'

'And who might be——'

Even as these words issue from his mouth, the correspondent regrets their utterance, for the larger man has forcefully pulled open Whitty's tweed trousers; the smaller man reaches carefully into his jacket pocket with his one hand, extracts something soft and drops it inside the opening provided by Will – something warm, moving, something the size and shape of . . .

'Now you're dancing, Jimmy!' exclaims the smaller man, stroking his whisker with the bad hand. 'We were hoping we'd see you dance – am I not right, Will?'

'True for you, Norman. Nothing better than a good dance.'

'Though not too energetic. Rodney bites harder when he is shaken about.'

Whitty is dancing in the square, dancing with great leaps and twitches, trying to work the dreadful thing down his trouser leg and away from his person. He hears someone screaming.

'Look at him go, Will! There is nothing like a rat in the trousers to move a party to dance. Do you see? What he is doing is very like a jig.'

'True for you, Norman. And he be singing as well. Would you listen to him sing!'

17

Coldbath Fields

Most men desire fame, to have themselves known to strangers and recognized in public; yet in practice it is the unknown about a man which is of more value to himself than that which is known – especially a man who, for one reason or another, finds himself a member of the criminal class. For one thing, the unknown has more than one side to it. One never knows when a piece of the unknown will emerge to one's advantage or disadvantage. For this reason, William Ryan has always had a great respect for the unknown – specifically, the need to lessen it in others but not in himself.

An unknown such as the fact that, while a ward of the parish, William Ryan occupied the position of climbing-boy or chimney-sweep – which occupation he chose over farm labourer, sewer-hunter or dredgerman, on the theory that the ability to gain access to a house through a small opening might come as an advantage later in life, with the potential to produce a profit; more so than the ability to feed animals.

His career as a legitimate chimney-sweep came to an end by the age of ten, before he could be deformed, or killed by fire, or smothered. Ill-used by his master-sweeper, one day young Ryan found it expedient to hit him over the head with a brick when his back was turned, necessitating a change of employment, for his employer could no longer talk properly, nor could he manage the accounts.

Such it is with a general education in the school of life that one can never know what knowledge will prove useful in future. Now, twenty years later, in his prison yard, left alone after twilight by his over-confident turnkey (counting the day's bribery receipts), and having over past weeks strengthened his upper torso by means of assiduous work on the crank, Mr Ryan is about to make surprising use of his childhood vocation.

Crouched in the corner of the wall beneath the cistern, having previously noted every irregularity in the stonework and memorized the pattern, Ryan pushes his back hard against one wall, braces his feet hard against the other, and secures his fingers in a pair of small indentations established earlier for that purpose. Thus poised, he begins to levitate, inch by inch, working his way slowly up the rough stone, using the angle of the wall to brace himself in the way that a climbing-boy uses the turn of the chimney to gain a purchase. At length he reaches the cistern and is able to clamber onto it. Crouching atop the cistern, without hesitation (he has mentally rehearsed the action countless times), he lunges for the bar which holds the *chevaux-de-frise*, thus gaining a purchase for both hands between the sets of spikes. Hanging from the instrument, his feet against the stones, he now makes his way painfully along the wall, crab-wise, hand by hand, three-quarters around the yard. An arduous business: unable to avoid the intermittent revolving blades, by the time he reaches the wall abutting the press yard building, Ryan is deeply lacerated about the chest and arms and bleeding copiously therefrom; he sustains further injury in pulling himself onto the bar over the top of the spikes. Many men would grow weak from loss of blood, yet after weeks in a cell he feels his strength return, together with the rage for survival and the animal smell of freedom.

From the wall (stone embedded with shards of glass) he leaps some eight feet to the roof opposite, scrambling over the lead tiles and the gutters of the prison and adjacent buildings until he finds himself above a nearby street. Seeing a woman hanging her washing on an adjacent roof, he hides by a chimney stack until she completes her task, then follows her down into the house and into the kitchen, by whose stove an older man and a young boy are sitting down to a meal of boiled mutton. The woman, the man and the boy are sufficiently alarmed by Ryan's wild and bloody appearance that they remain silent; indeed, the boy obligingly shows him to the door.

Ryan winds his way down Mount Pleasant, possibly the most sarcastically named piece of geography in the British Empire; nothing can compare with it for meanness, melancholy and inexplicable dread, with its peculiar smell of past ages, a murky closeness that arises from deep decay. He keeps to the alleyways wherever possible to Guilford Street, where a convenient trough affords him the means of removing the most conspicuous evidence of blood from his clothes.

In the street nearby, the prisoners' van known as Long Tom's Fraser passes by, a gleaming black omnibus manned by two crushers; a moving pest carrier whose halfway house is the gaol and whose bourne is the gallows.

Sing ventilator, separate cell
It is long and dark and hot as well
Sing locked-up doors – get out if you can
There's a crusher outside the prisoner's van . . .

Still a weary distance from Russell Square, he enters the Grave Maurice, an ancient gin palace covered with advertisements for 'The Out-and-Out', 'The Makeshift' and 'Medicated Gin – Strongly Recommended by the Faculty!'

He passes through a heavy door held part-way open by a leather strap and pauses in its shadow to survey the room inside – the long zinc-topped counter backed by piled casks painted green and gold, at which sits a line of customers, bent over as though to say grace and drinking in this fashion, being too drunk to raise the cup to their lips. Along a narrow, dirty area beside the bar and out of the publican's sight (a florid man with a bottle-nose from sampling the product), customers recline on old barrels, having received full value for money. It is here he directs his attention to a lone, sleeping gentleman in shirt-sleeves and waistcoat; his heavy coat, which appears to have been a naval officer's, has been tossed carelessly across the table in front of him . . .

Concealed within his new coat, William Ryan can afford to take the main thoroughfares as far as the Holy Land, where the sight of a man bleeding from wounds inflicted by a sharp instrument is nothing uncommon in any case. Though weakening from his wounds, he none the less moves at a brisk walking pace through the familiar neighbourhood, the better not to attract interest on the part of the spectral, feral young men who lurk everywhere in the dark, standing in doorways and seated on rotted steps, waiting for the source of their next drink. Upon emerging onto Regent Street he turns north, adjusting his pace to that of a man with an appointment or other specific business. Down Regent Street it is but a short way to Portland Place and the woman who has occupied his thoughts, in one way or another, for fifteen years.

Finding the strength that often accompanies an improvement in prospects, William Ryan breaks into a run.

18

Camden Town

Whitty has often asked himself how he become an opium-eater. Was it attraction, defiance, ignorance, misery, fraud?

In actuality, all of the above – combined with, of course, availability. In these fast-paced modern times, there is hardly an anodyne in the chemist's shop which does not contain a generous quantity of that useful substance; and as a man who is never more than a week away from utter ruin, who lives by his ability to generate new and interesting material upon demand, Whitty deeply values the drug's efficacy in silencing, temporarily at least, that black cormorant of despair which will, when least welcome, perch itself upon a writer's shoulder and cackle into his ear: *Naw! Naw! . . .*

As with other pleasures, the drawbacks of opium are discovered well after its advantages, not the least of these being the growth in required dosage for desired effect. For his part, Whitty manages on a relatively modest level of three hundred drops of laudanum per dose (an alternative to the raw drug, which would constitute a form of euthanasia); this represents his chief disciplinary accomplishment since he was sent down.

Another detriment to the taking of opium is the dreaming: hours spent in a damp bed with lunatics and vermin, or revisiting, in the most excruciating detail, events one should never have lived in the first place. Such memories occur as moving pictures, whose horror is not mitigated by the awareness that it is all but a dream.

So vivid have these nocturnal horrors become that Whitty has seen fit to consult a medium over the possibility of possession, a hirsute Romani who counselled a programme of 'luminary adjustment'. This he underwent for a fee, but to no avail.

EVERY MAN HAS HIS FANCY
RATTING SPORTS IN REALITY

In front of his face is a placard containing a programme of the evening's events. The sign, with which he is all too familiar, hangs above a bar made of mahogany. He turns to gaze upon the pit, a small horseshoe-shaped circus some six feet across, fitted with a high wooden rim to the height of a man's elbow. This too he knows well. A series of gas lamps overhead render the white-painted arena stark and shadowless, the better to discern movements almost too quick for the human eye.

The ratting parlour again. How he wishes he had never seen the place. He has sworn off ratting since – why then must he re-enact the whole catastrophe again and again? What has he failed to learn from the experience?

Around the rim of the pit he discerns the heads and shoulders of several gentlemen – one in costermonger's corduroy, one in a soldier's uniform carelessly unbuttoned, another in coachman's livery – each holding in the crook of his right arm a small terrier, squalling and barking and struggling to gain access to the lighted playing-area, while a rusty cage full of live rats is brought to the arena. The cage is opened and the rats are pulled out one at a time by their tails. This is done by the Captain, the owner of the establishment, who presides over the proceedings like a cleric.

'Careful, Captain,' sounds a voice above the din. 'These ones are none the cleanest.' By this it is meant that the creatures are not the favoured country rats, but city wharf rats of the kind that outnumber the population of London, swarming through the drains, tunnels and sewers beneath the city.

'Sewer rats is notorious for giving dogs the canker,' cautions the Captain to Whitty in a confidential voice. 'Do you still wish to participate, Sir?'

Why did you not heed the Captain's warning? Why did you risk your animal and make such a wager into the bargain? Fool! You fool!

While the rats are being counted out, those rodents which have already emerged from the cage frantically circumnavigate the arena, trying to hide in the gaps of the boards surrounding the pit, and scrambling up the sleeves of the Captain's coat. 'Get out, ye varmint,' the Captain cries out, shaking them off.

'Chuck him in, then.'

Over goes Tiny – a terrier of mixed parentage, five pounds and a half in weight, whip-like in structure, scarred from head to toe, and in a perfect fit of excitement. Whitty's prize, his fortune in the making, the dog upon whom he had invested far more than he owned – indeed, were this a legally sanctioned speculation, the wager alone would be more than enough to assure him a sojourn in debtors' prison.

Loose in the pit, Tiny becomes quiet and goes about his task in a businesslike manner, first rushing at the rats, then burying his nose in the mound of those who have fled until he brings one out in his mouth.

Twenty rats with wetted necks lie bleeding on the floor and the white paint of the pit has become stained with blood. However, Tiny has a rat hanging from his nose, which, despite his tossing, still holds on with its teeth and claws. *Let it be, Tiny, let it be!* Enraged, Tiny dashes his tormentor up against the sides until finally he has shaken the rat loose. There is a patch of blood like a strawberry upon Tiny's nose . . .

Whitty awakens with a spasm of self-hatred, and it comes to his attention that he has been miserably bruised, cut and scratched – not in the nose, but in a more intimate region of the body.

Is he about to follow Tiny, the victim of an infected nibble?

What fiend within induced him to gamble so ruinously? Did he hope to remake himself? Was that it? To acquire a sudden fortune, redeem the family estate, extinguish the memory of his own disgrace and be welcomed back into the family bosom, to his father's open arms, the Prodigal Son returned? *Fool!*

Whitty curls into the foetal position and awaits the rebirth of hope, only to have his mind return to that dreadful scene . . .

'Time!' shouts the Captain. Tiny is snatched up, panting, neck stretched like a serpent, the remaining rats crawling about while the Captain endeavours to rinse the terrier's mouth and nose with peppermint water, then catches Whitty with a baleful look: *Abandon all hope, ye who enter here . . .*

The peppermint water did no good. Tiny came down with a fever which sent the most promising ratter in London to join the choir invisible and, along with it, Whitty's foolish hopes.

He reawakens with that bone-deep shudder which accompanies the passage to dreaming and back, like the skeleton attempting to shake free of the flesh and hop about the room.

Again the pain in his groin. Dancing, they called it – a terrified man with a rat in the trousers, dancing in Ingester Square. He gingerly touches the lacerations, which burn beneath the covers. He can only pray that they heal, that Rodney was not of the sewer variety that did for Tiny . . .

The ratters threatened much worse. The Captain's claim, with accrued interest, has expanded to £400 – a staggering debt whose mounting increments place him in the position of a man trying to outrun a speeding train.

The ratters once forced a defaulter's hand into a cage of starved rats and held it there for half an hour.

Whitty slides off the bed, shuffles to the wash-table and examines the face in the glass – stricken, not by alcohol and medicine, but by fear. He probes his skull with his fingers, noting a marked diminishment in the region of Hope.

He pours cold water into the washbowl, splashes it upon his face, then uses the pitcher to prepare himself a morning healer of gin and water. As a further precaution he takes a measure of Acker's Chlorodine.

He returns to his bed and sits upon the edge, warming his feet upon the rug, awaiting relief. Glancing absently about the room, his eyes rest upon his coat, draped over the chair in front of the dressing-table with a bulge in the side-pocket. It reminds him of something . . .

Bigney. Mr Bigney gave something to him: papers. In return for an obscene stipend.

Whitty lights a cigar, rises to his feet and retrieves the package of clippings.

Yet another deluded wager? More money down the cess-pit when he might have employed those funds to keep the ratters at bay? What can he have been thinking of?

Calm. Remain calm. He opens the packet and examines its contents. The first clipping is not encouraging, given that its by-line happens to be the contemptible Fraser, whose turbid observations are the last place to which one might turn for illumination on a delicate morning.

THE PUBLIC ORDEAL OF MRS COX

by

Alasdair Fraser
Senior Correspondent
Dodd's

Seldom in memory has your correspondent observed such an orectic conventicle as the mob which slavered outside the High Court of Judiciary this July 30 morning, snarling in vulgar whispers, cackling at anything that might pass for humour, pressing their filthy hands upon the heavy doors, vying for choice positions from which to view the coming spectacle, in which a rare specimen of female licentiousness endures the most solemn ordeal society has to offer since the regrettable abolition of heresy: to be on trial for the murder of her husband.

Naturally, to the rabble (many of whom could do with a spell in the stocks themselves), the issue of justice being done or not done stood a distant second to the prospect of coarse titillation.

At the stroke of eight o'clock precisely, as the oaken doors opened and a dense mass of humanity in its rudest form spilled inward, mutton-faced louts ruthlessly elbowed their way to the few available seats, with no quarter given to the niceties of age, gender or physical limitation.

With another two hours to wait, spectators availed themselves of breakfast – cheese, bread and meat pies consumed on soiled handkerchiefs as though at a picnic, while watching a parade of their betters enter the well of the court.

Below, high Scottish clergymen took their places as well as the country's finest journalists and illustrators, preparing their sketchbooks to render their now-famous profiles of the legal duellists on the case, as well as the fascinating form of Mrs Cox herself.

Finally at ten-twenty, the packed courtroom turned to sudden silence and rose to their feet upon the order of the clerk of the court – 'Court!' – followed by the stately, bewigged procession of the Right Honourable John Lord Hope, the Lord Justice-Clerk, together with his two fellow judges, Lords Handyside and Ivory. However, to the public gallery neither ancient ritual nor judicial eminence could distract spectation from the small, square patch of flooring directly in front of the prisoner's dock.

Slowly, like an eyelid opening after sleep, the patch of floor began to rise, revealing itself to be a trap-door, below which one could discern a flight of steps leading to the cells, located in the dank depths of the building. From this dismal interior there arose a sombre policeman, his face flushed by the effort as well as by the unaccustomed public attention. Then a few steps behind rose the central protagonist of the drama: Mrs Eliza Cox, the Accused – or, in the peculiar legal terminology of Scotland, 'The Panel'.

As it has been throughout the trial, the sensuous features by which her true character might be read and understood (at whatever cost to public decency) have been, no doubt on the advice of her counsel, concealed by a full widow's veil. One hand, gloved, clasps a lace handkerchief perpetually to her throat – no doubt to divert attention from her famous bosom. Such features, had they been displayed in their full hedonism as living evidence of the obscene passion smouldering behind the dreadful crime of which she stands accused, might have produced a more decisive verdict than that which was about to transpire . . .

Expelling a derisive snort, Whitty sets the piece aside in favour of a second clipping, a standard news item containing a brief explication for the British reader of the 'Not Proven' verdict peculiar to Scottish courts. Trust the Scots, thinks Whitty – savage brutes, yet able to equivocate like the Swiss!

Not Proven: it is clear that, far from exonerating Mrs Cox, the woman stood effectively convicted of a foul, contemptible murder; all that separated her from the gallows was the inability of a male jury to envisage a wife capable of such an outrage – such a possibility had the potential to infect the peace of every home in the realm.

Hence, the third clipping, in the form of a satirical poem such as is commonly written by advocates of one movement or another as a means of gaining promotion for their cause:

Upon the Acquittal of Mrs Cox
Lucy Aikin

Once more England, lift thy drooping eye,
The tilted scales of Justice to descry;
As to the might of feminine deceit,
Twelve good men fall humbled in defeat;
And yet what different verdict might be given
What tissue of deception might be riven,
The reason of a female to address,
The subtle forms of delicate distress;
A calculated tear may bring to grief
The commonplace of masculine belief;
In examining a woman in the dock,
Less credulous the chicken than the cock.

Thus does the woman stand convicted even by those shrill harpies, the feminists – who would have women become club members, smoke cigars, bet on the horses, run for Parliament; for whose satisfaction the House of Lords would become the House of Ladies! So universal is the presumption of her guilt, even the hags of militant feminism find political capital in condemning one of their own sex!

Our Mrs Cox would not inherit, nor could she return to her former life, nor to any life a woman might willingly choose for herself. Under the circumstances, her best option would have been to disappear, to merge with others of her kind, to swim together down the drain of social misery all the way to London.

Hence, the third clipping, an advertisement from a gentlemen's quarterly catering to Oxford men, commonly sold under the counter on Halliwell Street:

THE GROVE OF THE EVANGELIST
Discipline for Wayward Boys
Manners and Horsemanship
Mrs Eliza Marlowe, Governess

Clearly Mr Bigney has assembled a narrative wherein Mrs Cox became Eliza Marlowe. Having experienced utter ruin, our temptress discarded her honour forever – though not with the emphasis with which she discarded Mr Cox:

> *Corrupt and mean, a libertine,*
> *Ancient, bald and stout;*
> *A suitor from a class above -*
> *For him I was cast out;*
> *And in my wrath then from the path*
> *I stumbled and I fell,*
> *While in her pride, my would-be bride*
> *Did sell her soul as well.*

If ever there were good reason for an Inquiry into the State of Girls' Fashionable Schools, here it is – especially when taking into account Sir Henry Stork's admirable concern over the unfulfilled woman's natural and well-documented tendency to duplicity and malice. Notwithstanding the corruption and meanness of the doomed Mr Cox, his widow has sold her soul for certain, and other accoutrements as well.

Thus, Mr Owler's Sorrowful Lamentation, however unwittingly, holds true, assembled as it was from inadvertent scraps and details, and with no context to guide it. Moreover, Mr Ryan, up to this point at least, has not been proved a liar – which of course does not mean that he is telling the truth, any more than it makes him innocent. The most duplicitous of men are forthright in all respects but one.

What may or may not be true, however, occupies at this moment a distant second place to the prospect of having found a story that is worth at least £50 – which would permit him to put the ratting débâcle behind him for a time and to get on with life, such as it is.

Whitty pours another gin and water, relights his cigar, and prepares to reread the material, raising a glass to the appalling, essential Mr Bigney.

19

The Grove of the Evangelist

... to reanimate the torpid circulation of the capillary or cutaneous vessels, to increase muscular energy, and favour the necessary secretions of our nature. Flagellation draws the circulation from the centre of the system to the periphery...

Having given his coat and hat to a footman, the patron, notwithstanding his patrician bearing and leonine head of silver hair, stands meekly in the centre of the reception room, awaiting permission to enter.

As always, the door (insulated with velvet) opens and the maid appears, like a tiny severe gentleman, a parson in widow's dress, with a luminously pale cast to a face which, though by no means young, displays the open indifference of an introverted child. Clearly this is a maid by choice, not necessity. As always he is alarmed by her silence, which is not simply a lack of sound but an aura she carries wherever she goes. As always, he is intrigued by the bright scar on her left cheek – the result of a burn, not an incision, to judge by its colour and thickness, almost like a brand.

'Good evening, Mrs Button. I am pleased to see you again.'

Mrs Button nods briskly and steps aside so that he may enter.

'Good evening, My Lord.'

As the door shuts quietly behind him he stands in the room and waits to be noticed, like an obedient child, which pause affords him ample time to watch her every movement and to remind himself why he is here.

As always he is startled and intimidated by her appearance, which is of a kind seldom seen these days, when any figure may be built of any fashionable dimension, being constructed of horsehair, whalebone and other materials, then crowned with false hair, such architecture of form and line to be accomplished by the milliners and dressmakers and hairdressers of Regent Street and Mayfair.

Not so with Mrs Marlowe, formerly Mrs Cox, née Eliza Hurtle, whose naturally severe beauty transcends all fashion – scorns it as the moon scorns gaslight. Her skin, that which she permits to be seen, appears as white and chilly as marble; as does her bosom, proudly outlined beneath a garment of black silk seemingly thrown on in haste. A cliché of course, the pubescent dream of an adolescent; precisely what the gentleman, standing in the doorway in his shirt-sleeves and awaiting instruction, has purchased in advance.

'Well? Are you coming in or not? I grow tired of these absurd hesitations of yours.'

Tentatively he steps onto the red Turkey carpet. The velvet door swishes shut behind him – Mrs Button has been standing behind him all the while. What was she looking at?

He proceeds just far enough onto the Turkey carpet that he may see her more clearly, seated upright on the divan beneath a lamp, indifferently reading a book covered with black leather.

Abruptly she glances up with those startling green eyes, then arches one dark eyebrow, then returns to her book.

'There are a great many things left to correct in you. I can see that. We may require the nettles, for utrication.'

Delicious. 'Whatever you think best, Madam.'

'I have been thinking about your case and have decided you require special attention. When I am ready. Wait there while I finish my page and we shall begin the lesson. Stand very still or, I warn you, I shall know how to be firm.'

He watches her read, growing warm as though standing next to a fire. She is very lovely, very dark. Her hair, jet black, spread in a thousand curls about her head and neck, seen against the red velvet of the divan. Her cheeks and lips are full, her white neck giving way to the softness below. She can be soft, but she can also be severe. He must stand very still, for that is what she told him to do.

She closes her book, lays it aside and surveys him again from head to toe. 'You are not precisely a treat to the eye. Yet I suppose we shall find some way to make use of you.'

Her bust is full and beautifully shaped, yet she dresses as though oblivious to it, always in black – not a sad widow's garment, but well-fitting and, especially, simple. A majestic woman, a pleasure to serve.

She rises and walks around him, looking him over like a mediocre piece of furniture. 'How dare you look at me like that! How dare you! I can see what you are thinking – Do you know how a well-bred women responds to such looks?'

Suddenly and with impressive strength she slaps his face. He lurches backward and falls onto the carpet as though having received an electric shock.

'Get up on your knees, Sir, your thoughts offend and disgust me. Do not look at me unless I tell you to, or I shall deal with you as you need to be dealt with.'

Kneeling on the Turkey carpet like a Muslim, he stares down at the pattern, or series of patterns, which reminds him of the entrance to an Oriental temple. His cheek burns as though scalded. In the heat of his burning cheek he can breathe the lotion she rubs into her hands to make them smooth.

'I wish to make myself comfortable before we proceed. Come here and take off my shoes. Do it immediately. And remain on your knees, Sir.'

A light, elegant, buttoned shoe with a riding heel appears beneath the folds of her clothing and points in his direction.

Eagerly he approaches the waiting foot as though having not yet learned to walk. Taking his place before her, his hands tremble as he removes the shoe, slips the soft leather away from her shapely, warm foot, then places it before her. Her smooth toes, toenails sharp, move as though to stretch themselves, then disappear beneath the folds of her crinoline. Now her other foot appears and demands its turn. He slips the shoe off the foot – even warmer than the first! – as slowly as he dares, using his left hand, while holding her delicate, naked ankle with the right. The second foot disappears. Now he carefully arranges the shoes – still warm! – side by side in front of the divan. Now he remains still, staring at the carpet, awaiting her pleasure, studying the warm leather shoes before him.

'I shall return directly. If you remain absolutely, completely still, and if you behave as you know you should, then we may not have to administer punishment – indeed, we may be pleased to administer a reward . . .'

She disappears through the door to what he knows to be her dressing-room, for this entire procession of events has occurred previously, many times, in the same sequence and form, with occasional improvements and variations to elicit surprise.

Her shoes. Black leather against the red of the Turkey carpet. He reaches out his hand – he can feel their warmth on his fingers even without touching them. But he must touch them. Now is his chance. He picks up one open shoe, still warm, holds it to his face and smells. Now the other. He lifts the two to his face and breathes their perfume, like water to a man dying of thirst, sounding an audible *ohhh* . . .

'For shame, Sir!'

She stands in the doorway to her dressing-room, framed in mirrored light, seemingly taller than before, clad in a long dressing-cape, deep red with a small hood, its folds unbroken from her shoulders to the floor, her white limbs bare to the shoulder from two openings in the sides.

'What is it you think you are doing with my shoes?' In her right hand she holds a whipping-cane made of the most flexible rattan, steamed and suppled with brine as are whipping-canes in the better public schools, and with the characteristic curve of the handle, but slightly longer to give it more spring.

'This obscene behaviour must be corrected by means of the severest punishment. Take down your trousers, Sir – and do it quickly, do not enrage me further, I warn you! Look down at yourself, at the evidence of your debauchery! Do you think that I mean to indulge your disgusting lack of self-control?

'Now we will begin your correction. Kneel over the divan. I did not know that I should have occasion for the harness quite so soon.'

He obeys without a sound, taking position, bent low over the end of the divan, which, unlike its domestic equivalent, has been bolted to the floor and has been laid with a white towel to receive his spendings.

From behind her back she produces a harness of narrow, strong leather, fitted with brass buckles so that it can be precisely fastened around the neck and across the torso, around the genital apparatus (now in a painfully swollen state), thence to the ankles, there to be affixed not by a buckle but by a cinch. She performs this manoeuvre with swift, expert movements, then, standing behind his back, she pulls the cinch tight until he cries out, in a voice higher than its normal resonance.

> She laid him flat on a gorse down pillow,
> And scourged his arse with twigs of willow,
> His bottom grew white, then pink, then red,
> Then bloody, then raw, and his spirit fled.

'Please, Miss – I cannot bear it!'

Bracing her bare foot against his behind, she pulls the cinch even tighter. 'Oh but you shall, Sir. You shall! How dare you disobey me! How dare you use my shoes for your filthy purpose!' Having completed her task, she stands above and behind him, readying the cane as though about to strike. She pauses, knowing what a pause can do in certain circumstances.

'Do not think for a moment that I enjoy having to do this.'

She strikes. Again – each blow from her strong and cunning wrist bringing him closer to the ultimate humiliation, until at last the Earl of Claremont cries out in agony and rapture with the voice of a small boy . . .

A knock on the window. Voyeurs are a common nuisance at the Grove of the Evangelist, men who like to watch but not to pay for it. It is a disadvantage to working on the ground floor.

'Cease this crying and sobbing, I warn you. I shall give you a moment to consider your misconduct and vow to amend it.'

Slipping on her shoes, she steps briskly across the Turkey carpet to the corner window, heavily draped with red velvet, both as insulation and as an assurance of privacy. She grasps the hem of each drape, throws aside the curtains, steps forward – and faces the gentleman on the other side, whom she has not seen face to face in fifteen years.

Despite the blood on his face and the years and the grime accumulated during his escape through London, the recognition is instant. A sound escapes from her lips, a voice from long ago.

20

Camden Town

Thinking is a chore requiring patience with the limitations of the mind; or to be more precise, patience of the spirit with the limitations of the brain.

The spirit longs to throw off the blinkers of rational discourse, to see fully, to employ the entire mind and not simply that part of the brain which thinks it is thinking. Thus it is fitting that the spirit, upon occasion, deceive or manipulate the brain into surpassing itself. Hence, man has been endowed with alcohol and other 'spirits', with which to reconcile the disparity between the demands of the spirit and its chief instrument – albeit at some cost.

With perseverance, the correspondent has laid before him several lines of enquiry, each with its own singular attraction:

THE FIEND AND THE PAUPER
Chokee Bill's Strange Confessor

by

Edmund Whitty, Correspondent
The Falcon

THE LOWLIFE OF LONDON
Inside Rat's Alley – A Shocking Report

by

Edmund Whitty, Special Correspondent
The Falcon

A WALK THROUGH THE STEEL
Science, Fiendishly Clever
Edmund Whitty Reports from inside Coldbath Fields

RYAN TO WHITTY: 'I TOO AM A VICTIM.'
Cruel Upbringing Nurtures a Convicted Murderer

WHITTY'S ASTOUNDING ASSOCIATION
A Fallen Woman in the Shadow of the Fiend

THE FIEND STATES HIS CASE
Would Implicate Prominent Person

RYAN CLAIMS INNOCENCE

Never mind that last, thinks Whitty, it is too implausible. On the other hand, one does well to test the range of public credulity, to give the imagination a stretch.

Notwithstanding, there lie buried in these obvious lines of enquiry more nuggets of productive employment than the correspondent has encountered in months. Whitty has not the faintest idea where any of it will lead, for he is not a clairvoyant; on the contrary, he is a man whose lot it is to stagger from one question to the next, from one fact to the next, sniffing for crisp copy, barely able to see his own feet.

Tell that to the Editor. Tell it to the Captain. Tell it to the Master at Christ Church, Oxford.

Whitty takes a sip of gin. For the greater good.

The Fiend, the patterer, the rookery, The Steel, the madam, the murderess – not to mention a shocking girls' school dalliance: such an embarrassment of riches . . .

Someone is knocking. Someone is at the door. Four knocks, evenly spaced.

Blast. That is Mrs Quigley's knock. He recognizes her spongy knuckles, not to mention the implied rebuke in the rhythm, the calculated urgency of attack. And of course it would require the insensibility of a walking-stick not to recognize the nasal whine now invading the premises, which music has caused Whitty such joy throughout his sojourn at Buckingham Gardens. Call it 'The Song of the Suburban Twit', if you like, or perhaps 'The I of the Wheedle', lending superb expression to the suburban attitude of flatulent self-congratulation . . .

Where am I? What was I thinking?

'Mr Whitty! I can hear you talking to yourself, therefore you are within! Your attention if you please! There is a gentleman to see you, *sniff*, if I may deem the term to be appropriate in this case . . .'

The wooden teeth of the proprietress go against the grain. Whitty hears himself emit an involuntary oath, which elicits a predictable gasp of shock from the other side of the door. Recovering his composure, he crosses the Turkey carpet (in his night-dress and bare feet, gin in hand, cigar in mouth), and flings open the door.

Remain calm.

Her crinolined form entirely fills the entry as she glares at him, wearing an expression calculated beforehand to inspire miscellaneous guilt.

'Ah, Mrs Quigley, cheering as always, such a delight to behold. Please state your business.'

'I hope, Sir, that I did not hear the words my ears tell me I most surely did.'

Stepping into the room without an invitation, she sniffs the air conspicuously, brushing aside clouds of smoke with the palm of one hand as though the carpet were on fire; her glittering eyes observe in every detail the correspondent's red-eyed state of disarray.

'I smell an unusual brand of tobacco, Sir.'

'An acute and penetrating observation, Madam, lending an air of innocence to the act of prying into other people's business. What exceedingly brief service may I offer you, Mrs Quigley – engaged as I am in vitally important work?'

The eyes travel upward and in silent enquiry as to what important work might be sensibly undertaken in Whitty's condition.

'The police are here to see you, Sir.'

Whitty suppresses the urge to heave. 'A most ominous pronouncement, Madam. Are you certain it is the police?'

'Sir, I know a policeman when I see one, I can assure you of that. Mr Whitty, when we entered into our arrangement, I regret that I was not apprised of your line of work. I believe you intimated you were in banking.'

'You mistook me, Madam. *Drinking* was what I said.'

Mrs Quigley does not find this amusing, indeed there emerges a steely aspect to the woman, a quality Whitty has noted in others of her sex who undertake a commercial enterprise late in life – what one might call the battle-axe within.

'I shall indeed provide for alternative accommodation, Madam, the moment I have completed my exposé on suburban lodging. And now, so that I may prepare to greet my guest, allow me to draw your attention to that useful portal, the door.'

Having thrown on a dressing-gown, cravat, slippers and a splash of toilet-water, Whitty descends the stairway into Mrs Quigley's fussy, under-heated foyer.

Wouldn't you know: Under-Inspector Salmon, of that nest of snakes known as New Scotland Yard. Salmon, whose technically handsome features – patrician nose, strong jaw – have placed him in charge of entertaining the press, or harassing them, or breaking their arms, as necessary.

In his straight hat, straight coat, straight chin-whiskers, and his straight and dangerous stick, Salmon aspires to resemble some Cromwellian Iron Duke. Yet to Whitty the under-inspector is a man like himself, a professional who walks a dark street, wringing a living out of misery and death; indeed, put together with the Editor and taken as a group, Salmon, Whitty and Sala somewhat resemble Burke, Hare and Knox, whose frightful commerce in cadavers chilled the public's blood in the early part of Her Majesty's reign.

> Up the close and down the stair
> But and ben wi' Burke and Hare.
> Burke's the butcher, Hare's the thief,
> Knox the boy what buys the beef.

At Whitty's appearance on the stairs the under-inspector smiles: not a reassuring expression in his case. 'Mr Whitty, Sir. I thank God to have found you at home.'

'Indeed, Policeman, I assume a godly reason for your visit.'

'Ungodly I am afraid. The Fiend has escaped from Coldbath Fields.'

'Shocking. And which fiend might that be?'

'As though you don't know.'

'Indeed, Policeman, I do not.'

Whitty has heard that even the crushers regard the under-inspector as unnatural and bloodless, with an incorruptible, cruel rigidity to his character.

'Indeed, Sir, I have come to congratulate you.'

'And what is my achievement, Sir?'

'A bit late to plead ignorance, given that it was you who predicted it.'

Thinks the correspondent, *Did I?* If so, then the game begins in earnest – whatever it is.

'Mr Whitty, I'll thank you to favour me with a reply.'

Salmon gestures with his stick while speaking, stopping just short of the bric-à-brac, figurines and other bourgeois affectations that clutter every horizontal surface of the room, thereby signalling his willingness to do damage.

'Please enlighten me further, Mr Salmon. I write many pieces in the public interest, and I make many predictions of varying discernment.'

'A disappointing response, Sir. I assumed we could speak intelligently and with a measure of mutual respect.' So saying, the under-inspector produces a neatly folded page of *The Falcon*, opens it, and proceeds to read aloud:

> *However valid, such objections are soon to be eclipsed by a scandal of sheer incompetence, the which is destined to jolt London to its foundations . . . Due to rampant negligence and petty corruption from the highest official to the lowest crusher, the public remains at the mercy of the true fiends who stalk the streets . . .*

Salmon refolds the clipping carefully and slides it in his pocket as though it were evidence for the Crown. 'When you saw fit to compose those words, Sir, to what were you referring, if not to the escape of Chokee Bill?'

'Chokee Bill has escaped? The deuce, you say!'

Salmon's stick cracks Whitty behind the ear with sufficient force to put him on his knees. 'Please do not play cute with me, Sir. Please do not.'

Whitty rubs his throbbing temple while awaiting the ringing in his ear to subside. 'I fear, Mr Salmon, that you give me more credit than I deserve.'

The under-inspector speaks with exaggerated politeness – never a good sign in a thug. 'Please allow me to assist you, Mr Whitty, I believe you slipped upon a wet spot on the floor.'

'Sir, I swear to you as a journalist that the piece in question was social criticism of a general nature, noting inadequacies in the security of the British penal system, with the obvious conclusion that no good will come if it is permitted to continue.'

Salmon seizes the back of Whitty's dressing-gown, ripping the collar: the correspondent now stands or rather dangles before him, face to face, receiving the full benefit of the officer's metallic breath. (*Mercury? Arsenic? Ether? Ether: Of course.*) As well, he has the benefit of the officer's stick, inserted skilfully into an intimate place which would cause pain in any circumstance, let alone with the injuries previously inflicted by the ratters and their little friend Rodney.

'Policeman, I swear to you on the grave of my mother that I know nothing! Nothing!' Unencumbered by feelings of manly pride, Whitty can bleat for mercy with conviction, and is willing to swear to anything at all by his poor dead mother.

Still sensing a lack of sincerity, the officer twists the stick forcefully upward.

'I know nothing! Policeman! I beg you, stop!' The bric-a-brac clatters around him – surely Mrs Quigley is within hearing. 'Mrs Quigley! Please come at once!'

The door to the rear of the building remains closed.

'That is not the way I read the situation, Sir. Nor, might I add, does the public read it so. If I remember correctly, you played a prominent role during the terrible panic that attended Chokee Bill – indeed, the man was virtually your creation. You assiduously fed the fear, eagerly shovelled fuel on to the general alarm over profligate crime in the streets of the city – garrotting, rapes, beheadings, anything to shake the public's confidence in the Metropolitan Police. Thanks to your work in that particular, the business of the city did not return to normal functioning until the arrest and conviction of Mr Ryan.

'With that in mind, should it transpire that you participated in his escape, or had word that there might be an escape but failed to inform the police for reasons of professional gain – a 'scoop' as you like to call it – I fear that outrage among the constabulary will be such that I cannot vouch for the continued safety of your person, Mr Whitty, Sir.'

The under-inspector underscores his points skilfully with the stick, executing the manoeuvre in such a way that it will not show bruises, outside the bathhouse at any rate – an exercise designed to leave the correspondent with a full appreciation of how relative and contingent is the freedom of the press.

21

Near Leicester Square

Tucked into a cranny down a narrow lane off Orange Street, curled up like a child in its cot, it is a wonder she was found as quickly as she was. What with the ubiquitous sight of recumbent forms in doorways and niches, it is often the case that a corpse is taken for a sleeping vagabond until it is betrayed by the stink.

The crusher, in a Peeler's top hat and tails, stands above the young woman like a coachman attempting to awaken his drunken mistress. As is customary, he halloos three times, then employs the end of his stick to dislodge one arm, whereupon the body as a whole rolls toward him and suddenly he is looking into the ruined face. Mr Wells does not like what he sees lying there at his feet, for he has daughters of his own.

'Dear Lord in Heaven,' he whispers to calm himself, while he turns to the fellow Peeler at the entrance to the lane: 'Another one, Mr Chesney.'

'More of the same, Mr Wells?'

Mr Wells's attention turns to the scarf, tight around the throat. The Fiend did not take the trouble to close her eyes – and the rest of it. Hence, his weary acknowledgement.

'Correct, Mr Chesney. The silk scarf, the nose cut off, she has all the markings of Chokee Bill.'

'Then we are to alert Mr Salmon. Them is the orders, Mr Wells. I shall go to the constabulary directly.'

Whereupon Mr Chesney disappears, leaving Mr Wells with the melancholy chore of passing time with a corpse.

Gazing into the empty eyes of his mute companion, Mr Wells reflects on the nature of death as deeply as his imagination will allow. What is now gone that once was present? For it cannot be denied that there exists an inordinate stillness to her, with a quality to it unlike the stillness of a stone or other object. It is as though someone has retired, leaving behind an old, torn coat.

In a gesture of respect, there being no witness to an unprofessional display, the Peeler removes his top hat while thinking: She must have had a pretty face. Could he not have left her with her only advantage in life? *Bless you, poor thing, wherever you are is better than where you were.*

Preoccupied by these dismal thoughts, some time passes before the Peeler becomes aware of another presence nearby, in a cranny opposite and down the lane. Small, sooty hands cover her face, almost invisible in a tangle of brown hair. Tears ooze between her fingers, though she makes no sound.

The sight of intense grief being commonplace for a man in his line of work, Mr Wells secures his hat to his head and calls to her in the manner he employs to establish authority, the implacable bark of the Metropolitan Police.

'You there! What is your business? Do you know anything of what has happened here?'

Mr Wells is about to shout at her again, but she speaks: the Peeler must draw closer for it is but a whisper.

'No, Sir. I 'as found her and am keeping watch'

'Were you an associate of the deceased?'

'Aye, Sir. Her name were Flo. She were my benefactor.'

Mr Wells, who has seen much, looks her over and puts two and two together. For it is the way with whores this young that most have been abducted from the country. It is usual for such a girl to find herself reduced to nothing, owning not so much as the clothes in which she toils, so that her whoremonger may control her activities and prevent her escape. Even were she to escape, she could not return home, now that she is ruined.

'You are being over-generous to your whoremonger, Miss. You are well rid of her. On your way, then. Make out on your own. Find for yourself a pegging crib and earn your supper.'

Thinks the Peeler: With her whoremonger gone to her reward, at least the girl can keep the profits, which is an improvement.

'I'm not that kind, Sir. I'm a lacemaker. I done that as little as I could.' The girl glares defiantly at the constable with an ordinary face for such as she, distinguished by a peculiar mark on the upper lip and nothing more.

'A subtle distinction, Miss.' At a loss for more to say, Mr Wells returns to stare at the dead woman, until comes the welcome bellow of a Metropolitan policeman at the lane entrance. 'Well then, what do we have here, Constable?'

Upon recognizing the outline of Under-Inspector Salmon, the Peeler assumes an aspect of calm diffidence, the better to make no impression one way or the other.

'Murder of a prostitute by garrotting, Sir. Maiming followed death

143

if we may judge by the lack of bleeding. Seemingly our man has wasted no time getting back to work.'

'I'll thank you to leave the speculation to me, Mr Wells.'

'Yes, Sir,' replies, Mr Wells, who wonders where Chesney went, the rascal.

The under-inspector steps briskly into the lane, nudges the Peeler aside and takes a closer look at the corpse. Mr Salmon does not remove his hat. Bending down (knees crack audibly), with gloved thumb and forefinger he picks up one end of the silk scarf which has been twisted about her neck with considerable force. Slowly he unwinds the scarf, then glances at the label – then turns abruptly, having sensed the presence of Etta, still in the cranny, curled up like a tot.

'What is this one over here, Mr Wells?' Mr Salmon rises to approach the girl, while carrying the scarf in one hand.

'Only a fellow judy, Sir. Appears to have been acquainted with the deceased.'

Turning his back to Mr Wells, the under-inspector contemplates the girl. Then, to the surprise of the Peeler, he leans forward and almost gently drops the scarf over the girl's narrow shoulders.

'It is from Henry Poole's. You should get at least five shillings for it.'

'Begging your pardon, Sir, but should not the scarf be retained as evidence?'

'No need, Mr Wells. It does not tell us anything we do not already know.'

22

Camden Town

Climbing the stairs back to his rooms – slowly, carefully, painfully – while massaging the tender spot with one hand, Whitty reflects on the fact that there exist two versions of the myth of Pandora's Box: one narration concludes that the opening of the box released all human evil into the world; the other claims it to have been the source of all human hope. A distinct alternative, which one would prefer to have settled before lifting the lid.

That is not Whitty's way, if indeed his method of working can be so termed, being based neither upon observation nor deduction, nor any other form of human or even animal cognition. Instead, like an insect in trousers, he relies upon the quivering of a set of invisible antennae, which lead him forward until, well before the mind has ascertained what is happening, the body is already in the middle of it – and, as in this case, taking a beating for it as well. For not the first time in his Promethean career, Whitty curses his 'method', while at the same time curious as to why it provoked such an inordinate response from the under-inspector of Scotland Yard.

At the minimum, he takes satisfaction in the fact that the current line of enquiry has been settled, and that it is, as Mr Owler would say, fly.

RYAN INNOCENT
Police conceal evidence; revelations
implicate prominent gentleman.

Capital: a narrative that connects the factual dots into a plausible picture, providing its author with the possibility of selling *The Falcon* on an investigative serial – always the most lucrative form. And there is the welcome prospect of inflicting harm on a certain policeman . . .

So thinking, Whitty opens the door to his rooms.

Speak of the devil: before him paces the patterer in an excited manner, his ruined hat in hand, his face set in an expression of rueful melancholy.

'Mr Owler. How do you do?'

'Good-day to you, Mr Whitty. Are you in poor health, Sir? For I must say you do look pale.'

'Something disagreed with me is all. Indeed, I was about to contact you about a new development.'

'Sir, I come on the same particulars as you. I saw the police carriage outside and so gained access up the back drum. Your house mistress were listening by the hall door and did not see me as I passed.'

Confound her!

'Mr Owler, I have it on good authority that our man Ryan has escaped from Coldbath Fields.'

'Werily, I heard it this morning.'

'It is a rare opportunity.'

'Or a rare disaster.'

'*Sniff.*' Mrs Quigley, hovering in the open doorway.

'Mr Whitty, I see that you are entertaining a second visitor. Here at Buckingham Gardens it is not customary for guests to employ the servants' entrance.'

'Mrs Quigley, it is a privilege to introduce to you Henry Owler, Special Inspector, City of London. Do not be misled by the officer's appearance, for he is incognito.'

Mrs Quigley's small eyes dart sideways, betraying a doubt, upon which Whitty pounces like a cat.

'A murderer is at large, Madam, a fiend who preys on elderly women such as yourself. Believed to be stalking Camden Town at this very moment. Please be so good as to prepare tea while the officer and I take urgent counsel here in my rooms. Otherwise we will be forced to take tea elsewhere, leaving Buckingham Gardens unprotected.'

'Sir, this might not be the time for tea.' Although admittedly hungry, Owler would not dream of dining in Buckingham Gardens, whose opulence he finds intimidating.

'Oh, but it is tea-time, Inspector. Is that not so, Mrs Quigley?'

Mrs Quigley departs to the kitchen, there to exercise her spite upon the scullery maid, while boiling her cheapest tea.

Cradling Mrs Quigley's teacup between his palms as though it were a small, delicate animal, Owler seats himself upon the soft chair opposite Whitty's desk and wonders at the luxurious solitude of a correspondent's personal cocoon.

A soft, clean bed with feather comforter, on a Turkey carpet. A blazing fire of large, whole lumps, warming the air, already fragrant with cigar smoke – that masculine incense which, to the patterer, might just as well be bank-notes, burning. How is it possible, he wonders, for a party to have advantaged himself with such comfort and ease from morning to night, to bask in such softness and warmth like the pampered cat of a duchess, and yet to scorn his life – nay, *discard* his life, as though it were a piece of bad meat?

On the other hand, thinks Owler, waste is the hallmark of a gentleman; hence the term 'wastrel'. Such a privileged party as this is the more to be pitied, in the way one might pity a man with a huge, empty stomach, below a tiny neck, who in his life will never fill the vacancy within. It is possible that the man is not so much a wastrel as *wasted* – in the way that London has ways of wearing a party down, of laying him *waste*. On balance, Owler deems himself the more fortunate of the two, having experienced satisfaction from time to time. This conclusion Owler resolves not to mention to the correspondent, for men of the quality are a proud people, and disdain the sympathy of others.

For Whitty's part, his recent acquaintance with police brutality, now past, has caused his spirits to rebound with a renewed sense of purpose, not to mention the possibility of material redemption. The correspondent pours a measure of gin into his tea, then into the cup of the man opposite, not without a pang of pity for Owler's limited potential. Whitty is careful that his expression does not reveal such thoughts, for the poor are not lacking in dignity – but what a filthy cubby-hole of a world such a man must occupy! With what limited movement, with how low a sky! Fleetingly, Whitty attempts to picture the depleted psychic universe of such a man as this. Having one suit of clothes, does he dream of having two? Festering and itching throughout the summer night, does he dream of a private bath? As a man of thirty-five who looks sixty, is it his ambition to see his forty-fifth year? How does life appear to a man whose hopes for his daughter have no greater object than that she might keep her body as her own, and not as a thing to be sold on the street?

In this way do men of divergent stations in life pity and patronize one another, simultaneously.

'Mr Owler, may I suggest that we consider our options at this stage calmly. I am certain you can discern the wisdom in such a move.'

'Indeed, Sir, though there's a powerful uneasiness to be certain. It is no easy thing to trim the mind against so complete a disaster.'

'Would it alleviate some of the uncertainty were I to assure you that, whatever the outcome, you will turn a better profit than that which would accrue on your own?'

'That would indeed be very fly, Sir, but I have no confidence of such a thing. I've not ever called out a Sorrowful Lamentation but that it is 'orrid or *stunning*. My readers are wery conservative in these matters, Sir.'

'Be that as it may, Mr Owler, in this case you will be working with a writer with *The Falcon*, whose task it is to lash the ignorant, the presumptuous and the corrupt, with a rod pickled in classic brine.'

'You don't half go on, Mr Whitty, Sir.'

'My point is this: unlike the rabble who devour your 'orrid particulars, our readership looks to *The Falcon* for the truth, and damn the consequences. We go to battle, and damn the wounded. I invite you to join me: put your confidence in this enterprise and you will not regret it.' So says Whitty with assurance, having little of it himself. While lighting a cigar, he can only marvel at the fabulous mirages he is capable of spinning, in snaring for himself a reliable source.

'To speak the truth, Sir, I have no option but to join in your enterprise. With Ryan escaped from Coldbath Fields, I have no enterprise on my own.'

'Allow me to put a splash more gin in that tea, Mr Owler, it will buck you up.'

'Thank you, Sir, that is welcome. In the matter of which we speak, what particulars do you wish to know from me?'

'I need to understand what is known of the escape itself, not what is reported in the press, but what is heard on the ground – for it has spread about the Holy Land, has it not? The nearer to its source, the closer a rumour is to fact.'

'From what I can discern, Sir, it were a stunning escape – though hardly a clean one, for he left a deal of blood in his wake. Scaled the wall like a salamander, then took the spikes and blades with his body as need be is what he did. Succeeded to the roof of the house adjacent, walked down the stairs while the family was eating their dinner, like he was the lodger in the attic. The young nipper 'as confirmed the party was slashed wicious, so bad that, as he walked, the blood hit the floor without dripping. From Mount Pleasant, the Fiend must have kept to the alleys, for he remained unseen by a soul until he stole a coat at the Maurice, from a gonoph, name of Lanky Hillman, a rampsman and footpad known to possess a powerful thirst.

'Lanky's was a heavy Navy coat with extra pockets, conwenient for stolen goods. Soon after, a strange operative in Lanky's coat was sighted in the Holy Land, once by the stick-man on St Giles High and the other by a whore on her way to Nailer's Lane. Just west of Nailer's Lane, some Irish toffs contemplated lifting Lanky's coat off the fellow, but he was gone before they 'as made up their minds to it. From there, he headed more or less in the direction of Regent's Park, and that is all that is known.'

'Going back a distance, you say that our man was on a roof and covered with blood, having scaled the wall with its various steel deterrents.'

'Exactly so, Sir. Them things is like razors, you saw it yourself. He might yet die from it, I expect.'

'Then it follows that he must have known exactly where he was going. With no refuge to be gained in a timely fashion, either he would be quickly recaptured or his body would be found in the street next morning. This much is excellent.'

'I don't know what is excellent about it. Even if caught, he'll wind up in Newgate for sure, in the hole, out of communication.'

'Forget your Sorrowful Lamentation, Mr Owler. Now you can have a half-interest in a far more propitious story than the self-pity of a condemned man.'

'With respect, Mr Whitty, half of naught comes to naught, is my calculation.'

'You are sinking into despair, Sir. I have a medicament that tones the system wonderfully.'

'Just the tea and gin for me does fine.'

'Take some more, then. When did you avail yourself of what you call the 'full particulars' of the escape?'

Owler gratefully pours another splash of gin in his tea. 'It was known within the hour, I should think. Blind Dalton came to me with it by dawn, and all St Giles was a-buzz of it by nine. I left my girls to ascertain the way of it further, then walked directly to where we now sits.'

'How did it come about that you knew where to find me?'

'The coster at Fleet Street heard you give directions to your cabman. As a party seasoned to the city you must surely be aware that nothing is said aloud but has more than two ears to hear it.'

'The ears of ratters among them, I should imagine.'

'I don't know what you mean, Sir.'

'All the better for you,' replies the correspondent, squirming uncomfortably in his chair.

Off St Giles High Street

Our two little criminals (or 'female operatives' as their betters would have it) spent a mainly frustrating afternoon, owing to an article printed a few days earlier on the pages of *The Illustrated London News* and subsequently echoed in *The Times*, concerning a marked increase of pickpockets, rampsmen and other thieves, on which subject journals print every rumour going, no matter how vague or preposterous. According to the current version, so abundant are the snatch thieves in Piccadilly that, in experiencing the necessity of entering a public urinal, a party might as well throw his watch into the ditch, for it will be no longer his by the time he has taken his piss.

Civic officials responded to this climate of alarm by loosing into the streets a competing swarm of crushers and detectives, as though the Metropolitan Police (underpaid, undertrained, overworked, and uncompensated in case of injury) did not include a sufficient number of footpads, rampsmen and bug hunters among their own ranks.

In this way does the atmosphere of a society deteriorate with the evil expectations of the privileged, and streets which ordinary Londoners happily walked a fortnight ago are transformed in the public imagination into an untamed jungle inhabited by wild animals. Thus is the city governed by fevers of malignant righteousness, and London returns to a time when the heads of traitors and Jacobites adorned the spikes on Temple Bar.

In sum, now is the worst possible time to be nicked.

Phoebe and Dorcas have therefore eschewed all but the most glaring opportunities: the gentleman whose silk handkerchief was about to fall out of his pocket anyway, the fish merchant for whom Dorcas's bodice possessed such magnetic appeal that his nose nearly disappeared down her cleavage.

By day's end, for all their efforts, Mrs Ealing can offer them but a few pennies. Having come to a previous agreement on disbursal of the spoils, the two girls part company according to plan: Phoebe will return home with pilfered scran for her father's supper; Dorcas will venture to the Crown, there to invest her money in spiced gin, while in hope that a certain sporting young gentleman will be in attendance to refill her cup, in return for a talk and a bit of a look.

As the street around them repopulates from day traffic to night traffic, the two girls kiss one another in parting, for they really are the best of friends.

'Well, Miss Phoebe, I fears I must bid you good evening.'

'And what suitor occupies your engagement calendar this evening, Miss Dorcas?'

'My prince awaits, Miss Phoebe, to ask for a kiss. And to ask, and ask again.'

'Have I met the gentleman?'

'That you have, my dear. There were a handsome prince and a toad prince, and I have drawn the handsome one.'

'Have you let him kiss you? I can tell by your eyes that you have.' Phoebe blushes at the very thought of what they must be doing.

Dorcas giggles at her innocent friend. 'Only as necessary, Miss Phoebe. For a gentleman is run by fascination.'

'And by withholding. Be careful of his behaviour and watch for signs. You know the rumours that are about.'

'I shall watch him like a falcon, my dear. Wish me good luck.' And with a giggle and a wave, Dorcas is gone.

In Phoebe's view, Dorcas has been over-fond of the Crown of late, a place frequented by fast gentlemen of the quality – not to mention the lowest rakes and scoundrels. There is nothing to fear, it is true, within the Crown's four walls; but upon venturing forth from that secular sanctuary, a girl with a belly full of gin must pass through a half-dozen narrow, dark streets before she reaches Leicester Square – and there was a body found on Leicester Square, or so Phoebe has heard . . .

None the less, she says nothing about her worry. Between her own dream of a career on the stage and Dorcas's hoped-for attachment to a well-heeled gentleman, she cannot honestly say which is the more realistic. On what basis would she assume her own dream to have merit, and not that of her prettier friend?

But the gin is a worry. In these times, young ladies have become more generally fond of gin than boys, a little fuddle on Monday being no longer a disgraceful practice – especially spiced gin, hot with lemon and nutmeg, more satisfying for some than laudanum in its languorous effect.

And the other is a worry as well – the kissing and all that follows. Oh the thought of it! In Phoebe's mind, Dorcas stands on a border, about to cross into an unknown land from which no return is possible.

In this way Phoebe worries over her best, her oldest – nay, her only friend.

The Crown

Situated within sight of Cranbourne Street, amid a row of dishonour-able netherskens with rentals by the hour, the Crown is a large public house frequented by an unusual variety of the London citizenry. Within its walls, affluent sporting gentlemen may disport with equanimity amid the swell mob, as well as among vagrants, whores, dollymops and scrubbing-women – the cheapness of these women acting as an aphrodisiac for the jaded palate.

Here of an evening, there is dancing under the gasoliers, in whose seductive glimmer vastly mismatched couples cavort amid the glamour of the Crown's chipped golden cornices, its crumbling stucco rosettes and its bright advertisements (*The Famous Cordial, So Recommended by the Faculty*). Here a young man of good family can satisfy a yen for the lowlife in comparative safety, thanks to the figure of Stunning Joe Banks, the proprietor, an ex-pugilist who exerts as powerful a dominion over the Crown as he once wielded in the ring.

Cold and wet from walking, Dorcas pays the barkeeper for her cup of spiced gin 'The Cream of the Valley', meting out her coins one by one, calculating that she has enough money for one more. After that she must depend on the generosity of a gentleman, or go without. Choosing her customary table, next to a pillar and in sight of the door, she settles in, crosses her legs, and arranges her skirts, having already pinched her cheeks and unbuttoned her bodice one extra button, for effect.

She takes a tentative, delicious drink of the hot gin – breathing the fragrant steam, feeling the liquid warm her chest and her head and calm her uneasiness. Already she feels her shoulders settle, while the blood returns to parts of her body which have felt nothing since morning. She half-closes her eyes, the better to attenuate the sensation that life is good . . . But now the uneasiness comes over her once again, for her cup is becoming cooler and lighter with each tiny sip.

And now it is empty.

She rises, her head swimming ever so slightly, yet still steady on her feet with her last pennies ready in hand. Should she be condemned to remain alone for the evening, then the next cup will be her last, and she must return to two people who have become her family – nearly, but

THE FIEND IN HUMAN

not completely, for the kindness of Mr Owler will always be in some sense the charity of a strange man. One can never entirely eradicate the suspicion that the charity of a man is not without its underlying object. So imprinted is this suspicion that it requires daily testing, masked as teasing. It is not a comfortable situation for a girl; yet the presence of Phoebe makes it bearable and it is the best that can be hoped for. She must not think too long upon this subject or she will be sad throughout the whole next drink.

'Excuse me, Miss.'

Him. She recognizes the slight limp without looking directly, yet she pretends not to know the gentleman.

'I beg your pardon, but would it be impertinent of me to ask if I may offer you a drink?'

She pulls back her shoulders, the better to open the button just a bit; she smiles uncertainly, as though unaccustomed to an approach by a strange gentleman. In truth he is by no means a stranger, but that is the game he likes to play, so she does.

'Oh Sir, I don't know as it would be quite proper.'

He leans against the pillar in that offhand way that shows the splendid cut of his trousers. With a lucifer he lights a cigar which cost the equal of what Dorcas makes in a good week. Now he resumes play-acting: 'I confess to having admired you for an entire hour. Surely it is only fair that I pay some sort of tribute for the pleasure you have given me.'

'Well, Sir. Since you put it that way.'

'Capital.' He calls to the barkeeper: 'A brandy if you please, my good man, and your best spiced gin for a splendid young lady.' He removes the cigar from his mouth and raises his glass to this lovely girl whom he simply has to have. And by God he will have her: it is as simple as that.

> There was a little maid,
> Looked like a little dove;
> This little maid felt something queer -
> She called the feeling love;
> There was a very little man,
> Who felt a little smart;
> He told this pretty maid
> She'd stole his little heart.

154

25

Plant's Inn

The smoke-cured wooden panels that envelop the establishment reflect the watery light seeping from a window in the roof, for it is audibly pelting outside, a painful mixture of rain and hail – Ah, spring!

The warm glow of gaslight and firelight, reflected off the coloured bottles behind the bar, does not present the welcoming prospect it did, before the unfortunate incident with Mrs Plant – of which Whitty still retains no recollection. None the less, something must be done, for a clubman's drinking-quarters is of vastly greater significance than his sleeping-quarters, or any other quarters for that matter. The significance of this particular venue to Whitty's well-being is not lessened by the face and form of its owner.

Standing in the doorway while surveying the room, he shakes out his hat and gloves in an assured manner, nodding in the direction of his colleagues who have paused to look over the new entry, before turning once more to the exchange of non-sequiturs and *bon mots*:

– *The unemployed are becoming unpleasant.*
– *The institution of aristocracy is based on injustice and moral debasement.*
– *That demented scribbler has long since lost the way to Bohemia.*
– *He is an old bottle-nose, and a braggart besides.*

Whitty is uncertain how to proceed with Mrs Plant. Unlike the gentlemen-commoners, with their gold tassels and their ample allowances, Whitty was required actually to *study* while at the university; this, during the years when young men are expected to acquire temporal experience. Therefore he can boast of no greater, and more often less, experience with the opposite sex than that of his contemporaries.

This much he knows: Mrs Plant is a proud woman, capable of inflicting not inconsiderable damage, both mental and physical.

What must be done, will be done. He will not be removed from the premises unless it be to the mortuary.

Looking on the positive side, recent events have lent the correspondent confidence, a result of success and not medicine.

Suitably impressed by Bigney's research (presented as Whitty's own, of course), Sala, over the inevitable objections of Dinsmore, jumped like a trout – with the result that the correspondent exited *The Falcon* with a mandate for a six-part series; in return he is to receive a stipend sufficient to mollify his creditors and their little friend Rodney for at least a month.

Time to move forward, with the wind at his back, to score a triumph of Wellingtonian scope.

The barkeeper, engaged in the studious wiping of a glass, notes the correspondent's approach with misgiving: 'Still bad weather for a visit if I may say so, Sir. Chilly hereabouts.'

'Good afternoon, Humphrey. The weather notwithstanding, I wish to speak privately with Mrs Plant, please.'

The correspondent leans across the bar to effect a confidential whisper, not to attract undue notice from patrons from competing publications; he descries Banning and Cobb watching from a corner table, with Hicks surely not far away.

'Man to man, old chap, how do you rate her disposition?'

The barman's eyes swivel sideways, meaningfully. 'As I said, Sir, it is rum weather, damnably chilly.'

Having failed to heed the barman's ocular warning, he is startled by the voice at his shoulder, though it speaks *sotto voce*:

'Whitty, you have some nerve coming in here.'

'Ah, Mrs Plant, the very person I seek. I'm very glad to see you, Madam.'

Which is for the most part true. Despite her advanced age – easily thirty, well into her middle years – Mrs Plant remains an unusually comely specimen of her sex, with straight features, a generous crown of copper hair, and remarkable skin, the latter lending radiance and freshness to what he imagines to be a taut yet womanly physique, somewhere beneath the petticoats and corset.

'Get out of here afore I take the tongs to you.'

Speak calmly. Do not feed the fire.

'Mrs Plant, if something I may have said or done has in any way contributed to your distress . . .'

'Of course it's all about my distress isn't it? And I'm not the blowhard killing myself with drink.'

'I assure you, Madam, I have absolutely no memory——'

'I am not surprised. It is the source of all your happiness, that you can do or say or write anything you like and not remember a shred of it.'

'I beg you, Mrs Plant, if you would at least intimate to me what it was I did to offend.'

'Oh you are a slippery one . . .'

So saying, Mrs Plant, unaccountably, lapses into tears.

Faced with a weeping publican, utterly at a loss, Whitty becomes uncomfortably aware of other patrons, competitors in the trade who have now grown quiet, their eyes scrupulously averted yet recording every detail, none of which favours his reputation.

'Mrs Plant, I beg of you . . .' He places his hand on her arm as though to comfort her, which she rejects with a vehement slap. 'Madam, I entreat you that we may discuss this in the privacy of your snug. Please believe me, I would not for all the world have caused you a moment's anguish or concern.'

Removing from her sleeve a handkerchief with which to dry her eyes, Mrs Abigail Plant turns away so that he will not see how flushed her cheeks have become; and indeed she does retreat to her snug, behind the glass window etched with angels, having said nothing to render him specifically unwelcome.

Whitty follows. On balance, he has made progress.

Seated at the table opposite, after taking a restorative sip from her ever-present glass of whisky, Mrs Plant dabs her eyes, blows her nose in a ladylike manner, then settles into a brittle silence, eyes cast downward as though reading a message in the table's scarred surface. Whitty determines silence to be the best course, while not in full possession of the facts.

At length she speaks calmly, while steadfastly refusing to look at him, for fear that the sight of him might provoke a new outburst.

'You are a fool, Whitty, which is more dangerous than a devil. A devil knows the damage he does while a fool remains happily ignorant.'

'I regret, Madam, that I am at a loss to explain myself, even to myself.'

Whitty adopts a penitent yet watchful stance, certain that she will come out with the information soon. And sure enough, she leans toward him to speak in a sharp whisper, the lower part of her face in shadow, her aquamarine eyes watching him closely, glittering in the firelight with a renewed welling of tears.

'For one thing, you asked me to marry you.'

Oh, the deuce!

'I beg your pardon, Madam. I did what?'

'Asked me to marry you. As though it would make up for what he did. As though you would make a decent woman of me.'

'To make up for what he did? Of whom do you speak?'

'Your friend, the swell – the one who thinks his hands belong on any woman he pleases.'

Whitty is dying for a drink, but to signal for a gin now would betray weakness. He must think clearly and calmly: of the many indiscreet utterances a man can commit, save a challenge to a duel, a rash offer of marriage is the most unnerving.

'I beg you, Madam. Please refresh my memory.'

'It was after the last hanging. You reeled in with your young toff and his friend. Introduced them as classmates – easy to see why, as the fat one paid for the gin.'

Thinks Whitty: These details have a familiar ring; Harewood, Sewell. It is starting to come back.

'The handsome one took a look around, saw nothing better in the room, and so became increasingly familiar while you muddled yourself with drink. I slapped him off me and was reaching for the coal shovel when, momentarily sensible, you leapt between us in a righteous fit; suddenly you, as my self-appointed protector, denounced your companion as a knave (yes, you used the word *knave*), breaking several cups into the bargain. Whereupon the two of you faced off like boxers. Your friend knocked you down without difficulty.'

'A man collects unsavoury companions when he is half seas over.'

'And toadying to the quality besides.'

'Quality? I tell you I was utterly mortified by Harewood's behavior, that your protection was uppermost in my mind.'

'My protection? The impudence of it! The nerve!'

'Madam, I am confounded by your response.' Which indeed he is. *In vino veritas*, indeed.

'Mr Whitty, I had thought ours an acquaintance with respect on both sides. I will not bore you with a review of the path which led me to where I am, but I can promise you it was not an easy one, and with many a reptile on the wayside. And what respect do I receive from you? First you presume to defend my honour, then you insult me with facetious and maudlin talk of marriage! Get out of my sight! Kill yourself! Get it over and be done with it! Hang yourself from the chandelier, you surely know how to do it, you've seen enough of Mr Calcraft . . .' Again her voice falters and she falls to weeping.

Whitty sticks his head around the glass partition and signals urgently to the barkeeper: 'A large brandy, Humphrey – now, if you please. And the usual for Mrs Plant.'

158

The correspondent is out of his depth. Married men of his acquaintance confess to being utterly confounded by the women who have occupied the adjacent pillow for years: how much greater is the bewilderment of a bachelor from Christ Church?

'Madam, I regret that I cannot unsay what has been said, undo the injury, or humiliation, or insult, or whatever I inflicted upon you. I do respect and admire you, and find you in no way deficient – other than in your choice of myself as a friend. Please understand, Mrs Plant, that I admire you not only as a publican, but also as a woman. This is what no doubt prompted me to misspeak myself so presumptuously. Call it besotted grandiloquence, an excess of zeal, the raving of an idiot, but do not call it a sign of disrespect.'

Mrs Plant's brilliant eyes shine into him with an expression both sad and amused. For some reason, he finds this as unsettling as her anger.

'You poor man. What a correspondent, who digs up the truth about others, but knows not the truth about himself.'

To this Whitty has nothing to say.

Humphrey clears his throat discreetly. 'Your brandy, Sir. And your whisky, Madam.' The barkeeper has been hovering nearby, the Devil knows how long.

26

The Holy Land

Situated a few steps from Rat's Castle, the Owler garret on Scalding Lane, in more fortunate times, served as quarters for the meanest scullery maid in the service of a quality household. Such being the course of property development in the St Giles rookery, it is now the spacious domain of a superior provider, a man able to afford the privacy of three to a room, and with its own tiny fireplace. The latter convenience, with the addition of an ancient heating grate acquired by the girls from a shop in Cheapside, now serves as a stove, upon which Phoebe places her father's two herrings side by side – and a smaller one for herself – above an accumulation of coke which she gathered in the street.

Whatever the social milieu, a superior position exacts a spiritual penalty. In her mind Phoebe follows the aroma of the cooking food, as it wafts through the air, under the door and thence down the stairs, down, down, until at last, at the bottom of a succession of stairways, a hundred noses twitch with envy (hooked noses, bottle-noses, the dirty button-noses of stunted children), while a hundred stomachs growl, until the fragrance of the fish finally reaches the basement, whose crush of miserable humanity – eating, sleeping, dying, lying openly naked in the summer months on straw billets and mounds of swarming rags – cannot smell anything.

Owler lights his pipe with the lucifer he used to light the coal chips, stooped over by the single window – such being the slope of the roof that he cannot reach his full height in any but one part of the room. By habit he puffs his pipe so as to fill the room comfortably with the smoke, then half-reclines on one of three ancient wooden hospital cots, lacking room for other furniture.

For the sake of decency, the room has been divided into two sections, the two cots occupied by the girls being separated by means of a makeshift curtain strung across the room, an accumulation of colourful swatches of cloth upon whose origin Owler does not care to speculate.

Against the far wall leans the patterer's board, now displaying *The Affecting Case of Mary Ashford*, the ever-popular account of 'The young Virgin who was diabolically Ravished, Murdered, and thrown into a Pit'.

The three remaining walls have been covered, by his daughter and her companion, with pictures removed from books and calendars he has never seen, depicting famed performances by Charles Kean, Ellen Tree and Agnes Robertson in the plays of Shakespeare. Owler cannot help but view the famous theatrical trio as a mocking reflection of the three occupants in this attic, contrasting the squalor of one with the dash of the other. Yet comparing one's position to that of one's betters will not help a party get ahead in life.

'*The poor rogues talk of Court news, who loses and who wins, who's in, who's out . . .* Who said that, my girl?'

'Shakespeare, *The Tragedie of King Lear*, you asked me that once before today is when you asked it.'

'Werily, I did. My little learning is what I have heard, my girl, and it makes me prone to repetition.' Her father puffs his pipe in a thoughtful manner as he does when unsure how to speak to his daughter. 'Now my mind is centred on another particular. I'm thinking on our Mr Whitty. I would have you put your mind to this, Phoebe, lest I enter in an unwise partnership, for you are a sharp judge of such things.'

'I'm listening, Father. Continue, please.'

'Mr Whitty is a smooth man, where I'm a rough-made man. Mr Whitty has been lucky in his life, whereas I have not. Mr Whitty is a party as slides through life alone, where I'm a man what has picked up attachments along the way. Given as I have you girls, your two lives being my obligation in life, what rash thing am I doing to form an association with a party what has scarce regard for his own life, let alone another? Funny thing to say, but it is a fact that he has nothing to lose. It is myself has the greater wealth, in a manner of speaking.

'And there is another particular: Mr Whitty is of a crafty, subtle nature and I have no confidence that he is fly. I am not putting it well, my girl, such is the confusion of my mind in thinking through it.'

She turns the herring over with her father's knife and thinks upon the correspondent – who, to her eye, is a most cultivated and attractive gentleman. In the privy she touched his hand while helping him to his feet and they were like the hands of a woman, that unscarred they were, yet like the hands of a man in their shape and strength. His hair, though it had tousled about, fell into a becoming shape all on its own; his speech was likewise that of a man of quality, not to mention his smell, of cologne and good tobacco. And yet she knows him to be a man unhappy with himself . . .

'You make me think, Father, of a piece from the Bible: *My brother is a hairy man, whereas I am a smooth man.* It *is* from the Bible, is it not?'

'I've not read the Bible, as you know.'

'Yet you told it to me – Jacob nicked his brother for the birthright, with the connivance of his mother as well.'

'These stories are told to children to make them sleep. I've no knowledge of them, really.'

'Jacob and our Mr Whitty are both smooth men.'

'And what lesson do you draw from the comparison? Am I the hairy man what is deceived?'

'Indeed, Jacob was smooth, and dishonest, and something of a thief into the bargain. A sorely disreputable person would you not say, Father?'

'That trick he did with the goats was a wicious thing. I would never stoop to such a thing meself.'

'Because you are . . .'

'Because I am a rough man, is what you are going to say.'

'It was you who said it, Father.'

'Yes, I suppose it was.'

She takes two fish off the fire, places them on the tin plate and hands the plate to her father, whom she can easily reach, the walls being about two yards apart; now she spears the third fish with the knife and blows it cool. 'I remember Jacob wrestled with a dark angel in a dream.'

'Yes, my girl?'

'Is it possible Mr Whitty wrestles with a dark angel too?'

'I would think he might. The gentleman's face, when in repose, turns melancholic.'

'Even so, over the long run Jacob became a stunning successful man. God saw to it.'

'God meant it to be is what you are saying.'

'And from this we learn, Father, that even the smooth man . . .'

'May well be part of God's plan, whether he is fly or not. I think Mr Whitty himself would be surprised to hear that.'

Thus does a daughter become mother to her father, she with the more nimble mind and the stolen books. Thus is a young girl drawn to an older man of the quality, as a step beyond wherever she finds herself.

A moment later, daughter and father reverse places again, as a girl appeals to the hard-gained wisdom of her father.

'Are we in God's plan, Father? The place we live in – is this God's world?'

The patterer does not reply until after the eating of his fish, for the girl has him thinking now.

'I believe so, girl, yes I do. Even I what has little to do with Him and don't have the full particulars, and even though things is confusing in these times, what is good and what is not, I, who have never set foot outside London since I came here as a boy, have seen this one thing to be true: there is a good place, and there is a dark place, and all of London is both them places at the same time. Even we who occupy the Holy Land, even we must choose which London is ours. And out of what we have chosen . . . life goes on.'

'How is it that there can be a plan, and yet ours to choose?'

'You have me there, girl. I have not the foggiest idea.'

Phoebe puts her own fish before Father. She is not hungry. She is thinking about smooth Mr Whitty, and of her only friend Dorcas. She is not certain whether God has a plan, and, if so, she does not wish to think about what it might be.

27

The Grove of the Evangelist

The house is one of several stone structures of a dark and anonymous appearance on the east side of Portland Place, whose street façade has been made to appear as though the occupants are absent, or ill, or dead.

In the case of the Grove of the Evangelist, so carefully contrived is the illusion of disuse that, upon peering into the cast-iron letter-box, Whitty descries a pile of out-of-date advertisements and unopened invitations, as though the occupant were unavailable or unable to reply; which impression is belied by the fact that, in two days' scrutiny from across the street, Whitty and Owler (the latter burdened with papers and sandwich-board) witnessed sixteen gentlemen to enter the building and fifteen gentlemen to exit – all of whom disappeared with all dispatch in their carriages (which magically appeared from a nearby lane), south in the direction of Warren's Hotel, or north to Park Square and the Outer Circle.

'In the last of the carriages rides a member of the legal profession. I have seen him hold forth at the Chancery.'

'Werily, that would be the operator with the buff waistcoat. And did you catch the stunning silk choker on the toff what went off in the brougham?'

'Sir Charles Boyle is his name. Prominent in the Freemasons, I am told.'

'Blimey.'

'God may blind you indeed, Sir. He has blinded many to the sins of the mighty.'

'It is shocking to see the quality in such a light.'

'I am touched by your idealism, Mr Owler,' says Whitty. 'I could do with some of it myself.'

Having returned to their post across the street, a lengthy period having passed without the furtive arrival of another visitor, Whitty determines that it is time to make his move.

'Wait here if you please, while I put a theory to the proof.'

'With respect, Sir, I haven't earned my supper yet, nor supper for my girls.'

'Can you not sell your deuced papers while keeping watch? There are pedestrians and carriages here as well.'

'This is not my territory. It is no good to work outside one's territory. A party gets a sense of a place, what is called for in certain weather. There is no good in my working this territory any more than a riverman working the sea.'

'Mr Owler, try to appreciate the situation. Chokee Bill may lurk behind these walls. It is a rare opportunity for us both.'

'I don't see it as such. For one thing, I can only watch the front. The moment he gets a whiff of us he'll be out the back drum for certain.'

With effort Whitty remains patient with the sheer conservatism of the man, the unwillingness to move beyond his habits of mind and body for the sake of a lucrative piece of work, even to the extent of leaving his customary corner. Odd, the way common knowledge and biblical teaching depict the poor as wastrels and indigents, when the truth may be that they are poor simply because they are too careful.

'Listen to me please, Mr Owler. In the first instance, your purpose here is to note who comes and goes generally, and whether or not anyone else is watching the house. In the second place, if his condition is as you describe, it is a miracle he has enough blood to go from one room to the next. Our greater fear is that he is dead.'

'True for you there. 'T'will be days before he is moving by the accounts I hear.'

'In any case, where on earth would he escape *to*?'

'I deem he has a plan in that particular, and that the destination must needs be foreign, for he will come to no good in the city, nor in the country, neither. There lives many a man in England what would like to tell his mates what he is the one what did for Chokee Bill.'

The correspondent produces a coin as an end to the discussion. 'Quite. Excellent analysis. Here is a shilling so that you will not concern yourself with supper.'

'Begging your pardon, Sir, it is not my practice to take charity.'

'That is tiresome of you, Mr Owler, I have never shied from it myself.'

'Good evening, Sir. And how I may assist you, please?' The liveried footman is of Caribbean origin, to judge by his accented English and his features – sharper and lighter than the African, taller than the Indian. A handsome, athletic specimen, Whitty judges him to be in his late teens, but with a face inscrutable beyond its years. Indeed, the eyes betray only a flicker of interest, with a trace of mild amusement.

Whitty places his card into the white-gloved palm of this muscular impediment. 'Edmund Whitty of *The Falcon*, here to enquire after Mrs Marlowe.' Under one arm he carries a copy of that newspaper with which to fortify his position.

'Very good, Sir. I shall see if Madam is in.' So saying, the young man disappears from the entryway into a décor which, from what the correspondent can discern from the doorstep, appears to consist of nothing but the colour red in various shades and textures. Absent-mindedly, Whitty extends one hand, causing the heavy mahogany door to swing further open. Purely in order to return the door to its former position, he steps into an entryway of white marble, whereupon he feels magnetically drawn into a receiving-room, for it is like entering the interior of a woman's mouth . . .

His upper arm is clamped by iron fingers in a white glove. 'I do not recall your having been given leave to enter, Sir. I hope that this is not a prelude to unpleasantness and that you will go now.' So saying, with his other hand the servant deftly places the calling card between the correspondent's lips.

Whitty removes the card and turns to face the footman, whose grip on his upper arm has tightened and whose eyes no longer reveal a trace of amusement. 'I beg your pardon, my good fellow, I can see that I may have been in error.'

'Indeed, you are seriously in error, Sir. Please leave now.' And the correspondent finds himself gently but surely propelled back whence he came.

'Upon consideration, it may not be Mrs Marlowe I seek, but rather a Mrs Cox. Or then again, perhaps I should enquire after Miss Eliza Hurtle. One can so easily become confused when confronted with a bevy of assumed names.'

The face reveals no surprise, yet the hand behind Whitty's back hesitates. 'Please you will wait upon this spot.'

This time the door closes firmly and the latch slides shut.

Whitty turns to face the street, where a well-maintained brougham slows to a halt, curtains part, and a man's face appears in the window, unrecognizable but for the twice-about white neck-cloth of a clergy-man. Noting the presence of the correspondent, the face disappears abruptly and the brougham resumes its journey at a brisk pace. Whitty notes with satisfaction that, across the way, the patterer has just sold a Shocking Outrage to a gentleman walking his terrier.

At length the mahogany door opens, and in place of the athletic young man in livery now stands a strange little widow with hair cut short in the way of men who work with machinery, and a curious scar on one cheek. Not Mrs Marlowe, surely – and yet such a thing is possible. Whitty has nosed out many a notorious seductress only to be confronted with a moustache, hare lip or advanced tooth decay, rendering incomprehensible her vaunted allure.

'Have I the honour of meeting Mrs Marlowe? Mrs Cox? Miss Hurtle?'

An unnaturally long consideration ensues before the woman does him the favour of a reply. When it comes, it is by no means an enthusiastic welcome.

'Please enter.'

Whitty steps into the red reception room again, having surrendered his hat, stick and gloves to the footman, who has been lurking behind the door.

The little woman turns to Whitty with kernel-like eyes. 'Wait here, please,' she bids him in a dry voice, and disappears down a hallway. Her footsteps recede out of hearing. A door opens, then closes faintly in another part of the house.

He directs his gaze from the Chinese carpet embroidered with red dragons to the portrait of Victoria above the fireplace, to a replica of something by Michelangelo beneath the fern in the corner; a surprisingly lush fern for a house lit solely by gaslight, in which the night, and its conjunctive desires, obtains from dusk to dusk. As well, he notes the lack of a mirror or other reflecting surface to remind the visitor as to his true identity and station. The red walls above the wainscoting and the red velvet drapes (red velvet being at one time restricted to the gentry by law) overwhelm the white gauze curtains and the cream tablecloth like blood on a sheet. As an example of interior design the effect goes well over the top, yet it is undoubtedly effective, like the décor of a theatre in its intention to arouse anticipation of the coming entertainment – not a comedy but a melodrama, a tale of shameful desire in a foreign setting, indulged with utter abandon.

Of course: De Sade. Bound in human skin.

Footsteps. More decisive footsteps now, not the brisk click of the little widow. To effect an offhand appearance, the correspondent examines the second painting in the room, a water-colour by that pretentious ape Rossetti; he maintains this position until an odd sensation in the nape of his neck causes him to turn and to greet his hostess – who is the selfsame woman in the water-colour. Thinks Whitty: A splendid entrance and a splendid effect, orchestrated to perfection. He becomes aware of how closely she has been regarding him. *Touché, Mrs Marlowe*. Whereupon Whitty reaches into a pocket for his packet of powder, to steady the nerves.

'I do not permit the taking of stimulants in my house, Sir. Nor do I permit smoking, nor alcohol nor opiates. Can you imagine why this might be so?'

'I should very much like to hear it,' he replies coolly, returning the chemist's packet to his pocket as though it is but a trifle, the easiest thing in the world.

'I find that men take up such habits for their numbing effect on the emotive faculties. Women also, for that matter – but with a different objective in mind.'

Steady.

'Madam, if you refer to the principle of mind over matter and science over passion, then I for one am committed to it.'

The eyes flash. 'Do you know how a well-bred woman deals with thoughts of the sort you are entertaining now?'

Maintain calm.

'Allow me to come directly to the point, Madam,' stammers Whitty, determined to recover momentum. 'I shall not insult you with facile prevarication, nor by withholding facts. Put plainly, I am aware that William Ryan, the condemned murderer, resides in these premises. He has been followed here and has been seen to enter. I am aware of Mr Ryan's past connection to yourself of – please excuse me – an intimate nature, which occurred several years ago. And I am aware, Madam, of the events which took place between then and now, of Miss Hurtle, Mrs Cox, and Mrs Marlowe – now, perhaps, with the ambition of becoming Mrs Ryan. With so many names, Madam! One would think you aspired to the German aristocracy!'

Momentarily Whitty worries that the woman might faint, for the white skin of her cheeks and throat has turned ashen and the eyes momentarily blurred; however, after a lapse of half a second she executes a contemptuous shrug.

'Congratulations, Sir. You have spied effectively. I commend you for it.'

'Thank you. Now I request that you take me to Mr Ryan at once. Otherwise, I shall be obliged to notify the authorities – and of course the public at large.'

Having thus established himself as other than a paying customer, the correspondent boldly lights a cigaret and observes his hostess with interest: a pale, statuesque woman with a remarkably smooth brow and eyes like ice floating in the North Sea – and yet the nose is a touch too long for true prettiness. With remarkably full lips, almost swollen, which turn up at the corners as though forming the beginning of a smile – and yet a chin too prominent by half, set in an expression of unbecoming, almost masculine determination. With long, lustrous, plaited hair, almost blue in colour, wound above her head with seeming carelessness (by the little widow no doubt), leaving a few dishevelled wisps in the current fashion, revealing a long, proud neck, abbreviated by a lace collar fastened with a brooch decorated with a Chinese motif; the same lace which decorates her neck reappears at the cinched cuffs above her strong, white hands, one of which taps a closed Chinese fan upon the palm of the other as though keeping time with an unheard piece of music. Her figure is a shapely one, boldly uncorseted.

A dangerous woman. Or rather, since all women are dangerous, more dangerous than most.

'You are with *The Falcon*, Sir.'

'Correct, Madam. That is the paper I have the honour of serving.'

'I regret that we have confined ourselves to *The Illustrated London News.*'

'I assure you it is to my regret as well.' Whitty sighs inwardly, it being one of the Deity's little jokes that no correspondent may enter a room without a copy of the competition in sight and none of his own.

Again the half-smile. Again the fan, tapping a brisk tempo. She makes no secret of sizing him up, therefore he sizes her up in return.

Her dress is of silk – midnight-blue, a generosity of fabric defined by a wide belt at the waist, permitting one to glimpse the merest hint of movement in her bosom. He judges her height to be slightly above his own, enhanced by the elevated riding heels on her buttoned boots.

The ensuing pause extends longer than he expected. His hostess remains in the wide doorway, regarding him with an expression neither displeased nor pleased. Beneath the coil of thick hair he can envisage, phrenologically speaking, equally distinct formations in the regions of Amativeness and Calculation – an unusual and dangerous combination.

'Will you take tea, Mr Whitty?'

The corners of her full mouth turn upward again to form a bare suggestion of a smile. Without awaiting a reply, she exits, leaving the door open and affording him a view of her receding figure as she moves down the hall. She pauses at a doorway, glances quickly in his direction, then disappears, leaving the impression that he should follow.

He turns back to the portrait on the wall: he is about to take tea with a woman who stands unacquitted of having poisoned her husband. A woman to whom, a very few moments ago, he uttered a threat which was tantamount to blackmail.

Touché, Mrs Marlowe – unless, God forbid, you are Mrs Cox.

Whitty seats himself at the tea-table, noting that china and silver have already been laid out by his hostess's companion on a pressed linen table-cloth, with milk, lemon, sugar and an array of cakes. Everything – cups, spoons, napkins – appears immaculate and orderly, as if to offset the nature of the activities taking place elsewhere.

Like the reception room, the sitting-room has been decorated in shades of red, excepting the glass cupola in the corner looking onto the garden, where stands a lush fern identical to its colleague in the reception room: hence, the relative health of the many large plants in the house despite the almost total lack of daylight, their having been alternately placed here. Seated beneath the fern, Mrs Marlowe pours. For not the first time, Whitty experiences the discomfiting feeling that he is acting according to her script and not his own, that any strategy he might undertake will be incorporated into her overall design, like a musician improvising on a theme.

'Cream and sugar, Mr Whitty?'

'Sugar, please, Mrs Marlowe. Two spoons.' He replies as though confident that the white granules in the bowl are indeed sugar.

She stirs his tea with a silver spoon in her capable fingers. Are they the hands of a murderess? Did those hands stir arsenic into her husband's tea, day after day?

Thinks Whitty: Poison is the most intimate violence, and the most repellent, for the murderer must be sufficiently trusted that the victim will accept food or drink. Hence, it is said, poison is the weapon of women, to whom the role of providing food customarily falls. Arsenic is an especially appropriate weapon for the weaker sex: unlike strychnine, whose effects are felt after a short while, arsenic may be administered over a period of weeks, so that the victim gradually falls ill and dies, unaware of the cause of his symptoms, while the murderer feigns womanly concern, giving him his medicine, tucking him in each night as innocent and ignorant as a baby . . .

'Be careful, Sir. Be careful of what you are thinking.' Surprisingly, this warning comes, not from the lady before him, but from her bleak little guardian, hovering in front of the cabinet.

'Mr Whitty, I believe you have met my companion, Mrs Button.'

'Indeed, Madam, though I do not believe we have been introduced.'

'Mrs Button, this is Mr Whitty. A journalist with an enquiring mind.'

'That is not all that is on his mind.'

'That will be sufficient, Mrs Button.'

The little witch executes a stiff curtsey. 'Good-day to you, Sir.'

'And to you, Madam. A pleasure to have met you.'

In a house of illusion, odd and disturbing encounters are only to be expected.

Mrs Marlowe sips her tea. She has not taken sugar. 'As a newspaperman, Sir, I ask you: What is your professional opinion of Mr Acton's report on the debilitating effects of self-abuse? The gentleman writes that it is the cause of idiocy and death, and that it is rampant among the upper classes, and that Britain is losing her leaders of tomorrow . . .'

'Madam, on that matter I have no opinion, except to say that Mr Acton is a fraud and a nincompoop.'

'Since I am only a woman I lack first-hand experience in such matters. However, it has been my experience that the more well-born a man, the more peculiar his tastes.'

'Indeed, it is a startling paradox that high-born children suffer indignities unknown to their inferiors. Such punishments as take place regularly in the halls of Eton and Rugby, were they perpetrated in a school attended by boys of the lower orders, would inspire headlines such as *Atrocious Cruelty of a Schoolmaster.*'

'Perhaps for the upper classes such experiences are a means of inuring one to future suffering – of oneself and of others. Such practices might also solidify membership in the class to which the boy was born. I have heard it said that in the better public schools, tradition demands that a boy must surrender his every possession to his school – including his cock.'

She pauses with a trace of amusement. 'Oh dear, Mr Whitty, You spilled some of your tea.'

'How clumsy. I do apologize.'

'Allow me to refill your cup.'

Whitty sips his renewed cup of tea and swallows. It has a bitter taste.

'More sugar, perhaps?'

'No, thank you. It is excellent.'

Again, silence falls between them as Mrs Marlowe sips her tea, replacing the china cup noiselessly in its saucer. The correspondent reminds himself that the upturn of her lips does not constitute a smile.

'This is Oolong tea, Mr Whitty. It has been partially fermented, to allow some of the bitterness to remain.'

'I try to avoid bitterness in food. I find enough bitterness elsewhere.'

'An ability to appreciate bitterness is the key to a cultured taste. Or rather, an adult taste. Children always display an eagerness for sweets.'

What is she insinuating?

Whatever her meaning, the intent of her manner of speaking is that of a field cannon – to wear down and weaken the position opposite. Accordingly, Whitty reaches into his coat, retrieves his notebook, opens it to a fresh page, produces a pencil, and gazes at it as though thinking profound thoughts. Not that he has anything to record in his notebook; the point being to inspire in the opponent feelings of uncertainty and a fear of the written word.

'Mrs Marlowe, since you seem in no hurry to fetch Mr Ryan, I wonder if you might allow me to inquire: When you administered poison to your husband, was it at tea-time? Or did you make use of some other occasion to do the deed?'

The eyes remain locked upon his for eight seconds (by Whitty's count), then break away while she sips her tea.

'Neither, Sir. I did not poison my husband.'

A direct hit. Fire another round.

'Then how, in your view, Madam, did your husband's corpse come to be saturated with arsenic?'

She holds his gaze, this time for eleven seconds. A slight flush rises to the cheekbones. He braces for retaliation.

'Mr Whitty, may I speak candidly?'

'I assure you, Madam, at *The Falcon* our sole aim is to uncover the truth in the public interest.'

'What utter rubbish.'

'You are, of course, at liberty to disagree.'

'Then here is a story for you, Mr Whitty – I believe the term is, 'an exclusive'. My only request is that you promise to print all of it or none.'

'If it will be of interest to the public, by all means.'

'Mr Cox was in the habit of taking Fowler's Solution – do you know the remedy?'

'Arsenic in a base of oil of lavender. Said to effect an improvement in deficiencies of an intimate nature.' Whitty has used it himself for melancholia, though arsenic must be taken with exceptional care.

'That is correct. You see, unknown to myself previously, Henry had contracted syphilis years earlier, while sowing his wild oats. This you will find in his physician's report, though it was not generally known, nor was it read at the trial, for reasons of public decency. Mr Cox, after all, was not on trial. Nor was it made public the various scientific remedies my fiancé undertook from the point of our engagement – principally chloride of mercury and quicksilver, of which, by the day of our joining in holy wedlock, Mr Cox's cumulative dosage exceeded a pound a day. The most noticeable effect of this valiant regimen was that my husband's gums turned purple, while his breath assumed an odour I shall not describe. As well, by the time of our nuptials, Mr Cox had turned quite plump, and had acquired a delightfully childlike sense of humour. At dinner, he would pull chairs from under his guests to general amusement, or he would stand up suddenly and in a loud voice declare himself an onion. These antics my father enjoyed greatly. After the unpleasantness at school, of which you seem to be acquainted, he considered himself fortunate to acquire a son-in-law of Mr Cox's rank. And besides, my husband gave exceedingly good dinners.

'Less scientific, perhaps, was Mr Cox's adherence to the still-common belief that the disease might be cured through sexual conversation with a virgin. Nor was this brought to the public eye – again for reasons of decency. For as you are no doubt aware, a husband who knowingly and wilfully infects his wife commits no crime. Am I proceeding too fast for you, Mr Whitty? You do not seem to be taking notes.'

Touché again, Mrs Marlowe.

Of course there is no point in writing any of it down, since none of it will pass the Chancellor. Whitty none the less maintains an aspect of calm confidence. 'I am, Madam, aware of such a belief. A product of that savage time in human history when children were sacrificed on Waterloo Bridge.'

'And what do you do with your spilled salt, Mr Whitty? And what is your opinion of a black cat? Fortunately for the blushing bride, another common symptom of my husband's disease was impotence – which frustrated Mr Cox considerably, and which he treated with the afore-mentioned Fowler's Solution. Indeed, so eager was he to consummate our marriage, at times he took nearly a teaspoon, which would have been fatal in itself for someone less accustomed to its use.'

'An intriguing narrative, Madam. Yet, as I am given to understand, a search was undergone following his demise, with no Fowler's Solution found on the premises.'

'Are you familiar with the incidental effects of arsenic, Mr Whitty? Skin disorders. Anaemia. Boils and swelling in the loins. Wart-like appearances all over the body. Vomiting. Flatulence. Hardly an erotic prospect for the new bride – but then, as Mr Acton points out, the respectable woman is devoid of such feelings, is that not true, Sir?'

'May I say, Madam, you have a charming and baroque way of avoiding questions which you do not wish to answer.'

'Who made the bottle disappear, you ask? I am surprised, Sir, I had thought you clever. Why, Henry did, of course. When he understood what had happened, when he divined the truth, he smashed it to pieces. My husband's little joke, don't you see. His childlike sense of humour.'

'Why on God's earth, Madam, would your dying husband do such a hideous thing?'

'Because his bride was not a virgin, Mr Whitty. Because the damned fool had poisoned himself for nothing.'

Whitty has no reply at hand. His notebook remains blank . . .

'Good evening, Mr Whitty. I trust that my fiancée has kept you entertained.'

Ryan.

The speaker has situated his entrance so that Whitty must turn awkwardly in his chair, thereby exposing his back to Mrs Marlowe. Again, the correspondent experiences the sensation of playing a part in a performance.

'Good-day, Mr Ryan.' Whitty addresses the handsome, haggard gentleman as though his appearance were a minor and not unpleasant surprise. 'I am glad to see you up and about.'

'Thank you, Sir.' Ryan places the pistol on the table and sits. 'How did you know where to find me? And what do you hope to accomplish, now that you have?'

28

The Haymarket

It is not an uncommon practice for a gentleman, in seeking to purchase the favours of a lady, to do so under an assumed name; indeed, it may not be an exaggeration to suggest that it is a rare gentleman who does otherwise. The names chosen for such an alias might someday make a potential area for academic study.

In such a study, Reginald Harewood would belong to that category of gentleman who adopts a new cognomen for each encounter, out of an impulsive need for novelty and variety, not to mention the innate caution shared by all Harewood men.

Hence, it is no great wonder that Reginald Harewood chose to pursue his flirtation with Dorcas under a name other than his own; what stands out as unusual in this particular is that on this occasion the name he produced as his own was the name of his good friend Roo.

He will never know why he did such a thing. Upon receiving the girl's not-unexpected enquiry, the name 'Roo' sprang forth all on its own. A slip of the tongue, a human error – one which cannot be subsequently amended, for that is the way it is with pseudonyms.

In any case, the situation is not without its poetic aspect: Reginald Harewood, boffing a girl in his friend's rooms, in his friend's bed, in his friend's name, as if Sewell were losing his virginity by proxy . . .

– *You talk improper, Mr Roo.*
– *Mr Roo, you old beast, let me go.*
– *I must go home, Mr Roo, or I'll catch it.*
– *What is the matter Mr Roo? You're all red.*
– *I cannot do that, Mr Roo. My sister would catch me.*

Although wildly out of her element at a Mayfair address, Dorcas takes care not to stare about, for she would rather the gentleman think she is accustomed to such luxury, that such places are nothing special to her. Instead of trying out the furniture as she wants to, she lolls indifferently upon the soft bed and smells the clean linen. She longs to look at herself in a mirror, but the room has none – strange for a gentleman's room not to have a mirror, how does he keep his whiskers so perfect? Still, the dark mahogany wainscoting has been waxed to such a shine that she may see her reflection almost as clearly as though it were a looking-glass.

He is stroking the nape of her neck, to which Dorcas responds in the mahogany reflection with seeming indifference: 'What did you take me all the way here for, Mr Roo? Always before you was happy with it done in the carriage.'

'My blossom, I wanted to be with you where nobody can hear us, and where we cannot be disturbed. For I am much taken with you, even if I am a bit cross. Why did you not come to meet me in Leicester Square yesterday as we agreed?'

'I was ill yesterday. I drank too much spiced gin and ate too much sugar and cakes. I lied down in the afternoon.'

'Are you sure you were not with somebody else? A pretty girl like you must receive many attractive offers from gentlemen.'

'I only gets money from you. From nobody else. I'm not that sort of girl. I'm not gay and I have never before done things like you have me do. Never once.' She does it for him because he is so handsome and so clean, and such fun, and because if she refused, then he would find someone else, and that would end the game, and there would be nothing left for her to do but to sit in the Crown and drink what little gin she can afford and wait for someone else. Yet there remain things she will not do for a man until he is her husband, for she is not that sort of girl.

'Here is a golden sovereign, my darling. That comes to twenty shillings. I swear you shall have every bit of it, if you will only let me do the other. Please?'

It makes her feel strong when he begs her for it. She touches the gold coin he holds between his fingers as though it were a piece of jewellery. 'Oh, no. I ain't going to do that, Mr Roo. You try to make me and I'll scream.'

'You can scream all you like, by Heaven, for there is nobody to hear you.'

'Then I will go where there is someone who can.' Whereupon, to Harewood's surprise, she abruptly gets off the bed and marches to the door, and with some determination; he has to move quickly in order to place himself between her and escape.

'Forgive me, my dear, that was wretched of me and I am so terribly sorry. That I could say such a thing! You do not know your own power, my dear, you have a way about you that brings out the beast in a man. I am utterly at your mercy – O Dorcas, don't you like me even a little bit?'

'I likes you well enough and I will do some things for you, but if you become a beast and try the other then I will fight you off and scream out the window and you will be in trouble.'

'My darling, I swear that I shall be as good as gold.' He holds her tenderly in his arms for a long moment (she can smell the scent he has put in his whiskers), until he can feel her relax against him; now, drawing her back into the room and onto the bed, he takes out a second coin and holds it beside the first. 'What if I gave you *two* golden sovereigns?'

She stares at the gold coins, more money than she is likely to see in a year, then pushes them away.

'I won't. That much is no good to me anyway.'

'Why is that?'

'My sister would know what I did for it. Already my sister is onto me with hints all the time, she knows I kiss you and suspects the rest that I do. Whatever you give me, if I cannot drink and eat it away, it's no good to me. You stop! Take your hand away from there!'

'Dorcas, is that what you've been doing with the money?'

'I already told you as much. It is why I was sick yesterday.'

'What is it you eat? Where do you go?

'I eats things my guardian cannot buy, though he works hard for what we has. Pies. And sausage-rolls – oh, my eye, ain't they prime! And I take a cab and sit and look out while it goes through Mayfair while I eats them, and then I have spiced gin at the Crown where we first met.'

'These two sovereigns would buy wonderful food for all three of you – for quite some time.'

'It don't matter. They would know what I did and would not eat it.'

'You can wrap a sovereign in a piece of paper, make it muddy, and say you found it in the street.'

'That might go past my guardian, but my sister is more clever. Once she seen me come out of the carriage after being with you, putting my clothes right, and I was hard pressed for an excuse . . .'

He sits closer to her and savours her intoxicating natural scent, nothing like perfume. As a child living in the country he once hid in a haystack, from which position he watched a stallion mount a mare. They hobbled her feet so that she would not kick the other and do serious damage, while he snorted and roared like a man in the greatest pain. Though confused by the spectacle, it was not lost on him that something extreme was taking place – frightening and painful, and yet, to go by the faces of the men in attendance and the cries of the horses, stimulating for all concerned . . .

'Get your hand out of there, I told you! Don't do that you beast, I'll scream!'

'Please, Dorcas, let me do it! It won't hurt a bit, in fact it will feel jolly good, and I will give you the coins and some shillings extra.'

'I already done enough, Mr Roo. Has any other girls done what I done with you already?'

'At least a dozen.'

'Lor'!'

'In good society, this happens as a matter of course, by the time a girl is fourteen. If you and I were in society we could do it all we want and it would not be unusual.'

'Even in the wealthy classes? Does girls of the quality do it?'

'A girl among the well-to-do classes who bothers to hold onto her virginity does so only in order to command a higher price.'

'How you talk, Mr Roo! Then they are but dollymops.'

'Love removes all social distinctions, my dear. Can you not see that, Dorcas? Look about you: With so many rooms available for hire in the city, would a gentleman such as myself invite a girl into his own private rooms if he did not hold her in the highest esteem? If he did not love her very, very much?'

At this she falters, for she has not the vocabulary to argue with him. 'That may be true and may be not . . .'

In her confused state of mind, she does not notice his hands at work until he has her in a fever and what is going to happen is going to happen, even though she does not know precisely what it will be.

She has surrendered! He has won!

Reginald Harewood reflects upon the advantages in bringing a girl to a room of one's own – that he then has the time to bring her over to his way of thinking, and then he can enjoy her cries fully, in the certainty that no one will hear them but himself. Her expressions of pain upon his entering her caused him inexpressible pleasure, and he spent almost immediately. Now they are lying together under the sheet as though they were lovers, while he kisses away her tears to silence her whimpering (*You've done for me now, Mr Roo, I'm undone for certain!*), and an all too familiar uneasiness begins to creep over him, which he knows will grow, until one day it will be too much to bear . . .

With affecting naivety, now she begs him to take her away, swears she would live alone in a room if he would see her but once a month. Momentarily his uneasiness verges on remorse, but this too passes, giving way to a general anaesthesia, with hardly a tinge of any feeling in particular.

Now comes a slight distaste. He reflects upon the knowledge that she will spend the money he gives her to gorge herself with food, will use his tribute to her beauty to become fat and pasty, like the pies she consumes; that her breasts, now so firm and delicious, will take on an unappetizing, mealy consistency, like pears that have missed their season.

> Gather ye rosebuds while ye may,
> Old Time is still a-flying:
> And this same flower that smiles today
> Tomorrow will be dying.

The Grove of the Evangelist

Seated opposite at the tea-table, manifestly debilitated by loss of blood (and open to death by blood-poisoning), William Ryan presides over the meeting by virtue of his pistol, a .44 calibre by Nock if Whitty is not mistaken, of the type known as an 'overcoat pistol' and common to officers in the Royal Navy.

'I did not know you served in the Navy, Mr Ryan.'

'Another example of your clairvoyant powers, Mr Whitty?'

'No. Your pistol is Navy issue.'

'Is it, now? Pure luck, in actual fact. I borrowed a coat from a party, stuck my hand in the pocket, and there it was.'

Whitty remains unperturbed by the pistol, reasoning that if he has not been poisoned then he is unlikely to be shot. 'The existence of an advantage depends not upon what is present, but upon what will come next. While the machine at your disposal confers an unassailable advantage at present, other machines mean certain doom later on.'

'How so?' asks Mr Ryan, picking up the pistol and if to examine it.

Says Mrs Marlowe, 'I am curious about those other machines.'

'As an example, the electric telegraph.'

'I had thought the electric telegraph an instrument of communication, not a weapon.'

'And yet, what communication it offers! Since the beginning of time, the maximum distance anything might cover – whether a man or a word – was that which could be accomplished on horseback. A fugitive on a fast horse – or, better yet, a fast train – could flee his pursuers indefinitely. But with the telegraph, information is instantaneous and the world is the size of London.' So says Whitty, striving to recall Sala's excellent rhetoric on the topic. 'As a fugitive you will never outrun your name, Sir. Wherever you go, your past will await you, in every station, every dockyard, every constabulary in Britain.'

Whitty can discern Ryan's quick breathing, the rattle within; clearly the man is not getting his health at all. Desire, not biology, is keeping him in the game. But desire for what? For vindication? Revenge? Mrs Marlowe?

The latter, in all probability. The correspondent discerns an uncommon heat in the way they gaze at one another.

'I had not thought of fearing that, Sir.'

'But you must, Mr Ryan, include it in your plans. Assuming that you recover; assuming that you venture farther than the back garden . . .'

Mrs Marlowe interrupts: 'What is your reason for relating this information, Sir? I had not taken you for a scientist. Surely you have something in mind, other than to provide a reason for it to be Mr Whitty who remains in the back garden.'

She sits back, exchanging with Mr Ryan a smile of mutual understanding. Whitty feels an unwelcome chill. That was not the understanding he sought.

'Let us be candid: I am not suicidal. I notified a colleague of my intended destination, with the proviso that he should contact the police should I fail to return. But even absent that precaution, surely such precipitous action is against your own interests: why should I have placed myself in the present position, were I not confident that I can be of use to you? Before you embark upon your brief, doomed elopement, will you entertain an alternate course of action?'

'What be your suggestion?' Ryan places the pistol upon the table.

'Give yourself up to the police. Reassert your innocence, with the support of *The Falcon*.'

'In a pig's eye, Sir. Go to Hell.'

'How predictable, Mr Ryan. You would rather drown than accept a life-line.'

After a tactical pause, the correspondent performs his standard speech in overcoming the reluctance of a potential source: the power of the press, etc., its capacity to right wrongs, exculpate the wrongfully accused, etc., etc., the moral weight of posterity, etc., etc., etc . . .

'Mr Ryan, in your cell at Coldbath Fields you declared an overriding intention to protect a certain lady from harm, that your lack of a defence in determining your guilt or innocence had a chivalrous origin. May I be so bold as to assume the lady in question to be present in this room?'

'You may, Sir. Die for her I would, and without regret.'

Mrs Marlowe's cheeks flush slightly as he covers her hand with his.

Mrs Button has appeared with hot water to add to the tea; having witnessed the previous exchange, she raises one eyebrow approximately a quarter of an inch.

'What harm might come to me, my dear, that has not happened already?' enquires Mrs Marlowe.

'My love, I wonder if you might leave Mr Whitty and me for a moment, to discuss this delicate matter. Only a moment, I promise you.'

'Very well, William, but if there's something I ought to know . . .' At a warning look from Ryan she stops in mid-sentence. 'Excuse me please, Gentlemen.'

Mrs Marlowe exits the room with a troubled aspect; her little woman like a shadow, following close behind.

Whitty takes a sip of his cold tea. 'I assume, Mr Ryan, that the lady views you as something other than a murderer evading the just outcome of his misdeeds, or a coward who permits others to die while he savours his dubious freedom.'

'No, Sir, for I am nothing of the kind. No woman has ever died by my hand.'

'And Mrs Marlowe believes you? You are a charming and persuasive man if I may say so, Sir.'

'To this I swear on my honour and before God.'

'Quite. Allow me to appeal to your honour then, such as it is. Have you given any thought to the notion that, if you are not Chokee Bill, someone else is?'

'Indeed I have, Mr Whitty. It is the police who have placed innocent women in peril by pegging me for it.'

'But now, Sir, you are not without influence in this. Mr Ryan, do not underestimate the power of the Fourth Estate. Your escape, while a doomed prospect in itself, provides you with an opportunity of public vindication, and all that follows. The opportunity to live in freedom, with the woman you claim to love. I suggest to you that a man who would refuse such an offer is a liar, a coward, a murderer, or all three.'

Ryan grows thoughtful. Weariness overtakes him. His handsome features have turned the colour of stucco. 'I shall think upon what you say, Sir. I shall give you an answer presently. I am not yet fit for a stay in Newgate I am afraid.'

Indeed, thinks the correspondent, you would not last a night in that fine institution.

'Mr Whitty, assuming we enter into some sort of arrangement – and I do not admit to this – I insist that anything you write or do on my behalf must exclude any mention of Mrs Marlowe's name, history, or current employment.'

Whitty agrees to this easily, for few of Mrs Marlowe's particulars would pass the Lord Chamberlain.

'Nor may you inform Mrs Marlowe of our arrangement, for she is a proud woman.'

'You have my word of honour. In return, may I invite you to reveal the name of the gentleman you and your murdered accomplice attempted to swindle.'

'I shall not.'

'For the protection of a lady, no doubt.'

'Because I have reason to believe that the gentleman in question is the Fiend in Human Form.'

'Quite.'

Whitty can hardly contain his excitement at the emerging outline, an assembly of narrative fragments which combine into a stunner of the first water.

A condemned murderer executes a daring escape from the most modern prison in England. Metropolitan Police are at a loss. After a period of public alarm and at the daring behest of a prominent member of the press, our man surrenders, still resolutely proclaiming his innocence – which claim gains weight by his surrender. The correspondent eloquently takes up the challenge, sowing doubt as to the guilt of the condemned man, together with hints of a conspiracy to conceal the Fiend's true identity. Editorials appear. Questions in Parliament. London is a-twitter.

As the execution date approaches, the public devours each successive report on the case. The correspondent is the focus of a *cause célèbre* which reaches a shuddering climax on the day of the hanging.

At which point the true Fiend is brought forward. Or not, as the case may be.

Most likely, Ryan is hanged. Whitty has not forgotten Mr Hollow's description of Ryan (over the most dreadful meal he has ever eaten) as an unregenerate scoundrel who should have been hanged a dozen times already had justice prevailed.

Any journal in London would pay a considerable sum for this. Prepare the presses, Sala! Open the coffers, Dinsmore! Look upon your rival, Fraser, and weep!

Having accomplished that which he set out to achieve, Whitty takes his leave of William Ryan and proceeds down the hall, there to encounter his hostess as she emerges from a room whose door is ajar just enough to afford the correspondent a momentary, unwelcome glimpse of an elderly gentleman in a woman's corset.

After a murmured good-day from Mrs Marlowe and an inscrutable nod from the widow at her elbow, then having retrieved his hat and stick from the liveried footman, Whitty rejoins Owler across the road, positioned as Whitty left him over an hour ago, his sandwich-board proclaiming a Most Sanguinary Outrage of the Laws of Humanity.

Despite the damp and chill of late afternoon (it is raining again), despite the weight of the murderous menu he carries, Owler has remained as watchful as a Beefeater on duty. Not for the first time is the correspondent struck by the man's tolerance of discomfort.

Whitty, for his part, is in a state of preoccupation. Notwithstanding the heady elation that accompanies a potential triumph, he is bothered by the same curious unease that disturbed his equanimity upon entering the Grove of the Evangelist: that somebody's plan is proceeding perfectly; that somehow he is performing as somebody expects.

'And what were the situation as to the fugitive, Sir?'

'Though I don't quite have the particulars, fundamentally it is as suspected: Mr Owler, our man is within.'

'Lord dismiss us. We must go to the constabulary at once.'

'I beg your pardon?' With a cigar and a lit lucifer poised in mid-air, Whitty watches in astonishment as Owler makes for the corner. 'Where are you going, Sir? What the deuce do you intend to do?'

Owler turns at the corner of Foley Street; in his sandwich-board he resembles a walking door: 'Sir, is there any question? There is a murderer in that house!'

Whitty catches up to the patterer near Langham Place and what remains of Lord Foley's gardens, there to restrain Owler with the crook of his walking-stick, for our man must be set right at once.

'Mr Owler, I insist: contrary to what you propose, we must leave Mr Ryan exactly where he is.'

'But Mr Whitty, Sir, to harbour a murderer is akin to the act itself.'

'Oh, the deuce, Owler! Are you an aspiring clergyman? Your life is awash in petty crime. You and your charges should not survive but for fraud and theft.'

'That is a sin we commit to live, not out of greed.'

'Surely you are not serious.'

'I wonder the same of you, Sir. A man has naught without his honour.'

Whitty removes his flask from his pocket and drinks, unprepared to discuss honour with one of the costermonger class. From their position on the corner, the two men watch while a running footman appears from the direction of Great Portland Street at full tilt and proceeds to the Grove of the Evangelist, whose door he raps with the end of his long stick. Mrs Marlowe's formidable servant opens the door and the two footmen compare livery while a mustard-coloured chariot with a trail of liveri ed servants comes to a stop at the kerb, another footman opens the carriage door, and none other than the Earl of Claremont enters the establishment.

In the meanwhile, Whitty attempts another line of reasoning. 'There is one other particular that you should know: as you are aware, our man claims innocence. And there are facts which support his claim.'

'What facts might those be, Sir?'

'I am not permitted to reveal them at this time. It is a major scandal, I assure you.' Whitty sighs inwardly: how he wishes he were able to lie, comfortably! His colleagues do it without a qualm – indeed, with pleasure!

On the other hand, thinks Whitty: well at least it has brought Owler to heel.

'And you give credit to such a thing, Mr Whitty, Sir?'

'Indeed, I view it extremely seriously. New information has surfaced which casts doubt on the validity of his conviction. If he returns to prison now, England might hang an innocent man.'

'I am thunderstruck at this.'

'So am I, Mr Owler. In the meanwhile, Mr Ryan has sworn on his honour to remain on the premises. Upon his recovery he has agreed to permit *The Falcon* to escort him to the Metropolitan Police for a scene of unexampled drama.'

'Mr Whitty, I have in my time dealt with over two dozen condemned men; and hardly one went to the scaffold believing he killed a soul – even after confessing it.'

Whitty wonders what British justice might look like should such faith infect the Chancery at Lincoln's Inn Fields. 'Indeed, Sir, I grant that the British judicial system is without equal. Yet surely you must see that if we turn our man over to the constabulary, and he continues to be presumed guilty, then our story is, as you might put it, coopered.'

'Werily, Sir, but the man *is* guilty – that is the facts as they stand. For ourselves, seeking our own profit, to permit the Fiend to run loose – or even run the chance of such – and I a father with two girls? The thought is not to be entertained.'

Whitty's eyes roll upward. 'Dear Jesus.'

'I ask you not to take the Lord's name in vain.'

His patience worn past endurance, the correspondent extends this humiliating bluff to its limit: 'Sir, in the first place, our man is severely injured and can barely walk, let alone stalk the streets with a view to murder. In addition, allow me to reveal that, before we came here I secured permission at the highest level for the course of action we are about to undertake. The highest level, Sir.' So saying, Whitty places his finger beside his nose, indicating he must say no more.

30

The Falcon

The office appears precisely as Whitty left it after the previous request for funds, as though in suspension, as though even the cigars between the sub-editors' teeth have maintained their length.

More stifling than the ever-present smoke is the atmosphere of stale contempt Whitty knows he will encounter, whatever he proposes. With his lacklustre record of return for advances, he might produce proof that the Queen were a Jewess, a Negro or a male in disguise and still it would be greeted with close-fisted indifference by Dinsmore's college of ha'penny-clerks.

'A Ryan exclusive would indeed be a coup,' agrees the Editor. 'Yet I don't see how we can advance you on it, old chap.' Sala rolls his eyes in the direction of Dinsmore with a long-suffering wink. 'You haven't delivered *The Falcon* anything on the Inquiry into the State of Girls' Fashionable Schools, nor have you produced one instance of a wife putting rat poison in her husband's soup. Petty I know, but there it is.'

'Nor has Mr Whitty favoured us with his sensational series on the relationship between a condemned murderer, a patterer and a woman of low repute,' adds Dinsmore, like a mortician inserting a tube.

Sala cleans his monocle, scowling at the correspondent from within his beard. Replacing the instrument, he executes a rueful, apologetic shrug. 'It's a rum business, old chap, money and all that – but that is the way of it. Speaking of money, Edmund, what on earth do you do with it all?'

'Much research has been required at considerable overhead.' Indeed, this last declaration approaches the truth. Between the sum owed to Mr Bigney and the money sent by post to the Captain to keep his brutes at bay, the correspondent has barely the price of his dinner.

And so to work.

Whitty executes an elaborate sigh as though at the chore of having to explain that which is obvious, seating himself, not upon Sala's precarious wreck of a stool but upon the edge of Dinsmore's desk, which presumption inspires much throat-clearing from the sub-editor and his college of crows.

'Gentlemen, I invite you to make like truffle pigs while I put the facts

187

under your nose one by one. I have demonstrated the possibility of a connection between William Ryan, the convict known as Chokee Bill, and the Cox case. Which connection has *everything* to do with the Inquiry into Girls' Fashionable Schools, because that is precisely the institution at which the outrage occurred. In addition, I have produced the figure of Mrs Cox – a woman with only a Not Proven verdict between herself and the gallows. And I have produced the prospect of an exclusive interview with William Ryan.'

'A strong beginning, Edmund. Yet not a word has issued from your pen. Nothing beyond the occasional social snipe from your London clubman persona, together with a series of dark warnings, gathering clouds and all that sort of shite.'

'Sir, would you expect me to post a narrative while the denouement awaits?'

Contributes Dinsmore: 'Whitty, you're like a man drawing upon one account to pay for the next. Sooner or later the game is up, Sir.'

'Try to comprehend, gentlemen, that while you sit at your desks awaiting news of the outside world, it is my duty to enter that world. This is what a correspondent does. I don't write stories, I find them – otherwise what would *The Falcon* print? With what would you occupy yourselves, if it were not for wretches such as myself, groping blindly for the truth? What the deuce would you *do*?'

The Editor lights the reeking end of a cigar, the better to distract himself from the discomfort of conversing in this tone to a former friend and classmate – and himself a former correspondent, besides. What a lot of formers we acquire in life! And how they come back to discomfit us!

'Gentlemen, may I be allowed to speak from my humble corner?'

Dinsmore has been waiting for his opportunity, for there is nothing he resents more than the Editor's friendship with the most overrated journalist in London.

'Whitty, *The Falcon* finds it troubling that, whenever you come in with one of your so-called stunners, it happens to coincide with a financial emergency of some sort.'

'You do me an injustice, Sir. Nothing could be further from the truth.'

'If one may be so bold, Sir, there exists an issue of credibility. When a somewhat erratic – though of course brilliant – correspondent approaches one's desk claiming to have a confidential connection with the Fiend in Human Form . . .'

Adds Whitty: 'As well as a sensational exposé of the system that set him loose. Do not omit the broad context.'

'In any case, it all rests on whether said correspondent in fact *has* contacted the Fiend in Human, don't you see?'

It has come to this.

'I understand now, Gentlemen. You doubt my word. That is the case, is it not? You suggest that my report is a . . . a *cock*.' Whitty tries to approximate the level of indignation displayed by Owler under a similar circumstance. 'Mr Sala, I regret that I must herewith post my resignation.'

'*The Falcon* accepts,' says Dinsmore, with glee.

'Easy now, Gentlemen,' cautions the Editor. 'This begs the fecking question.'

'As for the first instalment, Sir, allow me to withdraw it. I shall take it immediately to Reynolds, who has expressed keen interest.'

Sala removes his cigar in order to consider the possibility of a bluff. 'You wouldn't go to Reynolds, would you, Edmund?'

'I must, Algernon. I have lost the confidence of *The Falcon*.'

'Was that your inference, Dinsmore? I did not think so.' The Editor's tone does not offer the sub-editor a choice of reply.

Having called Whitty's bluff, and having his own bluff called in return, Dinsmore purses his lips as though passing lemon seeds. 'I should be distressed if Mr Whitty were to think me disrespectful of his brilliant work. If Mr Whitty's discovery should produce crisp copy, I should not hesitate to offer a stipend upon inspection.'

'On inspection? I say, what a devastating insult!'

Sala winces as though pained by the meanness of it all. 'Dinsmore, that does seem rather hard. Clearly Mr Whitty has not managed his funds well – the creative mind rarely does.'

Replies Dinsmore to the Editor: 'If the result is as I fear, then you shall be held accountable.'

'This man is our best correspondent. He must live on something. Edmund, what do you say to a guinea now and the rest upon inspection, as a show of good faith.'

'That is not satisfactory, Algernon. I need two guineas now and eight upon inspection.'

'Very well. Two guineas and eight upon inspection.'

Whereupon the correspondent promptly produces the first instalment (which he completed the previous night) and tosses it upon the Editor's desk. At the rate he is going, he could keep the ratters at bay for months.

Algernon Sala adjusts his monocle and scans the first page.

'Dinsmore, you'd better have a look at this.'

'Ten guineas, please,' says Whitty, smiling, holding out his hand.

ESCAPED MURDERER CLAIMS INNOCENCE
EVIDENCE MOUNTS

by

Edmund Whitty, Correspondent
The Falcon

Since the escape of William Ryan, the convicted murderer known as 'Chokee Bill', excitement has risen almost to the level of the garrotting terror which seized London prior to his capture. Were it known that a Bengal tiger were at large in Piccadilly, the reaction could be no more severe, so freely has terror blossomed anew in the public mind.

Given the opportunism rampant in these times, it will come as no surprise that the various journals comprising the cultural landscape of the city have made the murders a prime object, in their determined quest for an enhanced financial return. Even so, once the initial arrest of Mr Ryan took effect, we note the ease with which London chose to declare the subject closed. In a stroke, all questions about the gruesome murders were declared answered, and even the fevered voice of *The Illustrated London News* turned its attention to a thumb-twiddler on Mr William Acton, as though the habit of self-abuse among youngsters were equivalent to the murder of helpless women.

And yet the question remains: Does the arrest of Mr Ryan truly fulfil the demands of the evidence gathered by the constabulary – all of the evidence? If so, why has the constabulary not come forward with a complete accounting – commonalties of the method of killing, witnesses in the areas where the killings took place, the observations of acquaintances – thereby assuring the public that every one of these appalling acts can be explained through the mind and actions of one William Ryan?

To what may we ascribe this unwillingness among the gentlemen of the press to do their duty as the dissecting room of English morality? What has rendered them so squeamish?

We who are not squeamish must take up the scalpel of truth with which to cut the skin, to lay bare the muscles, to probe and to penetrate, to see all – even to the grinning skull!

AN OPEN LETTER TO WILLIAM RYAN

Edmund Whitty,
Offices of *The Falcon*,
Ingester Square, London.

Mr William Ryan,
At Large

Dear Sir,

A man flees from prison for one of two reasons: if guilty, it is because he
fears the truth; if innocent, it is because he despairs of the truth's emerging.

Evidence has come to my attention supporting your claim of innocence,
and *The Falcon* has determined to take up your cause. Only your fugitive
circumstance stands between you and the truth upon which you claim to
stand.

I challenge you, Sir, to throw yourself upon the mercy of the British People, the
conscience of the Metropolitan Police, and the courage of the British Press.

I remain, Sir, your most obedient servant,

Edmund Whitty,
The Falcon

'That ought to hold their interest, Gentlemen,' says the Editor.

'It is tolerable,' replies Dinsmore.

Someday the correspondent will enter the office with explosives
covering his body: upon hearing the word 'tolerable', he will release the
switch and level the building.

Adds Sala: 'It depends, old chap, on what you have waiting in the
wings. *Do* you have something in the wings, Edmund?'

'The future looms before me like the dome of St Paul's.'

'On a foggy night.' The Editor holds a lucifer to his stump of cigar,
producing an aroma of burnt whisker. 'Assuming that we commit *The
Falcon* to your Quixotic quest, may I ask where you intend to proceed?'

'If I knew that, Algernon, I should be writing fiction like Boz.'

'No need to get shirty about it, old boy. We trust your judgement –
is that not so, Mr Dinsmore?'

The sub-editor, immersed in a copy of *Lloyd's*, reserves the option to
declare himself strenuously opposed, in case circulation fails to meet
expectations.

It has been a while since Whitty has carried so much weight in his purse, yet he does not proceed directly to his chemist. That is because he truly smells a stunner worthy of further investment. Hence, after putting money aside with which to ward off the ratters, he has requested the additional services of Mr Bigney. (Such being the disparity of their social positions, only prior remuneration will maintain the engraver in the correspondent's service.)

Hence, upon concluding his business in the office, he makes his way directly to the rear of the building and down the stair to the engraver's steamy, inky, metallic domain.

In a small storage room, sheltered somewhat from the shattering noise of the presses, Mr Bigney counts the proffered money in one blackened hand, the palm a lighter shade like the palm of a Negro. 'I see, matey, yor explorations has borne fruit as anticipated.'

'I admit that your material has attracted mild interest.'

'Mild, is it? Then prick up your ears for what is to come.'

'Never mind your dramatics, what do you have?'

'For one, I have the "undisclosed location" of the Fiend in Human.'

'So do I. You will have to do better than that.'

'Oh, to be sure there be more to tell.'

'What is it about to cost me?'

'A guinea and it's yors.'

'For that price it should implicate the Royals.'

'There be an inference in the reports as to certain deceased women of low repute, what led to suspicion as how the Chokee Bill killings never stopped altogether, but that the crushers be under pressure not to make the link.'

'What sort of pressure?'

'The merchant class, possibly – who suffer a loss every time Madame Tweedle and Lord Dum refrain from visiting the city. The curious thing of it is, even those as know the victims keep mum on it out of the same concern.'

'That would seem a short-sighted policy.'

'As long as the victims is members of the excess female population, the price of peace don't seem too high. That is the thing don't you see: the oppressed co-operate with their oppressors, being also in business for themselves.'

'I suppose it becomes a choice between the murder of a few or the starvation of the many.'

'Very good, matey. Yor must save that line for a good cut. That is how we does business, is it not? I supplies the meat, yor gives the cut.'

'I say, Mr Bigney, you make me out to be some sort of butcher.'

'There is a shortage of English butchers, so I am hearing. A pity, with such a surfeit of fat meat at Westminster, oinking and ready for the chopper.

> 'When the levers of power is master'd,
> And the slaughter-house houses a Pope;
> We shall see the baronial bastard
> Kick heels with his throat in a rope.'

The correspondent thinks on Bigney's inflammatory doggerel as he makes his way up the cellar-way with its attendant smell of ink and earth, into the narrow alleyway and thence to Ingester Square. A plausible narrative indeed. The existence of a tactical, self-interested silence among the merchant class and its official lap-dogs of London goes some distance to explaining the under-inspector's violent response to an unexceptional piece of speculation: that the line of enquiry leads to mortifying revelations concerning the Metropolitan Police . . .

'Do what you like for a penny, Sir? For I am a nice clean girl.'

The whore is seated under the forlorn scrap of a tree. Her smile is a young girl's approximation of seductiveness. She might be no more than fourteen, yet her face has already begun to show premature lines and the pinched look that comes of tensing against the cold. Her hair and face are drab and common; an unusual mark on her upper lip imparts a slightly foreign quality to her demeanour, which might please some. Certainly she receives little assistance from her cast-off, once-stylish clothing; her little hat appears horribly dirty and, worse, ridiculous.

Whitty can remember a time when such was his despair that he might have put a few pennies to such base use. However, with a little learning and a functioning imagination one becomes bleakly resistant to the lure of such tatterdemalion romance. Gazing upon the figure before him, he feels only the vicarious despair of a fortune-teller who sees death in an expectant palm, as he envisages the creature she will surely become, wandering Hyde Park after nightfall, consenting, for the sake of a few shillings, to practices which gratify men of morbid or diseased imagination.

Is anything less sexually exciting than pity?

Rendering matters more uncomfortable, the young woman mistakes the correspondent's not unfriendly regard for interest. She releases a button, though she has little enough to display beneath her bodice.

When she speaks she has a way of phrasing as though asking questions, a mannerism which comes of taking shallow breaths.

'That's a good gentleman. Sit beside me and I will show you a nice time. You will see.'

'What is your name, child?'

She bristles at the description. *Such dignity.* 'I ain't no child, am I? Done it more times than you.'

'I expect you are correct, Miss. I apologize. And your name?'

'It is Etta. Might you be Mr Whitty?'

'How did you know that?'

'I been waiting. An organ-grinder on Fleet Street? He fingered who you was. What wrote up the particulars. On Chokee Bill.'

'How did you come across it?'

'The fishmonger 'as read it to us in Covent Garden.'

'Was there something in the piece of particular interest?'

'Chokee Bill done for my benefactor. He done Flo. The Peelers as said so. They said Flo was the first since he scarpered.'

Thinks Whitty: If Ryan did for anyone since that night, then he was in better condition than he appeared.

'Are you certain, Etta?'

'So said the Peeler what found her. Excepting, Chokee Bill done my Flo while he were in gaol.'

Whitty sits beside her. At close quarters he examines her small face. Her skin smells of coal dust and gin (of which he undoubtedly smells himself). And there is another smell too, of the young girl that remains somewhere inside.

'Perhaps it was not Chokee Bill, Etta. Perhaps it was someone else.'

'They did not believe me either. When I told them it were while he were in gaol.'

'Do you mean the Peelers?'

'Aye.'

'When did you talk to them, Etta?'

'One week ago. On the morning they found her.'

'And they did not believe you?'

'No.'

He allows a silence for her to collect herself. After casting her gaze about the square, she resumes in a quiet voice, as though someone else may be listening.

'It is said he is a ghost. That prison cannot keep him.'

'Are you referring to his escape?'

'To tales previous. I heard as he comes out at night. And does girls. Prisons is nothing to Chokee Bill.'

Of course. Thus does the plague spirit continue to wander the streets, while witches spoil the crops and Jews steal away the children . . .

'Etta, I assure you that whoever did for your friend is a man, not a ghost.'

'Ghost or man, he should pay. She was good to me, was Flo. We was to meet, after work. And I sees her. The scarf twisted about her neck so cruelly. He didn't need to pull so hard. Nor did he need do that to her face.'

The girl frowns as though listening for something – or perhaps to picture the memory with greater clarity, like a valuable object given to her in trust.

'So I watched over her. Until the crusher found her, two days after.'

'Two days after? Please tell me more, Etta.'

'Mr Salmon? He takes the scarf off her. And gives it to me. "It is from Henry Poole's," says he. "You can get five shillings."'

'Mr Salmon the under-inspector?'

'Yes.'

'He did not wish to hold it as evidence?'

'He said as it was not needed.'

'And did you get five shillings for it, Etta?'

'I did not wish to sell it. I run after Mr Salmon and says to him how it done my benefactor, that it was before Chokee Bill escaped and how he should keep it. "Never mind," he says. "Take yourself out before you find yourself in the workhouse."'

She has begun to weep.

'What did you do with the scarf then, Etta?'

'I sold it. To eat and such. No good to me, was it? The keeper of Perkin's Rents was owed four shillings. And I have sold the rest of her things since. I cannot make my board the other way. Men doesn't want me. Unless for something I won't let them do.'

She weeps harder, huge sobs. The correspondent gives her his handkerchief with the instruction that she is to keep it.

'Times is altered for me since I came into the city. I wish I was dead, is the truth. I wish I was in my coffin.'

Whitty does not protest her sentiment. 'What other things did she have, Etta? Your benefactor?'

'The dresses and . . . such . . . and . . . and . . .'

'And?'

'And the things what she took.'

'Took from whom?'

'The gentleman. The young man's things? Of the quality, see. She as would lift things? For a joke mostly. A joke on the gentleman. The last few things gave her especial pleasure to have.'

'What were they, Etta, these things she saved?'

'A watch and ring. I sold them already.'

The deuce. Of course, he can hardly blame her.

'Excepting the flask. She took particular pleasure in it, so I will keep it in her memory. No matter what, I will not sell that.'

So saying, the girl produces from her skirts a silver flask, of a common type – indeed, Whitty owns something like it himself.

'I remembers when she got it. It was my first time. Flo had the handsome toff. And I the pudgy one? With the spectacles. Had to practically push me into the cab, Flo did, I was that scared. "Don't worry." she says. "Plant him a kiss. With the tip of your tongue? And you'll be on your way." '

Whitty gently takes the flask from the grimy little hand and turns it over: *Hallo.* A crest on the surface, of the kind that wealthy families commission to disguise their low beginnings. This example contains what might be Masonic symbols; by turning the object's surface in the gaslight, he can make out a surveyor's sextant.

Ah, the pungent aroma of scandal.

'Etta, I will give you five shillings for this flask, does that seem fair?' Indeed, it is twice what the piece is worth.

She dabs her eyes with Whitty's handkerchief. 'I cannot sell it. I will never sell it.'

'I am sorry, Miss. I meant no harm by the offer. Here, you may have five shillings anyway, with my compliments, for you are an admirable young woman despite your circumstances.'

He returns the flask with the cash. She twists the money in her fingers, embarrassed. 'Thank you, Sir. You are kind.'

'Have you thought of visiting a Refuge?'

'Too much preaching. I'd sooner starve.'

'I salute your good taste and your courage. Good luck to you.'

'Goodbye.'

She gets up and walks away, then turns back at the edge of the square. 'Mr Whitty, Sir?'

'What is it, Etta?'

'I may lend it to you. Flo said I may. Just now.'

Without another word she hands him the silver flask, and now hurries away across the square, to disappear down the narrow court, leaving him wondering how he will ever find her again to return it. How she might believe that, having partaken of the morals of the city, he will even bother to try.

3 1

Plant's Inn

Fraser is, as always, pontificating.

'Nothing justifies the natural physical dominance of men over women so much as the recent census. Mark, Gentlemen, that the city dweller lives longer than a country dweller, and that men live longer than women. And note the following: *City women live shorter lives even than country men!*'

Whitty did not enter Plant's to engage with Fraser's reactionary sophomorics and thereby contribute to *Dodd's*, yet he cannot resist. 'Well-simplified, Alasdair. Worthy of an idiot.'

'Not so simple as a correspondent who takes the part of an escaped murderer.'

'That was a presentable crack,' whispers Hicks of *Lloyd's* to Cobb of *The Illustrated London News*, pencils scratching on their laps.

The moment Whitty's first instalment appeared in the streets, pennies began to pour into the coffers of *The Falcon*, necessitating, by mid-week, an extra printing. The prospect of reading words from the mouth of an escaped murderer, with titillating references to poison and scandal, created an irresistible narrative; for no experienced reader of *The Falcon* doubted that a reason existed for the juxtaposition of these items – a way an editor has of intimating some fact which cannot be communicated by reason of public decency. Thus, thanks to censorship, what the correspondent withholds takes on greater value than that which is revealed.

As a result, Whitty's reception at Plant's is that mixture of envy and contempt with which all journalists acknowledge a more successful colleague.

'Well done, old chap,' ventures Hicks, employing the bar to remain upright. 'Not a cock, surely?'

'Question in Parliament,' adds Cobb. 'Thing has taken on a life of its own . . .'

'Of course Mr Whitty is fully in command.' Fraser arises to clap the correspondent's shoulder in comradely fashion. 'My sincere congratulations, Edmund.'

'Kind of you, Alasdair. Generous indeed.'

'Not at all, old chap. Credit where credit is due.' Fraser shows his little teeth, eyes glittering with feral bonhomie.

Why is Fraser smiling?

'Quite. Buy you a drink?'

'Don't mind if I do, Edmund. A drain of pale if you please, Humphrey.'

Whitty produces the borrowed silver flask. 'By the way, this was left at the club after whist the other night. Wonder if you might recognize the crest, popular as your opinions are with the upper classes.'

Fraser turns the flask in the light, then hands it back with a snort. 'Confound it, Whitty, thought you knew the fellow. Saw him with you some time ago, a 'classmate' you called him . . . It was after the Walden hanging I believe. You put on quite a performance that night, I must say.'

Whitty, finally, has come to remember all of that dreadful night, in mortifying clarity. The liberties taken with his publican and all that followed. And now, here before him, a scandal – with Reggie Harewood at the centre. It is at times like these that a journalist believes in the existence of God.

'Humour me, Alasdair. If you please, continue.'

Fraser turns to the barkeeper: 'A dram of malt, Humphrey.'

'You may put it on my account,' says Whitty.

After accepting his expensive whisky, Fraser continues. 'A family of land buyers and sellers, rent their holdings, made a medium fortune in the shadow of the Duke of Bedford. The old man, notorious skinflint, keeps a house near the park. The son you know – another precious Oxford sort, frequents the divans and the supper rooms off the Haymarket.'

'Yes of course. It all comes back to me now.' It does not. Other than that unfortunate evening, he knows precious little about either gentleman, the latter being gentlemen-commoners, for whom Oxford is not a university but a private gaming club. Hence, throughout Whitty's truncated academic career, they occupied quite another dimension in space and time.

Naturally averse to supplying information to an enemy, Fraser escapes to the rear snug with another whisky, leaving Whitty with the suspicion that our man's brief moment of congeniality served as cover for an attack already underway. To calm his stomach, he drains his ale and signals to the barkeeper, who gets up from his stool beneath the amber bottles, with a deep weariness in his jowls.

'Awfully generous, Mr Fraser, wouldn't you say, Humphrey?'

'Very generous indeed, Sir. Of course you are aware of the spoiler.'

A spoiler. Of course.

'Not entirely, Humphrey. Please refresh my memory, and my glass.' A half-crown rattles upon the deep chestnut surface, rubbed to a gloss.

'*Dodd's* seems chuffed about it apparently . . .' Glancing about the room, the barkeeper leans on the bar in such a way that the half-crown discreetly disappears beneath one hand. 'Before your arrival, Sir, Mr Fraser entertained the company on the prospect of a devastating riposte to yourself which he views with more than the usual satisfaction.'

Humphrey's gaze lifts to the party immediately behind the correspondent. 'Am I correct, Madam?'

'Like lobsters in a pot you lot are. One rises to the top, the rest pull him down to boil.'

Whitty turns to face the proprietress. 'Ah Mrs Plant. A bit of cookery advice is always welcome. A pleasure to see you.' Which is not in any way untrue.

'Watch your mouth, Mr Whitty,' replies the latter. 'I'll not abide sarcasm.'

'Madam, I could not be more sincere.'

'That is true. Sincerity is quite beyond you.'

Whitty sips his ale carefully, for he must keep his wits about him. The barkeeper retreats. Whitty's half-crown has disappeared.

She watches the correspondent sharply as he writes in his notebook; he deems it prudent to avoid her gaze by recording his conversation with Etta, while it is clear in his mind.

'Mr Whitty, is it true what you say about Chokee Bill? Or is it all a cock? I worry, for you have a tendency to gamble from a position of weakness . . .'

'Your concern is misplaced, Madam,' says Whitty. 'The situation is well in hand.'

'Two gentlemen were asking for you.'

'Excuse me?'

'Two gentlemen, neither of whom would be mistaken for members of the clergy. Parties of a type with which you seem over-acquainted.'

Blast. Whitty really must speak to the Captain, for the last remittance should have bought him at least a month's respite from the ministrations of his men. Unless this pertains to someone other than the ratters. For such is the double-edged sword of success: one becomes all the more visible to one's enemies, both known and unknown.

'I say, Edmund,' calls Fraser from his position in the centre of the room. 'If someone is catching up to you, I recommend that you request police protection.'

An unseemly chorus of laughter erupts from the table. Whitty is aware that Fraser has told a joke, but does not see the humour in it.

Outside Plant's Inn

The key to manoeuvring while drunk is to choose one's points of support, for a set of legs which serve reasonably well in motion can buckle of a sudden when called upon to remain upright and still at the same time. Therefore it is well to have a lamp-post or other stable object on hand at the right moment. By this rule of hand, or foot, Whitty totters down Tudor Street to Bouverie Lane on his way to the Strand, the most convenient throughway for locating a cab at this time of night.

Ryan or no Ryan, Chokee Bill is still at work – unless there are several Chokee Bills, an original and his imitators. That is the problem with whores – they provide opportunity and cover for any mimic with the desire to murder a woman.

Whoever Chokee Bill is, he is not William Ryan. This much seems certain . . .

Where am I? Whitty embraces a lamp-post, the better to regain his bearings, his sense of what is vertical and what is horizontal and what is in between.

Bracing himself in an upright position, he pushes firmly on the lamp-post, thereby securing sufficient forward momentum to propel his body down the street, while his feet move beneath him as though walking, as far as the succeeding lamp-post – to which he clings with the crook of one arm as though embracing a tall, narrow-shouldered acquaintance.

He covers an eye to avoid seeing double. He is at a doorway, at the end of a series of vaults called the Adelphi Arches, a succession of subterranean chambers leading through the embankment to the Strand. He remembers this doorway, for it was once the back exit of a notorious coffee- and gambling-house, where visitors were befriended by thieves, blacklegs and prostitutes, then swindled, drugged, thrown from the rear door into the darkness, and left to find their way home as best they could.

Whitty's recollection is distracted by the exclamations of a woman near the river, which echo off the stones. Curious, he stumbles down the embankment into what appears to be a stable, where the outspoken female, seated on the steps of a wagon, is engaged in an altercation with a cab owner – several of his vehicles are lying about – whom she claims to be her husband.

Notes the cab owner: 'Yer were common when ah met yer, lying as what you was, and is since the most drunken slut-hag what is possible to meet.'

Whereupon the woman brandishes something in his face made of paper, going so far as to slap his cheeks with what she triumphantly claims to be her marriage-lines.

Aware of the presence of a spectator, the womanly combatant turns abruptly to the correspondent: 'It don't matter if I were one of Lot's daughters afore. I don't say I wasn't. But I'm his wife now, and this 'ere is what licks 'em.'

Man and wife produce flasks of gin and toast their future together, reminding Whitty of the nostrum: *When drunk a Frenchman chatters; a German sleeps; an Englishman fights.*

He staggers onward, for to obtain a cab at this location is impossible. He is about to proceed back up the embankment when a coach slows on the road beside him, then comes to a halt. Perhaps it is black, or perhaps it is dark blue. In either case, Whitty is not aware of having signalled for transportation.

He gazes up at the driver, who is indistinct; Whitty's lips are somewhat numb, rendering his consonants indistinct.

'Ah good, my man. Evening to you. Most appreciated.'

'Evening, Guv. Where to, then?'

Whitty's right foot paws the step in an attempt to gain purchase. 'To Camden Town, Sir, that sour, frigid bitch of a community. Be in no haste, for I believe I shall avail myself of a brief nap.'

His foot finding the step at last, he propels himself in one motion, head first, into the open doorway of the carriage – where two men await. Or perhaps it is four. And a boot comes down. When he lifts his hand to his eye, the finger is bent in an unnatural direction.

The driver cracks his whip with an automatic flick of the wrist, and the carriage continues to Fleet Street and the Strand, thence to Piccadilly, to Regent Street, to Portland Place, around the park and back again, while the two gentlemen, or perhaps it is four, hammer the correspondent's flesh by means of neddies – or rather, two types of neddy, one a traditional cosh, the other a short metal bar with a welded knob. Each weapon is designed for work at close quarters, in which the leverage of elbow and wrist can break a rib; such efficiency would cost many lives were it not for the stiff hats worn by fashionable gentlemen.

In Whitty's case, though their intention is not to kill, his assailants are comfortable with that eventuality, and desist only when they are tired, at which point the victim's injuries include broken ribs, nose, teeth, some internal injuries, and a broken finger.

Having been thus serviced, Whitty is thrown headlong from the swiftly moving carriage, to skip along the cobblestones as far as a trash heap near Plant's, minus his hat, there to be examined by an emaciated black cat. A woman atop the rubbish heap with a clay pipe in her mouth straightens up to examine the correspondent . . . no, that is not so. She is looking at the cat, mumbling to herself that there walks two pounds of meat.

His life has been not a bad one on the whole, thinks the correspondent, who closes his eyes and surrenders to whatever lies beyond. A merciful end, really. God bless the drink: even during the worst of it, he did not feel a thing.

WHITTY, J'ACCUSE

by

Alasdair Fraser, Senior Correspondent
Dodd's

Following the escape of the Fiend in Human Form known colloquially as Chokee Bill, the incitement of the public continues unabated, not least as a result of the efforts of one Edmund Whitty, who marks upon the pages of a rickety, tottering weekly, notorious as the most corrupt, profligate, contemptible publication that was ever palmed upon any community, the aforementioned gentleman's most recent outrage being to induce the distinct, if wholly unfounded, impression that a person or persons other than William Ryan perpetrated five foul murders, and has murdered since.

One expects a measure of credulity from the great unwashed, and a measure of cynicism from the lower orders of journalism. However, when members of the House begin to take such piffle seriously, when such inflammatory ramblings o'ertop the considered verdict of a court of British Justice in the minds of serious men, then it is time to cry, 'Enough!'

Much has been written about the obvious danger of excessive free speech, when it takes the form of a cry of 'Fire!' in a crowded theatre. It is no small achievement on Mr Whitty's part to have joined that cautionary exemplar in illustrating the criminal perversion of a founding principle of English civilization – to wit, the deliberate spreading of false news, with the object of furthering a nefarious agenda, to sell newspapers at any cost. For this much is true: that a false report can prove as murderous as the deed it professes to discover.

Whitty, *j'accuse*.

Decent Londoners accord to the police the most admirable tenacity in working toward the arrest of Mr Ryan. English justice pursues its quarry with steps swift and sure. Although deeds of violence may be concocted with the greatest premeditation, they cannot for long escape.

The law and its officers have conferred a high benefit upon society, not merely in punishing present offenders, but in deterring others from committing such crimes in future. It is a duty far higher and more important than anything conferred by the organ on whose pages Mr Whitty sows public doubt as to the folly of crime and the justice of punishment.

We trust the esteemed proprietor of *The Falcon* will not permit the charade to continue. We trust that Mr Whitty will not pursue such vital and delicate public issues, lest modern journalism eclipse middle-age witchcraft in the atrocity of its superstition, and the cruelty of its ignorance.

> *For Whitty's writings prove his creed,*
> *That men who write should never read,*
> *Just as Whitty thinks it bosh*
> *That men who write should ever wash.*

33

The Falcon

Algernon Sala adjusts his monocle, turns to his sub-editor and sighs: nights of shuddering pessimism, not a wink of sleep, nothing but bleak projections ahead, all causes doomed. No man on earth can have this effect upon him the way Whitty can.

'Dinsmore, I am worried.'

Sweet music to the ears of the sub-editor, who lowers his copy of *Dodd's* with an expression of sympathy upon his face: 'Indeed, Sir. I should be worried sick were I in your place.'

'Fraser has got off a good crack. A good crack indeed. Edmund will need to advance a compelling piece of rhetoric to top a crack like that.'

'A most ominous indication, that we have not heard from Mr Whitty in nearly a week.' Dinsmore adopts an expression of worry, while planning his own future.

Sala lights a cigar, ignoring the stub burning in the tray. 'Mr Whitty will respond decisively and at any moment.'

'Your loyalty is most gratifying.'

'We Oxford men stick together.'

'That is generous of you, Algernon. For it is well known that the man was sent down in disgrace. His intemperate habits got the better of him, I expect.'

'Not a bit of it. Damned promising fellow, won the Boulton Scholarship – Christ Church, you know. Some expected him to end up in the clergy if that is plausible.'

'It is not.'

'In any event, the question became moot when he published a lampoon portraying the Archdeacon in inappropriate situations involving choirboys. Under a pseudonym to be sure, but of course it all came out.'

'And for concocting a piece of satire he was sent down? That seems hard.'

'The deuce of it was, every word of it was true.'

'Oh dear.'

'That is the thing of it, you see. Whatever else, Whitty is an honest man, in his fashion.'

'He is a fool.'

'That too. And it is not unreasonable to call Whitty a wastrel and a reprobate – but a charge of endangering the public by concocting lies? This must be rebutted with vigour.'

'Yet what rebuttal can there be?'

'Indeed. And there is another worrying development, Dinsmore. I have in my hand a note from the proprietor. He asks for a casual meeting in precisely an hour and a half.'

'Concerning Mr Whitty?' Dinsmore's plump little hands are folded on the desk before him as though in prayer.

'It is no laughing matter,' continues Sala, who thought he heard someone snicker.

Mr Henry Ingram of Broombridge & Paternoster Row, with an office in the Temple and rooms on Pall Mall, is a small party with sharp features, bright eyes and a hatchet-like demeanour designed to indicate that all decisions are final. His clothes fit him ill; he wears a white beaver hat with a long nap, like a farmer, and an incongruous, patterned silk *cache-nez*. Although spectacles lend him a studious air (provided one ignores the hat), he has no claim to education, for which commodity he turns to his secretary, Mr Lemon, a well-built man of thirty with a Cambridge pedigree, an epicene manner and an air of unctuous adroitness – which, in Sala's opinion, renders him extremely dangerous. The Editor suspects that Lemon, in moments of repose, looks fondly at the prospect of an editorship should Sala fail. Which, if Dinsmore has anything to offer, he will.

The proprietor drums his fingers upon his desk in an attitude of purse-lipped concern, as though examining the future in its buffed reflection. Mr Lemon looms over Ingram's shoulder in an attitude of benign stewardship, like the doctor of a wealthy patient in precarious health.

Sala stands on the rug like a man in the dock. Nobody invites him to be seated, and three empty chairs in sight.

The proprietor speaks without glancing up, the inference being that when he does favour the Editor with a look, it will cut to the quick and render the final verdict. Any Temple bully with a capacious purse can command an influential journal, and thereby purchase a degree of respect for the cut of his mind.

Sala is to receive a lesson in journalism. The little shite has read newspapers, knows his own likes and dislikes, can describe successful papers he has perused; and such is the traditional relationship between editor and proprietor that the latter's judgements, informed or not, hold sway on any topic known to man.

Here resides the real power of money and the supremacy of business in modern life – that the market-place of ideas is controlled by cunning idiots who have read little and learned less, who experience the city, the country, the empire, the universe, as a series of conveyances, luxurious rooms, and conversations with gentlemen as ignorant as themselves.

The little shite finally makes eye-contact with the Editor. '*Dodd's* has made an ass of your friend Mr Whitty, Sir. How do you intend to bring the ship back on an even keel?'

Adds Lemon: 'What Mr Ingram means to say, is that this will not do.'

The Editor heaves a deep, inward sigh.

'Exactly,' agrees Ingram. 'It will not do.'

On the word *do*, Ingram stabs his forefinger on to the desk, breaking a fingernail in doing so. Curiously, he does not appear to notice. This is the sort of occurrence that haunts the Editor's days and nights with the suspicion that Ingram is but a Punch puppet, that the hand of Lemon, the secretary, is firmly stuffed into the back of little shite's head.

Lemon wishes him ill. Lemon wants Sala's head on a spike above Temple Bar.

'Gentlemen,' counters the Editor, 'I am pleased to report that circulation on the current issue is up by half. Only Mr Whitty can account for this result.'

'My good chap.' Lemon speaks as though addressing a public school dolt. 'Advertising is down. Please do remember that, at only a penny an issue from the reader, the advertiser is the key to our future. When the advertiser worries, *The Falcon* worries. And we expect you to worry as well.'

Sala would like to leap at Lemon's throat with his penknife and slit it like an envelope.

The proprietor nods vigorously. 'Saw Atchison at the club – the clothier, good for a quarter-page as you know. "Deuced business," says he. "Never thought Broombridge & Paternoster Row would put the business of the city in jeopardy for the sake of a sensation."'

'What Mr Ingram means to say is that Broombridge & Paternoster Row has a reputation which must be sustained by its subsidiary holdings. This is your editorial responsibility.'

'Just so,' agrees Ingram. 'At all costs we must have editorial responsibility.'

Sala sighs anew, for he understands the mathematics involved: only if sales to the public equal or better lost advertising revenue, may he continue. For any hope of this, the Editor can only rely upon Whitty. But where is he? Where?

Sala reassures the little shite with a confidence he does not feel, hinting darkly of a matter of privileged information that does not exist. Our correspondent is onto a piece of crisp copy that will galvanize London and, of necessity, attract advertisers to the paper in unprecedented numbers.

'Of course we trust in your judgement,' says Lemon, indicating that Sala may choose the noose by which to hang himself.

'I appreciate your confidence, Gentlemen.'

'Of course you do, Algernon,' replies Lemon.

'Quite,' agrees the little shite, returning to an examination of the desk-top. 'Good-day, Algernon.'

'Quite,' agrees Sala, smarting at the use of his Christian name.

34

A Room above Plant's

Whitty has awakened in misery in his life, yet is in no doubt that something relatively serious has happened, a judgement rendered the more worrying by his body's seeming paralysis; this state of incapacitation has not decreased during the normal waking process, when the soul rises from unknown depths to its daytime station behind the eyes and ears. He feels pinioned to a horizontal surface, upon which his inert body throbs and swells with each heartbeat.

Prudently, Whitty adjudges it not a propitious time to open his eyes for a look at the world. Better to turn inward, take stock of the present, and plan the future. Only then will he open his eyes . . .

He lies on a narrow bed, his head resting on a clean pillow, facing right. Both his eyes are blackened and shut. The bridge of his nose is swollen and inflamed, as are his lips and cheekbones. A film of oily sweat shines upon his forehead, indicating fever.

Thinks Mrs Plant, watching him: Please do not die.

Within his private, dark encasement, the correspondent takes stock: of bruising there can be no doubt; ribs cracked though not necessarily broken; possible torn shoulder muscle. Such is the utility of a neddy as an instrument of underworld chastisement that the injuries it inflicts never fail to impress the recipient with their variety and extent. Worryingly, his body still refuses to move. *Pray, not the spine. Pray, not the brain.* So thinks Whitty's soul as it retreats to the region of the solar plexus.

Surely there is nothing more hilarious to God than a praying agnostic.

Whitty awakens. Therefore, he must have been asleep.

New pain! A stabbing, insupportable pain in his arm!

He opens his eyes and is blinded by the light from a window, pouring over the shoulder of a man whose face, albeit in shadow, appears slightly older than his own: a wide, bland face with the smug intensity of a medical practitioner. The man is stabbing him in the arm with a long instrument.

'Sweet Jesus, Sir, what the devil do you think you are doing?'

'Excellent!' The bland face reveals a set of ivory dentures, which appear too large for the face and emit an odour of rotting meat. 'Never fear, old chap, it is pure morphine and nothing more. You are experiencing the hypodermic syringe, the most recent thing. This one came directly from France. I have used it six times today, already.'

No good can come of any device made in France, thinks the correspondent. 'Please remove it at once.'

'By injecting morphine into the vein, we ensure that addiction will not result. This is scientifically proven fact. You may thank your stars that you have enjoyed the latest in modern medicine.'

So saying, the unknown gentleman removes the instrument, which resembles a pair of scissors but with a long darning needle where the blades should be.

A most sinister contraption.

The correspondent came by his suspicions of medical men long ago. As a child, he contracted fever and a physician nearly bled him to death. In a dream his soul escaped through his mouth for a time, to hover over the foot of the bed while the body slept, as though making up its mind.

One of the servants, an ancient Scottish crone who kept the poultry, clipped a lock of his hair, put it in a sandwich and fed it to the spaniel. The boy recovered the next day while the spaniel died. Of course, for Master Edmund's cure the physician accepted a substantial sum from his father, though he had had nothing to do with it.

However, at present he possesses neither the will nor the means with which to dispute the administration of modern scientific methods, as he closes his eyes and the morphine wraps about him like the warm arms of a woman.

As a matter of fact, he senses a woman in the room.

Whitty awakens. Unlike his previous emergence he now experiences nausea worse than any morning sickness he has suffered of late, while breathing with difficulty – the result of a burning weight on his chest, whose protective cage-work stabs him with each beat of the heart. He opens his eyes, and now comprehends his sensation of nausea, for the familiar, bland face with ivory teeth looms directly above, exuding an odour of tobacco and ale-fart.

'Capital,' remarks the unwelcome *pater patriae* to someone else in the room. 'Do you see? His constitution is coming around.' The self-satisfaction pours out like honey, as does the stench. The latter alarms the correspondent, who is of the firm opinion that disease is miasmic: that the various odours that emanate from the human body constitute nothing less than a continuous volley of infection, like a malignant firing squad, one malady to strike should the others miss their mark.

'Damn me to Hell, Sir, what the devil are you doing now?'

'I am administering a cataplasm on top of a tisane, Sir. The blistering effect of the decoction will draw out toxins in the kidneys and bowels, and prevent an ague.'

'I don't agree. Leave me alone at once.'

A familiar voice emanates from before the window: 'It's a poultice, Mr Whitty. This is the physician Dr Gough. Now shut your gob and lie still.'

With difficulty the correspondent turns his gaze in the direction of that exquisite voice.

'Mrs Plant. Dear Mrs Plant.'

'Enough of your malarkey, Sir. Although you seem to be recovering.'

'Truthfully, Madam, what is my present condition, in your view?'

'As though you jammed your face in death's door, you bloody fool. Is that not like you, vanity from start to finish . . .' She turns away from the light, not to let him see how worried she has been.

Happily calculating the enormous fee to come, the physician removes his spectacles, dons his filthy coat and bows, like a seedy magician who has performed sleight-of-hand. Whitty shudders at a fresh stain on the doctor's waistcoat, an ominous, dark fluid.

'The fractures and contusions will restore themselves once the patient has a good blistering. The broken finger, which is very bad, has been strapped to its neighbour and, barring an influx of poison, may be saved. We have administered a herbal purge to treat the fever, which condition – of this there is not the slightest doubt – has been brought about by morbid excitement of the organs occasioned by the shock of the fall from a moving vehicle, and inflamed by unhealthy exposure to the night air. In short, Madam, the patient's condition remains serious but not critical. It was a very near thing – indeed, I have just this morning come from performing an autopsy on a man who died from a similar complaint.'

Thinks Whitty: Hence, the splatter on the waistcoat, which, at more than one point in the proceedings, stood within an inch of his nose.

As the physician's footsteps recede down the stairs and out the door, Whitty examines his hand, whose fingers have been strapped together as described.

Never mind: to have survived an English physician is a miracle in itself.

Whitty awakes. Therefore, he must have been asleep.

Collecting his senses one by one, he determines himself to be situated in a small bedroom above the main drinking-room at Plant's. A steady rumble of discussion filters through the floor in tantalizing vowels, as though the gentlemen were holding pillows to their faces; and he recognizes the familiar hollow echo outside – of horseshoes, boots, iron wheels rasping on the cobbles below.

As well, he recognizes what he takes to be Mrs Plant's personal taste in home furnishings – spotless lace curtains, walls the same green as the snug downstairs (thus saving the cost of paint); he notes the picture beside the mirror above the wash-table, depicting an Irish castle in a sentimental landscape of rocks, heather and sea.

Clearly the assailants returned him to whence he came. How nice of them – but if so, how did they know it would be, for him, a circular journey? For it was not from Plant's that he was abducted, but from several streets hence. Therefore he must have been followed from Plant's. Was he followed by the black carriage (or perhaps dark blue), or did accomplices proceed afoot? (In all probability the one signalled the other according to the drill favoured by teams of garrotters on the Ratcliffe Highway.) Hence, the enemy was present while he drank gin downstairs. Yet there were no strangers there whom he can recall, Plant's being not the sort of place in which a stranger goes unnoticed, particularly one whose clothes, aspect, smell, accent, race or vocabulary are suspect.

Therefore his assailants had the co-operation of somebody known to the correspondent.

Fraser? Salmon? Dinsmore? The Captain? Mrs Quigley? Dear Heaven, the enemies accumulate like lint!

His chest burns painfully, which puts him in mind of the medical practitioner, whose memory draws his attention to the evil-smelling poultice applied to his chest; which, in turn, puts him in mind of . . . the pain! Sweet Jesus, the scalding pain! With a cry, he sits bolt upright, and instantly regrets his haste with another roar: the ribs!

Cracked as neatly as stonework: there's a neddy for you.

Remaining upright for the moment, thus minimizing movement, Whitty lowers the bedclothes – slowly – in order to expose the poultice in its unwholesome ugliness, sticky and pungent, the colour of iodine –

which abomination he slowly peels downward. Unhappily, the action tears the hairs from his chest, individually and to excruciating effect, inflicting further damage upon a skin already inflamed by quackery. Choosing swift, cruel punishment over slow torture, and with an additional, emphatic imprecation to Jesus, he rips the poultice from his body in one excruciating stroke and casts it aside, where it lands on the floor with a damp, heavy thud.

'Mr Whitty, if you must take the Saviour's name in vain, will you pipe down? You can be heard as far as the scullery.'

'The Saviour and I have reached an understanding, Mrs Plant. We call upon one another when needed.'

'I doubt that you're first on His address book.'

'Nor last, Madam.'

Gingerly he places himself back on his elbows, the better to take a good look at Mrs Plant, who once again (or possibly still) stands before the window. Daylight illuminates the copper in her hair, leaving her lovely face in shadow. Even in his reduced condition he cannot but notice that she is not wearing a corset. It comes as a mild shock to him, that a woman, in private, might choose not to wear that healthful garment. Which inspires Whitty to a remembrance of Mrs Marlowe, who likewise assumed such *dishabille* about the house . . .

No doubt he has been blackened with denunciations from his competitors – Fraser, huffing and puffing over Press Ethics, an oxymoronic proposition not unlike Police Protection . . . Beyond this room, Whitty has no doubt, his colleagues have judged his career to be at an ignominious end with the workhouse in sight – hence the easy laughter from below.

And yet, thinks Whitty, the story continues. Or, as goes the Hebrew maxim, look for the ending after the ending. In which one's bespoke narrative takes an unanticipated turn . . .

Whitty peers out at the world like a knight through a visor. Mrs Plant stands in front of the window – still or again, as the case may be. The light from the window has changed its direction since his last awakening. And she wears a different dress, the sort of dress in which she customarily appears while working downstairs – corseted, thankfully.

'Mrs Plant. It is indeed a pleasure to see you again. I seem to have nodded off a moment.'

'Three days, Mr Whitty.'

Three days? 'Madam, surely you exaggerate.'

'You bugger, you nearly died, you had me so scared . . .' She holds back the tears, not to give him the satisfaction. 'Hit your head, you did, in the fall from the carriage. Might do you good, a few less brains – think of it as a form of pruning.'

Whitty, in the meanwhile, makes a collection of remembrances from the last day he had his health: the pathetic little bunter and her startling gift of a flask – which, as it transpired, belonged to Harewood; the prediction of a spoiler from Fraser, with others inevitably to join, like baboons in heat. What must Sala be thinking in his absence? He remembers having taken notes at one point . . . His sense of time seems to have deserted him. For all he knows he might now be an elderly man.

Three days?

'Mrs Plant!'

'Whitty, quiet down or the street will hear you.'

'I beg you, I must be away now on urgent business. Please fetch my coat.'

So saying, he sits upright, slowly, bracing himself against the pain.

'Mr Whitty, you misunderstand the situation. This isn't a hotel. You're an invalid. As such you are my responsibility, and you shall leave when I decide you are fit.'

Whereupon, to his horror, it comes to his attention that, underneath the bedclothes (presently draped around his waist), he is utterly naked, not so much as a pair of drawers to cover his most private organ. He falls back onto the pillow, groaning with the pain of sudden movement, and pulls the bedclothes over his reddened chest, for it has become clear that he and Mrs Plant occupy a most indecent situation – which, if it were known, could do serious harm to both their reputations.

'Mrs Plant, I beg to apologize most abjectly for my condition, but I fear I am in a state of – if I may speak frankly – of complete undress.'

'Do not apologize, Mr Whitty, for it was I who undressed you. You needed a bath. You stank and were all bloody.'

'Dear Heaven, Madam, I hardly know what to say.'

Whitty has, in idle moments before this, imagined himself and Mrs Plant, first as lovers, then as a cantankerous married couple in endless competition for the upper hand. And now this indignity – here is this selfsame woman, having viewed his privates at leisure, having bathed him like a toddler! It does not bear thinking about. He must leave the premises at once.

'I beg you, Mrs Plant, please return my clothes now, so that I may retire with whatever face I have left.'

'I regret that your clothes were not wearable, Mr Whitty. Everything was burned at once.'

From below comes a muffled cackle, from either the Devil or the correspondent from *Dodd's*.

'Do they miss my presence downstairs?'

'No, you are there in spirit, for the number of times your name comes up.'

'In what context? Prince among men sort of thing?'

'A public flogging appears to be the way of it, Mr Whitty. One of your preludes to a hanging.'

'My reputation has suffered before. Reputation is an elastic commodity.'

'True for you, Sir. After all, you are not dead yet.'

From below comes the sound of unpleasant laughter.

The notes.

Breathing with difficulty, he resists the urge to leap from his bed and fling himself into the street. 'Mrs Plant, I have a somewhat important question to ask you about my coat – did you burn the coat?'

'Indeed, Sir, the coat was the first to go.'

'Quite.'

'Of course I removed the notebook.'

Bless you.

'There wasn't, I suppose, a sum of money in the pocket?'

'No money.'

'Are you certain?'

'Do you think me a thief?'

'No, Madam, I think you are an utterly magnificent woman.'

'You are delirious, Sir. I have put you in mind of your mother. She too has seen you naked.'

What the Devil can she mean by such language? Naked, indeed! Is he being patronized? – For the tone of her conversation hints at a form of mockery common to base sensibilities. What unilateral power is vested in a woman through the intimate, one-sided knowledge of a man's naked body!

'I shall have you understand, Madam, that the word 'naked' is not a permitted expression at *The Falcon*.'

'*Disrobed*, then. Head to toe. Back to front.'

'Quite.'

To Whitty, one thing seems self-evident: in mankind's relations with the gentler sex, a threshold has been passed in his lifetime, beyond

which no man may feel entirely at his ease with a woman – where a man
can no longer predict what she knows, and what she will do.

'Mrs Plant, I wonder if you will allow me to be candid.'

'From you, Mr Whitty, that would be refreshing.'

'I wish to say that I am most grateful for your assistance in the course
of my difficulties. In light of what has passed between us in the past, I
am truly amazed.'

'Amazed by what, Sir?'

'Kindness, I suppose. It is a rarity.'

'Not for a woman. In every second house in Soho there is a sick,
injured or drunk man, tended by his deluded Mary. For women, such
kindness is a sort of hobby.'

'Like tatting, I suppose.'

'No, a frailty one is born with. Like a club-foot.'

'Mrs Plant, you make reference to relations between the sexes in
general, and I concede to your superior understanding. Yet, if you will
permit me, I beg to become specific – to wit, solicit your view as to the
accuracy of my suppositions on a matter of some urgency.'

'I do not understand you, Sir. You're talking Spanish.'

'What I mean to say is that I beg to solicit your opinion of events as
they have transpired, and what I think about them.'

'That is acceptable. Please do so.'

'Prior to a previous visit to your establishment, I happened to be met
by a young woman of ruined character.'

'Hardly a rare occurrence, Mr Whitty.'

'Rarity or not, this young woman – who, I hasten to add, is not to
blame for her situation – provided to me information of an extra-
ordinary character. As a result of which I have reason to believe that,
whatever his character, William Ryan and the infamous Chokee Bill are
not the same man. Indeed, following and as a result of Ryan's conviction, I believe that the latter has been conducting his activities at will.'

'Rumours of such a thing have been circulating for weeks among the
Radicals.'

'Madam, the Radicals can detect a conspiracy in the weather.
However, this unfortunate went on to recount a circumstance of which
the Metropolitan Police are quite aware, and which, through agreement or collusion of interest (virtually identical in effect), similar
institutions chose to ignore. I believe this young woman, because to
construct such a narrative from whole cloth would require a cunning
quite beyond a ruined doxy on the embankment. Indeed, if the young

woman invented the tale she should be Mayor. For who can deny the feasibility of such a circumstance – in which officers of the city become selectively blind and deaf, with the blessing of officials in Whitechapel? Which would enjoy the complete co-operation of everyone who has a livelihood to lose – down to the last costermonger. By Heaven, it is even possible that the Fiend is a member of the police!'

'A quaint theory, Sir. You could be a Radical yourself.'

'Forgive me. I have not been well.'

'Would you care for a cup of whisky? I appreciate the exertion it requires to speak plainly to a woman.'

'Delighted more than words can express, Madam.'

Mrs Plant proceeds to the dressing-table, allowing Whitty an unhindered inspection of her form. 'Please continue.'

'Shortly after having published my observations (and, I'm obliged to admit, in a condition of slight over-refreshment), I took what I thought to be a cab. Later I awoke as you witnessed me – if *witnessed* may be deemed sufficient in this case.'

Mrs Plant approaches the bed with two cups made of blue glass, smiling to herself for an unknown reason. 'I assume you have discounted simple robbery as a motive. That would be too straightforward for Edmund Whitty.'

'It might have been my first thought – indeed, a hurtful amount of pounds were taken from me. Yet it doesn't narrow the possibilities: surely no scoundrel who will break the bones of a stranger would flinch at robbery.'

'Mr Whitty, I've become tired. Do you object if I am seated?'

'On the contrary. Pardon me for not getting up.' He takes a sip of the precious liquid, which tastes of peat and old library books. He reflects that perhaps it is good to be alive, even in reduced circumstances, if only to savour a decent whisky once more, to lie in a soft bed.

Whereupon Mrs Plant, no doubt to further test his tolerance for intimacy, sits on the bed right beside him!

Whitty had not for one second expected her to do this – after all, there is an empty chair in the room; which unforeseen development causes him anxiety over the situation beneath the bedclothes – the lack of a night-shirt or other insulation increasing the danger of an unwanted tumescence, rendered readily apparent by his prone position, which he cannot alter without severe discomfort; which danger has already become a horrifying possibility for, truth be told, Mrs Plant is a well-made woman . . .

'Mr Whitty, it seems probable to me that, one way or another, you have displeased people who don't brook displeasure gladly. I do not know how I might be of assistance . . .' Mrs Plant pauses, having flushed somewhat, for the room has become warm.

'Mrs Plant, have I your leave to make an unusual request?'

'I am willing to entertain it, Mr Whitty.'

'Please understand that I would not for a moment impose, nor cause offence.'

'I shall take that into consideration.'

'Madam, having emerged from death, so to speak, I find myself uncommonly aware of the sensations of the moment . . . so to speak. Furthermore, having, upon an earlier occasion, made mention of my high regard for yourself, I wonder if we might put behind us one certain precipitous and tasteless request, in order to entertain another?'

'Whitty, are you going to ask me to kiss you?'

'Madam, that was indeed my intent.' He braces himself against the possibility of a blow to the face.

'That is acceptable to me. Provided it don't lead to further liberties.'

'I assure you, Madam, in my present condition I am at your mercy.'

'Very well, then.'

And so she leans toward him, and he strains upward toward her, as far forward as the situation permits, just far enough that their lips can meet, however tentatively, while closing their eyes – not only to maintain decorum but also to give themselves fully to this exceptional moment.

Whitty is no sensualist as a rule; he avoids Turkish baths and is not partial to the scent of flowers. And yet, to hold his mouth against her soft flesh, tasting of whisky, gently moving with his own, all touch between them concentrated in an area of approximately one square inch, while the scent of her fills him like smoke, infusing his head and loins with a sensation which does not compare with the sensation of opium or laudanum or alcohol or any other medicament with which Whitty customarily renders life acceptable, awakens a sensibility of which he has only the vaguest memory, having partaken of it as a child, at which time it might have been termed *joy*.

After an interval of uncertain duration, she returns to an upright position and straightens her hair. 'Well, Mr Whitty,' she says. 'I'm sure I do not know what to say.'

'I too am at a loss for words. Madam, I am at your service.'

Mrs Plant rises to her feet and smoothes her dress. Through the corner of her eye she notes that a small military tent has been erected in the centre of the bed, despite orders to the contrary.

'Sir, might I speak plainly?'

'Madam, you have my undivided attention.'

'I know not what meaning to attach to this. It is a mystery and I am not sure I like it.'

'I assure you, Mrs Plant, that I remain in the dark as well.'

'In any case, I count on your discretion.'

'On this matter I am as mute as the Sphinx.'

'I'm a business woman. Smutty rumours of an attachment are not to my advantage.'

'Indeed, Madam, I'm well aware that I have nothing whatever to offer you.'

'You're presumptuous, Sir. I shall decide that for myself.' So saying, she kisses him again!

Whitty awakens. Therefore he was asleep. With eyes closed he can sense somebody standing over him – not Mrs Plant, nor the physician, Mr Gough, both of whom he would identify by smell, though not with equal relish.

He opens his eyes, and is surprised – nay, astonished – to see before him the androgynous Mrs Button. Thinks Whitty: Is he awake? For Mrs Button is the stuff of unpleasant dreams.

'Good-day to you, Mr Whitty.'

'Mrs Button. Such an unexpected pleasure. Is your mistress well?'

'Mrs Marlowe is moderately well, Sir, and sends her compliments to you.'

'To what do I owe this unexpected visit?' (Whitty struggles to maintain composure, for the pain of his excited breathing is quite excruciating.) 'Is it a message by any chance?'

'Indeed, it is a message. My lady asks the honour of your attendance in two days' time on a matter of some urgency.' Mrs Button produces an envelope from her sleeve and lays it upon the bed beside him. 'I am instructed to await your response.'

Clumsiness is a damnable thing with a set of broken ribs; as a consequence, some time elapses before he manages to tear open the envelope, while allowing for minimal movement and avoiding the broken finger. In the meanwhile, Mrs Button's mien of vague disapproval does not alter, nor does she break this silent torture with an offer of assistance. But no matter: when the correspondent finally retrieves and unfolds the message, the three words which comprise its entire content expand to fill his mind entirely, as though with a euphoric gas.

MR RYAN ACCEPTS.

35

Chester Path

Sewell alights on the Outer Circle and crosses to the iron gate. As usual, the upstairs curtains flutter.

He is beginning to feel used, like fifth business in a smutty little comedy from the Restoration. With greater frequency he returns to his rooms to find his food eaten, his drink drunk, his cigars smoked and his bed sticky. It never occurred to him that sexual intercourse might prove so messy, slipshod and insanitary; nor that two people might perform the act so often.

If indeed there are only two.

Again he reminds himself why he lets Reggie use him, why he does not complain. David and Jonathan. Friends for life.

This modern utilitarian age does not understand the pure, lifelong friendship that can obtain between one boy and another, akin to the instinctive bond between brothers, yet deeper in that it does not rest upon an accident of birth.

All men are naturally drawn to those examples of love in nature and in art that represent lifelong fealty and sacrifice, that exist as monuments to it: the love of a dog for its master, of a soldier for his comrade.

At Eton, Reginald Harewood rose to the defence of Walter Sewell a second time: an incident in which Sewell stood accused of putting a noxious substance into another boy's food. Harewood swore that Sewell had undertaken nothing of the sort. It was thereafter at Sunday service – a moment he relives almost daily – when Sewell, burning within, found the courage to ask Reggie whom he liked best in their row.

'Lumsden?' whispered Sewell.

'Only third best,' replied Reggie.

'Etheridge?'

'Fifth.'

While the chaplain droned out the true meaning of the Eucharist, they traded names down the row to the end, until Sewell (and, he feels certain, Reggie) realized not only that each had omitted his 'first best', but that the only boys remaining had been each other! In that moment

Sewell experienced the thrill, not untinged with apprehension, which occurs upon first discovering the existence, or at least the possibility, of reciprocated love.

Such absolute, unimaginable joy. Caught in the moment, Sewell laid his hand gently on the back of Reggie's soft blue blazer, then on the waist – Oh, Heavens! Did Reggie feel Sewell's hand, did he know what had transpired between them?

Yes. Surely, yes. Deep down, he had to have known.

Despite this heightened intensity of feeling, their association continued to adhere to the highest possible standard, as it has since. Sewell would never have allowed such a thing to take place, even had Reggie expressed such a desire – the things that other chaps did on cold nights while bedded double. Reggie and Roo did not do that appalling, dirty thing. Indeed, Sewell remained pure in body, even while his friend spent into available women, almost at random. It does not matter – do you see?

Nor does it matter that Reggie uses him. Their friendship will continue undiminished when his friend can no longer manage the grubby act with his darling wife Clara; when the latter, with a high collar to hide her wattles, is having it off with the ostler. Even then Sewell will still be there, and nothing will have changed.

Which is not to say that Sewell is enthused by the current situation.

When first he laid his rooms open for Reggie's copulations with his cousin, he imagined the act as a relatively dry affair involving a mixture of pleasure and pain, along with a certain abandonment and noise. However, to go by the evidence, one had to wonder at the sheer outlay of human secretion. In the interests of research, one evening Sewell hid himself in the study with a glass tumbler held by the wall, the better to overhear the goings-on in his bedroom.

It turned out to be a long evening. Indeed, at some point during the activities, Sewell fell asleep on the couch. When he awakened, he resumed listening, and it became clear that the young woman in the next room was no longer Cousin Clara. Then it dawned upon him that Miss Greenwell was not the only young lady featured in these exercises. The evidence of this is now inescapable, to the extent that, having changed the sheets, still he cannot sleep for the smell.

Sewell reaches for the brass knocker, set in the jaws of a lion. After three strikes precisely, the door swings open to reveal Bryson, long-faced and impeccably liveried and impersonal as always.

'Good afternoon, Bryson. Walter Sewell to see Miss Greenwell.'

'A very good afternoon to you, Mr Sewell, Sir, and may I say welcome.'

'Thank you. I am pleased to be here, and pleased to see you as well. By any chance is Miss Greenwell at home?'

'Please step inside, Sir, and I shall be extremely glad to determine that for you.'

As always, the servant examines Sewell's card as though he has never encountered its owner; satisfied that Sewell is not an intruder, Bryson admits the guest into the ante-room, then exits to obtain instructions. Alone, Sewell bites a fingernail while rereading the framed verse on the marble wall:

> God moves in a mysterious way
> His wonders to perform;
> He plants his footsteps in the sea,
> And rides upon the storm.

Presently he hears the voice of the footman: 'Miss Greenwell is in her chambers, Sir, and regrets to say that she is unwell.'

'Quite. Oh dear. Thank you, Bryson, I shall not trouble her further. Please convey my hopes for her speedy recovery.'

'Kind of you, Sir, but Miss Greenwell indicates her wish that you should follow me.'

It has already occurred to Sewell that Clara knows about Reggie's indiscretions, for she possesses a fair degree of animal cunning. If so, what now? Of course a woman is less blinded by love and has a higher tolerance for physical messiness. Thus, it follows that Clara will seek not to end the problem, but to limit the damage. If so, why is she about to perform a sick-bed scene for his benefit? What will she ask of him now?

He follows Bryson upstairs, wiping his palms with his handkerchief to keep them dry. The stairwell seems unheated and smells strongly of varnish. They proceed onto the landing and down a hallway, rendered tube-like with its rounded Paladin ceiling and maroon velvet wallpaper.

Having entered Clara's boudoir, he stops to assimilate the unfamiliar feminine hideaway, a décor he has not visited since his mother's dressing-room, to which he would be summoned for periodic chastisement; both rooms redolent with that peculiarly feminine reek of perfume, powder, musk and scented linen. Lit by gaslight, doubled by a large mirror, sit a row of dolls in frilled dresses, staring fixedly at him with painted blue eyes, while the curling iron steams on its iron stand.

Not too ill for hairdressing, seemingly.

Comes a weak voice from within the bed-curtains: 'Roodie, is that you? I beg you to come closer so that I may see you.'

He hates the way Clara has further diminuated his schoolboy name, which he never gave her permission to use in the first place. To her he is less than a schoolboy, more like a prodigious toddler. He pushes these caustic thoughts to the side upon the appearance of Miss Brown, with her perpetual crewel work.

'Roodie, you remember Miss Brown – my companion, protector, and confidential friend. Miss Brown, perhaps you recall Mr Sewell, an acquaintance of my cousin Reginald.'

'Delighted to see you, Miss Brown. And to see that you are looking extremely well.'

'I am well within reason,' replies Miss Brown. 'I am obliged to you, Sir.'

Holding his gaze a further instant as though to read his thoughts, Miss Brown parts the bed-curtains; in reaching out she reveals a pair of white arms with the bones clearly visible beneath transparent skin, like a membrane through which the skeleton is about to emerge. Having performed this service, she retreats to the corner of the bed, whereon she sits, motionless as though she has become a part of the bedpost.

Filled with misgiving, Sewell peers through the curtains.

Reclining upon a bolster and pillows, Clara Greenwell has become in her own mind the consumptive heroine of a French novel. Her breasts are clearly outlined beneath the silk bedclothes, lit by a candelabra on the side-table so that her features are thrown into relief, her golden ringlets spread about the pillow, dishevelled yet symmetrical, the eyes gently closed, the lips slightly pursed as though she is waiting to be awakened by a kiss from a prince.

'Is it you, Roodie?' she whispers, as though asleep.

'Clara. What has happened? What is wrong?'

'Don't you know, Roodie?'

'I assure you that I don't, Clara.'

'Such a child, so innocent and kind. That is why I love you so.' She opens her eyes slowly and quotes in a whisper:

> *'I hear a voice you cannot hear,*
> *Which says I must not stay;*
> *I see a hand you cannot see,*
> *Which beckons me away.'*

'Dear Heaven, Clara, you frighten me! When last we met, you were never better.'

'Give me your hand, Roodie, that I might hold it.'

He wipes his palm hurriedly with his handkerchief and feels her little soft hand slip into his. He wonders how firmly he is expected to hold it, while Clara resumes her ghostly monologue.

'Three times it appeared to me. Last night I beheld it for the third time. 'Prepare, Clara,' it said. 'Prepare for death.' I know you must think me a foolish girl . . .'

Stooping awkwardly within what amounts to a small, heavily perfumed tent (to sit upon the bed is out of the question), grasping the young woman's hand, Sewell makes sympathetic, pigeon-like noises, while Clara whispers half-remembered passages from novels featuring spectral appearances and premonitions of death.

At length, she focuses her lovely eyes upon his. 'Dear Roodie, please, you mustn't worry.'

Comes a voice from the foot of the bed: 'Miss Clara has received a severe shock to the system, which occasioned an ague, which weakened the young lady's heart.' Miss Brown pronounces the memorized sentence crisply, for it will earn five shillings.

'Oh, Roodie, I don't understand any of it. Am I dying?'

'Dear Heaven, Clara, please tell me what happened.'

'He has another. I am certain of it. Did you not know?'

'Reggie? Surely not! It is not possible!'

Clara begins to weep genuine tears, in great, childish sobs – for, beneath the performance, she feels truly humiliated. 'You are much too kind to admit that it is so. Hold me, Roodie! Hold me, for I am betrayed!'

'I assure you, Clara, Reggie has never spoken of you in other than the most affectionate terms.'

'You are so good. You do not see the evil in others. But I saw the marks of his betrayal.'

Thinks Sewell: To what, exactly, is the woman referring?

'Roodie, I am undone! Hold me, my dear, for I am dying!'

Out comes another torrent of sobbing until even Sewell becomes aware of what is expected. With the greatest reluctance he sits on the edge of the bed, whereupon she wraps her bare arms around him and sobs into his chest.

'There, there . . .' Sewell, whose chest has tightened and who has reddened considerably, is at a loss for words, as well as for an appropriate place to put his hands. His arms, of necessity, wrap themselves about the soft flesh encased in warm silk, whereupon she pulls him downward, gradually but inexorably, onto the bolster.

'Hold me, Roodie! Please hold me!'

Miss Brown crosses to the window and examines carefully the traffic swishing back and forth on the Inner Circle; for supper she will have a joint from the master's table.

Reeling from the shock of Reggie's betrayal, and against the possibility that she might not succeed in reawakening his affections, Clara determined it the wisest course to prepare other arrangements just in case. Sadly, upon resuming her at-homes with various young gentlemen, it became apparent that word of her indiscretions with her cousin had reached their ears, in however vague a form, thereby depreciating her value. Having reviewed Sewell's family history and his considerable establishment, Clara Greenwell has begun to view Reggie's friend in a new light – not as a laughable foil but as an alternative position. Indeed, if necessary she could come to find him rather adorable and sweet.

As the position becomes clear in Sewell's mind, he resists the urge to flee pell-mell out of the house. Of course it is inconceivable to Clara that this unlovely young man might be moved by anything other than desire for her.

Thus, Reader, we leave our two young people, holding each other in a most intimate posture, each wishing the other were somebody else.

WHITTY TO FRASER: 'PUBLISH AND BE DAMNED'
Questions Spark Vicious Attack

by

Edmund Whitty
Senior Correspondent
The Falcon

Your correspondent begs the reader's absolution for having failed to reply promptly to the vile calumnies uttered in print by the columnist for *Dodd's*, then to be aped by his desperately vacant imitators, an absence necessitated by a period of recovery from serious injuries arising from differences with certain parties – who, like Mr Fraser, disagreed with our presumptuous scepticism, albeit with sharper teeth than any yapping Scotch mongrel.

For our presence on this page and not the Obituary page we owe nothing to our libellous friend and much to the estimable physician Dr Gough, together with the most modern medical equipment British ingenuity can devise.

In keeping with *The Falcon*'s standard of utter integrity (as opposed to another organ, its eye peeled for ever-darker shades of black), we propose to set down a series of unembroidered facts, later to be followed by irrefutable proof, when health permits.

When one's accuser's viewpoint is limited to the bottom of his glass of gin, how may he be disproven by rational argument?

We find ourselves likewise paralysed when we attempt to unravel our friend's self-serving pieties and fortuitous suppositions, which belong to another era, in which men believed that the world was flat and the plague was caused by the Jews. Let it suffice to note that, if Fraser's proof will sink a reputation, then heaven help Her Majesty's Navy; and if our Mr McSodden supposes that his flaccid assertions amount to penetrating journalism, then heaven help his employer.

By way of contrast to our friend's amalgam of unfounded pronounce-ments, behold the particulars by which any reasonable citizen might question William Ryan's guilt of the offence for which he is condemned to die. We appeal to the Englishman's native common sense and inborn judgement of character – quantities notably absent from consideration in today's criminal courts, as well as upon the pages of certain journals.

William Ryan, to be sure, is an unsavoury character whose fellows may be seen on any evening, propping up the bar of a Soho gin palace, men characterized by a distaste for honest work, a gift for fraudulence, and a lack of common morality.

I have seen Ryan, in the flesh. I have sat across a table from him, and I can tell you that his fingers are permanently scarred, as a result of skinning them for the purpose of deciphering a marked deck of cards. This is the sort we are dealing with. I have spoken with this reprehensible cad at length and can report one fact with utter assurance: here is a man inspired by one consideration alone – Money.

Is this not obvious? Can any man who has spent a day in London deny the existence and the ubiquity and the mentality of such a character?

However, does such a man commit murder? Possibly – but under what circumstances?

Dear Reader, place in your mind for a moment the spectre of five, then six women, murdered in the most foul and barbaric manner, with disfigurements inflicted for the sheer devilish pleasure of it, the signature of satiated rage. Identify these women with William Ryan – who never made a move since he took his first step but for personal gain!

Now let us direct our gaze to the Metropolitan Police, whose investi-gation of the murders subsequent to Mr Ryan's arrest, under the direction of the phlegmatic Mr Salmon, was conducted in such a half-hearted manner as to suggest that Mr Ryan's trial had already taken place.

And yet, what a tangle of dangling threads remain!

The victims were all murdered by strangulation, which outrage was accomplished by a silk scarf – which, in each and every case, had been purchased at Henry Poole's. (The Fiend cannot be faulted for his haberdashery.) Yet, when your correspondent took the minor trouble of consulting with the proprietors of that excellent establishment as to the existence of a customer with Mr Ryan's distinctive aspect and station (a swell, as opposed to a dandy), Poole's can recall NO SUCH CUSTOMER.

(And yet, what superior official of the City does not frequent that fine establishment?)

Now let us turn to the melancholy, fallen creature, discovered by police and subsequently contacted by your correspondent, seated beside the body of her murdered friend on the morning following Ryan's escape, her friend strangled by means of a scarf WHICH CAME FROM POOLE'S. Undoubted proof of Ryan's guilt, were it not for the fact that our fallen young woman had, by this time, conducted her lonely vigil beside the body of her friend, for TWO DAYS!

Reader, are you in possession of a calendar? If so, then you have the advantage of Under-Inspector Salmon, and my Gaelic detractor, for whom it must set an uncomfortable precedent that *The Falcon* might uncover for itself a prospect unavailable at the bottom of a bottle.

And the crowning argument: With his simple mind and his naive enthusiasm for British justice, your correspondent appears to have occasioned the vituperation of certain parties, to the extent that he was set upon and injured within an inch of his life. Coincidence, I ask Mr Fraser?

Accusez-moi, Monsieur? Fraser, *J'accuse.*

36

The Falcon

Algernon Sala is a frayed man, his spirits having fallen prey to metal fatigue, the result of trying to reconcile divergent and competing objectives over and over again. Caught forever in the tentacles of administration, Sala now lives in hope that Whitty will revive, however briefly and tenuously, the Editor's position with the little shites.

For this reason, Sala has not grasped his friend by the collar and thrown him out the window for having reduced him to this state. As well, he is disturbed by his friend's deteriorated appearance – the result of a descent down a dreary vortex of drink and debt and pot-house dissipation.

'Have you had lunch, Edmund?'

'I never eat it. You know I hate lunch.'

'Great mistake, that. One should eat whenever one can.'

'Who was it said that lunch is an insult to breakfast and an injury to dinner?'

'A confounded fool. I hate fellows who talk in epigrams. What the devil did you do to your finger?'

'I thrust it where it was not welcome.'

'No need to pursue the subject further. Cigar, old chap?'

'Kind of you, Algernon, but I prefer one of my own.'

Whitty is in good spirits, having treated the effects of his injuries with a few drops of laudanum, for the ribs pain him. To offset the languor, he applies a lucifer to one of his cigarets.

'You for one should avoid the smoking habit altogether, Edmund. I have seen corpses with a more salubrious aspect.'

'Nothing that modern medicine cannot cure. Took a bit of a thrashing is all.'

Both men have understated the case. To enable Whitty to rise from his bed, Dr. Gough, in his wisdom, strapped the correspondent's ribs in a kind of corset, as a result of which the patient cannot breathe properly and is easily made faint. Hence the application of new medicaments, the effects of which have lent him a gaunt, poetic, rather Keatsian mien . . .

'Still with us, Edmund?'

'Fit as a fiddle, Algy.'

'Are you saying that because our man is a thief, it follows that he is not a murderer?'

'Don't be absurd. Of course he could be both. However, other facts will soon emerge.'

Maddeningly, Whitty places one forefinger beside his nose.

'This is what troubles me, Edmund. What we seem to have here is a bubble inflated by an absence. As Dinsmore once suggested, you are like a man who borrows money from one account to the next, so that no banker becomes alert to the fact that there was no money to begin with.'

'I say, Algy, that is very hard.'

'Tell me, is *The Falcon* commissioning an investigation, a documentation, or a polemic? And if you call it poetry, Sir, I shall never speak to you again.'

'An excellent question: How many facts are required to make a thing true, and in what order? I have given you the truth of cause-and-effect – and the effect is standing before you. A casual reader is not generally inspired to break the bones of a correspondent over a work of fiction.'

'Agreed, Edmund. Excepting that cause-and-effect has inspired you to implicate the police, the aristocracy, as well as officers of the fecking City. Why stop there? Why not the Prince Consort? Or do you intend to mount a broad attack against Established Order in general, like a bloody Frenchman?'

'I beg you to rest assured that my thinking reflects nothing remotely French. But who knows, Algy? The investigation is at a delicate stage. What can we know for certain in life?'

'If you bring Bishop bloody Berkeley into the discussion you will get a fist in the belly.'

'Mr Whitty is venting nothing but wind,' says Dinsmore, his little plump hands folded before him. 'If I were you, Algernon, I should compose an ignominious retraction for later use.'

'Shut up, Dinsmore. Shut your fecking trap.'

'Very gracious, I'm sure.'

Watching from behind the vacant desk of an absent sub-editor, Whitty notes how, in the interval since he last visited the office, Dinsmore seems to have acquired an air of increased strength at the Editor's expense. Given that the sub-editor has made no secret of his disdain for his immediate superior, and given Dinsmore's seeming companionability with Mr Lemon, is it any wonder that the Editor is not getting his health?

In the meanwhile, bent over his desk as though against a heavy wind, Sala secures his monocle, lights a fresh cigar, and examines once again the correspondent's collage of observation and innuendo.

'Not a shred of this would pass in court, you know.'

'I was unaware that we were working for the Chancery.'

Comments Dinsmore: 'Edmund appears to have accorded the status of fact to an alcoholic hallucination. By the way, the piece reads like a translation – is it a crib from the French?'

'No more French than your masseur at the baths, Mr Dinsmore.'

'Haw!'

Though uncertain what he meant by that last cut, Whitty is pleased that it amused the Editor. A vague recollection inspired his mouth to move: anything for a defence. Which motto – *Keep them Startled and Brass it Out* – might appear on the Whitty family crest: a mouth rampant on a field of brass balls.

'Algernon, allow me to sum up the narrative as it has unfolded thus far: other than William Ryan – and the question of his guilt or innocence for the murders of Chokee Bill – who is the principal character in the drama? Through whose eyes does the reader view the world?'

'Please out with it, Edmund. I detest riddles as much as epigrams.'

'He is making this up as he goes along,' comments the sub-editor.

'The thread, Gentlemen, is your servant. Myself.'

Dinsmore groans, theatrically. 'I am becoming nauseous. Mr Whitty's megalomania knows no bounds.'

'Shut up, Dinsmore,' snaps the Editor. 'It may be a new idea. Something outside the perimeter of your bantam mind. Pray continue, Edmund, what are you talking about?'

'The survival of *The Falcon*, Sir.'

'Survival, in what sense?'

'The dailies have taken the field in an unholy alliance with the electric telegraph. You have remarked upon this many times. No man in London today opens *The Falcon* in expectation of news.'

Dinsmore groans again. 'Might I remind you, Algernon, of the employer's directive: "to render common sense to the common man." I do not see how Mr Whitty's theory takes us in Mr Ingram's direction.'

Whitty notes that the sub-editor has addressed the Editor by his Christian name twice this afternoon. And he recalls grotesque rumours rattling about the printers – that the porcine Mr Dinsmore and the epicene Mr Lemon have entered into, if such an expression may be decently employed, a bath-house alliance, as well as a quest for dominion.

Dinsmore's smile is of an assured victor who has decided to humour the vanquished before crushing him like a beetle.

Sala focuses upon Whitty with a desperate intensity.

'Carry on, Edmund. Ignore the little shite.'

'I remind you that life is, by definition, chaotic. This fact makes a correspondent necessary – one who digests facts as they appear, mulls them over and brings them forth as a coherent mass.'

'You make it sound like a problem of the bowels, but continue.'

'A correspondent is not a factory worker, nor a clerk, nor a dustman. He is a lightning-rod, Sir, constructed and placed to receive and to channel the prevailing current, the latest signals – to sensational effect.'

Noting the correspondent's dilated pupils, the Editor marvels at Whitty's ability to render plausible a viewpoint which is his alone; the narrative has drawn the Editor into a world defined by Whitty's self-conception – an achievement not to be sniffed at. Contrary to his own judgement, the Editor is giving in.

If the little shites would pay for a secretary to record these conversations for later study, perhaps the Editor might discover how it is done.

'Edmund, if you don't mind I shall attempt to untangle the narrative you have put before me. First, we have the business of the scarf from Poole's. A fine scarf – indeed, a rather popular scarf about town; an object of theft, I imagine, for every jail-cropped buzzer on Oxford Street.'

'Possibly. However, the facts indicate otherwise.'

'What facts?'

'I'm in the process of stirring them up.'

'Jesus wept, Edmund. You're an *agent provocateur*.'

'I beg you, Algy, to heed your own warning: when an electric telegraph is situated in every home in London, where will Londoners turn for the latest shipwreck, and the biggest turnip in Scotland? And for what will they require a newspaper? By reporting the news, *The Falcon* dooms itself. To survive, *The Falcon* must *be* the news.'

Like any worker on the front lines of an institution, Whitty fails to fully appreciate the underlying strength of his position, based on the fact that no editor truly wishes to know how little anybody knows for certain. The thought that a substantial investment rests on such a precariously shifting foundation does nothing for investor confidence – to say nothing of the little shites.

'You should be in politics, Edmund. Perhaps you already are.'

So says the Editor, having been drawn disastrously into a general discussion of journalism, which subject cannot but advantage the correspondent. Trained by hours of gin-soaked debate, such questions are mother's milk to men such as Whitty.

Situated at his desk behind an opened newspaper, Dinsmore permits himself a small smile. Mr Ingram will appreciate this.

The Grove of the Evangelist

'Good evening, Sir. And how may I be of service?'

The Caribbean footman, neither sympathetic nor unsympathetic, steps aside, allowing the correspondent to enter the foyer. As a born Englishman, Whitty shudders at the inscrutability of the man, who, for aught he knows, would as soon tear out his throat as take his coat.

'Edmund Whitty of *The Falcon*, at the invitation of Mrs Marlowe.'

'Very good, Sir. I shall enquire if she is in.'

The correspondent does not have to tarry long. In a moment he is whisked into the sitting-room, where Mrs Marlowe awaits, in a dress of red satin cut to emphasize an unexpected *décolletage*. Beside her stands William Ryan, in a sober black suit, his beard trimmed and his health noticeably improved: indeed, Whitty would like to know the name of his physician.

'Mr Ryan. I am glad to see you in improved health.'

'I fear that I cannot return the compliment, Sir.'

'I concede the victory. My congratulations to you.'

'Not to me but to my dear Eliza, who has been my saviour.'

Whitty turns to Mrs Marlowe, who wears a distinctly unangelic expression upon her full lips.

'How do you do, Madam?'

'I am tolerably well, Sir.' The tension, not to say malevolence, is evident. Clearly she is not pleased to see Whitty – hence, whatever is about to transpire will take place at Mr Ryan's insistence.

'May I be so bold as to conclude that a decision has been made on the subject of our previous meeting?'

'You may, Sir, and it has. It is my intention to surrender myself to the police and to accept your offer – which I assume to have been an honourable one.'

Excellent.

'If I may be candid, Mr Ryan: While my offer stands, it contains no guarantee against the gallows.'

'I am ready for the gallows, Sir, if that is my fate.'

Whitty is momentarily nonplussed at such a sentiment expressed by one of his ilk. Has he misrepresented the man as a scoundrel? How easily is an opinion dislodged by an incidental remark!

The pause which follows is broken unexpectedly by Mrs Marlowe: 'Mr Ryan read of another atrocity in the pages of *The Falcon*. It altered the cast of his intentions.'

'I believe I am the author of that report, Madam.'

'Indeed, and I believe it was written to achieve exactly this sentiment in Mr Ryan. Sir, you display admirable cunning.'

'You do me too much honour, Madam.'

William Ryan shakes his handsome head, sadly amused. 'Mrs Marlowe and I are of two minds about you, Mr Whitty.'

'Indeed, Sir. I am of two minds about myself.'

'Mr Whitty, when last we met you advanced a telling argument – that my escape serves as a mask for the Fiend. I cannot in conscience run away, physically or morally, and leave such a legacy behind. I must see the thing through. I pushed the thought aside for a time. But then came . . .'

'Then came news of another,' says Mrs Marlowe with unusual bitterness. 'You timed it perfectly.'

'A sixth woman dead in the most beastly fashion.' Ryan's face struggles for composure. 'Why are you not laughing, Sir? Do you not see the humour in my position? An innocent man stands convicted of murder – yet the longer he asserts his innocence, the more women will die. While free, he becomes a murderer's accomplice – and freedom becomes a crime.'

Mrs Marlowe speaks with undisguised bitterness: 'Whatever his past, my husband-to-be is a man of integrity, Mr Whitty. You have seen this, and have used it against him, and in so doing have overpowered a woman's love. I congratulate you, Sir. Now you may reap your reward.'

RYAN SURRENDERS, ELOQUENTLY PROCLAIMS INNOCENCE
Correspondent Vindicated, Denounces Metropolitan Police

by

Alfred Hicks, correspondent
Lloyd's Weekly

The eleven o'clock chime at St Sepulchre's on Wednesday serenaded an unusual throng of journalists gathered together before the massive, solemn entrance to Newgate Prison – fewer in number, it is true, than the thousands who arrive of a Monday morning to witness a hanging, and yet representing thousands of readers all over the Realm – of *The Times,* the *Telegraph, The Illustrated London News, Lloyd's,* down to the most scabrous weekly in Scotland, who wish to understand the event, to know more about the subject than an Aberdeen crofter.

No less empty, in its vacant portentousness, was the presence of Under-Inspector Salmon of the Metropolitan Police, presiding over the ritual of an arrest, with a battery of uniformed constables ready to join the choir.

Resentments and rivalries temporarily put aside, this diverse assemblage of press and police, of comment and custody, maintained an easy familiarity; normal distinctions of rank and protocol having been o'ertaken by a universal satisfaction in the event to come – to wit, the final denouement of a narrative which has throttled the public interest for months, and is certain to provide crisp copy, an enhanced reputation and a generous stipend.

None of these august gentlemen can maintain a non-partisan spirit, having so much to gain from the result. In this regard, a log of the company present revealed that detractors of Mr Whitty's claim outnumbered any other opinion by a factor of fifty to one: a not indefensible position, given the spotty reputation of the gentleman at whose summons the gathering has taken place; for Mr Whitty has conducted surely the most visibly chequered career of any journalist in London.

Indeed, so unanimous and emphatic was the general opinion, it seemed to your servant that this Wednesday group betrayed a sentiment not unadjacent to their Monday morning counterparts; in eager anticipation of another sort of hanging – that of a fellow correspondent, hoisted upon his own petard.

In the role of Mr Calcraft was Mr Fraser of *Dodd's,* whose evident glee crossed that boundary which separates good cheer from bad taste – especially in one who has everything to gain from his rival's humiliation. Mr Fraser's morbid enthusiasm proved infectious among his colleagues to an unattractive degree. Following deliveries of refreshment from the nearby Saracen's Head Inn, and in a conspicuous lapse of objectivity, the correspondent for *Dodd's* was heard to join Mr Bogg of the *Monthly Packet* and Mr Whidden of the *Dundee Evening Examiner* in a disgraceful chorus of *O My! O My! I think I've Got to Die!*

Disgraceful – and well beneath the standards of *Lloyd's,* where we keep an open mind.

At last St Sepulchre sounded eleven, and hardly had the last chime echoed when up from Smithfield Market approached our protagonists (in a carriage driven by a Negro), the appearance of which was greeted with a coarse cheer of dubious welcome.

The coach having come to a smart halt before them, our men of the press produced pencils, notebooks and cigars, together with expressions of miscellaneous concern, while Mr Salmon descended the steps with his retinue:

'Gentlemen, I am Under-Inspector Salmon of the Metropolitan Police. I respectfully direct you to step forward where we may see you. Furthermore, I advise you to refrain from suspicious movement . . .' Here the under-inspector trailed to a halt, in mid-sentence, having lost his drift, his statement having no purpose other than as newsprint.

I leave you to imagine, Dear Reader, the gasp of astonishment, the choking hack of poorly inhaled cigar smoke followed by a cadaverous silence, as the Negro hopped from his perch, with all the nimbleness of his race, opened the carriage door – and our two protagonists stepped down.

First came Whitty of *The Falcon*, wearing a light blue coat, fawn trousers and an aspect of adamant, dry defiance:

'Good morning, Inspector. And a good morning to you, Gentlemen. My friend and I are honoured to have piqued your interest.'

So saying, the correspondent stepped onto the street while turning gracefully to the carriage door, from which aperture, wearing a sombre black suit and an aspect of forbearance, came Mr William Ryan, the fugitive known as Chokee Bill.

In the description of such a scene, *Lloyd's* regrets not having engaged Mr Dickens.

As the constables dutifully stepped forward to make fast their captive, pandemonium erupted among the correspondents on the square, with Newgate's relentless stone wall in the background, its forlorn expanse broken only by grated windows and recessed statuary. Were these scuttling gentlemen viewed from above, they would have resembled the spectacle of a stone thrown upon an anthill – an undignified scramble for personal advantage, while the most prominent journalists in London desperately revised their positions, retroactively, of course. Suddenly each and every correspondent, thinking back on Whitty's case, discovered himself to have viewed the Ryan trial all along with the utmost scepticism. Indeed, were it not for vague and sinister pressures from on high, these worthy men would have given voice to their thoughts long ago.

Thus do a pack of hyenas recast themselves as lone wolves, howling at the moon, each a lonely voice in the crowd.

Amid this visibly shifting atmosphere, the gentleman from *Dodd's* and the under-inspector for the Metropolitan Police grew visibly uneasy. Sensing an unwelcome scrutiny, they became wary and skittish and gloomy, like workmen in a tunnel who hear the distant sound of rushing water. For surely it is evident that, should the reputation of the correspondent soar to the heavens, so will the reputations of Mr Salmon and Mr Fraser plummet to the floor.

And make no mistake: the gentlemen of the press smelled blood. Where one might have expected the notorious Mr Ryan and the victorious Mr Whitty to have dominated the scene, our recent arrivals found themselves curiously relegated to the position of spectators, while the relentless eye of the Fourth Estate turned its implacable gaze upon their accusers, now ripe for evisceration.

In replying to Mr Whitty's analysis of the case, Mr Salmon attempted a lame defence, which crumpled like a meringue under close questioning:

Mr Hicks of Lloyd's: 'May I ask, Sir, what measures have been taken by your office in view of recent revelations in the Chokee Bill affair? Have you lost the scent?'

Mr Salmon: 'Sir, I assure the public that we have taken recent events most seriously, and that enquiries are ongoing.'

Mr Hicks: 'By "ongoing", Sir, are we to understand that you are in doubt as to Mr Ryan's guilt of the crime for which he has been condemned to death?'

Correspondents: 'Hear, hear!'

Mr Salmon: 'I am not prepared to say.'

Correspondents: 'Shame! Shame!'

For his part, the Scotsman from *Dodd's* – who, in a prematurely celebratory frame of mind, had partaken of a quantity of gin – seemed at a loss to make a case for himself in any language.

At which juncture did Edmund Whitty, the actor-manager behind this entire opus, lift one gloved hand for silence – which action caused the general uproar to cease and the gentlemen of the press to take up their pencils once again in the expectation of crisp copy.

Surprisingly, the gentleman from *The Falcon* refrained from his usual false bravado. On the contrary, he seemed almost diffident; when he spoke it was as a man humbled by the events in which he had played a part – and by the courage of the man standing beside him. Let it suffice to say that this was an unfamiliar Edmund Whitty before us today, a man with a newly discovered sense of purpose and destiny.

After him spoke William Ryan and, in deference to journalistic veracity, I shall here reproduce the text, delivered extemporaneously and transcribed via the miracle of short-hand by your servant, for you, Dear Reader, to judge at your leisure:

'Mr Salmon and distinguished members of the Press:

'It is not often a man has the opportunity of speaking to such a redoubtable gathering – especially a man born in an orphanage, the whelp of a fallen woman, whose profligacy set him upon a downhill journey to the lowest flesh-pots of London. I do not claim myself as victim, nor do I undertake to defend my actions, which have been of the lowest kind – short, I say to you, of murder. Of that one crime I am innocent, even if 'innocent' may seem scarcely the term to apply in my case.

'But if innocent, why did I escape? For every Englishman knows that there is no honour in flight. Gentlemen, my answer to you consists of one word: Despair. Of British justice. Of God. Of life itself. I invite you to pass judgement, you who have passed time in a death cell.

'It took Mr Whitty to set me right. He has been an inspiration to me, and I should not be here but for him. Mr Whitty gave me to understand that what is at risk goes beyond the hanging of an innocent man. What is at risk is nothing short of the truth, Gentlemen – and the lives of defenceless women, who, however low they may have fallen, deserve our protection . . .'

Your obedient servant was unable to record the remainder, obscured by the din of sycophantic cheers.

38

The Crown

Undefeated but once in his fighting career, Stunning Joe Banks is one of a few retired pugilists in England who actually prospered from the craft. Moreover, in becoming a publican he shrewdly chose the one social arena which affords continued value – both to his former glory, and to the skills which he acquired in the process: while the Crown plays host to many a bully-boy, the most vicious tout in Britain turns diffident as a schoolboy when facing the disapproval of Stunning Joe Banks.

Despite the damage wrought by bare fists hardened in brine (which seems not to have affected his mind), Stunning Joe cuts an exquisite figure: situated behind the bar of French-polished mahogany, in a tailored lavender coat, tweed trousers and a silk neck-cloth, the publican glows as a living monument, a symbol of British pluck.

When he speaks, which is seldom, a strangled whisper issues forth – the result of a bare fist to the Adam's-apple courtesy of Sweeny in '44 – and yet all listen, such being the latent power of an ugly, silent, well-dressed man with a reputation.

'The young lady before the pillar?' he whispers into the barkeeper's ear.

'Indeed, Sir,' replies the barkeeper. 'A comely little piece. Drinks every penny she earns. Singularly well-favoured, however.'

'And her escort?'

'Oxford, by the accent, or pretends to be. Jolly taken with her to the tune of three gins and a twelve-shilling bottle of Moselle.'

'A glass of the best gin and peppermint for the lady, Basil, and another for the gentleman. Later we will take the prospect aside and acquaint her with the advantages of a room upstairs. That it is safer, if this is the road she has chosen.'

The barkeeper nods agreement, drawing a cup of 'The Out-and-Out'. Indeed, the young lady will fill out the dance floor nicely, beside Miss Fowler with the beautiful leg, the Amazonian Miss Bolton, and the singularly genteel Miss Parks – who, for an extra pound, is capable of the most uncommon exertions . . .

It is the proprietor's judgement of horseflesh that enables such a varied, spirited, profitable gathering to occur of an evening, beneath the gasoliers and the stucco rosettes.

No Peeler can vouch for one's safety in the streets – whether it be from the thieving Irish, who will strip a clerk naked and throw him in a cess-pit; or the well-born, upper-class beast who wanders the streets with his friends, provoking fights with the lower orders; or the touts who break heads and molest women of all ages; or the roving bands of cruel children, who are the worst of all . . .

Within these walls, ladies and gentlemen of all classes seek their business and pleasure in a state of truce.

Unaware of her recruitment as a prospective associate under the protection of the establishment, Dorcas accompanies her escort past the dancing couples, across the floor, and out the door, just as the barkeeper was preparing to bring glasses to their table.

Thinks the barkeeper: An opportunity lost. But not to worry. He will draw the little fox aside when she comes in tomorrow, white with morning sickness, and she will be pleased by the offer of a free gin.

39

Plant's Inn

No English journalist exists who does not long for the pamphlet wars of the last century, when a correspondent was truly relevant to the business of the nation: not, as obtains in the modern era, as a salesman for watches and corsets and the latest cure. Who does not wish to hold forth in the days of the Old Jewry, jousting with the emerging vocabulary of methods and ideals: Liberal, Conservative, Socialist, Capitalist, Anarchist, Liberty, Equality, Fraternity: juicy, chewy, portentous words, like fatty cuisine and a legacy of the bloody French.

Oh, for the days of Burke, Priestley, and Macintosh, who coined the term 'counter-revolutionary', and lived to see it in the dictionary! Oh for the days when scribblers were philosophers!

Whether or not Whitty's current campaign will achieve its purpose in gathering support for a reassessment of the Ryan case, sufficient to the day that it has redeemed both the reputation and the marketability of its author. The latest issue of *The Falcon* has already outsold its predecessor; circulation can only increase as readers eagerly devour the narrative from one issue to the next. As for Mr Owler, the patterer's first-hand acquaintance with a sensational case will assure the popularity of any number of revelations and lamentations.

Content for the moment, the Captain – having received Whitty's stipend – assured him by return mail of a period of grace from the visits of Will, Norman and their little friend Rodney. His creditor denies having been party to Whitty's thrashing – which supports the correspondent's hitherto flimsy assumption that the attack in the blue (or black) carriage occurred as a consequence of his investigative activities.

There is nothing like an unseen enemy to hone the mind: in past days, the correspondent has partaken neither of stimulants nor depressants, neither of emulsions nor amalgams, hypnotics nor narcotics, anaesthetics nor beneficial smokes. Only the occasional gin, administered to calm the nerves, sullies the purity of his rubbery vessels and veins.

Holding a handkerchief to his face to ward off the poisonous, opaque fog (it is barely mid-afternoon), Whitty swings into Plant's, his entrance announced by the little brass bell over the door; whereupon he perceives the babble within to decline precipitously and many eyes to turn – first in his direction, then to the rear snug, then to one another.

The degree of Whitty's success is apparent.

Among his colleagues, with the possible exception of Mr Hicks the contrarian (who, it is said, keeps beetles in his pockets), Whitty is the most despised correspondent in London.

Excellent.

Regard the dark portentousness on Cobb's flushed countenance, the knowing cynicism of Brewster. Regard Stubbs, Beresford, Mellon: of this spiteful congregation, Fraser has now appointed himself Pastor. And behold: there he stands in the doorway to the rear snug, a glass of gin in hand, a glitter of madness in the eye, displaying his little teeth in what passes for a smile.

'Whitty, my good man. Lovely to see you, old chap.'

'And yourself, Alasdair. How have you been keeping?'

'Top drawer, I should say. And I trust you prosper?'

'Flush with the bloom of capital and collateral.'

'Excellent. And no wonder, with the smashing narrative you have going. I expect they are ecstatic at *The Falcon*.'

'It was not without assistance, I assure you. For instance, I had the opposition of a spoiler from *Dodd's*. Can't do without drama, old boy.'

Fraser absorbs this crack with that Celtic ability to think sharply while unable to walk in a straight line. 'Taken altogether, Edmund, the narrative has a new lease on life, I should think.'

'The game is not over, Alasdair. Plenty of turns to come.'

'Quite.'

The collegial, ironic pleasantries continue, with the heads of Cobb, Hicks and the rest wagging back and forth, nostrils quivering for a killing shot, an artful parry. Of which there will be neither: having prepared a gin and water, the barkeeper lifts an eyebrow to the correspondent for a brief word.

'A constable from the Peelers came to see you moments ago, Sir. Name of Mr Wells. Left word that that there has been 'another of the same', as he called it. Situated off the Ratcliffe Highway, on Cannon Street Road. The gentleman intimated as how you would understand.'

'Thank you, Humphrey. Although it is a stale, trivial bit of material, it might result in a line or two.'

Thinks Whitty: This can only mean one thing, given the location. *Capital.*

40

Cannon Street Road

Her murderer, once he was done with her, deposited the body, dumped it rather, in a field situated in between the London Hospital for Seamen, Watermen and Dock Labourers, and the Whitechapel Mount – a Brobdingnagian dust pile dating back to the Civil War. Clearly her murderer chose the site with an eye to facility of disposal and unlikelihood of observation. Perhaps he paused here to spend extra time with her, for she has been mutilated with more than the usual savagery, as though Dorcas merited special treatment.

Primed by the reputation of the Ratcliffe Highway (the site of, among other enormities, the infamous Walker murders), interested citizens began to appear from all over, as soon as the corpse was discovered and reported by a muck snipe in a scavenger's tent. Eager spectators arrived from Stepney and Whitechapel, then from more distant parts as word spread – like a ripple in a pond, thanks to a little-understood phenomenon known as a *chaunt*.

It was only a matter of an hour before the chaunt reached the ears of Phoebe Owler.

Having made the journey to Whitechapel on foot, she works her way sideways through a kind of maze made up of the tightly packed bodies of men, stinking of sweat and tobacco and wet wool. As she squeezes through, anonymous hands grasp and feel her until she wants to scream.

Strangely, when she sees Dorcas, and what has been done to her, she does not scream . . .

She is lying down. For how long? Cold stone hurts her cheek. She is on the ground. Someone is poking her with a stick. Before her, the heavy boots and blue coat-tails of a Peeler.

'Now then, Miss. Are you in need of assistance?'

She rises to a partially seated position – carefully, for she is dizzy. Her head and right shoulder throb where she hit the stones. What was it that made her faint so?

She sees the blanket on the ground – a horse-rug spread across the stones, with something under it. A foot and a hand protruding. And now she knows. By reaching out and leaning forward she can touch the lifeless hand. Now she knows what lies under the rug and remembers what she saw . . .

'Wake up, Miss. You can't just keep falling over. This is no place to sleep.'

Someone is crying, in great, gasping sobs.

'Knew the victim, did you? Pity you had to see that. Sit over there and keep warm. And stay back from that thing, Miss, you don't need to see it again.'

So saying, Mr Chesney turns to address several onlookers: 'Gentlemen, show some human feeling if you please. Step back and make room so that this young lady may breathe. She has, as you can see, sustained a bad shock to the system.' With a Peeler's tone of authority he forces the crowd to retract somewhat, though they are certain to inch forward to their former position the moment his back is turned.

Thinks Chesney: Where in bloody London is Wells?

Whitty alights from the cab at the corner – gingerly, to avoid the pain that accompanies sudden movement. Mr Wells awaits, as agreed, at the kiosk north of the intersection. (With informants, clarity and reliability are essential.)

'Excellent, Mr Wells. Good to see you. Good of you to inform me of this new development.'

'As agreed, Sir, for I am a plain man with children to feed.'

'Well done. Here's a crown for you.'

'Be so good as to slip it into the left coat pocket, Sir, while looking in another direction.'

'I trust you've given the situation the benefit of your experienced eye?'

'I have indeed. All consistent, Sir, a procession of familiar object. The scarf was twisted for slow strangulation. A silk scarf from Henry Poole's.'

'Are you certain, Mr Wells? Are you certain it was from Poole's?'

'Do you suggest that I cannot read the label on a scarf?'

'I mean no such thing.'

'It is not as if I did not see Chokee Bill's work before this. Though for the first five I was off-duty.'

'Mr Wells, you are a stalwart ally and the press salutes the good that you do.'

'I hope it is good, Sir. I have a daughter of fifteen.'

The crowd thickens as they approach Whitechapel Mount, then

peters out as they reach the site, having wearied of the spectacle and craving a drink. Even front row spectators have turned away from the horse-blanket and what lies beneath.

Having examined the corpse, Under-Inspector Salmon, a lean, black column bent double, tosses the horse-rug back in place and straightens to full height. He replaces his top hat – which he removed, not out of respect for the dead, but against the chance of its falling into the dirt.

Salmon notes Whitty's presence with neither surprise nor pleasure.

'Good-day, Under-Inspector. Such a relief to see that you are conducting enquiries. It appears as though you have another scarf to give away.'

The under-inspector's mouth forms a lipless line. Whitty notices for the first time that he has no eyebrows.

'Good-day, Mr Whitty. There has been a murder, as you see.'

'Indeed, Policeman. Seven murders. Five plus two. On this occasion, I trust that you can accept the notion that William Ryan may be otherwise occupied.'

'I take your point, Sir. Yet this does not disprove him of any of the others.'

'You leave out of account, Sir, the existence of a scarf with a specific label.'

'Thanks to you, Mr Whitty, scarves from Henry Poole's are familiar to anyone in London. With such a cover, I should be surprised if a garrotter used anything else.'

'For this you blame the press, Sir?'

'Do we blame a hyena for chewing dead meat?'

'You have supplied *The Falcon* with crisp copy, and we thank you for it.' Whitty is about to add something scathing, when he notes that the under-inspector's attention has shifted to someone else, someone immediately behind him . . .

How long has she been standing near the blanket on the ground, watching and listening with that peculiar expression on her face?

The deuce.

'Crisp copy is it, Mr Whitty? Otherwise you should not be here, wallowing among us lower orders. How much you care! And Mr Policeman – the both of you. What bloodsuckers!' Phoebe wheels about and disappears into the crowd. Whitty lunges forward to detain her, but is immediately prostrate with the pain in the chest.

'You seem sadly out of condition, Sir. Who was that young judy – an acquaintance of yours?' Salmon views Whitty's discomfiture with bitter

THE FIEND IN HUMAN

satisfaction, a small recompense for the trouble which must be dealt with as a result of this. 'I see that in speaking to the debauchery of the lower orders, you write from experience.'

The correspondent does not reply, being occupied with getting sufficient air.

'On reflection, I am not surprised, Mr Whitty,' continues the under-inspector, 'that a notable such as yourself might run in such company as that thing under the blanket.'

With difficulty the correspondent turns to the horse-rug, drops to one knee and lifts up the corner, so that he can see.

And now he knows.

Plant's Inn

'A very large gin if you please, Humphrey, and pour one for yourself.'

'Indeed, Sir, you appear as though you have sustained a shock to the system. Your colour is not the best.'

Whitty downs half the gin in one go. Too many shocks to the system. Humphrey is correct. As a precaution he takes a pinch of restorative powder; he counts himself lucky to have some on hand after his period of enforced abstinence.

'I wish to speak with Mrs Plant. Is she in?'

'She wishes to see you herself, Sir, on a matter of some consequence.'

Leaving two shillings on the bar after accepting a splash more gin as a healer, Whitty steps behind the frosted glass; there sits Mrs Plant, her whisky before her, her luxuriant hair piled carelessly with combs, her mouth pursed as though contemplating an unexpected problem.

'How do you do, Mrs Plant. I'm very glad to see you and hope you are well.'

'I'm doing nicely, Mr Whitty, but you appear to have relapsed. Do you have fever?'

'No fever, Madam, thank you. It is another matter which concerns me.'

'No more than I, Mr Whitty – a situation upstairs.'

'Please elucidate, Madam.'

'A gentleman has come to see you. Of the costermonger class.'

At which, Whitty experiences a terrible feeling.

Continues Mrs Plant: 'I put him in the room upstairs. Here is the key. Something ghastly has happened, Mr Whitty, it made me weep just to look at him.'

Having ascended the stairs by threes, having fumbled with the key with his damaged hand, having entered the room with a great clatter (when it became apparent that the door was ajar), having peered about the unlit, silent room, Whitty faces the patterer – seated, or rather slumped, on the chair by the window.

Strangely, even in shadow Owler's face has become almost luminous, in the way of the doomed stick-men of Seven Dials. His normally ruddy complexion has acquired the pallor of tallow and the shine of tarnished silver. His ponderous shoulders are folded inward like the wings of a dead bird. His hands rest on his lap as though they have been broken.

Reluctant to disturb the man yet barely containing his own distress, Whitty sits quietly at the edge of the bed, on the spot which the body of Mrs Plant once occupied – an impression which remains fixed in his mind.

'Mr Whitty, Sir. Is it you?'

'It is I, Mr Owler. And how goes it with you?'

'Things could be better, Sir. Much better if truth be told. I 'as been waiting to tell you, for you will want to know.'

'I have already heard the terrible news, Mr Owler.'

'Wery bad news, Sir.'

'I extend to you my deepest sympathies. Dorcas was . . .'

At the sound of her name, Owler's face crumbles like a dry biscuit; Whitty must now wait some few miserable moments before the man recovers his composure.

'My Dorcas has been done for, Sir,' says the patterer at last. 'She were murdered. It was cruel and foul, in the way of the others, but worse yet.'

Whitty maintains his composure, with effort. 'Mr Owler, this is the most dreadful thing I ever heard.'

'The short of it is that it were Chokee Bill done it. It were none other. The scarf and the . . . the other things he done. It were Chokee Bill.'

'Pray, Mr Owler, do not continue.' Thinks Whitty: what a fearful triumph, to see an invention, Chokee Bill, come to life.

'My Dorcas were a good girl. She were not a bad girl. Resisted her state in life, wanted a bit of fun, to get ahead – what girl wouldn't, a pretty, spirited girl like that?'

Again Whitty must endure the sight of an adult gentleman weeping with complete abandon. In pursuing his profession the correspondent has heretofore witnessed such displays with clinical interest, in the way that he might observe an animal for a report on bear-baiting. Such detachment has now left him.

'May I offer you a whisky, Mr Owler?' Here comes the ever practical Mrs Plant, who has been watching silently in the doorway, goodness knows how long.

'You're kind, Madam, and I'm most grateful to you.'

Removing a bottle and glasses from the dresser, Mrs Plant pours three fingers for Mr Owler and two each for Whitty and herself. 'It is a terrible thing to lose a child. A misery of devastation and loss. There is nothing to compare with it.'

'Werily, Madam. The more so with oneself to blame.'

A silence ensues, broken by the muffled voice of Fraser under their feet: he advances a quip, which earns a volley of hard laughter from the company.

'Mr Owler,' says Whitty at last. 'May I ask if the blame you have taken upon your shoulders bears any relation to your mention of 'others', in speaking of Chokee Bill?'

'Oh you are a cunning gentleman, Sir. I have always thought that of you.'

'You knew, did you not? You set out to record William Ryan's last confession, giving no credit to his claim of innocence, fully aware that the murders of Chokee Bill continued. You impress me, Sir; you have the markings of a journalist.'

'True for you, Mr Whitty, and how I regret my cleverness! I knew, just as you say – as did the Peeler on the Haymarket and the offal-eater on New Oxford Street and the beet-seller in Covent Garden. We all knew, every coster in the Holy Land, but none of us did say so – not even to one another, not even to ourselves. Oh Mr Whitty, Sir, the depths one sinks to in the course of making a living!'

Mrs Plant refreshes the patterer's whisky. 'Mr Whitty does not grasp how children make cowards of their parents. Being a bachelor, his principles are as fresh as a daisy.'

'That is true, Madam,' says Owler. 'If any fear unmans one, it is the fear that one cannot put food on the table. And during the garrotting panic it near came to that. Had the arrest come a week later, it would have been the workhouse for us, with starvation to come. Best that Ryan confess and hang for it, was my judgement.'

'And that of every father in London. Are you following any of this, Mr Whitty?'

'I take your point, Madam. There is no need to harp on the shallow egotism of bachelorhood.'

'That is your interpretation, not mine.'

'It is well known, Mrs Plant, the tragic effects of a superficial con-fluence of interest, especially among the poor.'

'True, Mr Whitty. There is among the poor a shared interest in remaining alive.'

Whitty does not accept poverty as an excuse for immorality; none-theless, he maintains a professional aspect. 'Mr Owler, did it not alarm you to see your girls unprotected, on the very streets you knew Chokee Bill to wander at will?'

'No, Sir. The Fiend is but one man. With one murderer loose, what has changed? What greater menace is Chokee Bill to a child of the Holy Land, than is ordinary life? Like others I balanced the sums. I weighed risk and the benefit. And for my blasphemous calculation, I lost my lovely Dorcas . . .'

Whereupon Owler cannot continue.

Whitty partakes of his whisky and accepts another, having nothing further to say.

At length, Owler recovers his composure. 'Sir, I have no doubt that you will take a dark view of me. Bear in mind that I am not the quality, I'm an ignorant man who has no ethics what have been bred into a gentleman like yourself.'

Whitty manages neither to laugh nor to cry. 'You embarrass me, Sir. I had assumed you to understand that a journalist's ethics are but a tactic for the purpose of obtaining co-operation from the public. I am no honest man, Sir. Nor am I a moralist, nor a pastor, and in the course of a day's work I regard ethics as pests. Dear Mr Owler, I beg you to see me as I am – a dissipated, curious chap, whose adherence to any code of conduct is a matter of context and whim.'

'And drink,' adds Mrs Plant, helpfully. 'In his cups, Mr Whitty presents no ethics whatsoever.'

'Very helpful, Madam,' replies Whitty, evenly. 'A further splash of whisky, if you please.'

Mrs Plant pours the last of the bottle equally into three glasses. While filling Owler's glass, she looks him over carefully, then proceeds: 'You have a second dependant, I'm told, Sir. And what is her situation?'

'Phoebe will have taken it hard, Madam.'

'Indeed she will,' replies the correspondent, choosing not to say what he knows.

'She is a good girl, but I despair of what she will take it into her head to do.'

'To what do you refer, Sir?' asks Mrs Plant. 'What is it you fear she will do?'

'I fear she will go in search of him, Madam. And I fear that she might indeed find him – for she is that clever. And that would be the end. If she was to go the way of Dorcas, that is the end of the world.'

'Dorcas was your ward I believe, Sir?'

'Werily, Madam, she were, though she took my name.'

'In other words, you are not her father.'

'True, it were a former associate, long dead, as left her in my care.'

Whitty watches and listens and takes notes, saying nothing. Crisp copy indeed, thanks to the perspicacious Mrs Plant.

'Mr Whitty, I believe there may be another bottle in the drawer.'

Four large whiskies having gone down the neck, Whitty makes his way with care up Whitechapel Street toward the Strand, through a fog smelling of wet coal, a colour that turns the surrounding buildings to leprosy, a fog of sufficient thickness to provide a room-like effect, with a strange, muffled echo to the ubiquitous clatter of men and animals, the voices raised in anger, the rasp of metal, the perfunctory snort of a horse at the kerb, as though they were wrapped in bandages, head to toe.

The ear being thus rendered unable to distinguish one source of sound from another, the combined harmony becomes the utterance of the city as a creature unto itself, breathing, rolling and stretching its limbs. Thanks to medicinal powder, the pain in Whitty's rib-cage has receded so that he can move more easily now. Thus freed from the rigors of the body, the correspondent turns his attention to the pain in his mind – the perception that he did not have the moral courage to tell the patterer of the correspondent's encounter with his daughter, standing over the corpse of his ward, and what it may portend.

Whitty longs for an overview, to soar to some general truth, to rise above the muddle to the rooftops like a Hindoo on a rope, there to perch among the black cathedral spires that prick the overhanging cloud, to peer through the black smoke roiling upward from a thousand chimneys, and see everything . . .

Far below him Piccadilly churns in a grey whirlpool of hard-shelled beings like stones in a river, clattering across the cobbles. He fancies he can discern a pair of solicitors comparing fees, and the impatient curse of a gentleman upbraiding a crossing-sweeper, and the seductive laughter of a woman accepting an item of jewellery. As his ears become accustomed to sound in the way that eyes become accustomed to light, he hears in the surrounding narrow lanes and alleyways the growl of starving stomachs, the rustle of hands, groping for warmth or a weapon . . .

'I say, old man, are you quite all right?'

The deuce!

Whitty opens his eyes to discover that he is lying on the cobblestones.

Around him are passing feet. Above him dangles the cherry-cheeked face of a man – a clerk, to judge by the condition of his boots, his gloves, his collar, and the greasiness of his black suit.

'May I help you up, old man?'

'Bless my soul. Keeled over, did I?'

'Jolly well did, Sir. Felled like a tree.'

'Blast! Touch of ague I expect.'

'Shouldn't be surprised. A dose of the London particular is what I call it.'

'Quite. Much obliged to you.' Whitty retrieves his walking-stick from the cobblestones while waiting for his head to clear. A bit too much powder, obviously. Damn the inconvenience. Having deprived his body of a normal, day-to-day medicament, the correspondent must entirely recalibrate the dosage.

In the meanwhile, his rescuer continues to peck at him like a hen. 'Sure you're fit, old trout?'

'Fit as a fiddle. Cheerio, then.'

'And a good evening to you, Sir.'

Whitty continues on his way up the Strand, unsteadily, unnerved by the incident, a chilling reminder of what a disaster it is to lose one's health. His ribs are mallets beating on a thin membrane of alcohol. He will be howling soon if he doesn't partake of something. Morphine is called for, obviously – but how much? What is the correct dosage? Bloody Hell!

Having left Mr Owler, drunk, in the care of the surprisingly useful Mrs Plant (the latter having succeeded where the correspondent failed in extracting from the patterer a coherent picture of the situation as it stands), Whitty, upon consulting his notes (a poor substitute for a memory), begins in his mind to compose the most difficult narrative of his life, one which will require his undivided attention.

A SINISTER ASPECT
The Strand Transformed by Shocking Revelation
Notes on the Town

by

Edmund Whitty, Senior Correspondent
The Falcon

Following the terrible death of Dorcas Owler, it has become clear to every Londoner of sound mind that she is Chokee Bill's seventh victim. Hence, notwithstanding the identity of the Fiend in Human Form, he is at large. In spite of the urgency indicated by this self-evident fact, Under-Inspector Salmon, with the zeal of a deluded Muslim, persists in the persecution of a gentleman who, at the time of this selfsame murder, languished in a hole in Newgate Gaol.

An excess of zeal? Or is it the over-commodiousness of the ambitious, following orders from above?

While the health of an innocent man deteriorates in the most feared gaol in the realm, a murderer continues to take his grisly pleasure with the tacit approval of our city fathers. Having for decades countenanced and upheld the daily horrors of the rookeries, these fine gentlemen have little difficulty applying similar humbug to the murder of a Dorcas Owler, thereby turning Nelson's blind eye to the Fiend in Human Form.

All of which moves your correspondent to ask: If the worthy gentlemen of the City will tolerate such an enormity – what, then, is the City? Are we in Sodom? Are Londoners turning into pillars of salt?

While William Ryan continues to languish in a death cell, the City takes on a monstrous quality, which aspect presents itself plainly to your correspondent as he walks the Strand through poisonous wisps of yellow fog, exchanging nods with top-hatted sporting gentlemen – any one of whom might be a murderer – and turning away from strolling streetwalkers (a march-past of doomed women), any one of whom may be sacrificed to the Fiend.

Goode, Rochampton, Courvoisier, Chokee Bill: in truth, did these monstrous men, as we remember them, ever exist? Or did we make them into token villains, to be lanced like boils from the hindquarters of the City, then to disappear behind the walls of Newgate – while in London the infection continues? What folly, that such symptoms are hidden for cosmetic effect; that leprosy might be covered up so that the face of business can present a smooth smile to the customer.

When the City, to do its business, steps over the mutilated body of Dorcas Owler, is it so outlandish to imagine that the Fiend – whatever human form he takes – could be any man in London? Could he be, indeed, Everyman?

As your correspondent turns on to Piccadilly, a public omnibus passes, and for an instant he sees dreadful Greenacre seated within, a severed head carefully wrapped in a handkerchief and cradled in his lap, on his eternal journey about the City, flinching each time the conductor announces the fare as 'Sixpence a head!'

In the meanwhile, on the walkway near the omnibus, a workman pushes a cart containing a large trunk, eternally transporting a dissected victim of Mr Goode's.

Thus, as the city creates its villains for its own ends, it is in turn defined by them, at the cost of an ongoing procession of innocent dead. While William Ryan draws ever closer to the scaffold, while Chokee Bill goes uncaptured, the murders will continue. Savagery for the good of the city, and an ancient liturgy from our barbarous past.

And questions to be put to Under-Inspector Salmon.

A REPREHENSIBLE ACT
And a Nadir for British Journalism

by

Alasdair Fraser
Senior Correspondent
Dodd's

It is now clear that the correspondent for *The Falcon* intends to spread poison into every hearth in the realm with his outrageous allegations, the sum of which constitutes a monstrous insult to every Londoner, and to British Justice.

One can scarcely muster the dexterity to parse such twisted sentiments. It is as though, unconfined to the spectrum of Good and Evil, Decent and Fallen, Mr Whitty would treat the City itself (the greatest city on earth) as a village of damned souls, her policemen having become demons and her beloved Queen a predatory monstrosity with the claws of a dragon.

'It does not help our work,' laments Under-Inspector Salmon of Scotland Yard, 'that members of the press employ devious means to inflame the public.'

Of all Mr Whitty's deplorable pronouncements, for shamelessness and sham, none approaches the latest onslaught. It is as if a chemist were to proclaim the existence of a poison, then turn around and market it to the general public as a tonic – the poison in this case being that which fouls the public mind with all that is vile, corrupt and pernicious. And if that is the state of things, who will not steal? Who will not resort to unspeakable practices in the name of pleasure? And which among us will resort to murder, there being no reason to recoil from anything, here in the village of the damned?

'Our enquiries,' continues the under-inspector, 'are not made easier by the flawed and false conclusions of the correspondent from *The Falcon*.'

As with the cry of 'Fire!' in a crowded theatre, no good will result from the capricious exaggerations of Edmund Whitty. And yet why should he care, when such obscene provocations sell papers and thereby enhance his pocket-book, as well as that which is left of his reputation? Whether the victim be a debauched doxy such as Dorcas Owler or an innocent of good family, the death of every one of these women is a gain to him. How long will London authorities countenance such atrocious public mischief as this?

A VISIT TO WILLIAM RYAN IN NEWGATE GAOL

by

Edmund Whitty
Senior Correspondent
The Falcon

Surely not one man out of a hundred whose road to business takes him through Newgate Street or the Old Bailey passes Newgate Gaol without a furtive glance upon its empty recesses, its small, grated windows – yet how many give a thought to the wretched beings immured in its dismal cells? What gentleman imagines that, day by day, hour by hour, he passes within a yard of some fellow creature, bound and helpless, entombed within this gloomy repository for the guilt of London, whose misery will soon terminate in a violent and shameful death?

Ever inquisitive, your correspondent set about to discover where, precisely, William Ryan may be situated.

Having shown our credentials to the servant, we were ushered into the office of the Governor's House, where, after a delay, the officer arrived whose duty it was to conduct us – a man of about fifty in a broad-brimmed hat, who looked as much like a clergyman as a turnkey; which gentleman led us into a small room containing a desk and a book for visitor's autographs.

On a shelf over the desk, curiously, were the heads and faces of the notorious murderers, Bishop and Williams; their features have been depicted so as to supply sufficient moral grounds for their execution, with no other evidence against them . . .

Leaving the office, your correspondent entered a long room with a choice collection of irons, then passed through a heavy oaken gate, studded with nails and guarded by another turnkey. Together with our escort, we passed through a number of tortuous stone windings, guarded in their turn by gates and gratings, thereby dispelling the slightest hope of escape – if only by virtue of the maze of confusion to be undergone in doing so.

Down a flight of steps we proceeded past the chapel, where, but a few years ago, condemned prisoners were suffered to attend their last service seated beside their own coffins.

Further downward are the dungeons known as Stonehold, where the miasma is indescribable. Sufficiently poor the ventilation, sufficiently thick the stench, that prisoners must be doused with vinegar before they are taken to court.

We now pass through the press-room – a long, sombre space with two tiny, grated windows and a table, upon which sits a Testament with no sign of having received recent use. In this room, three wretches sit pinioned and awaiting their execution.

'They are dead men,' notes the turnkey, within his subjects' hearing.

A few paces away, through a dark passage in which a charcoal stove casts a lurid glow over the vicinity, lie the cells. In one of these sits William Ryan, in irons, attended by an experienced turnkey who never leaves him under any circumstances.

It is a stone dungeon, eight feet long by six feet wide, with a bench at one end, under which are a prayer book and a Bible, with an iron candlestick fixed on the wall to one side. The tiny grated window above admits neither air nor light.

On the bench sits William Ryan.

'Welcome, Sir,' announces the unfortunate. 'I regret that I cannot offer you refreshment, but my circumstances have been limited somewhat since last we met.'

Conceive the situation of this man, his state of isolation! Consider the thoughts which must weigh upon his mind! Imagine his feverish restlessness, the fear of death amounting almost to madness, together with an overwhelming sense of his own helplessness in the face of an implacable officialdom, yet tantalized by a faint hope of reprieve – faint indeed, for all the good that your correspondent has been able to effect!

Conceive, therefore, the heavy heart of your correspondent, who, after having received the most civil of greetings, must inform our anxious friend that there is no hopeful news, that the official line has not altered, that the under-inspector fails to see, or cannot see, or refuses to see, that which is patently plain to any man with a pair of eyes. What a temptation to fall into bitterness and despair!

Though noticeably weaker (the result of foul air, bad food and want of exercise), his fine features having grown ever more pinched and old, the condemned man rises to his feet and stands erect, grey eyes sharp as he shakes our hand, asks after our health, commends himself to persons dear to him, and speaks of the future with optimism.

Replies your correspondent: 'I am deeply sorry, Sir, for the disappointing manner in which your case has been dealt thus far. But we must not give up. Do not lose hope, Sir. For we are in England, where sanity prevails.'

Replies William Ryan: 'I am grateful for your assistance, Sir. Bring on the worst, yet still I shall be grateful.'

Grateful to me!

42

The Crown

Phoebe has not wept since she left Dorcas's side, not once, not a tear. There is no room inside for grief, such is her anger – which is for the best; being young, she is more equipped for the latter than the former.

Unlike grief, anger may be contained within an anaesthetic, almost pleasurable, calm; to look at Phoebe, a casual observer would see nothing other than another young woman naively determined to defeat poverty, using the one saleable commodity in her possession: dressed like a whore, but with no eye for the subtleties – that, for an example, it is of no use to unbutton a bodice when there is no cleavage to display, nor to paint lips red whose natural expression is of precise determination.

The girl in question would make a far more suitable prospect were she to have remained properly buttoned and to make use of her natural attributes – keen features, a quick wit, an sardonic eye – thereby to beguile some university gentleman.

For in truth there exists no young female (charwoman or countess, schoolgirl or flower-seller) in London who does not exist in some male mind as a tantalizing fantasy, in whose honour some schoolboy does not regularly engage in self-abuse – a fantasy which, when he becomes an old boy, he will seek to make real. Hence, the relation between the brothel and the theatre: success in both depends upon one's observation of the world, of the human mind, as well as one's own outward identity in the calligraphy of sex.

Given that Phoebe is a virgin who has never sought to acquire such insights, the weapon hidden in her dress (the knife with which she prepared her father's supper each evening) is but a useless extremity, her pose a trap improperly set – a trap which has not been set at all.

Yet this is her only hope if she is to look him in the face.

Dorcas once treated Phoebe to a ride in a hackney coach in their customary guise of well-born ladies – the price of the ride, Phoebe was assured, having been extracted from a gentleman's purse on Oxford Street. On that occasion did Dorcas point out the house off Bruton Street; then they rode around Berkeley Square again and again, having no place else to go.

'Ain't it prime,' Dorcas said wistfully of the house, momentarily allowing her accent to slip. 'And to think he is tall and handsome into the bargain! And he likes me, Miss Phoebe, so he does . . .'

The day and night following that terrible afternoon, Phoebe sat under a plane tree in Berkeley Square, not once taking her eyes from the four-storey corner building, confident that she would recognize Mr Roo on sight. Not until she felt certain to have inspected every occupant, both entering and exiting, did she admit defeat; for there was not one resident she could describe as resembling Dorcas's handsome lover.

Not that it is by any means certain that Mr Roo is her friend's murderer. As Mr Whitty demonstrated, one does not find the truth straightaway but blindly and step by step . . .

Now she finds herself at the Crown, pursuing her alternate course – taking Dorcas's place, literally so, at a table that she knows her friend favoured, from which position she hopes to encounter the gentleman she seeks. With the confidence of the young she knows she will recognize Mr Roo when she sees him.

On the dance floor, the ladies – Miss Fowler, Miss Bolton and a nameless blue-eyed girl with colourless hair – wearing short capes over their *décolleté*, dance with shop managers and the sons of shop managers, warehouse-owners and the sons of warehouse-owners. Unused to dancing and therefore ill at ease, the gentlemen don't speak as much as one word to their ladies; indeed, the atmosphere is oddly formal. But the hour is still early; by midnight these awkward gentlemen, emboldened by two bottles of champagne at ten shillings a bottle, will warm to the atmosphere on the dance floor, not to mention the *décolleté* before their faces, and the ladies will profit well.

Carefully Phoebe studies the faces of the women, their subtlety of expression and economy of gesture; so rapt does she become that at first she fails to recognize his voice.

'Good evening, Miss Owler, I am relieved to have found you.'

Anticipating the advances of a stranger, momentarily she panics, unable to formulate a sensible reply, nor to look the gentleman in the face; having been rendered in this instant paralysed at the prospect of a prospective gentleman – a *customer* – who expects her to carry out the unmentionable thing, a thing she blushes to speak of, even to another of her sex . . .

Mr Whitty.

The sudden appearance of that familiar and agreeable face comes as a not unwelcome shock. Her fury at his apparent sang-froid amid the stark horror of her friend's demise having abated, she has had time to make excuses for him. It is the profession which is heartless, not the practitioner. All men in public life are benumbed in certain ways; it is not his fault.

'Notwithstanding the events on Cannon Street Road, Miss, surely you're aware that, while I'm a hard gentleman with a bitter tongue, I am not a monster.' Whitty lights a cigaret, allowing the point to sink in. 'Surely you know that the death of your friend affected me greatly as soon as I realized it was she. Please understand that this dismal circumstance has only increased my determination to seek out the beast who would do such a thing.'

Whitty is a smooth man and she does not trust him; nonetheless, she gives him her full attention. Even in her present preoccupation with death and retribution and unimaginable loss, the young woman cannot help noting Mr Whitty's fine coat and haberdashery, his impeccable grooming – whatever the condition of the man within.

'I've been searching for you, Miss. Your father is in anguish. He needs you.'

'I'm on other business, Mr Whitty.'

'Evidently – you have assumed an uncharacteristic wardrobe.'

'It has accomplished me nothing, I regret to say.'

'To be candid, I found you presentable as you were.'

'Maybe so, Mr Whitty. Men's tastes, I'm told, vary.'

The correspondent pauses to nod a tribute in the direction of Miss Fowler and Miss Bolton, who smile over their admirers' shoulders. 'Indeed they do vary.'

'And how do you do, Sir? Well enough?'

'Somewhat battered by events, Miss Phoebe. As, I am certain, are you.'

A long pause ensues. Unprepared to withstand a tense silence under Whitty's gaze, Phoebe reaches for her glass – disastrously, for she cannot bring the gin to her lips for the trembling of her hands. The truth now being obvious, she buries her face into the crook of one bare arm and falls to sobbing upon the table; whereupon in an instant Mr Whitty has occupied the chair alongside, there to enfold her in a pair of surprisingly strong arms for an idle gentleman, arms whose attendant tenderness gives heart to her in the way her father once did when she was small, and her mother too, she supposes, whoever she was.

'Miss, I request the honour of your company, that we might speak privately on a matter of importance to us both.'

So saying, he rises and extends the crook of his elbow to her – which she takes, in the way she has seen with ladies and gentlemen of the quality. Thus appearing, to her own eyes at least, like any other lady of the evening in the company of a sporting gentleman, she climbs the open stairs to the mezzanine and thence down a carpeted hallway, which opens onto a series of supper rooms for private entertainment. One of these facilities contains two laughing young women, their male friend, and a 'guest' – the latter gentleman being entertained over food and drink, amid light-hearted games of chance, inadvertent touches and exposures of flesh – the object being to extract from the bedazzled guest everything he has in his purse and get a good dinner into the bargain. At the end of another short hallway they enter an office which is clearly that of the proprietor, for its walls have been papered with advertisements for signal matches in a career of over a hundred prize-fights, culminating in his two epic encounters with the Negro Narcissus – the last of which Stunning Joe Banks survived for thirteen rounds, despite a right forearm dislocated from prematurely putting his weight into a jab during the sixth.

The gentleman looming over his desk is of truly alarming propor-tions – greyhound-thin around the waist, yet massive about the chest, with pads of muscle seemingly overlaid like armour on the shoulders and arms; as well, she notes the ugly, inexpressive countenance, the imprint of its owner's former profession – the flattened nose, the cheeks covered by layers of scar tissue with the metallic sheen of a fish.

'Miss Phoebe Owler, allow me to present Mr Joseph Banks, an associate.'

'What manner of associate, Sir?'

'Mr Whitty and I exchange information to our mutual benefit, Miss,' offers the gentleman behind the desk. 'How do you do? I have the honour of serving as the proprietor of this establishment.'

While adapting to an unprecedented situation in the company of two such impressive gentlemen, Phoebe maintains what she deems to be an icy poise.

'How do you do, Sir? I am reasonably well and hope you are the same.'

The grotesque yet elegant gentleman rounds the desk to extend a hand which might be a lump of knotted hardwood, which she holds briefly, though unwilling at the same time to release the arm of the correspondent.

'Please sit down, Miss.' Stunning Joe gestures to a surprisingly delicate chair made of wicker. 'Might the Crown offer you its hospitality in the form of something to drink?'

'Spiced gin, if you please – I prefer "the Out-and-Out".'

The correspondent intervenes: 'A cup of punch for the young woman please, Mr Banks.'

'You are impertinent, Mr Whitty. The gentleman asked me and I requested spiced gin.'

Replies the correspondent: 'It was Miss Dorcas who customarily asked for spiced gin. May I ask, Miss, if you are contemplating this impersonation for some private purpose?'

'That is none of your business, Sir.' She maintains her calm: How does he know her so well?

A discreet cough from the proprietor: 'And something for yourself, Edmund?'

'A small whisky for the moment, Mr Banks, thank you.'

'How small?'

'Rather large, actually.'

'Very good, Sir.'

Phoebe waves a small thank-you to the retreating proprietor, who responds with a near imperceptible nod before closing the door. The correspondent, having worried himself white over the young lady's absence, then having calmed himself by means of forty drops of tincture of opium, therefore being insensible to the quiver of erotic content in the ambience at present, continues: 'You manage a fine portrayal of Dorcas, to be sure. However, at this time it is my wish to communicate with Miss Phoebe Owler, and not her tragic friend.'

'Such presumption, Sir. I don't recall having become your ward.'

'Miss Owler, under these difficult circumstances, what is it that we are attempting to achieve?'

'May I ask, Sir, what is it you mean by *we*? You and I are not in business together.'

'*Touché*, Miss. Yet my question stands.'

'I am not so unpresentable, Sir, and thought a gentleman would like me. That I might go with him to a room and let him do what he likes to me for money. Is that not how a girl makes a place for herself in this world?'

'I take your point. It is a dirty business and the great hypocrisy of our time.'

'Please don't talk to me in headlines, Mr Whitty, I don't like it.'

'Never reject a member of the press, Miss. A trite spokesman is better than none at all.'

She nearly laughs. Strange how one can still laugh.

'Miss Owler, allow me to express my condolences over your terrible loss. Such loss is meant for soldiers.'

'I don't understand you, Mr Whitty. Do you wish to make a joke of it?'

'On the subject of misery and death, jokes are all I have left.'

'Then you should make better jokes.'

'True. Now that I think about it, I never laugh at them myself.'

'Why did you wish to see me?'

Replies the correspondent: 'To congratulate you.'

'Congratulate me? What have I accomplished?'

'You have instinctively grasped that the fiend cannot be hunted but must be lured. A sophisticated concept and I commend you for it. However, if I may be so bold, there remain important particulars.'

'And what might they be?'

'For one, your father has no knife with which to make his supper. He has requested that you please return it to him, so that he may slice a bit of mutton.'

'I have no knife. He should look for it in the box next the fire.'

'I am relieved to hear it, for the implement will be of more use there than under your skirts. Which subject brings me to the second particular: May one take it that you seek to attract the attentions of one specific gentleman – as opposed to the male population at large?'

She feels her cheeks redden at the thought.

'Correct, Sir. His name is Mr Roo, and with my own eyes have I once seen him.'

'May I take you to mean that you would recognize him were you to see him again?'

'Indeed, Sir. I must.'

'Not if he chokes the life out of you, Miss Owler. For if he is the one we seek, you may have in your possession a far more deadly weapon than a pantry knife.'

'What weapon is that?'

'Singular knowledge.'

She notes wistfully that the gentleman did not mention her physical attributes. She is not surprised, however. That was Dorcas's speciality.

'If I may speak frankly,' continues Whitty, 'there is a man awaiting execution for a series of atrocities. Without your assistance, it is probable that our man will hang, while the Fiend continues to kill. Might one assume that this is not the outcome you seek?'

'That is a rhetorical question, Sir, which you may answer for yourself.'

Stunning Joe re-enters the room with a tray of drinks, which he sets upon the edge of the desk, his ruined face composed in an expression of interest, watching and listening as the correspondent undertakes to scour the young woman's memory for every particular, every fragment concerning her late friend's connection with this Mr Roo, the prince she claimed to have acquired, a member of the quality with such handsome features, manners and bearing, the swell who displayed such expressions of affection – in particular a willingness to entertain Dorcas in his own impossibly luxurious rooms.

'That is an odd name, Miss Owler – *Roo*. I don't think I know of it.'

'Whether odd or not, she would talk of nobody else. I suppose a pseudonym might not be an altogether rare device, when a fine gentleman chooses to seduce beneath his station.'

'True. Yet you say she mentioned a "frog" – a companion with whom this gentleman frequented the divans and supper rooms, in comparison with whom our Mr Roo was a prince.'

'Yes, she sometimes saw them together. However, I remember nothing of him. He was entirely unremarkable.'

'Given that he would venture a false name, it is inconsistent that he would entertain her in his own rooms.'

'Nonetheless, that is my understanding of it.'

'Quite. Did she mention the location of these lodgings?'

'Only that it was in Mayfair.'

'You have not seen the place yourself?'

'Certainly not, Sir, otherwise I should say so.'

Whitty produces an object and places it on the desk before her. 'Does this item signify anything to you at all?'

She picks up the silver flask and examines it. The face of the man who carried it is perfectly clear to her now.

'Mr Roo was drinking from this flask. I remember the crest, though I saw it mostly upside-down. It is how I knew him as a member of the quality.'

'Or a feigned member of the quality,' remarks Stunning Joe, towering above her. 'Such coats of arms be bespoken from any engraver on Oxford Street for £20.'

'True, Mr Banks,' replies Whitty. 'In any case, Miss Owler, I agree with you that it would be most co-operative were our man to approach his next victim in these premises. However, I am not confident that he can be that stupid – would you not agree, Mr Banks? – or he would be awaiting hanging in Newgate, and not a hapless coiner and crim-con artist named William Ryan.'

'Men are creatures of habit,' counters the proprietor. 'Once a man has selected a drinking place, there is very little will shift him from it.'

The correspondent concedes the point, being himself a loyal patron.

Continues the proprietor: 'Miss, may I emphasize that the Crown don't react favourably to brutal crimes, it is a bad business. Indeed, our reputation rests upon the confidence that any citizen may attend without fear. Thus you may appreciate our interest in seeing the matter resolved. Consequently, Miss, the Crown wishes to extend our invitation, not to say request, that you frequent the establishment as our honoured guest, our agent if your prefer – for which we are prepared to advance a suitable stipend, and, in the event of success, a suitable reward.'

'That is generous of you, Mr Banks. His capture would be sufficient.'

The proprietor turns to the correspondent: 'An impressive young lady if I may say so, Edmund.'

'Indeed, Mr Banks. Once again, Miss Owler, may we rest assured that you have availed us of the full particulars?'

'I beg your pardon, Sir, but no lady tells a gentleman everything.'

'I think you know of what I speak.'

'Indeed, you're a man who expresses himself clearly. That is your profession.'

'Quite.' The correspondent lights a cigaret in the stylish manner she has seen in the divans. 'Which allows me to return to our principal theme: you do nobody any good, least of all the memory of your friend, by acting as a goat in a trap. We are not in Africa.'

'Amen to that, Mr Whitty,' concurs the proprietor. 'Englishmen are not savages.'

'On the contrary, some are,' says Phoebe.

'She is a quick one,' says Stunning Joe Banks. 'Yet you would be surprised how many savages will put their savagery behind in order to stop in for a quiet glass and to have a look at the ladies. Sex is the lesser of many evils – if you will pardon my frankness to one so young.'

She replies, while directing her gaze to Mr Whitty. 'I am not so inexperienced as you think, Sir. I come of age next 19 October.'

'I look forward to it,' replies the correspondent. 'However, by

October I plan to have perished of a wasting disease.'

'That would be a pity, Sir. A waste, you might say.' Only in the ensuing silence does Phoebe realize that she is flirting.

'More significant, Miss, given that nobody paid particular attention to the man, is the fact that you are the one person in London who might conceivably point to the Fiend. However, I emphasize that we do not expect you to do for him in the way that the Frenchwoman Corday did for Marat . . .'

Whereupon he pauses, due to an interruption from the room next door, where certain entertainments can be heard taking place – the slap of a hand on soft flesh; the rustle of fabric; a ripple of sensuous laughter; the pop of a champagne cork.

Whitty clears his throat, delicately. 'Mr Banks, I note that the atmosphere adjacent to us has assumed a tone inconsistent with that which should occupy the ears of a well-bred young woman. Therefore, Miss Owler, if I may, allow me to conduct you home to your father by cab, so that you may return his knife.'

'Which knife do you mean?' enquires the young woman. 'Do you see a knife?'

Nothing is more incendiary to an ill-advised, unanticipated tryst than to be enclosed in a darkened, plush-upholstered, moving chamber. Privacy, Intimacy, Darkness, Transience: the Four Whoresmen of the Apocalypse.

Share a cab with a member of the opposite sex for twenty minutes, and no matter how inappropriate such untoward speculation may seem in relation to a man and a woman, still there will arise, if that is the word, an animal aspect inherent in the human spirit which the civilized man stifles with discomfort and ignores at his peril – for, however advantageous such a conveyance may be for an intimate assignation, that advantage becomes an alarming liability when the avoidance of such intimacy is an overwhelming necessity.

Standing beside Phoebe beneath the gaslight on Orange Street, already Whitty can sense that he has stepped into a delicate situation, as they await a cab in a mist which is not quite rain and not quite fog. Standing beside a young lady dressed for the business of the evening, he attracts looks of disapprobation from the open-air preacher at the corner with Bible and umbrella ('Yes, brethren, I was a sinner but the Lord's grace touched me' – etc., etc.), as well as the knowing winks and leers of the half-dozen clubmen who pass by, puffing their cigars.

Whitty shudders at the idea of such exploitation as he would at incest; the thought of such advances at such a time takes on a monstrous, deformed aspect. And yet such is his position that to refute such a possibility is to admit it as well.

The open-air preacher has a long face and a nasal voice and a small sign in front (COME TO JESUS NOW). In speaking he has a habit of casting his eyes into his umbrella. ('Jesus Christ came for us miserable sinners. Let us take thought for ourselves.') Inspired by the opportunity to deliver two souls from eternal perdition, he opens his Testament and, pointedly directing his gaze at the couple by the kerb, intones a passage concerning the Saviour and Mary Magdalene, in which a young woman of easy virtue washes the feet of her Redeemer and wipes them with her long hair – an unhelpful allusion, for, while the preacher draws from it edification to the effect that Christ is our refuge and our salvation, etc., etc., in the case of the correspondent, imagery of quite another order springs irresistibly to mind – of soft feminine hair on bare feet, etc., etc. . . . .

Phoebe, in the meanwhile, has found relief from her lingering grief in the form of a desire for the correspondent – a girlish combination of genuine affection and romantic fancy, not to mention the yearning to experience the pleasures of full womanhood. At the minimum, Whitty offers Phoebe a degree of freedom – the exhilaration of the over-whelming present.

A cab materializes before them. Mr Whitty steps off the kerb and opens the door for her. Momentarily she gazes into the charmed space within, suddenly shy of entering.

'Now then, my lovely, is you getting in or no, for we mustn't be keeping a gentleman waiting.' So says the bottle-nosed driver, wearing a heap of multiple cloaks topped by a horse-blanket, tiny inscrutable eyes behind several folds of skin, and one upturned corner of a liver-coloured mouth.

'Now, my man,' Whitty admonishes. 'How dare you speak to a lady in such terms.'

Phoebe smiles sweetly to the driver: 'Keep your bloody pants on, duckie,' she says in her doxiest manner. 'You is dealing wiff a lady.'

Which response earns her a long laugh from the driver, followed by a fit of coughing.

'Quite,' offers Whitty, handing the young lady up with a sensation of unaccountable unease. 'Leicester Square, please.'

Whitty closes the door and, as the cab lurches forward, settles beside the young lady, who is grateful for the darkness so that he cannot see her reddened cheeks. To Phoebe, a carriage such as this is a cocoon of impossible luxury – a room that does not reek of dried sweat, spilled gin, stale beer, rank breath, but instead virtually glows with a warm, rich, masculine smell of fine cigars, fine horses, grooming preparations redolent with lavender . . . Still maintaining her acerbic half-smile for his benefit while her eyes adjust to the woolly dark, she parts the curtains in time to glimpse a passing yellow phaeton – a violent splash of colour in an otherwise silver-and-black tapestry of movement and reflected light.

As for Mr Whitty, any reader who assumes that he would experience aught but misgiving at the inappropriate sensations which accompany this sudden intimacy would be widely at variance with the facts. On balance, with all flaws accounted for and when not in an inebriated state, the correspondent can lay claim to a relatively high standard of gentlemanly conduct. Yet, however honourable his intentions, the sensuous affection of any young woman for any older man must of necessity admit for the latter a painful longing for the Platonic essence of life (as opposed to Aristotelian actuality) – by which we mean that it is impossible for the older man to entirely resist a sentimental torrent of might-have-been, a yearning for a charmed realm of transcendent, youthful joy which once seemed possible but which has grown increasingly remote, as age, sorrow, circumstance and indulgence take their toll.

So thinks Whitty, sitting stiffly beside Phoebe, near enough to feel the warmth of her, glancing furtively and with uncertain eyesight at the transparently innocent, perfect face beside him – like a delicate window, so easily smudged.

Her heartbeat having increased somewhat, Phoebe looks her companion in the face for the first time since entering the cab – her Mr Whitty, in his lovely coat, his freshly brushed hat upon his lap, in the process of taking snuff with practised elegance. Yet in catching his eye with hers, she maintains an aspect of milky calm.

'Mr Whitty, what is the Fiend? Is he a human being?'

'On that score I am no wiser than you, Miss Phoebe. Nor is Mr Banks, who has seen much. However, unless our picture of Mr Roo is a case of girlish fancy making a prince out of a frog, we may assume this creature to dress, behave, and indeed live like any other gentleman – in all ways but one.'

'Do you think that if one were to look deep into his eyes it might be possible to detect the Fiend within?'

'I do not know, Miss. In my darker moments I suspect that there exists such a monstrosity in every man, which only the force of civilization and moral instruction keeps at bay – and imperfectly at that. To be candid, the purported innocence of the 'natural man' is altogether too French for my taste.'

'When I look into your eyes, I see a kindness which has always been present, or so it seems to me.' So says Phoebe, doing so.

During the ensuing pause it seems to Phoebe that she may have incurred a touch of fever, no doubt a shock to the system born of recent events.

'I beg your pardon, Miss Phoebe, but, if I may say so, you appear somewhat flushed. Do you wish me to stop the carriage? May I fetch you a drink, or offer a medicament for the nerves?'

'Nothing, thank you, Sir. However, I do believe . . .' Phoebe slips backward into the corner of the seat, for suddenly she is shivering.

Perceiving his companion to grow faint, Whitty secures one arm about her shoulders so that he may support her; in the meanwhile, the sleeve of his other arm accidentally touches her bosom as he attempts to warm her, so that, inadvertently, they are in a virtual embrace, his scented whiskers brushing her cheek, her breath soft upon his ear; whereupon she opens her eyes, now mere inches from his, wearing an expression she has seen on the faces of dancing ladies at the Crown – peering deep into his eyes, seeing only kindness there.

'Oh, Mr Whitty,' she whispers. 'I don't know what is happening.' So saying, as though to eliminate the uncertainty, she delivers the correspondent a lingering kiss, full on the mouth – it being the first time she has kissed a man, she wishes to experience it fully.

And the extent of Whitty's error occurs to him in full force.

Excellent. Skilfully done, old chap. You have blundered into moral quicksand. Such opportunities for making a cad of oneself! See them glisten!

True, his working method in pursuing this narrative has been no more chaotic than usual: like a hound, one detects a trail, which, by instinct, smells fresh. Off one goes with one's tail in the air in pursuit of the scent, until one comes to a fork. A pause follows; then, with an amount of prescience no more reliable than the insight of a threepenny Tarot-reader, one chooses left, or right; and so to continue to the next fork in the path, there to choose, and choose, and choose again . . .

Oh, dear God, and now he is kissing Phoebe. Long and deep – too deep to pass off as avuncular affection. Her small lips are moving with his, and with the utmost delicacy, and an eagerness to please – which fills the correspondent with an aching sadness, for he does not wish to be pleased by her in that way.

'I beg you, Miss Phoebe, this must stop.'

'Why would you wish it so, Mr Whitty?' So saying, she kisses him again; Heaven help him, he participates.

'Miss Phoebe, do I have your permission to speak candidly?'

'By all means, Sir, I should have it no other way.'

'In the first place, were this . . . this circumstance to go further, your father should have me unmanned with an axe.'

She laughs aloud. 'Do you really think so? How savage!'

'Well I shouldn't blame him. Perhaps I should do the job myself. To involve you further in this terrible business, and then to commit an intimacy into the bargain . . .'

Again she laughs – with regret now, for she can feel the moment recede. 'I am not a child, Mr Whitty. I know what is where, and I know what everything looks like, and I know where everything goes.'

'Of that I have not the slightest doubt,' he replies, ruefully, having for the moment lost the argument.

And so again they kiss – for Whitty a huge step backward; clearly it is one thing to settle on an ethical destination, quite another to summon the required strength to get there.

'I plead with you, Miss, do not kiss me again. You're hitting me below the belt,' says the correspondent, instantly regretting the metaphor.

'Might we discuss the matter rationally, Sir?'

'If only we could, Miss Phoebe.'

'Surely you don't suppose that I am a virgin?'

'Indeed, I am utterly certain of it.'

She frowns at the suggestion. 'Certain on what basis, Sir?'

'As a trained observer, may I say that you have the aspect, the eyes, and the spirit of an undefeated angel.'

She moves back in her seat, the better to determine whether she is being mocked. 'Undefeated, Sir? Whatever can you mean? For I assure you I am no angel.'

'By undefeated, I mean that nobody has yet taken away from you that which can never be returned.'

'*Yet*, Mr Whitty?'

'*Yet*, Miss Phoebe.'

They exchange a long look, the last between them of its kind, then a gentle embrace, one which he might reasonably term avuncular, again with his whiskers brushing her cheek – except that now they tickle her, they make her laugh a little, for the situation has grown humorous.

'I prefer your first excuse, Mr Whitty.'

'What excuse is that, Miss Phoebe?'

'That my father might unman you with an axe.'

43

The Holy Land

Henry Owler has not slept since the death. Nor has he moved since his return to the Holy Land, when he entered the room, saw and heard and felt its emptiness, and turned into a statue of grief. Odd, he thinks, emptiness being stronger than stone. For hours he has maintained precisely the same posture, in the way that a clown will impersonate a thinking man, perched on the edge of an empty bed, staring at another empty bed, behind him the makeshift curtain of patchwork, through which he has passed for the first time. The bed in front of him, which still belongs to Dorcas, remains precisely as she left it; therefore does the patterer cling to the sight of an unkempt blanket, as though the hand that moved it continues to exist in the room, hanging in the air like fog.

If only he could sleep. Yet he cannot, for his own daughter has not returned, nor has Mr Whitty sent word. Thus Henry Owler, father of Phoebe, sleepless, stares at what has been lost like a man perched at the edge of a cliff, chin in hand, awaiting the signal to leap.

'Father?' At first she thought the room empty, until she pushed aside the curtain.

He does not turn at first, believing the voice to have come from inside his own mind.

'Mr Whitty remarked as you needed your knife for supper.' Whereupon she drops the implement on the bed beside him.

He rises to his feet and reaches for her. His back temporarily declines to straighten properly and he finds himself bent like a hunchback until she steadies him, whereupon for a long time they hold one another, neither knowing precisely who is comforting whom.

He looks at the knife and apprehends its meaning. 'I will put this clearly, girl: I would rather the murderer go unpunished forever, that he live his cursed life in luxury and ease, than risk the loss of you.'

She puts her arms around her father and kisses him. There is no need for him to know what she intends.

The patterer has had the entire night in which to formulate his plan, for the citizens who frequent Carrier Square don't begin to disperse throughout London before eleven of a morning, nor return before daybreak of the next. Lying wide-eyed in his cot, heeding to the regular breathing in the second cot, and the silence in the third cot, he has ample time in which to contemplate the fullness and the emptiness and the impossible grandeur of life – a most intricate business. The resulting sense of wonder he expresses by the writing of a Sorrowful Lamentation:

> O heed ye to Henry, a man of your world,
> Charged with the care of two innocent girls;
> For the sake of a pound he directed his quill
> To the man who would hang as the Fiend Chokee Bill.
>
> While Henry did plot the condemned man to meet,
> Freely the monster was stalking the street;
> Yet for a story he shut up his ear
> To the villain who'd murder his innocent dear.
>
> And now he repenteth his seeking for glory,
> Repenteth the taking of life for a story,
> Thanks to the Fiend of a daughter bereft,
> Perhaps to be robb'd of the one he has left . . .

Having taken tea in the public kitchen, with his freshly papered sandwich-board with its Sorrowful Lamentation draped over his shoulders, the patterer awkwardly mounts one of the coster carts in the square, moving aside the indecently protesting figures of its two female occupants. So situated with a view of the buildings (which, in the morning fog, resemble sooty-faced, one-eyed wraiths, their empty sockets patched with rags), he glances behind at the now-empty clothes-lines of Rosemary Lane, lifts the iron pot and stirring-spoon which he has taken from Mrs Organ, the ancient keeper of the public stove, and proceeds to apply one to the other with such force that the clamour elicits a responding fusillade of protest from the whores in the nearby carts, and from hundreds of unseen occupants within the tottering wrecks of surrounding houses – the costers and the black Irish, the coiners and the magsmen, the rampsmen, bludgers, buzzers, macers, dippers, nobblers, mumpers and troopers whose vocation is to inconvenience, injure and infect the upright citizens of London.

Heads begin to appear in the windows and to poke up from the cellarways, yet the patterer continues his unwelcome tintinnabulation; only when he is certain that even the rats are listening does he begin his annunciation, speaking in a voice honed and hardened to penetrate walls, while gazing about with eyes filled with tears. Protest or no, they will listen.

'Come-all! Come-all! Look to Henry Owler, and contemplate his errors to your future betterment! Born in 1812, of humble yet industrious parents, what left him to the custody of a maiden aunt at a willage in Essex! Where in penurious circumstances his infant ears oft harkened to the Sunday schools of his native place, singing the well-known words of Watts' beautiful hymn:

> When e'er I take my walks abroad,
> How many poor I see. . .

'Thus did the boy set down the broad roadway what is walked by the poor, seeking to better his own condition! Made his first duckett at twelve he did, no effort too great for a fadge! Who, from ambition, did not marry until twenty-five, whose lovely Edith of Clapham was took by a fever what all the tonics on Camomile Street could not cure, and him with a baby girl!

'Yet such losses and blessings did not prepare him against the foul demon what ever haunts the footsteps of the ambitious, waiting to pounce! Hypocrisy, Sir! Lies, Madam – agreed-to for personal gain!

'Come-all! Come-all! Learn what price he has paid for his blindness! Innocent girl falls to fiend! Barbarous murder! Mendacity brings father life of regret! In pursuit of untruthful narrative, a man abets a murderer! Hear his sorrowful lamentation! Intimate details! Full particulars! Mystery revealed! Horrid and inhuman murder, with more to come! Wile and inhuman seducer slays innocent girl! Bereaved father can but watch and wait! Intimate details, full particulars guaranteed to move the feeling heart! . . .'

Slowly, still grumbling, the bedraggled populace straggle out of their suffocating lairs to gather about the patterer. Switching from one coster cart to another when required to vacate by the owner, Owler carries on his standing spiel for two hours in classic professional form – the exceptional circumstance being that in this case he has no broadsheets to sell. Instead, the crowd of interested parties gathers about his board and reads the narrative for nothing, then scatters throughout the city with the story firmly imprinted in the mind.

Thus informed go the multifarious citizens of the Holy Land: the widow whose husband has died in the hospital for consumptives as many times as Wellington saw engagements; the master of the Poxen Dodge, having applied acid to wounds punctured with a pin to cause the exposed surfaces of his body to present a mass of sores; Dry-Land Jack, who lost an arm in the Spanish Legion, never having been nearer to Spain than to Patagonia. Likewise the six shallow coves with twenty-seven stolen shirts, looking for a Welshman named Taff on Rosemary Lane; the twin orphan watercress-girls in matching dark print frocks, matching black chip bonnets and matching solemn eyes; the dextrous young wire (a picker of ladies' pockets) – an agile lad with beautiful hands who can crouch to half his height and creep up on his mark like a cat; the blind bootlace-seller, who for a ha'penny will tell of the day his eyeballs burst from smallpox; the screever with the shaved head and the coloured chalk with which to depict Christ with Crown of Thorns on flagstones; the family doing the Respectable Family Dodge, in their shabby yet scrupulously clean clothes, with a pack of pawn tickets to show they have parted with their all before coming to this, while the father stands silently with a paper over his face (*To a Human Public: I have seen Better Days*); and finally the lowly stick-men, off to Covent Garden for a 'tightener' of rotten oranges, to tighten the gut and hold at bay the awareness of starvation . . .

Amid the public's infatuation with the telegraph it is all too easy to disregard the near miraculous passage of facts, warnings and rumours that occurs daily among the poor; how the presence of an especially vigilant crusher or an especially generous almshouse or a butcher who cheats with his scale becomes generally known from one end of London to the other within moments of its revelation.

From this morning onward, Phoebe will puzzle at the inexplicable gaze of impoverished strangers, while the leisure hours of many a fine-looking young clubman will be rendered less hospitable by the seemingly inescapable presence of the most appalling wretches, eyeing his every move. Especially discomfited by this change in the atmosphere of his favourite hunting-ground is Reginald Harewood, having received from the barkeeper at the Crown some awfully distressing news.

A MEMORANDUM TO MR ROO

You have lost an object which may prove of considerable value to your personal assurance. Should you desire its return for payment of a suitable reward, would you please indicate to this effect, care of the Crown.

– A Friend of Dorcas

44

Sewell's rooms, off Bruton Street

Having spent an hour in the accomplishment of her errand, Phoebe smiles upon exiting the house off Bruton Street, imagining Mr Whitty's surprise were he to know to what degree he had served as her supplier of information and not the reverse – that the net gain had been hers. For though she knew precisely where Mr Roo lived, it is thanks to the correspondent that she now possesses a better picture of him, and a worthier commodity than her body with which to lure him in.

Of course, even with the knowledge of the flask to attract Mr Roo's interest (assuming it is the same flask he made such good use of on the night they met), still she faced the same difficulty as to how contact might be effected; therefore she took the simple expedient of slipping her message beneath every single door in the house.

With renewed hope, she runs to New Bond Street and thence back to the Crown. Were she to have proceeded at a more leisurely pace, she might have met the hansom cab containing the very gentleman she seeks – albeit in a somewhat dishevelled state – making its way to the house off Bruton Street.

Sewell finds it a worry whenever his friend fails to appear at his lodgings for several days in succession, at the minimum for a glass of brandy and the loan of a few bob. Unwanted images invade the mind, of Reggie garrotted in a ditch, or taken with cholera; in this instance Sewell's unease has been multiplied by the mysterious, cryptic note which someone slipped under his door, addressed to 'Mr Roo' in a female hand – which, together with his vague familiarity with the name 'Dorcas', induced the young man to experience that peculiar pulling in the chest which has occurred with greater frequency of late.

The message has remained open on the table in the sitting-room all day, awaiting an explanation from his absent friend.

Finally he hears Reggie's knock – three fast, two slow, one firm – a code they devised as schoolboys at Eton.

'Reggie, old man. Thank Heaven. I have just received a curious note concerning a young woman.'

'Confound your note. For the love of Jesus let a fellow in.'

'You do look a fright. What in Heaven has happened?'

'I've suffered the most beastly ill-luck in the world.'

Indeed, the young man standing unsteadily on the landing little resembles the dashing young Harewood whose face and form Sewell knows as if they were his own. This is not the irresistible rogue who chases Haymarket whores, watched over by his appreciative chum; this is not the sport on whose behalf Sewell gladly bet and lost £10 at cards a week ago. On the contrary, this is the face of a man who has been diagnosed with an incurable disease.

'I beg you, dear fellow, come in at once. By Heaven, you look as if you could make good use of a stiff brandy.'

'A capital suggestion.' Harewood stumbles into the room while lighting a cigaret with a trembling lucifer, his limp more pronounced than usual. 'It is a hellish thing, Roo. I've been most grievously used and am in dire peril.'

Sewell follows his friend into the drawing-room: by the rank smell of gin, tobacco and sweat, not to mention his friend's unkempt state, it is clear that Harewood has slept in his clothes – if indeed he has slept at all.

Sewell fetches a bottle and glasses, having noted that his friend has been drinking steadily and heavily enough to literally foam at the corners of his mouth. When a fellow has drunk this deep and this long, there lies a danger in attempting to become sober too quickly; indeed, such sudden abstinence can lead to dementia. Thus, additional alcohol is warranted.

Sewell administers to his friend two quick brandies in succession, then sits on the couch opposite, placing the bottle on the table next to the mysterious message.

'Reggie, you really must tell me what dreadful thing has put you in such a state.'

'I shall, indeed. But you must promise not to become cross with me, for it really is a devil of a thing that has happened . . .' Harewood's face once more crumples with despair.

'My dear fellow! Did Jonathan forsake David?'

'It's no laughing matter. I beg you not to joke about it.'

'Quite,' replies Sewell, for his friend appears inordinately serious, not like Reggie at all.

'Do you recall my speaking at one time or another of a . . . a certain young woman, in whom I had taken a . . . a certain interest?'

Indeed, how could Sewell forget, his normally impeccable bedroom having been drenched by their encounters.

'By this I take it you don't refer to your dear cousin.'

'I assure you, Sir, had I confined myself to Clara, I should not be as you see me now.'

'You did mention having relations with another female.'

'Actually, you might remember her yourself, from a fortnight or two back. Pair of ripe ones – except that one of them had a deuced filthy mouth.'

'That vile little thing? Dash it, you haven't taken up with her surely!'

'Hardly, I should say. No, the other. The blonde one.'

'What of her?'

'I'm blest if she isn't dead.'

'Dead? I say, that is hard. Not by violence, surely?'

'Very much so.'

'Well that certainly takes the fun out of it for you.'

'I say, Roo, at times your mode of expression is almost inhuman.'

'Sorry, old chap, don't mean it to be. Didn't know you were that fond of the girl.'

'How fond I was of the girl ain't the point. It's a rum thing to have your girl strangled, but that ain't the end of it. Damn it, Roo, I am associated with a grisly murder!'

'Such an association will go down poorly with the Governor, I am certain.'

'The Governor? Frig the Governor! I'm afraid, Roo, you lack a full appreciation of the gravity of our situation.'

Sewell notes with foreboding his friend's use of the first person plural. 'I beg you to explain the position more fully.'

'Sir, the young lady in question, with whom I have been seen in a public house upon various occasions and in transit to these very rooms, was done for by Chokee Bill.'

'That is impossible. The man was recaptured a week ago.'

'Then it was someone very like him.'

'An imitator is indeed possible, and the press will take care of the rest. Anything to put the masses in a frenzy.'

'To Hell with the masses.'

'No criticism intended, Reggie, but I do think you might appreciate the value of your social position *before* you get yourself into these things and not after.'

'Social position?' Reggie laughs – a hollow sound, thoroughly lacking in merriment. 'It is the fecking gallows I'm thinking about!'

'Reginald Harewood? Murdering women? I say, that would be a waste of horseflesh wouldn't it, old chap?' So says Sewell, affecting his man-of-the-world stance.

'Upon my word, Roo, there you go again. That you can joke about such a thing . . .'

Reginald Harewood begins openly to weep.

It would be an understatement to suggest that this development renders Walter Sewell uncomfortable. For an English gentleman of any breeding, such a display is like stumbling upon one's friend *in flagrante delicto*. Sewell notes, as though for the first time, an infantile quality to the trembling chin which does not show Reggie to good advantage.

He none the less does his duty, comforting Harewood with reason and patience, while thinking: A friendship sorely tested.

'Really, old chap, there is no point reckoning the position to be worse than it is. Granted, you were seen with the lady in a compromising circumstance – as were many other men, given her profession. Yet it don't follow that you choked her to death; indeed, the length of your association would weigh entirely against such a conclusion. A gentleman who murders his own mistresses? It flies in the face of good sense.'

Harewood reaches for the bottle of brandy. 'I'm less than confident that the Metropolitan Police will see it that way.'

'Very well, dear fellow, then allow me to put your mind at rest. In the unlikely occurrence of such an eventuality, I shall vouch for you. It is as simple as that. I shall say that you were with me the entire evening. How does that sound?'

Harewood nearly weeps anew, so sudden is the relief. 'Trusty old Roo! Dear old friend, may I say that you are simply the most capital fellow in all the world!' Harewood reaches across the table and gives his friend a pat on the knee. Now he raises the bottle in a toast, drinks – but another thought comes to mind, and he becomes solemn again.

'Actually, there remains something else about Dorcas which you need to know.'

'Dorcas, you say? What might that be?'

Sewell has picked up a curious scrap of paper and appears to be having some difficulty in breathing.

Harewood takes the missive from his friend's outstretched fingers, and reads it. 'Ah. Oh dear. There is another piece of beastly luck.'

'What beastly luck, Reggie? What beastly luck is that?'

'Shouldn't blame you if you're cross. Stupidest thing to do. But you're a man of the world, old chap. It was early days and I was desperately hot for a feel at any cost – deuced coy little piece don't you know, that was the beauty of her. Finally, by brute force I get my hand inside her petticoats and suddenly, apropos of nothing, the little tart asks me my name! Caught me utterly by surprise, don't you see, and while trying to put my hand further, I opened my mouth to come up with Stanley or Simpson or one of the usual monikers – and I'll be blest if what popped out wasn't Roo!'

Sewell is perspiring freely, cheeks burning, with that tightening in the chest; indeed, he thinks he may grow faint . . .

Harewood continues, oblivious to Sewell's distress: 'Stupidest damned thing. An accident really, when you think about it, a momentary lapse like a sort of fit. Not something to hold against a fellow, surely. Meant to say "Simpson" or whatever, and it came out "Roo". Simple as that. Once said, of course, no way to put it right.'

'For the love of Jesus, Reggie, would you kindly shut up?'

Unable to follow his friend's discourse for the sound of rushing water in his ears, Sewell downs a large brandy – too quickly, for the glass slips from his fingers and shatters on the maple floor, which sound alerts Harewood at last to the condition of his friend, now leaning against the mantel, supported by both hands, breathing in short, sharp gasps.

'My dear fellow, you've gone all red in the face! Can see why you're cross of course, but no point crying over spilled milk. . .'

'Shut up! Shut up! There is some powder in the top left drawer, bring it to me, now!'

The voice contains not the deference he expects of Roo but another timbre entirely, one which Harewood thinks it best to obey – indeed, he does not hesitate to do so. He retrieves the chemist's packet as requested and unfolds it upon an open notebook on the mantel, whereupon his friend takes two large doses as though it were snuff.

'Should I fetch a physician?'

'Wait, damn you!' The powder begins to do its work and each successive breath becomes easier. At the same time, Sewell appears to draw new strength from within, as though from a reserve supply kept for an emergency.

'Reggie, you've sorely tested our friendship with this blunder. I doubt whether vouching for you over the dead whore will be adequate to the situation.'

Reginald Harewood regards his junior colleague with incomprehension. It has never occurred to him that Sewell could lead an independent existence, let alone that he might feel ill toward him.

'Come now, old chap, you wouldn't refuse to vouch for your best friend in the world. Don't even joke about it!'

'Give us the facts, please. The object in question: can you think what it is?'

'It was the flask. Silver flask, don't you know, stolen by that dishonest whore. She took my rugby ring, damn her. Beside such a loss, never thought to bother my head about the flask.'

'Would that flask by any chance have carried the family crest?'

'Of course, old boy, never had any other one.'

'Quite. Let me sum up the situation as I understand it: first off, in addition to your dear cousin, you've been rogering this young Dorcas in my rooms.'

'Didn't think you'd mind, old boy. Same thing in a way, isn't it?'

'And in addition to admitting her into my rooms, in a moment of animal stupidity you identified yourself to the strumpet as Mr Roo.'

'I beg you not to harp on that. It makes me look something of a goat.'

'Now we've received what amounts to a demand for a pecuniary reward, from a person in a position to articulate a suspicious relationship between a dead whore and the inadvertently identified Mr Roo, as well as the Harewood silver flask.'

'A rum run of luck I must say, so many bad turns in one go.'

Sewell holds Reggie's gaze with a peculiar intensity. 'Shut up, Reggie. Shut your mouth, for you are indeed a perfect goat – and perfectly correct in your estimation that we, you and I both, are in extremely serious trouble. I wonder: is your stupidity general, or are there specific areas in your brain which are numb? Might you be a subject for phrenology study?'

'I beg you, old chap, a joke is a joke but there is no need to cut a fellow like that.'

'Do you have an opinion as to how a "friend of Dorcas" might have come by an item stolen by another of your filthy women?'

'Not the faintest, old chap. Complete mystery to me.'

'I see. Well, if indeed this person has your flask, her description of 'Mr Roo' is certain to resemble you and not me. Though I am sorely inconvenienced by your actions, yours is by far the greater peril.'

'Please stop, old fellow. You are being positively beastly.'

'Which puts me in mind of her beastly little friend.'

'Do you mean the impudent little slut? Oh, bad show.'

'There is your blackmailer, I should think.'

'What do you suggest we do?'

'*We?* If we are to sever this dreadful association, one of us will be required to contact this . . . this person, retrieve the flask and bring an end to the matter. And by "one of us" I mean that it will have to be the one of us who don't answer to the description of your Mr Roo.'

'Very sensible. Well said, my dear fellow.'

Eager to restore their association to a less prickly footing, Harewood moves to the opposite couch and places an arm about his friend's shoulder in a gesture intended to commemorate the new seriousness they have found this evening, the newfound depth of their friendship.

'Of course, it is no more than one might expect from such a capital fellow – best bloody friend a chap could have, by Heaven!' So saying, Harewood places a kiss upon his friend's cheek in the manner of one Frenchman bestowing a medal upon another. 'You shall be rewarded, old chap, goes without saying. Manage this business for me, dear Roo, and I swear you shall have whatever you like.'

Replies Walter Sewell: 'Reggie, do not ever again refer to me by that name.' So saying, he turns to Reginald Harewood and kisses him straight on the mouth.

45

Beak Street

For being of the honest few,
Who give the Fiend himself his due . . .

The fog on Beak Street is a yellow colour this afternoon. It will grow progressively darker down Regent Street, until by the time he reaches Trafalgar Square it will have the colour and texture of chocolate. Not strolling weather certainly; anyone out walking is scurrying home, or hurrying to office, committee or shop. Precisely for this reason he has decided to make the circuitous journey on foot.

Regent Street is enveloped in a fog of smoke irradiated by light, and he is struck by a mystical aspect to it all – the wide street of black macadam and sooty brick appears as a tunnel into the next world, fading into invisibility. As he quickens his pace, the intensified sun turns the fog golden while the rain becomes fine, close, pitiless. There seems no reason why it should not last until the end of time. He stops at Vigo Street to unfurl his umbrella – as do, simultaneously, a dozen or so fellow pedestrians within view. Thus sheltered, all resume walking, he among them, quickening the pace, bent beneath their umbrellas like mourners . . .

Nothing in London is natural, he thinks. Everything has been disfigured, transformed from its original state – the earth, the people who walk upon it, the very air they breathe; yet the present light transforms this necessary deformity, confers a strange grace upon the monstrous city men hath made, like a smile on the face of a Cyclops.

Even when there is sunlight, it is cold and damp. As a precaution, he wears two scarves – one for the walk home.

Though unpleasant in itself, the weather is of inestimable value in the accomplishment of his task, a drawn curtain to muffle the rough edges of what he is about to do, so that the act will blend with the muffled hum of the city.

It will be done in quiet and in privacy, in a hollow space where he will speak with her briefly beforehand, then take ample time during, then remain with her for a period afterward. His little rituals such as they are, his table manners as it were, small gestures to provide majesty and a sense of occasion to a melancholy event, in which a woman's attractiveness to a gentleman becomes her downfall, in which it would have been better for everyone had she been ugly.

Better love hath no man, than that he lay down a life for a friend . . .

As he walks south on Regent Street he feels his heartbeat quicken – not out of fear but of a kind of readiness, like the entrance of a gladiator; which illusion is enhanced by the curve of the street, like the approach to a Roman amphitheatre, its shadowed apertures filled with invisible, hushed spectators, shrouded in fog as though by a giant cloak.

He passes a tradesman, barely visible, to his right, who cautions: 'Watch out for your pockets, Sir.'

'I shall indeed, my good man. Much obliged to you.' So saying, he slips a penny into a coal-coloured palm, and continues.

The rain having let up somewhat, he re-furls his umbrella, which he now swings like a cane while increasing his pace, an exercise to stimulate the blood. The fog is now a thick buttery yellow, syrup impregnated with the smell of soot, so heavy that it sinks to the street and crawls along the gutters . . .

As he continues south, the cityscape around him becomes ever more massive and ponderous, with long ranks of black, blind windows above him like a charcoal drawing over which someone has rubbed his sleeve. Slowing his speed he passes through, but not among, the thickening crowd of pedestrians. Faces move in and out of his field of vision, in a pageant which is interesting for him to watch, but whose participants have neither time nor inclination to watch him in return.

At Piccadilly, the crowd has grown more dense. He passes a man with the set, impenetrable face of a businessman, massive as an ox in successive layers of wool, a top hat accentuating his height by at least a foot. He passes a group of women on a shopping excursion, dressed like stalks of asparagus or skirted lamp-posts, on their faces the customary sour grimace of the quality. He passes a pampered child of about ten, with the sulky, intent look of a young bulldog, incessantly yapping at his gaunt, miserable governess, a washed-out girl of sixteen. He passes two swells like hairdressers' dummies on their way to their club, their upper bodies executing a strangely motionless glide while their legs scissor beneath their coats. He passes three elderly ladies, Sphinx-like beneath their bonnets, with the complexions of nuns.

He pauses on Trafalgar Square – Nelson in the clouds above, planted high upon his column like a rat impaled on a stick – then resumes his pace, past more ladies: a girl with soft, angelic cheeks and deep periwinkle-blue eyes, conducted down the street by her mother, whose face is a red mask of inert flesh the colour of beefsteak. Close behind them follows a wealthy crone who might well be the grandmother, with heron's feet for hands, a stork's neck, and a great frontage of white teeth set in the prominent jaw of a carnivore.

Such would have been the fate of his own mother had she not expired while still a great beauty; it was not his intention that she should lure his grief-stricken father to the next world as well, leaving the family estate to their only child.

At the kerb, a ragged boy is performing cartwheels in hopes of a penny. A shilling falls at his feet. The boy fetches it eagerly, scanning the crowd for the invisible benefactor . . .

On the Strand the dispersing fog hangs like shreds of cotton from the lamp-posts, while the sun (which did not seem to proceed from any specific direction) skulks away forever behind the roofs of surrounding buildings, allowing darkness to spread so that, when at last he turns up Cranbourne Alley, he can hardly see his hand in front of him. Almost immediately, however, all is light and brilliancy as he approaches the Crown's fancifully ornamented parapet and the profusion of gaslights in richly built burners. A crowd of gentlemen speed past him to the light, like a school of eager fish, clerks for the most part, with mended coats and scuffed top hats and swinging worn walking-sticks.

He wriggles sideways through the dense, eagerly shifting crowd, by whose demeanour and by the excitement in their voices it is clear that an exceptional spectacle is taking place. By peering beneath the armpit of the man standing before him, he catches a fleeting, astonishing glimpse of two women, both stripped to the waist, hair tied behind with cords, standing up like men and facing off as though in a prize ring, their fists clenched like small clubs in front of their breasts, which seem, under the present circumstance, strangely irrelevant, like pouches under the eyes.

He notes that the gentleman acting as referee is none other than the proprietor of the Crown, presiding over a spectacle which in any other location would appear outrageous and bizarre, but which seems in this quarter to be a piece of acceptable entertainment.

The audience sets up a cheer as the two women fly at one another with that natural feminine inclination to tear and claw.

Capital. His timing has been perfect. Fifteen minutes after the hour, on the Saturday when the clerks about Fleet Street and Temple Bar receive their meagre stipends. Thus unchained from their scriveners' desks, their quill pens pried from ink-blackened fingers, they venture outside their prisons and proceed directly to the drinking-houses, divans and gaming-parlours, there to expunge a week of skull-sucking tedium with gin and ale, their consequent hangovers to see them through the interminable emptiness of the Lord's Day. All of this has been carefully planned on his part, which excellent timing is now augmented by circumstance – for who could predict or expect to have the additional distraction of a prize-fighting match between two Amazons?

Surely it is a sign that God smiles upon his errand.

He enters the Crown only to discover that, such is the lure of the outside entertainment, the place has emptied save for a scattering of nearly insensible customers at the bar and at tables. Without effort he instantly recognizes the young lady with the insolent tongue (*Why don't you go and pork your little fat friend?* – his cheeks still burn at the thought of it), seated at the table facing the dance floor, her back to a pillar, its elaborate Corinthian finial dripping over her head like a tropical tree. Thinks he: Some men might find her to be a pretty little thing with her hair parted in the centre, in a dress which has been made from many dresses. He, however, can recognize such vanity as an indication of a woman's overweening pride, her contempt for her station.

He thanks God to have been blessed with the quality of indeterminateness, a generality of countenance enhanced by a head of prematurely thinning hair – the forehead of a forty-year-old atop the face of a toddler. His fleshy countenance, lacking the definition afforded by prominent bones, can alter its aspect according to circumstance, so that it is unlikely to be identified from one casual interaction; which cultivation of changeable vacuity he augments with a wardrobe selected for its invisibility, its colours approximating the soot, rust and mud of the city; he tops his average coat with an average top hat, so that even his height is a matter for uncertainty.

And there is the advantage of knowing that the Mr Roo she anticipates is an entirely different gentleman.

Thus attired and with an expression of general affability, he steps across the empty dance floor and seats himself at a table whose only other occupant is asleep. He is now mere steps away from his prey, having attracted only the most cursory notice.

Notwithstanding his successful entrance, however, he senses danger.

A flash of heat strikes his right cheek, causing it to redden while his left cheek remains cold; he turns casually toward the barkeeper and signals for two cups of hot spiced gin; it is some few moments before he can attract the man's attention, during which time he puts a face to the danger: the gentleman huddled over his ale, glancing too frequently in the direction of the girl by the pillar, as though having made a resolution not to let her out of his sight.

Whitty. Wouldn't you know. The dissipated scribbler who came to the hanging. Not a gentleman's occupation – but of course Whitty is no gentleman. In all probability he means to serve as her accomplice in blackmail, for no Haymarket judy would muster the strength of purpose to launch such an enterprise on her own. A ticklish position to be sure, but it remains playable, for Whitty has not yet recognized him in return – indeed, has not glanced in his direction. Thus assured, with his back to the correspondent he collects his gin from the barkeeper, returns to an inconspicuous table, and waits.

There is a trick a man in spectacles can do. People assume such a man to be looking straight through his lenses, when it may not be the case. Thus, no matter how bad his sight, a man may observe the population of a room unnoticed through the corner of his eye, collect valuable impressions, and be thus at an advantage.

The young lady displays a winsome appearance: with her small, symmetrical features and the smooth arch to the brow, hers is an English, unobtrusive sort of beauty – which guise serves to conceal her low birth and animal cunning. Note that she pretends to be reading from a book: a clever touch, as is the gin before her which she seems not to sip.

Upon closer viewing, he can see her for what she really is.

There! Note the turn of the mouth, the determined – not to say ruthless – set of the jaw. Discern the contempt in the line of the forehead; and upon close inspection, see in her small features, despite their seeming harmony, that nibbling, rodent-like aspect. Take note of her hands, now that she has made the mistake of removing her gloves: see how the little claw grasps the book, while the forefinger of the other taps a tattoo upon the table, apparently at her ease.

> *For now we see through a glass, darkly;*
> *but then face to face . . .*

Were she to know, *even as also she is known*, he is certain she would fly at him like a bat.

The additional challenge – the presence of his college acquaintance across the floor – does not substantially alter the position, only the sequence and timing. And there will be no need to give her gin.

He waits without touching either cup. Outside he hears a chorus of hooting as a blow is struck, and a minute later a monstrous, extended cheer, which signals the end of the bout, for it is the sound of men delighted by a violent result. Warming his hands with a cup of gin, he listens to the babble outside and forms his plan – or rather, his instinctive course of action, for when one trusts in God one cannot rightfully be said to plan.

As expected, suddenly the doors explode inward and a thick swarm of clerks re-enter in an almost liquid rush of wool coats and hats; the room resonates with the click of walking-sticks, and the jocular palaver of satisfied gentlemen eager to savour their satisfaction, to relive it and comment upon it and commemorate it, then to sniff about for other entertainment.

'I beg your pardon, Miss. I am aware that we have not been introduced. My name is Mr George Stanley. If I may I be so bold, I believe you have advertised an object which is of more than passing interest to a certain gentleman . . .' So saying, he bows, placing his gloved fingers together before him in a way that makes him appear like a small, timid animal, positively the last creature on earth to give offence.

'Please forgive my disturbance of your repose, Miss. However, if you might please accompany me very briefly . . .' He feels his cheeks redden, yet it is from intensity of purpose and not from shyness, as she must certainly suppose. He adjusts his coat collar – though he is not chilly, for he is wearing two scarves.

The effect of his continuous, nervous patter is to set the scene in such a way that it is he who seems threatened by her and not the reverse; in the meanwhile he reaches tentatively with one hand, which she shakes out of politeness (but which he knows to be pure guile), not wishing to arouse his suspicion by appearing suspicious of him – especially given his evidently timorous nature.

'Dreadfully sorry to have kept you waiting, Miss. I should have arrived earlier but for the appalling business going on outside. Did you see it? Unimaginable, to think of such an outrage occurring not a mile from the Palace.'

Taking her arm, he helps her to her feet. Momentarily at a loss as to the appropriate response, she stands hesitantly, then silently agrees to accompany him, not through a decision having occurred, but in the way that water proceeds on a downhill course, it being the least resistant. He guides her quickly into the crowd, sidling crab-like against the tide of wool converging upon the bar for drink. The ambience of the Crown has turned to bedlam with the sudden crush and the undifferentiated din, as a further cluster of gentlemen enter, with the two pugilists straddled upon their shoulders, their faces and breasts wrapped with blood-soaked towels.

It is as if he and the young woman have gone to sleep and are now in a dream together, in which they move with exaggerated slowness through a mass of humanity, which closes around them like water.

'And where is the gentleman, Sir?' she asks with affecting innocence. 'For I have promised my protectors that I should not venture outside alone.' In truth, she has good reason to be prudent, for the street is all but deserted. The only human presences are the impoverished grotesques who loiter next the buildings opposite, hardly visible outside the ragged perimeter of gaslight that spills from the Crown, awaiting the opportunity to cadge or to rob some befuddled reveller on his way home.

'Very wise of you, Miss,' he says, and the assurance in his voice contrasts with the furtiveness displayed earlier. For it is only at these moments that he chooses to reveal his true strength.

'Sir, since I don't see the acquaintance of whom you speak, I believe I shall return inside.' At this he almost laughs, for seldom has he encountered such a shrewd one as this little witch. He reminds himself that this is not the time to show persuasive meekness; now is the time to show persuasive force.

'Indeed, Miss, his carriage will be along presently – a yellow phaeton, actually.' He speaks to her in a tone designed to create confidence in the stability of the situation, that all is well and all will be well. 'My friend is exceedingly well-born and well-known, as you yourself have shrewdly ascertained, and should be greatly harmed were it understood that he kept such company, in an area such as this. In return for your understanding and discretion in this matter, he is prepared to pay far more than you might have previously assumed. In fact, he has authorized me to present you with a gift, a small token – a family heirloom, don't you see. Utterly priceless . . .'

So saying, he guides her gently but firmly by the arm a few steps through the dense fog, the way one guides a recalcitrant child, further into Cat-and-Wheel Alley, to the secluded doorway of an abandoned lodging-house, where they may discuss matters without interruption by any human traffic which might issue to or from the Crown.

'Sir, I must insist on proceeding no further – indeed, your grip on my arm is hurting me.'

'Oh Heavens, where are my manners? Might I persuade you at least to step into this doorway so that I might present you with the small present I mentioned – which, I am certain, an assessment would value at no less than twenty shillings.'

'I don't know that I want your present, Sir.' Her tone of unease causes him to smile to himself, for there is nothing so delightful as the moment when they suspect that all is not as it should be.

'Actually, it is a scarf,' he whispers, controlling his excitement, the blood rushing to his loins in the anticipation of what is coming, while removing the white silk gentleman's scarf from about his neck and bestowing it around hers.

'I don't want it, Sir,' she says, trembling slightly. As his eyes adjust to the light he can make out the white face, the white scarf, the eyes widened like a small animal in the presence of a superior predator – utterly delicious!

'Oh but you deserve it, Miss. You do.' So saying, he wraps the scarf gently twice around her throat. And begins to pull.

'A pity there isn't a glass for you to see yourself in, Miss, for your new scarf looks so very pretty on you. But is it a bit snug? Does it chafe you somewhat? I'm sorry, but I cannot hear you. I can hardly understand a word you say. What lovely eyes you have – so wide, with not a trace of a squint! And how rosy your cheeks are becoming! Do I make you blush? Do I? Does my touch inspire certain urges? Do I excite you to indecent longing? Do I cause you to grow faint?' He pulls harder, while crooning on about how pretty she is, although in truth he cannot see her face for the fog and dark (a compliment to a lady is an acceptable untruth); applying ever greater pressure to the coiled silk scarf while inwardly marvelling at the sound of his own voice, the way it grows deeper and richer – as though the strength she loses accrues to him.

Delirious with the pleasure of utter command, he prepares to execute (appropriate appellative!) the final twist, in concert with his own spasms of pleasure, then to perform the little ritual that follows, in which he will cut off her nose to spite her face . . .

Inexplicably, seen only as a vague blur in the corner of his eye, her hand moves beneath her dress and now she leaps upward in a sudden sidewise motion, and suddenly it is as though his face has been inexplicably soaked with water.

O Heavens! It is not water, but blood! Blood!

A knife glints in her hand as she collapses backward with the now loosened scarf about her neck, while he reels in the opposite direction, his back striking against the stone wall of the doorway. Blood! The smell and stickiness of it, pouring over his cheeks and eyes! Blood!

He grows sick to his stomach and vomits, turning sideways not to foul his clothes – except that his coat is now soaked and greasy. Summoning his courage, he gently probes the wound with his fingers – a long, deep gash running from just above the eye almost to the jaw. It is all he can do to keep from fainting.

The girl! Where is the girl? In the initial shock – occurring as it did right at the climax – he released her and she fell, but where? Unable to see, groping with his hands, he feels for her on the stone steps where he left her – and, O God in Heaven, she has escaped!

He cannot see properly, for his fingers, in probing the wound which continues to gush, smeared his spectacles and fouled his eyes with the sticky, metallic substance; even so, through some primitive sensory apparatus he detects a presence, standing nearby – is it she? Is there hope? Please God, let it be she! With no further thought he lunges in the direction of the figure who is surely standing just a few feet to his left, and – O horror! It is a man, stinking with the most odious filth, who now holds him by the front of his coat while pouring fetid breath upon his open wound! Desperately he works himself free of the hands, wriggling and twitching like a small animal (tearing his coat), while gouging the eyes with his thumbs, for which he is rewarded with a roar of pain and a fresh dose of foul odour – and he is free.

And blind! In the struggle, his spectacles have fallen to the ground, and he cannot find them because his eyes are filled with blood! In this hysterical condition Walter Sewell flees into the foggy dark, looking for all the world like a giant decapitated fowl.

When the crush of excited drinkers has dispersed sufficiently that he may move from his place at the corner of the bar, it is a moment before Whitty truly comprehends the meaning of the empty table by the column; momentarily it is as if some feat of prestidigitation has occurred and she has disappeared by the touch of a wand, which gaping vacuity of disbelief is replaced by anger, as though the entire population of the Crown has conspired against them, which anger is overcome by dread, rising from the pit of his stomach, a dread the like of which he has never before felt in his life.

When he first devised this role for Phoebe to play, it was in the interests of uncovering a scandal – a young man of good family (against whom he holds a grudge), engaged in unspeakable acts; and, not incidentally, in the interests of keeping Owler's young lady out of harm's way. And yet, what if . . .

Blast!

Even in moments of journalistic excess, two sources of general terror obtain: the possibility that somebody might actually perform some frightful deed, or suffer some dreadful injury, as a result of the reading or misreading of the correspondent's text; the possibility that he has made a dreadful mistake, with similarly injurious consequences. For indeed, truth to tell, far more evil is perpetrated on this earth through negligent stupidity than through conscious ill-doing. Hang the incompetents and set the murderers free, and London would be the better for it . . .

Having recruited Phoebe to his purpose, at this moment the correspondent would gladly place the noose about his own neck.

Now he is running madly through the clutch of dancers with such force that one couple staggers into a table, overturning it and showering its outraged occupants with gin. He throws open the doors and plunges into the gaslit fog of Cranbourne Alley: it is all he can do not to scream at the glowering emptiness of it, this dank, stinking hole in the pit of the universe, bereft of life or hope, where exists not the faintest glimmer of beauty which is not to be instantly snuffed out. Surely it is not necessary to die in order to go to Hell.

At first he adjudges the figure coming out of the fog to be a will-o'-the-wisp, a ragged creature such as frequents the moors of Yorkshire, wailing for the dead; for indeed it is wailing, a sound of primeval distress. His second vision is of a looming tragedy, that he is to take her in his arms only to watch her die of whatever the Fiend has done to her. And then it is all nothing, nothing but this moment in which he is holding this keening young woman – who would not hold her? – wearing a white silk scarf from Henry Poole's.

He tastes her salt tears upon his lips. 'Did you see him, Phoebe, dear? Did you see him?' Even after the unprecedented desperation of the past few moments, Whitty cannot resist the awareness that the Fiend is receding even as he speaks.

'Might you recognize him if you saw him again?'

'Anybody will recognize him now,' she replies.

46

The Holy Land

Somebody is following him. More than one. He knows this, although he can see nothing; a sensation down the nape of the neck and across the shoulders. He must remove himself from the area at once, for she will alert the Metropolitan Police, who will surround him, for that is the purpose which the Peelers serve best – as a human retaining wall. St Giles will become a ratting-pit in reverse – with a horde of dogs in pursuit of a solitary rodent. He imagines a circle of top-hatted sporting gentlemen, peering at him from above the rooftops, looming over him with intense interest, waiting for the kill.

Someone is here! Someone is nearby!

'I have a pistol! Stay away, do you hear me?'

In reply he hears a slight rustling a little to the right. Pawing at his eyes with one hand, he uses the other to feel his way along the walls of buildings which seem to lean inward, so narrow is the street. Now he feels the outline of a window sash, and now he cuts his hand on a piece of broken window-pane! *And the Lord set a mark upon Cain* . . .

No. He will come through. He will endure. This is but a test of his faith – did not God say that *whosoever slayeth Cain, vengeance shall be taken on him sevenfold*? Thus he struggles forward, taking courage from the word of the Lord.

And now indeed he is beginning to see – a sign from the Lord that he is on this earth for a purpose under Heaven and that he will pull through. Now he can discern the outline of the street and thereby avoid obstacles before him, while feeling his way along, both hands extended, touching opposite walls – for the lane has narrowed even from what it was.

The street narrows yet again, so that he must move crabwise to avoid outcroppings, as though passing through a fissure in the earth, while avoiding the odious drain which bisects the lane, flowing with substances he does not wish to consider, let alone touch. At one instance the sides of the alley converge into a ramshackle wooden dwelling and a path continues through it; to his right he sees a cooking fire and a pot containing a malodorous meat substance. And still there is the rustling behind him.

It is easier for a camel to pass through the eye of a needle than a rich man to enter his kingdom.

How true that is. Wealth has made his passage to Heaven difficult. It is no easy thing to poison one's own mother, even when it becomes clear that she was acting as a whore.

> *More I require of thee.*
> *Thou shalt not suffer a whore to live.*
> *For who can bring a clean thing out of an unclean thing?*
> *No one.*

Hope appears as a splinter of light, a vertical cleft in the gloom; again he must turn sideways to progress past a window which looks into a bedroom filled with a coiling mass of sleeping humanity, whose collective breath pours through the broken pane like a cloud of malodorous steam.

He has emerged! He can breathe! He is free!

Squinting in the unaccustomed gaslight, he sees a kind of square, or court – really no more than a coincidental point of convergence for a tangle of yards, a series of narrow and tortuous shadows, much like the hideous passage he has just endured, each with its little rivulet of filth draining into a common, stagnant gutter in the centre of the square.

The square is filled with parties in ragged, dirty clothing, some famished and stick-like, others bloated and red, whose features he cannot discern without his spectacles: a woman, with a pipe in her mouth perhaps, holds a snarling dog by a piece of rope. Someone coughing in a blue rug. And silhouettes: a man with one arm, carrying a broom; a man in a broken stovepipe hat.

47

The Crown

She does not remember having entered the Crown, nor climbing the stairs to the office of Stunning Joe Banks, nor how she came to recline on his couch covered with a blanket, with Mr Whitty and Mr Banks hovering anxiously overhead, the latter extending a snifter of brandy to her lips so that she may breathe the fumes. She no longer trembles, nor does her mind occupy an animal state of absolute fear. Despite the events of the past hour she feels safe and warm – and decent, for the blanket covers the part of her dress which has been torn away . . .

Dorcas. The finding, stealing, matching and sewing of the squares of cloth was a thing they shared – both in the doing, which took many weeks, and in the wearing too, together or apart, as if they wore bits of each other wherever they went.

'He ruined my dress, Mr Whitty. I don't have another.'

Stunning Joe Banks speaks in a damaged growl: 'A new dress is forthcoming within the hour, Miss, never worn, selected by one of the more dignified young ladies of the establishment, courtesy of the Crown. I have given instructions that it be worthy of a schoolmistress, or possibly a governess, and that *décolletage* is out of the question.'

'I am not prepared to receive charity, Sir.'

'The Crown is not prepared to receive quibbles, Miss. D'you wish to traipse about in your skivvies?' So saying, the proprietor retreats behind his desk, there to busy himself with the accounts.

'Miss Phoebe, I apprehend that you have undergone a terrific ordeal and have occasioned a severe shock to your system. Your condition is one of great delicacy and must not be disturbed further. And yet, *tempus fugit* . . .'

'Do not speak Latin to me, Mr Whitty, I don't like it.'

'Then might I intrude with a question in plain English?'

'By all means, Sir. Ask anything you like. I am at your service.' So saying, she places her hand in his, at which the correspondent flinches. Stunning Joe Banks looks up from his desk, gazes significantly at the two joined hands, and lifts one eyebrow in Whitty's direction.

'Mr Banks, I know what you are thinking. It is incorrect.'

'I believe you, Mr Whitty. From what I am given to understand, womanizing may be the only weakness you lack.'

'I am touched by your vote of confidence,' remarks the correspondent, returning his attention to the young woman under his protection: 'Miss Phoebe, when you told me that any person might recognize your attacker, what did you mean?'

With her hand remaining in his (noting his discomfiture), she reaches beneath her dress with the other and retrieves the knife, now with dried blood along its edge, which stain will require ashes to remove. 'I meant that I have marked him, Sir, that he cannot conceal himself.'

'Am I to understand, Miss,' says the correspondent, glaring at the knife in her hand, 'that you did not return the implement to Mr Owler, as we agreed?'

'On the contrary, Sir, I did as we agreed. However, when Father finished his supper, I took it back again.'

'Point taken, Miss. With such a literal mind you belong in the Chancery. And in the struggle with your attacker, I take you to say that you wounded him?'

'I did. But not to kill, for I did not know where I should puncture him to make him stop. Instead I put the edge to his face, knowing that a cut along the forehead will produce a great amount of blood.'

'Very perceptive, Miss,' agrees the proprietor. 'Many a match be lost thanks to a simple cut over the eye.'

'You terrify me, Miss. The both of you terrify me.'

Continues Phoebe: 'Also I acquired these.' So saying, she reaches one hand under her dress, while still trapping Mr Whitty with the other; this time the hand emerges with a pair of round spectacles, smeared with blood and dirt, which she lays on the table beside the bottle of brandy.

'They dropped from him as he struggled with Dalton the monkey-chaser. I picked them up, and I ran. The Lady Lurker was also there, as was the dragsman Taff Spring.'

'Dragsman?'

'Stealing from carriages is Taff's speciality.'

'Friends of the family?'

'Acquaintances, rather.'

'It is a wonder that the attack occurred at all — with so many acquaintances at hand.'

'Not in the fog and dark, Sir. He would have done for me had I not my knife. He was surprisingly strong.'

'Still, it seems a remarkable coincidence.'

'I don't think it was a coincidence, Sir. It was Father. He put out the chaunt.'

'Put out the chant?'

'No, the chaunt. That I was to be watched. Father can do that. He is well-known in the trade. When he puts out a chaunt, all of London will know the tale in two hours.'

'And after you effected your escape – what then?'

'Certainly the Lurker and Taff would have put out the word, and he would be followed – and nibbed once they have him safe in the Holy Land.'

'And then?'

'He will disappear, Sir. That is the usual thing.'

'Disappear?'

'Into a cess-pit. Such as you encountered that first day. He will be hit on the head and thrown in with the rest of the shite, please excuse my language. And nobody will see him again, is what I am given to understand, although Father would never discuss such a subject in my presence.'

'Drown him in the cess-pit? It cannot happen.'

'The Holy Land is short of timber. We cannot afford gallows, nor graveyards, for that matter.'

Adds Mr Banks: 'One must admit that the cess-pit kills two birds with one stone.'

'That is not the deuced point! A gentleman is rotting in Newgate whose life depends upon the emergence of the Fiend.'

'I cannot help that,' says Phoebe. 'Mind you, there would be a trial first, it would be fairly done.'

'By this I suppose you mean some kind of local Inquisition, as occurs in the colonies?'

'The people of the Holy Land have tried their own since before your time, Mr Whitty. It is an old custom.'

Whitty turns to the proprietor: 'Mr Banks, do you know anything of this custom?'

'I have heard so. And from time to time I've noticed a particularly notorious regular to disappear of a sudden, no trace of his whereabouts and no knowledge from the Peelers. One chooses not to enquire further, as such customers are not missed.'

Whitty grasps both Phoebe's shoulders with utmost urgency. 'Look into my eyes, Miss: Do I appear serious?'

'Indeed, Sir. Astonishingly serious, for you.'

'Please believe me, it is vital that he not disappear.'

'Why, Sir? And to whom?'

'William Ryan is to be hanged on Monday. Your father knows this. If our man simply vanishes, an innocent man will die in his place. Your father will have traded one murder for another, and made a murderer of himself as well.'

She thinks about this, weighing her feelings for the gentleman against her native tendency to distrust such a complete outsider.

'What is it you wish me to do, Mr Whitty?'

'Go to the constabulary. Ask for Mr Salmon. Tell him everything that has happened. Give him the scarf as proof. Tell him where he should look.'

'And what will you do in the meanwhile?'

'I wish to speak to your father. Mr Owler and I have subjects in common.'

Stunning Joe Banks arises from his desk. 'Then I shall accompany you. Alone in the Holy Land, dressed as you are? Mr Whitty, you would be stripped naked inside of ten minutes.'

48

The Holy Land

As the two gentlemen make their way along Cat-and-Wheel Alley it is as if they are on parade, past a gauntlet of lead-coloured men and women no longer in a position to sell themselves, all eerily silent as they watch the passage of two examples of comparative quality, hungrily scan them top to bottom like wolves, with eyes like drops of mercury.

'Joseph, the route we have taken seems somewhat more degraded than most, if that is possible,' says the correspondent, somewhat unnerved.

'That is true,' replies Stunning Joe. 'But it is the fastest route, with the added advantage that these people are in general too weak to attack with any force. Keep your gaze forward, Mr Whitty, keep your hands free, and be pleased that we have not yet encountered the offal-eater.'

'That is indeed a blessing, Sir,' replies the correspondent, whose stomach is not constant.

As they turn down Mincer Lane, upon experiencing a flicker of moonlight Whitty stops to gaze upward at a slice of Prussian sky, against which he can make out the silhouettes of rooftops and washing, as well as rows of spikes driven into the walls immediately over his head, to facilitate passage from one window to the next; further on is a crescent-shaped bridge between roofs, and another behind it, built with the most paltry materials and in a state of near collapse, yet frequented as commonly as the street below.

Stunning Joe Banks notes the correspondent's upward pre-occupation: 'There are indeed faster routes from one part of the rookery to the next, Sir. It is said that an escaper may pass from Covent Garden to Upper Regent Street in a quarter-hour. But I don't know these ways, and they are littered with traps for the unwary.'

'Believe me, Sir, I am content with our present progress.'

At the end of Mincer Lane is a crumbling edifice which was once an elaborate fountain of the Italian style, a centrepiece for the garden of some elegant town-house; now the mansion is a nethersken and the fountain a plebeian source of drinking-water, from which a man is indeed drinking – not by using a cup, nor even the palms of the hands, but directly from the bowl; indeed, his face seems entirely submerged.

Sensing their presence, our man raises his head, streaming with water, to investigate these two strangers, whereupon Stunning Joe hands him a penny.

'I beg you to tell us, Sir, if we are near to Rosemary Lane?'

'Aye, that be so, my good Sir. I'm after there meself. There are important goings-on, you know, for a chaunt has gone up and many as is in attendance.'

'So we are given to understand,' replies Whitty, who has just now realized that the man was not drinking water but washing his bald head. 'If I may ask, Sir, what is your business or profession?' For the gentleman is oddly dressed, in tight-fitting trousers and an outlandishly coloured shirt. As well, his face and hands are streaked with a dark brown substance.

'Trueman Caul is my name, Sir, and I is in the nigger business. An Ethiopian serenader by trade.' So saying, he holds up the bones which are his chief musical instrument, consisting of two pairs of elongated sticks made of elephant tusk and shaped in a peculiar way.

'And where are your fellow serenaders, Sir?'

'They 'as took up with the chaunt. I was delayed by an unforeseen complaint . . .' Here the speaker pauses, having become distracted by the sight of Whitty's companion. 'Cor, Sir, if I may be so bold, would you by any chance be Mr Banks?'

'I have that honour, Sir,' replies the former pugilist. 'I am pleased to meet you.'

'Not so much as I, Sir. I were present at the bout against Caunt. It were a great moment, Sir. And a great moment it is for me now, Sir. I would ask the honour to shake your hand.'

'With pleasure,' replies the famous gentleman, extending his enormous, deformed hand, every bone of which has been broken and poorly set. To judge by the expression on the smudged face of the Ethiopian serenader, it is as if he has been granted an audience with the Queen, as if his life, however hard it may become, has now been touched by grace. The correspondent cannot help but remark on the paradox – that a hand that crushed the bones of one man may bless the life of another.

And so the two companions continue silently on their way, led by their recent acquaintance, whose ongoing announcement – *Make way for the distinguished gentlemen, please, Mr Stunning Joe Banks has graced us with his presence, do not disturb!* – appears to embarrass its subject greatly.

None the less, in response the denizens of the Holy Land step back and drop their heads slightly, and it is clear that the Iron Duke himself could not have provided a surer escort.

They turn another corner and now Whitty recognizes the court he visited earlier – the clothes-lines of Rosemary Lane, the coster carts and the stable-like structure which serves as the communal kitchen for the neighbourhood, now crowded with excited, expectant, ragged citizens, there being no room inside.

Notwithstanding the crush, their escort's pronouncements continue in their effect, for the throng obediently parts for them, while at the same time crowding over one another to catch a glimpse of a true hero of their kind, an exemplar of physical courage. Among the throng Whitty recognizes a woman who has a short pipe in her mouth and a wolfish-looking dog beside her; she nods to him in similar acknowledgement – which puts him in mind of the consumptive young man in the blue stable-rug, doubtless now deceased, such being the transience of life in the Holy Land, akin to a battle-zone. Now he sees that their Ethiopian serenader has disappeared – never, in all probability, will they meet again in this lifetime; whereupon it occurs to him that the chief difference between the Holy Land and proper London is neither one of ferocity nor squalor, but rather one of speed, in that the pains of a lifetime occur in swift succession here.

They pass through the green doors, jammed open by the pressing crowd, and already Whitty recognizes the heavy smell of fat and fish, augmented by the cheap tobacco of a hundred pipes, and the rancid odour of wool hardened by the combined sweat of a succession of wearers. The hole in the ceiling admits naught but the barest hint of moonlight. Gradually he discerns, in the inadequate gaslight, that in place of the culinary activities of his previous visit, what is in progress can only be described as a trial. Spectators crush upon them from all sides and fill the structure to capacity. They are muted, even solemn (with no drinking in evidence), as they perch attentively at and upon tables, those in the rear standing upon benches to obtain a better view, all facing the communal stove, where tables have been pushed together to form a kind of stage.

On a bench placed upon the table to the right and in charge of the proceeding perches the elderly, scrawny figure of Mrs Organ, whose customary occupation is to ladle out the substance Whitty could not think of putting into his mouth. Evidently it is the good woman's additional charge (perhaps by virtue of being the keeper of the stove) to deal out a measure of justice – an equally uncertain concoction. On the table to the left stands Mr Hollow, unsteadily, who appears to speak on behalf of the prisoner; Mr Owler, seated nearby, for his part plays a prosecutor's role, which he has evidently just completed, for he is very red in the face and wiping his eyes, while sweating profusely from tension and effort.

On the centre table, meanwhile, surrounded by two stout black Irishmen in tweed caps, a chair has been placed on which sits a man Whitty recognizes, squinting into the darkness. On his face is a serious wound, a long cut like the work of a surgeon, straight from forehead to jaw, which gives him the aspect of a Harlequin, the kind with a two-coloured face.

It is some moments before Whitty can discern what is happening, and that the voice is that of Mr Hollow. The distance of the voice lends an abstracted presence, something like the speech of a ventriloquist's puppet:

'My purpose here is to remind my brethren of this: notwithstanding that the offences of which the gentleman stands accused offend all Christian decency and civilized practice, that they have occasioned untold injury to persons present, still a man is innocent until shown otherwise; moreover his offence, if such there be, must be regarded as an offence, not to any person present, but to Her Majesty the Queen. I say this as one who has more reason than many to wish him ill. God save the Queen, Gentlemen! We will be governed by duty, and not rage, justice, and not revenge . . .'

Whitty listens in amazement. Provided one kept one's eyes and nostrils closed, the oration underway could be taking place in the House of Lords, declaimed by a senior eminence with the ministerial drone of a Methodist.

Covering the lower part of his face with his handkerchief to ward off the miasma present, Whitty glances at his protector, who seems unbothered and at ease: 'I say, old man, how do you bear the odour?'

'I have no sense of smell,' replies Stunning Joe. 'It was the Sweeney match what did it.'

'May I say that at present I envy you.'

'In my work it has advantaged me greatly. I can view the contents of a man's stomach without a qualm.'

Now Mrs Organ stands and speaks – whose air of dominance seems to possess some ancient root; indeed, the degree of deference accorded to the crone is not unlike that of an ancient village for the pronouncements of a witch. 'You may speak now, young master,' she says to the gentleman in the chair. 'What say you, Sir, to the charge what has been laid before us here, for which you have been marked by blood and seen by witnesses?'

At the sound of her voice, the young gentleman looks up as though dazzled by some bright light, into which he squints with effort. In the meanwhile, the muttering of the crowd in attendance grows tentative and silent, indicating a willingness to wait and listen.

Whispers the publican: 'Do you recognize the fellow?'

'Oxford man. I was acquainted with him once – only slightly, for we were not part of the same set.'

'So much for the benefits of a higher education.'

Indeed, on witnessing Sewell's bewildered, inarticulate condition Whitty feels a sort of misplaced pity, like the empathy one might experience for a blind hedgehog – which, having destroyed a vital crop, now finds itself in the open, cornered, and facing the ruined farmer.

The young man moistens his lips in order to speak, at first without success; his mouth seems muffled and dry, as though stuffed with salt biscuits.

'I wish to say . . . I wish to say . . .' He stops in mid-statement, surprised anew by the position in which he finds himself. Now he continues:

'No. Not possible. By which I mean to say that it is not right. I mean to point out that, with all due respect . . .'

Whereupon his small eyes widen as though a sudden inspiration has struck his mind. 'May I remind you that I am a fellow Englishman, of . . . of, with no disrespect intended . . . a distinguished family. It is not right that I be placed in judgement other than by . . . by . . . other than by a forum of my peers. That is the way of it, duly assembled, which is to say a court of the Queen's Bench, by authority of the Crown of England. I therefore request in the strongest possible terms . . .'

Here he pauses, overcome with alarm: 'Police! Help! Police! . . .' cries the prisoner hysterically, as though he were the victim of a buzzing in Covent Garden, which volley of cries occasions a corresponding shower of mirth from his delighted audience.

Notes the publican: 'Your classmate is due for the school obituary, by my reckoning.'

In the meanwhile, the crowd settles back into an atmosphere of ritual solemnity.

Comments the old woman: 'The young mister makes a joke of

himself, not of us. We know what we know.' The timbre of her voice, cuts through the smoke as scissors cut through paper.

'I only point out my position, Madam. By what authority——'

'You are out of order, Sir. There is no crusher to beat back the horde, nor a daddy to purchase your rescue. You are here before the citizens of St Giles what has suffered injury, being the effects of the actions of which you stand accused. That be our concern, and our dominion, and it is authority enough.'

'What Madam means to say, Sir,' adds Mr Hollow, 'is that we in the Holy Land can speak to the workings of the Metropolitan Police and the courts, to our eternal disadvantage. This is well known. Our confidence in those civic entities is of a restrained nature. Nor do you show yourself to advantage by invoking your membership in the quality, to we as have witnessed the quality at their leisure.'

In response, a whisper erupts of extended agreement, like the rustle of a thousand palms rubbed together, accentuated by more pithy and quotable phrases, which combine into a ripple of seething voices, like hot soup:

He's a downy little jemmy.
If the crushers nib him –
He as never get the fecking gallows.
Flam anything, they can.
Fecking scurf!
And my Jamie topped for passing snide!
They gets transportation.
Mizzle off to Canada.
Hear what he done to them girls?
Transport him to Hell!

Which utterances receive answering murmurs of agreement, invisible in the smoke, yet audibly growing in intensity:

Do the fiend now!
A rat, a beast, a dabino!
Stick him!
Give him the chiv!
See the colour of 'is guts, aye . . .

Whereupon Owler steps forward to speak – it comes as no surprise to Whitty, to see the patterer master a gathering, to receive a challenge from the masses and respond with intelligence and force.

'Be assured, Sir, that our court is rough, and we do not nose with the crushers . . . yet still you may rest assured that you will be dealt with fairly. Which must come as a comfort to you, Sir – unless it be the fairness itself which causes you worry, the thinking of the people, that you would prefer to hide beneath the skirts of the Queen. I ask you: Be it fairness or unfairness you seek for yourself?'

A wave of delighted laughter from the public, followed by an echoing chorus of coughing – indicating that the trial may continue with the assent of all present. Whitty now understands how the French mob managed to try, convict and execute their gentry with such dispatch.

> '*When the devil's riddle be mastered,*
> *And the charnel-house stinks of a pope;*
> *We shall see the baronial bastard*
> *Kick heels with his throat in a rope.*'

Following this surprising and familiar recitation from someone in the crowd, the voice of the accused cuts through the babble: 'Stop, please! I beg you, let me speak!'

As though to trump the sudden silence there follows an unnaturally shrill wail from the young prisoner, which resonates both within and without the packed arena, while he rises unsteadily to his feet, watched closely by his black Irish wardens. Approaching the edge of the improvised stage in this atmosphere of tobacco and sheep-fat, the accused peers blindly about the room, breathing in little gasps. Now he looks down upon his coat and attempts to brush away the encrusted blood and vomit, as though dusting himself before entering the parlour. Having thus completed his toilet he looks up again – and is surprised anew. Now he licks his lips, grimacing at the taste of his own blood – which, upon looking at his hands, comes to him as a surprise.

'I thank you, Sir, for your intervention on my behalf.'

'Please do not, Sir,' replies the patterer. 'Nobody wants your thanks less than I.'

At this the accused frowns somewhat, then turns to face the darkness, and enters his plea.

'Forgive my rude outburst, Gentlemen, in no wise did I intend to present a show of disrespect. Yet I beg you to place yourself in my position, and it will become clear that this assembly is unjust, and unworthy of Englishmen, which I know you to be. For at the least, I have not been accorded sufficient time to present you with the full circumstances of my case. Were I given a proper hearing, Ladies and Gentlemen, I have no doubt that you would conclude that, if I am guilty of anything, it is that I was too much the Englishman, too good to a friend, too loyal to my class, overly desperate to protect one whose name and reputation were about to be crushed by scandal. That I may be a fool, Sir, I readily agree. That I lack guile is without question. Yet I beg you, do not make me out to be a monster, but rather ask yourself what you might have done in my situation . . .'

So speaks the prisoner, and with such a remarkable tone of earnest gravity that the public of St Giles becomes momentarily confused, unable to summon a clear picture of the actor and the deed he is supposed to have done, the form and the content. Thus does the speaker gain time, in the way that a man experienced in politics or fraud will, purely by dint of apparent sincerity, temporarily overcome the empirical evidence of the senses . . .

'You are lying, Sir!'

Another surprising turn of events. All eyes turn to the voice, the first of her sex to have spoken out from among the spectators; indeed, once recognized, the young woman is lent a spectral quality by association with her murdered friend, the more so with the feeble gas flame burning directly over her head, in the light of which, Phoebe, in her new dress of green velvet, appears virtually to glow in the dark.

'I witnessed you, Sir. I stood before you. I looked in your eyes and I saw the bestial pleasure you took in what you were about to do. Murder and ravishment combined is what it was. So I say yes, Sir, you are indeed a monster.'

'Foul strumpet, I shall not be judged by you! How could you presume to do so? What would you know about honour – *that which is unclean cannot be made clean!* How can you know what it is to suffer under the burden I carry?' Here he turns to appeal to his unseen audience – whom, such being his deluded condition, he adjudges in some way sympathetic to his argument.

'Gentlemen, I appeal to you as men of the world. I speak to you of nothing less than the spread of disease – of infection both moral and physical, to which women such as this are self-evidently prone, who will go on to infect good men such as yourselves in frightening numbers. As the Bible says, *The harlot hast devoured thy life!*'

Cleave him up!

Skin him and boil him!

Like a fecking rooster!

Sputtering these and other less charitable imprecations, the inflamed throng surges forward like a grey tide about to swallow up the prisoner, who now shrinks back in fear – all of which Whitty watches in mounting alarm, notwithstanding the capabilities of his escort.

'Mr Banks, we must reach the young lady at once, for the position has grown exceedingly dangerous.'

'Seemingly, Mr Whitty. But we have yet to hear from the personage in charge. The power of these hags is well known.' So saying, the pugilist extends both arms in the shape of a wedge and begins to move forward with the stately indomitability of a locomotive, in the direction of the gas pipe with its feeble, flickering blue-and-yellow flame, followed as closely as humanly possible by the correspondent, greatly anxious not to lag behind, for each face he encounters in passing is like an artist's variant on a theme of dangerous malevolence; upon encountering any one such individual of an evening (and here are hundreds!) the sane person changes direction, clutches his purse and runs for a Peeler . . .

'Miss Phoebe,' he says to the young lady, 'Mr Whitty wishes to speak with you at once.'

'Good evening, Gentlemen.'

The correspondent notes the effect of this young woman upon the surrounding crowd – which, seen in the present context, might approximate the simultaneous appearance of Victoria, Miss Austen and Miss Kemble; it is she who is in her element, not the correspondent – and sad to say, when she looks up at Whitty it is no longer with the eyes of an infatuated girl.

'Miss Phoebe,' says Whitty, greatly agitated on all counts, 'as I made clear to you, an innocent life is at stake. This man cannot simply 'disappear'. To this combustible situation, I hoped you would provide water and not kerosene.'

She leans forward to whisper: 'I did what you asked me, Sir. Do you expect me to waltz in here in the company of the crushers? Do you wish me to write *informer* upon my forehead?'

'If I may . . .' The correspondent feels the weight of Mr Banks's palm upon his shoulder. 'I smell crushers about, who will not be bashful with their truncheons. It would be well for the three of us to move immediately hence.'

'Quite,' agrees the correspondent, who needs no further encouragement.

He locks arms with the young woman and together the three proceed through the green double doors to the courtyard of Rosemary Lane. Before exiting the premises, however, Whitty casts a long look in the direction of the patterer, who executes a subtle nod in return. Nearby, the Fiend squints into the darkness, muttering to himself.

Mr Hollow is nowhere to be seen.

In the meanwhile, on Rosemary Lane the festoons of used clothing have disappeared from the cave-like shops, entrances barricaded with any material their owners can summon up, and the coster carts have likewise been taken to higher ground.

However, at present the throng seems to have suddenly thinned with mostly beggars remaining, anyone able-bodied having been of a mind to exit the vicinity, with the look of preoccupation, the air of important business which is reflexively adopted by guilty men in the presence of the police.

'There, Sir, do you see?' whispers Mr Banks. 'Surrounded by crushers we are – do you see them in the entrance to Grubb Alley?'

Indeed, by peering vigilantly across the court Whitty discerns a vague outline: the distinctive top hat and tail-coat, its owner leaning inconspicuously against the wall; which collective presence is confirmed by the familiar and unwelcome voice at his shoulder.

'Well, well, Sir. You are in the thick of things, I must say.' Whitty feels the nudge of a familiar stick in the area of the kidney.

'Mr Salmon. Always a pleasure.'

'Whitty, you may present the police as a race of desk-mites, and yet we have been on top of your fair arse for many days.'

'After the ministrations of your louts, I count myself fortunate to have any arse at all.'

'You are fortunate to have a head. I warned you fairly that you were undermining police business, did I not, Sir?'

So the coach was black, not blue.

'Indeed, Sir,' Salmon continues, 'I cannot overestimate what a nuisance you have been.' The under-inspector is nudging the correspondent's kidney in earnest now, for emphasis; only the pugilist's strong grip maintains Whitty in an upright position.

'I think that is enough if you don't mind, Mr Salmon,' cautions Mr Banks.

Upon recognizing the renowned publican, the under-inspector puts away his stick. 'Very good, Mr Banks. Yet I assure you, this is a serious business. Certain statements by the gentleman have inflamed the public and impeded the course of justice.'

Snaps the publican: 'Not so, Sir. It was that ladies was topped, unacknowledged by yourselves, has impeded the course of justice.

Deliberately unrecognized, Sir – such was your zeal to calm a fever and to hang a man.' Mr Salmon holds his tongue, aware that his neck would be snapped, cause of death uncertain, by a single blow of that broken fist.

'Gentlemen, in the present circumstance, let us not dwell upon these things,' says Whitty, massaging his kidney with the tips of his fingers. 'Let all of us return to our good work and resolve to be better men.'

Stunning Joe Banks extends his arm to the young lady. 'If you will accompany us, Miss Phoebe, I should be pleased to escort you back to the Crown, where I have a proposition for you.'

'I am afraid I am not cut out for the work, Sir.'

'That is not the work I have in mind, Miss. It is your perspicacity and intellect I wish to engage in an official capacity. I require an assistant, with an eye for who is a scoundrel and who is not. And, of course, for light clerical duties as well. Might such a position hold your interest?'

'I shall need to speak to my father, of course,' Phoebe says.

In the meanwhile, the under-inspector has placed his face within inches of the correspondent, gripping his arm with one hand: 'You blunderer, you still don't know what you have done.'

'Very well, Sir, please enlighten me.'

'It is about the scarves.'

'Yes. Made by Poole's, all of them. Shocking, that you made so little of it.'

'Not all of them, Sir. Not all the scarves were made by Poole's. One was not. It was in for a penny, in for a pound, don't you see. To hunt for one murderer only to lose another is not an acceptable proposition, as I am sure you will agree.'

'I do not understand you, Sir,' replies the correspondent.

With a snort of contempt, the under-inspector turns and raises one arm – whereupon the Peelers swarm down Rosemary Lane and converge on Carrier Square like infantry, some heavily armed with weaponry, others with arms linked together, their combined effect being as a constricting human enclosure, in command of which Mr Salmon, tall and thin, like a whipping post in chin-whiskers and top hat, marches to the front of the communal kitchen, there to take charge of the whimpering figure of the Fiend in Human Form, seemingly unable to rise from his knees now that he lacks the support of his Irish escorts, who have surreptitiously left the building.

Mrs Organ, the keeper of the stove, remains, proudly, in her position of unassailable authority. As the angular old woman nods curtly to the crushers in greeting, it is as though she is in charge of them and not the reverse.

'How do you do, Mr Salmon? We have not seen you here in some time.'

'And a good evening to you, Madam.'

'This here is Chokee Bill, Policeman. Of that you may be certain.'

'I take you at your word, Mrs Organ. Is he an imbecile?'

'No, Mr Salmon, he is cleverer than we may ever know.'

The compliment having put his legs back under him, the Fiend rises to his feet and executes a bow, squinting in the direction of the policeman as though to a rescuer: 'Very good, Sir, and I thank you. Walter Sewell is my name. You might know the family. Your arrival has been timely. I am grateful for it and remain your humble servant.'

'Mr Sewell, Sir,' replies the under-inspector, 'I hereby place you under arrest, both for your own safekeeping, and as a suspected murderer.'

'Thank you, Sir,' replies the Fiend.

49

Newgate Gaol

Seated in the soiled elegance of a hackney coach situated in front of Newgate Gaol, Whitty peers between the ragged curtains at the empty Grecian niches in the wall: which gods and goddesses were they intended to contain? By the spirit of this place, one might expect demons and snakes of the inferno. But perhaps not. Perhaps absence is its best expression in the end.

Where are Cobb and Fraser? Where are Punch Crocker and Mr Hicks? Back at Plant's Inn is the correct answer. Because, for as far as their publishers are concerned, the freeing of an innocent man presents a far less noteworthy prospect than his arrest; indeed, the event pales in comparison to the truly vital interests of the moment: the couple who starved their kitchen maid and forced her to perform indecent acts; the elderly woman in a basement cubby-hole who stabbed a girl to death for urinating into her kitchen. Against such copy, what is the release of an innocent man?

Consequently, when at last Ryan's gaunt, ragged, yet handsome figure, having undergone the formalities of release in the Governor's House, steps between the iron gates to savour the smell of freedom – the smell of ale at the Saracen's Head Inn, the smell of cattle at Smithfield Market – only the correspondent is there to greet him.

'Mr Ryan. How do you do?'

'Well enough, Mr Whitty, for weeks spent in a cess-pit. I am pleased to see you, for I have not so much as the price of an omnibus.'

'I am surprised that Mrs Marlowe has not chosen to make the journey herself.'

'Unfortunately, it is unwise for my love and I to be seen together. A professional matter, of some delicacy.'

Ryan settles into the greasy velvet cushion, savouring its softness, while Whitty directs the driver to the now-familiar address on Portland Place. As the coach rattles down Snow Hill, the correspondent for *The Falcon* produces notebook and pencil:

'Mr Ryan, to business. For the benefit of our readers, would you care to place on the public record the impressions of the vindicated, acquitted, exonerated William Ryan?'

The grey eyes become amused and he considers his reply.

'First, Mr Whitty, I must thank you twice. I thank you for taking up my case, and for carrying it through to the end, despite all setbacks. There were times when it seemed only a sceptical remark in *The Falcon* stood between my neck and the rope. The power of the press, Mr Whitty! God save the power of the press!'

Having thus supplied a favourable quotation for publication in *The Falcon*, the speaker abruptly changes his tone. 'Got a cigar, old man?'

'Certainly.'

'Capital. Absolutely capital.' Ryan luxuriates in an all but forgotten pleasure.

'Quite.' A damp uneasiness slips over the correspondent, like fog.

'There is a second blessing I must thank you for, Sir. Mind, this one must remain between ourselves. Indeed, you are the only human being in the world I may tell it to.'

Odd, thinks Whitty, the need to confess. *Irish. Catholic. Of course.*

'It concerns a woman named Sally. You did not know her.'

'You refer to the fifth victim, Sally Hunger, your former partner in crime.'

'The very one, Sir! Well remembered!'

Whitty braces himself for what is coming.

'Oh, I done her, Sir. I did Sally, as we say in the trade. Dispatched her to a better world. Simple necessity, don't you see, a financial matter. I tell you this that you might comprehend the extent of your assistance to me. Why, what is the matter, Mr Whitty? You seem to have lost your colour, there is no bloom in your cheeks at all. Take care, Sir, for a man is nothing without his health.'

William Ryan smiles, with an aspect of smug, triumphant satisfaction. The grey eyes become brittle.

The correspondent, who would give anything for a drink, turns away, not to give him more satisfaction than necessary. 'I must have been a godsend to you.'

'You surely were, Mr Whitty, that is the truth. Your cleverness saved me from my own.'

'It was the crim-con game. Your little blackmail. All was as described, except for one small detail: the mark in question, whoever he was, did in fact pay the required ransom.'

'More than willingly, he did. The price, though considerable, was but a momentary inconvenience for the Earl of Claremont.'

A running footman. A mustard-coloured chariot with a trail of liveried servants. Portland Place. Of course.

'The Earl of Claremont is a wealthy man. Your dividend must have been substantial.'

'Oh it was a handsome sum, you're right there.'

'All the more handsome as an undivided sum.'

'You're a quick study, to be certain. In any case, the partnership was already winding down. Age in a woman is not the same as it is in a man. When a woman ages, she deteriorates, and becomes less valuable.'

'Therefore you disposed of her, murdered her, in a manner calculated to mimic the work of Chokee Bill in every detail.'

'The knife-work required a strong stomach. It is not easy to mutilate an acquaintance.'

'The scarf, of course, was not from Poole's.'

'Oh, that was not my only miscalculation. I have no doubt that the changes I made to her face did not exactly match the preferences of Chokee Bill. But my chief miscalculation was in underestimating the outcry for an arrest, the public fever whipped up by such as yourself. By the time I took care of Sally, any garrotter who topped a whore would have served Mr Salmon's purpose, at least for the time being.'

'Even if nothing quite matched.'

'Details Mr Salmon elected to ignore, until I was safely hanged. He knew I did for Sally, don't you see. A bird in the hand is worth two in the bush. The crushers are pragmatic in that way. I ask you, Sir, is there no greater injustice than for a man to hang for crimes of which he is innocent?'

'Indeed, you might have hanged for five murders, and not just the one you committed.'

'To be candid, I prefer not to hang at all. So you see, Mr Whitty, no cloud is without a silver lining. Thanks to these perilous events, I am now a free man, an affluent man, and about to be reunited with the woman I love.'

'Spare me the Byronics, Mr Ryan. You are a tick, Sir. You suck the blood out of every woman who enters your orbit.'

'That is hard, Mr Whitty, and I do not like it.'

'It makes no difference to me whether you like it or not. I intend to expose you.'

'And expose yourself into the bargain? As the dupe who abetted a murderer? I doubt if that will do much for your professional standing.'

'You overestimate my professional standing.'

'If a man desires to destroy himself, there is no stopping him. But be assured, I shall not accompany you. You cannot touch me, Sir. Allow me to point out that it is fundamental to Common Law that a man may not be tried twice for the same crime. This was central to my thinking, don't you see, when you made your proposal to me: that once acquitted of the whole, I should be free of the part.'

The coach rolls to a halt on Portland Place. William Ryan extends his hand, which the correspondent chooses not to accept.

'I do not expect that we will be seeing one another in future. You see, as luck or fate would have it, the Earl of Claremont was also a client at the Grove of the Evangelist. Isn't it a small world? Liked a good thrashing I'm told – though that wasn't Sally's line at all.

'So the worry is that, despite his generosity, His Lordship might take exception to having a blackmailer on the premises.

'The Earl may be a fool, but he is a powerful fool. So my love and I have decided to relocate in the New World. For the protection of the lady – don't you see? As I maintained to you from the beginning.'

Smiling at the irony of it, Ryan steps down from the coach and turns to the correspondent for the last time.

'What a shame, Mr Whitty! Your notepad is empty! You have not written a word!'

50

Chester Path

Having determined to ride his cob for a satisfactory entrance (the trip to the stables was a bother), Reginald Harewood canters about the perimeter of the park twice before proceeding to the Outer Circle and the family town-house on Chester Path.

Reginald Harewood's life is at a crossroads. The situation combines the direst urgency with a need for the utmost delicacy. With proper handling, he might emerge from his difficulty safe and sound. If handled poorly, he faces disgrace, disinheritance and ruin. The Governor's displeasure with his style of life is one matter, but an intimate association with a murderer? Worse, an intimate association with one of the victims? Harewood is in no doubt that, should the facts emerge for all to see, his life to come will be a rum business indeed.

In every life come crises in which the spirit must rise to the challenge and overcome adversity. *Courage, mon vieux.*

He alights from his mount in order to push open the iron gate, while tethering Raffles to the fence for the liveryman to deal with. Such is his preoccupation with his unenviable position in the light of recent events that he does not notice the movement in the curtains, two floors above.

He must marry Clara. This much is clear. However, the acceptance of such a conclusion does not render it any easier to bring about. After snubbing the girl for weeks (being hot for another – and they always know or at any rate suspect), it will require no small amount of persuasion to reacquire her favour.

So it is with a degree of unease that the only son and, it is to be hoped, future heir of the Harewood fortune (which he suspects to be greater than the Governor will ever acknowledge) approaches the town-house he stands to inherit. Nervously he smoothes his coat of robin's-egg blue and adjusts his fawn breeches. Assuming a posture of firm resolve, he grasps the brass knocker with one gloved hand, smoothes his whiskers with the other, and arranges his face into something noble.

The door swings open with startling suddenness, as though the footman were crouched within. 'Master Harewood. An unexpected pleasure, Sir.'

'Damn it, Bryson, must you startle a fellow so?' So saying, he thrusts his riding-crop, hat and gloves into the white-gloved hands of the footman.

'I beg your pardon, Sir. You were not expected this early. Unless I am mistaken, your letter indicated your visit would take place at tea-time.'

'Are you suggesting that I must make an appointment in order to enter my own home?'

Striding down the hall and into the reception room, Harewood is about to burst into the house proper with the usual *éclat*, but thinks better of it: he is seeking a woman's hand. For the moment, his demeanour must suit the seriousness of holy matrimony.

The footman, smarting from the master's unexpected cut, flutters about with a little clothes brush in one white-gloved hand. 'Allow me to brush the back of your coat, Sir.'

'That will do, thank you, Bryson.'

'Very good, Sir.'

'Please tell Miss Greenwell to come down directly, that I wish to see her.'

'As you wish, Sir.' The footman turns to leave, his face a blank façade.

'No, Bryson, amend that. Please tell Miss Greenwell that I beg her to come to me in the sitting-room, at her pleasure. And tell her that I appear unwell.'

'Unwell in what sense, Sir?'

'Sick at heart, sort of thing. Treat it as a worrying situation.'

'I shall do my utmost, Sir.'

'See that you do, and there's a half-crown for you.'

'Most kind, Sir.'

Stepping into the sitting-room with its swaddled, subterranean hush and its necrophiliac aroma of hyacinths, Harewood notes that two chairs have been set near the ferns, conveniently before the fire, on either side of a small drum table upon which someone has placed a Doulton comport containing mints by Callard & Bowser; the perfect setting for a *tête-à-tête*. His thoughts affixed to the forthcoming interview, he proceeds past the unfinished jigsaw puzzle to stand before the fire, removing his gloves. Savouring a mint, he contemplates the representations of the Queen, the Iron Duke and the Saviour above the mantel, the former duet gazing into the distance, the latter looking to Heaven as though for assistance.

Nobility, Courage, Forbearance: qualities upon which he must now draw deeply in this time of crises. For indeed, the enormities of the past week scarcely bear thinking upon – therefore he resolves not to think upon them, lest his self-possession falter. He lights a cigar, then turns away from the Saviour in order to warm his behind.

Upon hearing the crisp click of footsteps on marble, he turns back to a contemplation of the Queen. Presently the door opens behind him. He pauses for effect, then, with the goose-flesh rising on the nape of his neck, he turns to face a chilly welcome that leaves him in no doubt as to the challenge at hand.

'Clara. Dear Clara. You are lovelier than ever.'

'How do you do, Mr Harewood? It is my understanding that you wish to see me.' Her voice is a monotone; her eyes refuse to meet his, being cast down as though in prayer.

He gazes upon the young woman before him, framed in the door as though in a portrait, with an aspect inspired by *The Lady of the Lake*.

'To what may I credit this unexpected visit, Sir? For I have not heard from you in some time.' So saying, Clara executes a small shrug as though to say, *I am beyond this. Nothing can hurt me now.*

Harewood notes with relief that the girl can still get the blood going. The dishevelled blonde curls in appealing disarray; the fevered flush of the cheeks; the white fullness of the bosom; the slight puffiness about the eyes as though having just awakened: a package of sensuous vulnerability, wrapped in lace.

Harewood sinks to his knees. 'Oh, Clara. Dear, dear Clara.'

'Sir, I am astonished. Whatever can this mean?' Again she affects indifference, a few drops of laudanum having mitigated her excitement to good effect.

Only at this juncture does he note the presence of Miss Brown, half-hidden behind the veritable balloon of lace that fills the portal, peering at him from beneath her perpetual eyebrow. Harewood rises briskly to his feet, mortified. Blessed if he will humble himself any further with a servant in attendance.

'Miss Brown. Lovely to see you. You are well, I trust?'

'Much obliged to you, Sir, I am well within reason.'

'Madam,' he continues, 'I wonder if you would be so good as to have a word with Mother. Please tell her that I shall be visiting her in approximately a half-hour with an important announcement.'

'I beg your pardon, Mr Harewood, Sir, but my duty as Miss Greenwell's companion is to remain with her.'

To which her ward musters sufficient strength to speak: 'Go, Miss Brown. Go now.'

Continues the future master of the house: 'Allow me to assume that you feel at liberty to leave my cousin under the protection of a member of the family. Otherwise, I should wonder how you can bear to continue with us.'

'I only wish to do my duty, Sir.' With an imperceptible nod to Miss Greenwell, Miss Brown glides down the gaslit hallway like a small black cloud, and disappears.

An uneasy silence ensues. For a long interval these two handsome, proud, well-born young people regard one another with looks of solemnity and hurt.

Clara ventures a few steps toward him, then turns away: 'Oh, Reginald,' she says. 'It is all so degrading and beastly.' Whereupon, having nothing else to say about the matter, Miss Greenwell bursts into tears.

Gently, Harewood conducts the sobbing young lady to one of the chairs set conveniently before the fire, wherein she sits. He is about to take the other chair when, overcome by depth of feeling, he falls to one knee beside her and grasps her little hand in his.

'Dear Clara, please try to understand that I have been in a state of utter shock. Conceive of it! Sewell and I were schoolmates! The scoundrel was my oldest and dearest friend!'

She takes back her hand to brush away the tears which wet her cheeks. 'Yet you never suspected? You saw nothing that might warn you of his true nature? How ghastly – to think that I have been left alone with a monster in human form!'

'Upon my word, Clara, I was as utterly deceived as you. The man is devilishly cunning. If you had seen him on that day, how he transformed before my eyes, from an Oxford man and regular good fellow, perfectly good chap, to a brutal monster! I tell you, I doubt that I shall ever recover.'

'Have you spoken to him since? Has he explained himself?'

'Sewell is in Newgate Prison, Clara. I would rather throw myself into the Thames than enter the building. My reputation is compromised enough as it is. To be burdened with such a notorious association, in addition to my current difficulties with the Governor – I swear, Clara, on my honour, were I to see the man face to face I should give him a deuced thrashing. But of all the ignominy, most injurious of all is that which he has done to our love.'

'Why, Reginald, what do you mean? Though I confess to having been deeply wounded by your neglect. Indeed, I feared the worst.' A tear falls.

'Exactly so. You, like I, have been doubly deceived. It is as though the Devil himself were in this house!'

'What is it you mean, Reginald? Deceived in what way?'

'Think of it, Clara. Name the gentleman who arranged for us to be alone together under irresistible circumstances. Name the pander who egged us on, without whom . . .' Here Harewood takes a moment to summon his moral courage. 'Oh my dear, let us confess to each other that we were led astray, that our former conduct is something we must keep a secret for the rest of our lives. But who was it that led us? It was the Fiend himself, by Heaven! And to think that I never suspected! That I failed in my duty to the woman I love!' Overcome, Harewood buries his face in her lap.

'You were led astray by him. And I was led astray by you.' Clara thinks about this. 'I am disappointed in you, Reginald. I had assumed that a square man might recognize a crooked one.'

'Clara, I swear on my honour that I shall set everything right.'

'But how is that possible, Sir? You have intertwined my life and my reputation with that of a filthy murderer and . . . oh, it doesn't bear thinking about! I have been betrayed in the lowest possible way!' So saying, she launches into a fresh round of weeping.

'Betrayed you? Whatever do you mean? How have I betrayed you, Clara?'

'I cannot pronounce the words to describe it. It would foul my lips to do so.'

Reginald Harewood rises suddenly to his feet with an expression of horror. 'I understand. It was he, was it not? He set you against me!'

The weeping pauses momentarily. 'I must confess that the facts ensued from that, that beastly man . . .'

'It was he who told you that . . . that . . .'

'That you had . . . another.'

'Another damnable lie! I swear it to you upon my honour!'

'But why, Reggie? Why would he say such a thing if it were not true? It possible for one person to be so deceitful?'

'Oh Clara my dear, you are such a child.' So saying, he puts his arms around her. To which she does not object.

Victoria and Wellington look to the future. The Saviour looks to Heaven.

'What is it you came to say to me, Reggie?' she asks, wiping her eyes with a lace handkerchief. With her other hand she takes a mint from the bowl, and places it in her mouth.

New Oxford Street

As noted previously, the creation of dismal New Oxford Street bisected the great rookery, thereby doubling the population of the remaining half, while leaving the Duke of Bedford £114,000 to the good. New Oxford Street also had the inadvertent effect of re-establishing St Giles Church as the principal gateway to the Holy Land, a sort of interregnum between one world and the next.

St Giles is well equipped for this responsibility. There has been a house of prayer on this site since 1101, when Queen Matilda founded a leper hospital, whose chapel became the parish church. As well, convicts on their final passage to Tyburn for execution were traditionally permitted to stop at the Angel next door, to be presented with a St Giles' bowl of ale, thus to drink a last refreshment before passing out of this life.

How suitable to the memory of Giles, the seventh-century Greek whose insistence on living as a leper outside the walls of the town, and whose own damaged leg, established his patronage of cripples and beggars.

So thinks Whitty, loitering in the doorway of an abandoned shop on New Oxford Street, having followed the elegantly clad figure from Regent Street to Oxford Circus, thence to St Giles High Street, and to this church, with its spire thirty fathoms high and its reeking churchyard in which lies the poet Marvell, who employed the grave as an inducement to his coy mistress, and now experiences the truth of his contention at length.

After William Ryan alighted from the hansom and disappeared through the front entrance of the Grove of the Evangelist, his former travelling companion did not order the driver to take him home; rather, he took to the street himself and settled into a bush for a sleepless night of watching; which exercise has continued ever since, for it is not in Whitty's nature to let go of a narrative, whether it be of any use to him or not.

Hence, he proceeded to follow Mr Ryan at a distance wherever he chose to travel, over the course of nearly a week: to his tailor, to his tobacconist, to the various places of high living available to a vindicated murderer with a generous mistress. Impressive, thinks Whitty, the quickness and ease with which a man will create an agreeable daily ritual, then follow it to the point of religion.

In the meanwhile, over the course of his sleepless wandering, Whitty has gained an appreciation of the sartorial difficulties presented by outdoor living – how the poor come to appear in such a bedraggled state. Lurking in the shadows as Mr Ryan's observer, wrapped as a blanket against the cold, Whitty's fine green overcoat has deteriorated to the point where he may never again wear it in public. In addition, he now appreciates the importance of tobacco to ease the pangs of hunger and maintain wakefulness – and, of course, a drop or two of gin.

To be deceived so thoroughly! For Whitty this is not to be borne. If he cannot come to some understanding of what happened and how, it is an open question whether he will ever trust his instinct again. For when a writer's pride in instinct is pricked, the spirit literally splits in two, into the prosecution and the accused, the executioner and the condemned.

The evening fog has just begun to settle as Whitty retreats into a corner of the doorway, the better to render himself inconspicuous to his quarry – which action proves unnecessary in any case, for the correspondent's deteriorated condition renders him virtually invisible to passers-by.

William Ryan, for his part, wearing a dove-grey coat and matching top hat, spotless linen and a twice-around neck-cloth of blue silk (the current custom), cuts a figure which is the very essence of suave civility. With not so much as a glance at the figure in the doorway, he traverses the walkway, opens the heavy door of the church and disappears within.

The time approaches eight o'clock – or so says the clock. One never knows with church clocks, in this temporal era.

Having sharpened his concentration with a pinch of snuff, Whitty crosses the street and passes through the gate, noting the tableau overhead in which our Lord and Saviour presides over a tangle of human bodies, some playing harps and horns, others opening their clothes to reveal breasts of bone, all rising from their graves.

This is Resurrection Gate, through which coffins are carried to service. How appropriate.

Upon entering the church foyer he hears the unmistakable sound of a workman effecting repairs to a piece of wooden furniture. Upon entering the nave, he understands a great deal.

The pulpit, to the left of the altar, is enormous, made of mahogany, constructed as a tower from which the spiritual leader, standing at the lectern on a Sunday, hovers above the congregation, having reached his perch by a winding stair.

This stairway contains two landings: at the second landing Whitty observes William Ryan, having taken off his fine grey coat, lit by the dappled light afforded by the stained-glass windows above, in the act of removing one of several carved wooden panels, fitted into frames and concealing the interior structure; this particular panel is held in place, not by pegs like the others, but by means of a piece of leather, attached on the inside and acting as a kind of hinge. After peering inside, Ryan reaches underneath the second landing and removes a canvas satchel which has been lodged there, brushing off a light coating of dust.

'Good evening, Mr Ryan. I trust you found your blood money without difficulty?'

Having recognized the voice, William Ryan squints in the direction of the man standing in the shadows next to the rear pew. 'And a good evening to you, Mr Whitty, Sir. You've arrived a bit late, I'm afraid.'

'Late for what, Sir?'

'Having ascertained the hiding place from Mr Hollow, clearly you were after the prize. I am sorry to have outrun you.'

'Not at all, Mr Ryan. I learned nothing from Mr Hollow. You are welcome to the money, and welcome to go to Hell.'

'Whitty, allow me to warn you not to trouble me nor my wife-to-be, as we prepare for our journey. I wish you well, Sir, as long as you do not present a threat or inconvenience. If such is the case, it would give me some satisfaction to reveal the full particulars, about the correspondent who freed a murderer in return for a saleable narrative – and a share in the spoils.'

'Speaking of which, you will wish to safeguard the contents of your satchel, Sir. This is not a good neighbourhood through which to transport a large amount of money.'

'Save your concern for your own money, Mr Whitty. I shall manage.'

Unwilling to put down the satchel even for a moment, William Ryan shrugs his dappled coat awkwardly over one shoulder and proceeds down the aisle.

'By the way, Mr Ryan, I congratulate you on your fine suit of clothes. Especially the scarf – from Forbes, is it not?'

'Right you are, Sir. You have an eye for haberdashery.'

'I should have thought you would have purchased your scarf from Poole's.'

Ryan pauses at the top of the steps to regard the correspondent, with the aspect of a tolerant man whose patience has reached its limit.

'That is enough, Mr Whitty. Having served your purpose, you are becoming a pest. Accordingly, if I hear of you again I promise you a terrific amount of harm – in which effort I have already prepared a document as I have just described, addressed to a Mr Fraser of *Dodd's*, containing revelations what will put you on the street for good, Sir – if not in transportation.'

'I am acquainted with Mr Fraser. A good choice for a spot of blackmail.'

'You know more than I, Mr Whitty, about the power of the press.'

Whereupon William Ryan exits the church, passing through Resurrection Gate, and disappears into the dark emptiness of New Oxford Street.

CORRESPONDENT TO TAKE HIS LEAVE

Mr Edmund Whitty, Special Correspondent
for *The Falcon*, begs to take temporary leave
of his position for reasons of health. In his
absence, he directs the reader's attention to
the observations of his substitute, the eminent
and highly readable Mr Henry Owler.

The Grove of the Evangelist

Whitty examines Mrs Marlowe's library. Unusually for this part of London, they are not show-books. All bear signs of use: Milton, Thomas à Kempis, a much-thumbed Keats, Quarle's *Emblems*, Dante, Schiller, Tupper . . . The titles suggest a member of a reading set, while the Pre-Raphaelite daub on the wall suggests a Bohemian taste; no doubt the combination reflects the sensibility of the Fashionable Girls' School, about which much has been said.

'I compliment you on your library, Madam. Do you propose to transport these volumes to the New World?'

'No, Sir, I have already read them. Other than the poets, I have no wish to read them again.'

Mrs Marlowe reclines in a divan beside the fire, wearing loose jodhpurs and Belgravia boots, her glorious hair piled atop her head in suitable disarray. On the tea-table is a small yet alarming horsehair whip, with a handle made of glass and brass; next to it is another volume of Keats.

'I shall not take up a great deal of your time, for I see that I have interrupted you in the course of your studies.'

'I don't know why you have come, Mr Whitty, being informed that Mr Ryan is not on the premises.'

'I have come because it is you whom I wish to visit.'

'Oh, really? I did not take you for an Eton man.'

'That is hard, Madam, and I resent the insinuation.'

'I am a woman most men find of limited interest. Only Mr Ryan has ever valued me for myself. For what purpose do you wish to see me?'

'In the interests of my own peace of mind, Madam, such as it is, not to mention your security and happiness.'

'I am flabbergasted, Sir, by the depth of your concern.'

'Mrs Marlowe, let us be candid: I don't expect you to pay the slightest attention to what I am about to say. None the less, it is my duty to inform you that your husband-to-be is a murderer and a thief, though not necessarily in that order.'

'Forgive me, Mr Whitty, but are you delirious? You seem to be in the throes of a fever. And your appearance, Sir! Had Mrs Button not recognized you at the door, my footman would have turned you away.'

'I agree, Madam, that I am not looking my best at this moment. None the less, I have something of value to offer.' So saying, the correspondent produces a sheaf of paper, folded into a packet.

'What is that, Sir?'

'It is a narrative. An alternative narrative.'

'Alternative to what, Mr Whitty?'

'To the narrative advanced by Mr Ryan, which you have purchased with your future.'

'And which narrative is the true one, Sir?'

'I should leave that for you to decide, Madam, if indeed it matters to you. In any case there is some doggerel included which will amuse you.'

> Now I lay in Newgate Gaol
> As Chokee Bill to die;
> Though doomed to Hell I cannot fail
> To apprehend a lie,
> One fiend to wear a hemp cravat,
> Which the other fits;
> One fiend hangs for murder that
> The other fiend commits . . .

'I do not wish to read it, Sir. It is not a verse form which interests me, therefore I shall not take it. Mr Ryan warned me that you might appear with fantastic claims, displaying indications of dementia – the result of a shock to the system, compounded by overindulgence.'

Whitty shrugs, returning the packet to his coat pocket. 'As you wish, Madam. You are, it is plain to see, a shrewd woman with a hard-earned knowledge of the world, who will not be made an easy victim. As such, I suggest that you know a brutal and deceptive man when you meet one. Should you, in your travels with Mr Ryan, encounter a curiously large amount of money in his possession, or an unaccountable streak of brutality in his manner – think on me, Mrs Marlowe. Think on the events which have taken place in recent weeks, and use your best judgement, and decide who has been your friend. And now, Madam, please allow me to bid you a very good-day.'

'And to you, Mr Whitty.'

They rise in unison. Mrs Marlowe takes the little whip from the table in her strong white fingers. Her hand trembles, but quickly regains its poise.

Whitty crosses to the door, stops, and turns as though an after-thought has occurred to him: 'By the by, Madam, I wonder if you might allow me to present you with this.' So saying, he produces the scarf, an expensive scarf made of silk, which has been cruelly twisted and soiled.

'What is that, Sir? And why should I want it?'

'It is a very fine scarf, I assure you. It came from Forbes.' Indeed, the correspondent bought it from that establishment this morning, and a pretty price it was, too.

'Goodbye, Mr Whitty. Perhaps my husband-to-be will have use of it.'

'For your sake, Madam, I sincerely hope not.'

So saying, Whitty exits the room, leaving the scarf on the table, coiled like a worm.

The dark woman with the peculiar scar awaits him in the foyer. Without doubt she has been listening in on the proceedings in the sitting-room.

Whitty executes a small bow. 'Good-day, Mrs Button. May I assume that you will be accompanying your employer to the New World?'

'Yes, Sir. I shall accompany my mistress wherever she goes.'

'In that case I must bid you goodbye as well. I expect we shall not meet again.'

'I expect not, Sir. It is a big ocean.'

'In which case, may I have permission to ask a personal question?'

'You may, Sir, though I do not guarantee an answer.'

'It is about your injury, Madam.'

'Do you mean my scar?' She touches with one finger the deep red welt, as though to be assured of its existence.

'Yes.' Whitty is working on instinct, drawing upon a part of the mind not usually accessed without medication.

'A certain gentleman caused it while of unsound mind. For my mistress's sake, I shall not tell you who he was, nor what happened to him.'

'Mrs Button, you have been graciously forthcoming. As a token of my thanks, might you find a use for reading material on your way to America?'

'That is possible, Sir. While at sea, the time does weigh heavily upon one's hands.'

'Then I beg you to accept this trifle, with my compliments.' So saying, he removes the packet from his pocket.

'Thank you, Sir. I shall read it with interest.'

'See that you take care of your mistress, should she have need of you.'

'Do not worry yourself with that, Sir. I always take excellent care of my mistress.'

THE MURDERER'S CELL, NEWGATE: AN UNUSUAL INCIDENT

by

Henry Owler
Special Correspondent
The Falcon

Mr Robert Dow, merchant-tailor, deceased 1612, in his Will did charge the sexton of St Sepulchre's that he should pronounce two exhortations to the person condemned, and ring the bell while the prisoner was carted past the church, for which service was left the sum of 26s. 8d., for ever.

Furthermore, an exhortation was to be pronounced to the condemned on the night before his death, as follows:

You prisoner within, who, for wickedness and sin, after many mercies shown, are now appointed to die tomorrow, give ear and understand that the great bell of St Sepulchre's shall toll for you, to which end that all goodly people, hearing that bell, knowing it is for your death, may be stirred up heartily to pray to God. Therefore I beseech you to keep this night in watching and prayer for the salvation of your soul, while there is yet time and place for mercy, knowing tomorrow you must sit at the judgement-seat of your Creator, there to give an account of all things done in this life, and to suffer eternal torments for your sins committed against Him, unless through your hearty repentance you find mercy through the merits, death and passion of your only mediator and advocate, Jesus Christ, who now sits at the right hand of God to make intercession for those who penitentially return to Him.

> *Lord have mercy upon you!*
> *Christ have mercy upon you!*
> *Lord have mercy upon you!*
> *Christ have mercy upon you!*

It may come as an astonishment to the Reader that every word of the above pronouncement is distinctly heard by him to whom it is directed – through air choked with smoke and fog and through a succession of stone walls six feet thick – as though it were spoken in the next room. Such is the power of the Word over the constructions of human hands.

Your correspondent (in the absence of Mr Whitty, who is in recuperation) can attest to this, having spent the longest night of his life in the presence of the condemned man Walter Sewell, otherwise known as the True Chokee Bill, the Fiend in Human Form.

Surprising, the honours and trials which accrue unexpectedly to a man – being in this case the opportunity afforded to your correspondent of playing a raven's role, to perch o'ertop a condemned man's shoulder during the last hours of his life. It is by no means clear how this doubtful privilege came to pass, for the harm he has done to your correspondent, and to persons near and dear to him, would indicate otherwise. Conceivably, the condemned man saw in some action of your correspondent an inadvertent trace of human decency which, when communicated, had the effect of quelling a throng of citizens enraged by the enormity of his crimes. In no wise did your correspondent intentionally effect such a thing, who would gladly have watched the man cut into pieces and thrown into the sea.

And yet, in keeping with the right, accorded a condemned man, of a single visitation, an invitation was sent and received. Should your correspondent have refused it, the man would needs have passed the night alone, the night before he meets Our Blessed Saviour. Therefore, out of an obligation to honour the last request of even such a beast as this, and an offer from *The Falcon* to publish our observations, your correspondent acceded to the prospect of passing the night in the condemned cell of Newgate Gaol, in company with the True Fiend in Human Form.

In spite of the reek of the prison generally, the corridor leading to the condemned cell, although dimly lit, exudes a sanitary air, in keeping with a terminology in which the man about to die becomes the 'patient', and the execution becomes the 'file'. Outside the condemned man's quarters stands a warden – a muscular, experienced, yet kindly man who presents the welcoming gaze of a doorman.

'What is your business, Sir?' he asks.

'As you shall have been informed, Warden, I have been invited to write upon the file forthcoming.'

'Ah, yes, Sir. From *The Falcon*. You are indeed expected – though I am afraid you will gain little from the patient. Please to enter and see for yourself.'

The turnkey opens the door to the cell and we step inside a room which was built as for a monastery, without decoration save for a crucifix on one wall and a table containing a Testament, soiled and torn by use. Seemingly in defiance of the ruminative cast to the *décor* was the sound emanating from within: not a Sorrowful Lamentation, not a Defiance in the Face of Doom, but the incoherent, infantile, primitive wail of a terrified man.

Is it right to speak of cowardice at such a time and circumstance? Or has the word outworn its usefulness in the privileged world from which he has descended? In a world of comfort, is there honour to be gained in the defiance, or at any rate the stoic acceptance, of suffering and death? Or do the quality find honour in most conspicuously cringing from such? Your correspondent does not know, Dear Reader, if he ever did.

All the same, your correspondent took his place on the one available stool and, in the absence of a cushion, leaned his back against the stony wall, while the condemned man wept in the bed opposite. In the meanwhile, the bells of St Sepulchre rang their tribute: the message was spoken, and was heard.

I do not know for how long I sat across the room from the patient, curled like a newborn on his cot, a moist package of blubbering flesh, alternately gasping for breath then begging for his mother, then crying out the name of a prominent family forever soiled by his acquaintanceship. While clearly incapacitated by the sheer extremity of his situation, as the dreadful night wore on it became evident that the significance of the evil done by him, the bleak events which had taken place and were yet to take place on account of the Fiend, had entirely escaped his ken – or rather he had escaped them, having flown to some other part of his mind, some other world in which he is innocent; in which, however tormented, he feels the satisfaction of having been wronged, set upon, made the victim of a cruel world. I do not know when the Chaplain arrived, or whether our man did the patient any good, but suspect not.

In any event, there was no speaking with this person. Your correspondent does not know why he was invited, except as a possible diversion from the prospect at hand.

Like the bells of St Sepulchre, outside the walls could be heard, as clearly as though it took place in the next room, the hammering together of the black scaffold (one might expect such frequent usage to merit a permanent facility), the size and shape of a showman's caravan and with a similar purpose, if we are to judge by the anticipatory cries, the songs, the curses and imprecations, of the audience already gathered.

Especially does a hanging hold fascination for criminals – as an opportunity for boasting, and, in the case of pickpockets, for plying their trade. Older members of this set recall the days when the wretches were hung up in rows, when bets were taken as to which would die basely and which would die well. The spectacle holds yet another benefit for the criminal: now familiar with death, he is thereby equipped to deal with it himself.

When the bell of St Sepulchre first rang, the Fiend heard it – indeed, it roused him to momentary sensibility, for he sat bolt upright of a sudden and cried: 'One! Seven hours!'

So saying, he fell to his knees and seemed to pray for a very long time – until the next bell, at which he cried: 'Hark!' With a cry of despair he left off praying, fell once again upon the cot, and cried bitterly.

Worn with nervous excitement, not to say dismay, your correspondent drifted into an unsettled slumber and fevered dreams, to be awakened by the last bell. Upon opening the eyes it was as though the cell itself had grown smaller, or had been shrouded by an invisible tent containing the sadness within.

Even so, the opening of the cell door and the entrance of the officials came as a fresh shock to the patient – who, amid renewed prayers and imprecations, refused his breakfast, then resisted the attachment of chains with such unexpected force (and an unbecoming degree of squealing), that the warden and turnkeys grew short of breath in restraining him; so that when finally they ushered the patient from the cell, it was unclear whether he was walking of his own accord or being carried – down the stone steps, down the bleak stone passageway, down to the black metal door . . .

Upon opening the door, the sound is like a wind which roars into the building, then hisses, then roars again, as though coming from one enormous mouth. Before being led outside, the prisoner peers through the doorway – not at the ardent throng of factory-workers and servants, not at the tract- and refreshment-sellers, not at the frock-coated constables manning the low barrier in front of the black-covered scaffold, but at the windows opposite and above, where the quality reside, there to take in the spectacle at £10 per seat.

It seems as though he is searching for a familiar face.

Now his eyes focus upon the presence of the Chaplain before him, prayer book in hand. Now he is conscious of the presence of Mr Calcraft (who will earn a guinea for the morning's work), standing behind the Chaplain like a parson of lower degree, with his hairless brow and the pockmarks upon his cheeks. Now two helmeted wardens step to either side, take hold of the patient's arms, and nudge him forward. Thus encouraged, he steps outside – and the sheer size of his audience dawns upon him, while up goes the cry of 'Hats off!' followed by a resonating silence. Suddenly he becomes aware of pigeons scattering about as the procession takes its first few steps, across the stones to the waiting scaffold.

And he falls.

Your correspondent has seen such a fall before. When a man falls thus, it is not because he has stumbled. Nor is it the fall of a man who has suddenly grown faint. It is the fall of a man who has fallen out of the world.

Were his hands free, officials would perhaps have seen him clutch his chest – which seemed to bother the patient all night long. In this case, however, his hands being tied and his encounter with death thereby masked, the patient's abrupt demise occurred unannounced.

The initial response of the wardens was one of simple embarrassment, for such men pride themselves in their ability to maintain the dignity and the drama of the moment. Hence, the response was as though a pair of servants had dropped their trays; hence, they pulled the patient to his feet with a degree of roughness – and in doing so discovered that the man had lost his skeleton, that there was no purchase to be had in lifting, that their efforts resembled an attempt to sustain a long, heavy mattress in a vertical position.

Now the physician emerged from behind the curtain under the scaffold, to ascertain the cause of the delay. Stooping amid the black-coated officials, Mr Mortimer affirmed what the rest of the party, reluctantly, had grasped.

The patient was dead.

Therefore he could not be killed.

It took several minutes for the group to arrive at this self-evident conclusion, during which time the crush of spectators, craning their necks from beyond the circle of constables, made its feelings known with increased vehemence, rising to an extended murderous roar, awful to hear, amid which din the deceased man was dragged back through the black door where the official party could debate their next step, assembled above the prone, lifeless figure of the Fiend in Human Form.

It is surely unnecessary at this point to recall for the Reader the events of five and forty years before, when, having come to witness the execution of Holloway and Hagarty on this site, thirty persons were crushed to death in the crowd.

At length a worried official from the Sheriff appeared through the black door and the roar which poured into the hallway was like a flood. A moment hence, two more constables joined us: the position outside had been made much worse as a result of a group of young men from the country, who, in their eagerness to have an effect on the proceedings, had linked arms and moved toward the scaffold, thereby creating a kind of retracting fence, with the resulting panic within.

Such was the roiling push and pull of alarmed humanity, several persons had already lost their footing and fallen to the ground, thereby placing themselves at risk of being trampled to death. In addition, citizens in attendance on Snow Hill had begun to throw rocks and other objects into the throng, thereby increasing the sense that some kind of attack was underway.

It is not possible for us adequately to narrate how a decision such as the one which subsequently occurred in the stone confines of Newgate Gaol came to pass. Certainly, your correspondent could not quarrel with it – if one was to avoid the senseless loss of innocent life.

Thus it came to pass that the Fiend in Human Form was lifted upright, braced by a night-stick at his back and supported between our two substantial wardens, who carried him across the stones and up the metal steps of the scaffold. And though his feet dragged upon the ground, to the crowd in attendance it did not seem to matter, nor that he seemed unable to stand upright on his own upon the scaffold as the cap was placed over his head; nor that his eyes appeared to stare fixedly in a single place – at the seats rented by the quality. On the contrary, from the moment the condemned man reappeared, the crowd began to lose its fury, to turn docile as a herd of cattle, which proceeded to watch, wide-eyed, as a familiar ritual was played out for their benefit – the reading of scripture, the shaking of hands, and finally the springing of the trap and the descent of a man; whereupon the doctor beneath seized the legs to ensure the breaking of the patient's neck, going so far as to reproduce the kick, the tremor and the death spasm, followed by stillness, for realism.

Then, and only then, was the public satisfied, and willing to go home.

The Crown

Whitty adjusts his new frock-coat of violet (well regarded on Bond Street), in the hope that he will grow accustomed to the high silk choker, now the fashion. The cut of his pale yellow trousers is superlative, so long as he does not sit suddenly. Everything is new except the boots, which he judges good for at least another half-year.

He will be absent from public view for several days: he intends to take the water-cure, a good cleaning being the ticket to health. And the arms of Mrs Plant.

Aware that he has not been looking his best in past weeks, the correspondent wishes to leave in his wake the impression of a man on top of his game, among colleagues and enemies alike, and among certain young people who might have admired him for some reason, then thought better of it.

He watches Phoebe while she scans the room in a quick, professional sweep. (She notices him, yet gives him no special attention.) She moves behind the counter to have a quiet word with the barkeeper; now she disappears upstairs, with the preoccupied expression of a practical woman with several things on her mind.

Stunning Joe Banks, seated beside Whitty near the entrance, wearing a magenta coat (beside which Whitty might as well be a wet pigeon), holds his glass of Scotch whisky to the light in order to inspect its colour. 'As an employer it is an astonishment to me, how the nature of a position is defined by the one what fills it. The publican business is like boxing in that way.'

'Do you mean to say that Miss Owler has little to do?'

'Quite the contrary, Sir. From the morning she came into our employ, Miss Owler began to discover many things to do. Now she has sufficient to do that I don't know how I will replace her.'

'What makes you think that you will need to replace her?'

'Miss Owler seeks a career on the stage. When the stage comes into it, you cannot shift them. I have seen it before.'

Down the stairs she comes, balancing on the palm of one hand a bucket of iced champagne. She crosses the floor, past the dancers to an inconspicuous table occupied by a young Cambridge gentleman who appears alone, neglected and out of place in these surroundings. The sort of gentleman whose custom the Crown seeks; a gentleman who will pay well in future for a welcome now.

Whitty notes her velvet dress, the colour of coral, quite opposite to the green she wore on that night – which he will revisit more than once, both in memory and as crisp copy, the night a girl stared down the Fiend in Human Form . . .

'Good evening, Mr Whitty.' Phoebe smiles and extends her hand. Alas, she takes no particular note of his improved appearance.

'Miss Phoebe, may I say that you look splendid. Allow me to extend my compliments to you on your new dress.'

'It isn't such a luxury, you know. With a day between wearings, both will wear longer.'

'I'm sure that is so.' Whitty wonders: What was he seeking? Did he expect to bask in the infatuation of a juvenile forever as a kind of tonic? *Fool!*

'It is good to see you again, Mr Whitty. I should like to converse at length, for much has happened, but as you can see I have ever so many things to do. Would you excuse me, please?'

'I assure you, Miss, I excuse you utterly.'

And with a quick nod of acknowledgement to her employer, she is gone.

A pause, while two gentlemen of a certain age contemplate the relentlessness of time.

'So it goes,' says Stunning Joe Banks to his glass of whisky.

'So it does.'

'A drop more?'

'Please.'

'One can only make the best of things, of course. We all must work with what we have before us, Mr Whitty, and I encourage you to do so. Might I point out that there are women in this very room who might prove diverting. As an example, allow me to direct your attention to the vixen entertaining the young Cambridge fellow by the window: 'the Jewel of Morocco', they call her. Background a total mystery. And do you descry the mark over her upper lip? Said to be the mark of a sultan's daughter . . .'

'Very impressive,' agrees Whitty. So saying, he abruptly drains his whisky, retrieves his stick, and leaves without a further glance in Etta's direction.

Peculiar sort of fellow, thinks the publican, relighting his cigar.

54

The Falcon

In the darkened wooden hall Owler nods to the young, uniformed electric telegraph messenger, who, after rendering the patterer a quick glance from head to toe, rolls his eyes in disdain and continues out of the building.

Thinks the patterer: should this current run of good fortune continue, he will instruct Phoebe to purchase a suit of clothes from one of the shops on Waterloo Road – made of wool and not corduroy, in keeping with their improved situation.

He pauses before the green baize-covered door, having grown momentarily doubtful, forgetful as to his purpose in coming; but then reminds himself that he has been expressly invited by the Editor: he has an appointment. He has legitimate business within. No person, uniformed or not, shall have reason to turn him out.

Thus reassured, he pushes open the door and steps into a splendid room which has been lit by a guinea's worth of tallow candles, and is the picture of significant activity – a room in which telegrams are received, cigars are smoked, journals are considered, and the vital issues of the day weighed and discussed in their historic context. To Owler's ear the rumble of erudite conversation seems actually to vibrate physically with significant content, like a pump drawing upon an historic well of events transpiring in the depths of the earth.

'Ah, Mr Owler. There's a good chap. Over here, Sir. Good to see you.'

The Editor, from what one can discern from a face so utterly concealed by whiskers and a large monocle, greets him with unaffected enthusiasm, even going so far as to extend a cigar over the desk – which, as he draws nearer upon the Turkey carpet, Owler realizes is meant for him. The Editor's lens shines into Owler's eyes like the beam of a lantern.

'Thank you, Mr Sala, Sir. Wery kind of you I'm sure.'

'You are more than welcome, Mr Owler,' replies the Editor, holding a lit lucifer. 'Tremendous crack on the hanging piece, old boy. Bloody crisp copy to be sure. And I don't mind confessing that I was somewhat dubious – unknown quantity and all that.'

337

'It were a tremendous gamble for you, Sir, that is certain. One requiring no little courage on your part.'

'Indeed, so it was. Be that as it may, Sir, our friend Edmund Whitty staked his reputation on it. Pioneer of the new journalism he called you, and now I can see why. On-the-scene sort of thing, experience affecting the reader directly through the correspondent – trenchant, vivid, an account which does not simply report the news but *is* the news, don't you see. Haw! Hanged a dead man, did they? I tell you, man, Westminster is in crisis over it, and *The Falcon* is at the centre of everything! Sir, we are in the fecking thick of it! What else can the little shites ask for? I've got them, Sir, I have them by the bloody curley-wurleys and I'm damned grateful to you for it!'

'I don't pretend to entirely get your drift, Sir. Yet I can see you have underwent a rattling good stroke in a managing way and I salute you for it.'

'Well said. Fecking brilliant, I quite agree.'

'And on the subject of brilliance, Sir, how goes it with Mr Whitty?'

'On that, Mr Owler, you may speak with him yourself.'

Whereupon a familiar voice drifts across the room: 'Top drawer, Mr Owler. Absolutely top drawer.'

'Mr Whitty, Sir! I am wery glad to see you, I must say!'

Standing by the bookcase at the far end, leaning against the marble bust of some great person of the quality (who stares blankly into space as though astounded), Whitty puts out his cigar on the gentleman's bald pate and steps forward, hand outstretched: Owler is dumbfounded by the elegance of the man, in his new clothes – and himself just barely beyond corduroy!

'Equally glad am I to see you, Mr Owler, and pleased to report that, owing to the water-cure, the therapeutic ministrations of a close personal friend and the good efforts of yourself in my stead, I am restored to health: laudanum consumption down to an unprecedented sixty-five grains per day; no gin consumption before noon; Acker's Chlorodine suspended altogether; medicinal snuff and cigarets judiciously applied. Fit as a fiddle, Sir!'

Adds the Editor: 'And we must not forget the salutary effect of the recent information.'

'Quite,' replies the correspondent, relighting his cigar.

'Werily, Sir, am I to have the honour of knowing this information? I am certain it must be a stunner.'

'Certainly,' continues Sala. 'Mr Owler, circulation at *The Falcon* threatens to reach a level at which even the little shites are silent – at which even the fecking *investors* are silent.' So saying, Mr Sala turns to the gentleman at the next desk, concealed behind a copy of *Lloyd's*. 'Is that not so, Mr Cream?'

'Indeed so, Sir.'

'Mr Owler and Mr Whitty, allow me to present my new sub-editor, Mr Cream.' A man shaped like a vole smiles in greeting, then returns to his work.

'Begging your pardon, Sir,' says Owler, 'but Mr Whitty spoke about a sub-editor name of Dinsmore.'

'Mr Dinsmore is in France.'

'France, Sir?'

'Mr Dinsmore has chosen to take leave of absence in order to write a biography of Mr Balzac, a dead Frenchman. As well, another pillar of *The Falcon*, name of Mr Lemon, has chosen to accompany him – in the wake of certain rumours, baseless of course.'

'Once again, Sir, you have the better of me in this matter.'

'Politics, Mr Owler. Stay away from the politics of the office. That is my advice to you. In the meanwhile, a generous stipend awaits you with our cashier. Do not hesitate to submit to *The Falcon* again.'

'Thank you. I'm most grateful. Good-day to you, Sir.'

'One other thing, Mr Owler. Recent information has arrived.'

'Is there more, Sir? Then I hope you might part with it.'

'A telegram from Liverpool,' says Whitty, whereupon the correspondent produces an envelope, which he opens with difficulty. The broken finger is healing poorly – due, no doubt, to quackery.

55
Telegram, *SS Europa*

DISPATCH FROM
SS *EUROPA*
LIVERPOOL TO BOSTON
26 JUNE 1852

PASSENGER RYAN DECEASED STOP
SUSPECT CHOLERA STOP
SEA BURIAL STOP
WIDOW CONTINUE BOSTON STOP

Epilogue

THE SORROWFUL LAMENTATION OF WILLIAM RYAN
The Undoing of a Clever Man

by

Henry Owler

My name is William Ryan
And I were a clever man
And I suffer for Eternity
As only clever can
A charmer to the ladies
And the soul of jeu d'esprit
And now I charm the fishes
At the bottom of the sea.

Oh once I found a true love
Though I gained her love by guile
When I lost her to another
I found others to defile
Who did make their shabby sacrifice
While I collect the fee
Now I'm defiled by fishes
At the bottom of the sea.

By guile I murdered Sally
Who insisted she should share
Too clever by a fathom
This I found to my despair
Yet misfortune turned to favour
When my love came back to me
As a dream comes to a drowned man
At the bottom of the sea.

When faced with opportunity
A clever man turns brave
With the mastery of a mariner
Who dares to ride the wave

I rode upon the backs of fools
To freedom I did flee
And now I've found my freedom
At the bottom of the sea.

Triumph! Riches! Liberty!
And my devoted bride
Who followed me with only
Her companion by her side
We boarded for America
But landed two, not three
While I took up my station
At the bottom of the sea.

God can see the seer
A man sees what it seems
God knows actuality
A man knows what he dreams
Cunning cannot triumph
The Almighty did decree
Thus cunning brought a schemer
To the bottom of the sea.

Do the wicked know their wickedness?
Is half a Fiend a man?
How to measure innocence?
According to whose plan?
Like the tiny teeth of fishes
These questions torture me
In my solitary prison
At the bottom of the sea.

THE END

Reading Group Guide

1. The author has described *The Fiend in Human* as resembling distressed denim or leather: "something new that looks old." What seems new and what seems old about the themes and the story?

2. What do you think of Edmund Whitty, both as a man and as a reporter? What about Henry Owler? How are the two alike, and how do they differ?

3. Discuss the women and girls in the book. To what extent do the differing social positions of Phoebe, Dorcas, Clara, Mrs. Plant, and Mrs. Marlowe determine their fates? Do their strategies for survival ennoble or degrade them?

4. The title is based upon the phrase, "The Fiend in Human Form"— a phrase sensational journalists used in referring to a murderer. How does the meaning change in its shortened form? Is the "fiend" inhuman, or is he all too human?

5. Did the London environments described in the book seem authentic? On what basis do you think the author selected the details?

6. The author wrote the first draft of the book at a time when Vancouver was reeling over the murders of dozens of prostitutes, with no interest or action from the police. Does knowing this change your understanding of the book in any way?

7. How do the actions and attitudes of the Victorian sensational press compare with those of the media today?

8. The novel, unusually, is written in the present tense. Do you think John Gray's background in the theater influenced his decision to write it this way? How did it affect your experience as a reader— a historical novel, written in the present tense?

9. What kind of humor is evident in *The Fiend in Human*? Where does such humor stem from? What does the humor in the book contribute to your sense of the period?

For more reading group suggestions visit
www.stmartins.com

St. Martin's Griffin